Foluso Agbaje has been writing st[...] write. She loves London, but call[...] are shaped by these two cities t[...] When not curled up with her Ki[...] and a pack of chocolate biscuits, you'll likely find her in a bookshop, museum or restaurant. She is a big fan of period dramas, and has watched every episode of *Downton Abbey* more times than she's willing to admit. She also enjoys singing in her church choir, walking and swimming.

After graduating from the Faber Academy in 2022, Foluso completed her debut novel, *The Parlour Wife.* She has a Masters degree in Management and Human Resources from the London School of Economics and a Bachelor's degree in Accounting from Loughborough University.

Foluso lives in Lagos with her husband and two children, balancing her passion for writing with a full-time career in financial services.

instagram.com/foagbaje
x.com/folushh

THE PARLOUR WIFE

FOLUSO AGBAJE

One More Chapter
a division of HarperCollins*Publishers*
1 London Bridge Street
London SE1 9GF
www.harpercollins.co.uk
HarperCollins*Publishers*
Macken House, 39/40 Mayor Street Upper,
Dublin 1, D01 C9W8, Ireland
This paperback edition 2024

First published in ebook by HarperCollins*Publishers* 2024
Copyright © Foluso Agbaje 2024
Foluso Agbaje asserts the moral right to
be identified as the author of this work

A catalogue record of this book
is available from the British Library

ISBN: 978-0-00-865471-9

Printed and bound in the UK using 100% Renewable Electricity
by CPI Group (UK) Ltd

This book is produced from independently certified FSC™ paper
to ensure responsible forest management.

For more information visit: www.harpercollins.co.uk/green

Content Warning

Some scenes include references to sexual and domestic abuse.

PART I
September 1939-October 1939

Lagos was the centre of important port infrastructure and naval fuelling stations for the British Empire in Africa; the value of commerce in Lagos was well over £1,000,000. The significance of this coastal city was evident in its selection as a prime trade nexus for British West Africa in the strategically sensitive South Atlantic.

Journal of African Military History[*]

[*]   Coates, O. 2020. "The Threat of Aerial Bombing in World War Two Lagos, 1938–1943," *Journal of African Military History*, 4(1-2). Leiden: Brill

Chapter One

CENTRAL LAGOS, NIGERIA

September 3, 1939

T he banana boat drifted on the curves of the tide, rocking like a baby's cradle. Kehinde inhaled the sea air, lifting her face to the sky as the wind blew the ends of her cornrows off her neck. Seagulls squawked in the distance, their cries harmonising with the deep bass of the water, beating against the boat like a drum.

They sat at opposite ends of the boat, her father with his fishing net, and Kehinde holding the bucket of bait. For as long as Kehinde could remember, this was how they'd spent every Saturday morning. Unlike Taiwo, her twin, who was useless at fishing, Kehinde enjoyed being out here with their father. When they were younger, she would use the little fishing rod her father had fashioned out of a tree branch for her, while Taiwo spent the time talking about everything he would rather be doing, until he stopped coming altogether. Kehinde loved it, this was her time to shine, the activity she shared with her father alone. She helped him reel in a red snapper that looked like it had been caught unawares as she and her father gathered it up in their net. Kehinde tossed the fish into the creel with the dancing crabs, smiling as her father turned around to look at her, his face calm but resolute.

"Keke, we're done for today."

Kehinde nodded as they steered their boat towards the jetty. Her mother had reminded them to come back in time to start cooking for the party. And now hours had gone by, the morning sun sat in the sky, with dark clouds beginning to gather around them. She was looking forward to getting home before the inevitable rain started. Unlike the calm of the ocean, the wetness falling from the sky had never felt right on her skin.

"I invited Mr Ogunjobi to come to the house later," her father continued, the wind almost drowning out his words.

Kehinde felt her heart sink into her stomach faster than a rock dropped into the depths of the water around them. They had invited a handful of family friends and neighbours to their house to celebrate her and Taiwo's eighteenth birthday in the evening, and from their mother's frantic preparations she had suspected that Mr Ogunjobi would be there.

"Daddy, please. I don't want to marry him. I got a job at the *West African Pilot!*" Kehinde said.

"What job?" her father asked, frowning.

He had not yet accepted Mr Ogunjobi's marriage proposal, but Kehinde knew that he and her mother thought it was the best way to secure all their futures, especially as they had no idea that she had her own, completely different plans. She thought about the way the letter had felt in her hand yesterday, the answer to her prayers, salvation from Mr Ogunjobi. She finally had what she wanted most, an invitation to meet the editor to discuss her offer to join the *West African Pilot*, the newest newspaper in Nigeria.

"I submitted an opinion piece to the editor, and he loved it. He wants me to write a column for their female readers! Daddy, please, I might never get this chance again," Kehinde replied, sitting higher in the boat.

Her father paused as he looked at her. The look on his face was one of pride, and something else Kehinde couldn't decipher, fear maybe? He had always told her and Taiwo that they were born to do great things, and it had been her guiding principle all her life. But how could she do great things when she would much rather spend the day alone with a book than having to talk to people. In the last year of not being in school, one day, she had realised her life had no purpose. Kehinde had been listening to one of her mother's regular customers, who wasn't much older than she was, talk about how she was moving to Abeokuta to expand her raffia mat trade. While she joined her mother to congratulate the girl, it wasn't lost on Kehinde that she had nothing she was working towards, no real plans, despite the longing to do something meaningful with her life. How many more days, months, years even, would she continue to be just peaceful, quiet Kehinde, the daughter of the fisherman, the dutiful child that helped with the family business? She wanted so much more, a way to stop being the reserved twin, the wallflower, the one who cared more about what other people thought than her own ideas.

Then a month ago, Taiwo had seen the job advertisement for the *West African Pilot* on a flyer on his way to school. It was perfect, a job that would give her life more meaning, and one where she could get away with barely having to speak to anyone. Writing gave her a voice, a way to articulate the thoughts she was always too afraid to say aloud. Getting married was the last thing she felt like doing now that she had finally found a way to give her life more meaning, especially not to Mr Ogunjobi. It wasn't bad enough that he already had two wives, he was older than her father!

"Keke … war could be declared any day now."

"That's exactly why I should be accepting this job!"

"Kehinde, as an older person," he started, quoting one of his favourite proverbs in the preacher tone that Kehinde and Taiwo had heard so many times over the years. "Sitting down, I can see what you cannot see standing up. This isn't the time to be a political activist, war will change everything. Better to be settled and married, not doing an untested job."

Kehinde felt indignation welling up from deep within her. It always seemed like because she was a girl, her choices were to be made by someone else, first her parents, then her husband, the ultimate decision-maker in the chain of command.

"Mr Ogunjobi knows you're smart, he said so himself when I visited his Apapa warehouse last week. He will give you whatever you want, and everything you need," her father continued, wiping the sweat from his brow as they moved closer to the shore.

"I get to become a rich man's third wife, and I'll have whatever I want, even if I never wanted to marry him in the first place. How lucky," Kehinde responded, feeling moisture at the back of her eyes and a burning sensation in her nose. She couldn't cry now; tears never got her anywhere with her father. He believed it was a sign of weakness, a coward's way out of an argument.

As their boat approached the jetty, the wind continued to roar all around them, the dark clouds matching Kehinde's mood.

"Kehinde, what choice do we have? I should have listened to your mother when she told me to stop letting you read all those oyinbo books," he said, leaning forward and shaking his head. His movements were exaggerated by the wind as the loose fabric of his tunic flapped against his dark skin.

"I could be a writer, Daddy. A real, meaningful job! Why do I have to get married now?" Kehinde replied, turning away to hide the stubborn tears that had refused to stay behind her eyelids. Nobody ever said anything about what Taiwo was reading or doing, or what he was expected to think – his more radical ideas were simply passed off as him being adventurous, but any of hers were silly, because she read too much.

Her father softened as he watched Kehinde.

"Keke, the world is in trouble, every newspaper has said as much. The colonial government keeps coming up with new trade regulations every day, this European war is the only thing people are talking about in the market."

Kehinde hugged her knees, wrapping her arms around her body as she tried to hear what he was saying; that this marriage was his way of seeking to shelter her from the unknown, but his concern felt more like shackles than a path to safety.

"Keke, má sùkún. I've spoken to Mr Ogunjobi so many times. He's a good man. Even Uncle Ladipo and Aunty Laide think so. Get married first, let's see about the writing later," her father said, standing to tether their boat to the jetty.

Kehinde made a silent vow to hold onto her dreams, even as she felt them floating away. She wanted to say more but she knew her father would get upset if she pushed now, so she said nothing. He gave her shoulder a squeeze as they climbed out of the boat and she resolved to speak to him about it again, maybe tomorrow morning after the party. She was ready to take her life into her own hands, to have a purpose and a real voice. She was no longer going to sit and smile, keeping her opinions to herself. She had to make him see that she was ready to be free, before it was too late.

By the time they got off the boat, a light drizzle had started. Other boats lined the shore, with some of the fishermen choosing to remain on the ocean despite the rain. Momentarily putting aside any thoughts of Mr Ogunjobi and the *West African Pilot*, Kehinde and her father hurried home. Kehinde's sandals slapped against the untarred road, grateful for the shade of the gmelina trees above her. Also lining the path were small huts where less accomplished fishermen lived, mostly single men trying to earn a living.

It was strange for Kehinde to imagine that her parents had started off in one of those huts before they moved to Malumo Street, a small crescent of bungalows and one of the Lagos Island roads adjoining the fishing village along the coast. Her father, also known as Bàbá Ìbejì, had customers travelling from all around Lagos to buy his fish, knowing that they would get a fresh catch and honest prices from him. A self-educated man, he had risen in his trade by sheer luck, determination and, to use his words, the grace of God. In addition to his regular customers in central Lagos, he had special customers, colonial lords and big men in Ikorodu and Badagry. Once a week, he took the ferry to make special deliveries to his customers on the outskirts of Lagos who prepared seafood for exports.

As they walked by the fishing village, there were shouts of greeting sent in their direction, the other fishermen smiling at the familiar sight of Bàbá Ìbejì and his daughter.

"Come get your fresh, hot corn! Big, fresh corn and coconut!" called the woman selling boiled corn from the edge of the path. Kehinde could almost taste the corn; the rich, sweet smell of the cooked cobs wafted over in her direction, as they hurried past.

When they got to Malumo Street, Kehinde could already see their neighbour, Aunty Laide, sitting on the bench in her front garden, shielded from the rain under her porch.

"Happy birthday, Kehinde!" Aunty Laide called out, the warmth in her voice radiating through the rain. Kehinde could see the well-worn cover of *Pride and Prejudice* in her lap as she returned the wave. She made a mental note to return the two new books she had borrowed from her study.

Taiwo's green bicycle leaned against their fence beside Kunle's and Kehinde felt the familiar stab of resentment as she remembered that while she had to stay at home getting the food ready for the party, Taiwo would be going to the racecourse with his best friend.

"The way you boys eat eh!" her mother said as they opened the front door, shaking her head and laughing at Taiwo and Kunle as they finished their akara and ogi at the dining table. At the sound of the door, she turned and smiled at Bàbá Ìbejì, her eyes instantly lighting up. He crossed the room, embracing his wife like they had not woken up in the same bed that morning.

Taiwo caught Kehinde's eye as they laughed at their parent's inability to keep their hands off each other.

"Good morning, sir. Morning, Kehinde," Kunle said to them, smiling at Kehinde from the corner of the dining table. Kehinde wasn't surprised to see him there so early in the day. He had been a constant in their lives since she and Taiwo were five-year-olds.

"Morning, Kunle," Kehinde replied, instinctively rearranging the worn blue cushions on the two empty chairs for her father to sit on. A rush of flower-infused wind came through the open window above the dining table, making the white lace curtains flutter.

"Don't worry, Keke, I'll sit here," her father said, giving her mother's arm a quick squeeze before he crossed over to the parlour area. He sank into his armchair as the grandfather clock that her parents had won at a fair years ago chimed loudly.

"See the time, it's already nine! Oya, Kehinde, let's get your father breakfast before we start getting the rest of the food ready."

Kehinde followed their mother into the kitchen and almost tripped on the brown jute bag of rice and two crates of beer behind the door. None of those things had been there before she had set out with her father earlier.

"Small gifts from Mr Ogunjobi, for later," her mother said, not meeting her eyes.

Beer was expensive, not to mention the clearly imported bag of rice. Mr Ogunjobi was always sending these "small" gifts to the house, and it made Kehinde feel like a horse being sold to the highest bidder. These types of gifts and the treats reserved for the colonial masters, were things that only someone with access to the ports could get their hands on. Not that her mother minded. Lately, whenever they had visitors, she would throw in a casual comment like, "Kehinde, go and bring a slice of that cake, the one from Ikoyi Bakery, the one that Mr Ogunjobi sent yesterday." As Kehinde put three pieces of akara and a chunk of bread on a plate for her father, she almost started telling her mother about her job offer but stopped herself. It would be better if she won her father over first, she decided. Her mother would take it better from him.

Back in the parlour, her father was reading his copy of the

Daily Times. Taiwo stood beside the Rediffusion, peering over their father's shoulder. He looked up at Kehinde as she walked in with the tray.

"Hitler's troops have invaded Poland," her father murmured, as she arranged his food on the stool beside him. "We need to be prepared."

"Uncle Ladipo said the colonial administrators at Ikoyi Club have been receiving letters and telegrams all week," Taiwo said, swinging his satchel across his chest. Kunle rose from the table to shut the windows against the rain that was now falling softly, and the thud of the shutters coincided with the flutter in Kehinde's chest.

"Why are we fretting about something happening so far away?" their mother scoffed as she came out of the kitchen. She picked up her taffeta fan from the side table, muttering something about how hot it was even though it was raining outside.

Kehinde knew that unlike everyone else in the room, her mother would rather change the topic to the party happening later that evening. Taiwo on the other hand, was pacing the short distance between the parlour and the dining area, and Kehinde could feel the adrenaline coursing through him like it was her own. She willed Taiwo to remain silent, knowing that this was a bad time for him to explode after the conversation she had just had with their father.

"Please, let's stop all this, ah ah! No war has started yet!" their mother continued, when no one made any attempt to change the topic. She had placed her arm on their father's shoulder, and he visibly relaxed at her touch. Her eyes, so like those of the twins, had a sheen of uncertainty in them.

Kehinde sent Taiwo a warning look that doused the fire of his nervous energy.

"I'll see you later," he said, cocking his eyebrow at her.

"Don't stay out too late! You need to get home in time to take your picture," their mother said, already looking relieved.

"Don't worry, Ma. I'll make sure he's back on time." Kunle said.

As the door slammed behind them, Kehinde could hear the two boys riding off on their bicycles, the chains jangling against the sound of the falling rain.

"We still have a lot to do before our guests arrive," her mother said with the sigh of someone who secretly enjoyed the chores they complained about.

"I'm just going to lie down in the room," Kehinde's father said, smiling at her as she took his plate from his lap.

As Kehinde followed her mother into the kitchen she wondered if Taiwo had also told Kunle about his aspirations to become a military pilot in the Nigerian Army. She and Taiwo had spent increasingly more time over the summer talking about what a war might mean for them, for her writing career and for his flight path. Their father wanted him to have a respectable job, something safe and far from the physical labour of being a self-educated fisherman with a small income.

Kehinde had kept his secret, not telling anyone that he had been meeting with Captain Mackenzie, a Royal Air Force pilot who he had met at the racecourse over the previous summer and who had been filling his head with all sorts of mad ideas. Kehinde thought Taiwo was better off staying in school and becoming a lawyer like their father hoped and had said as much to him, but Taiwo as usual accused her of being the goody-two-shoes that always sided with their parents. Besides, she understood him, and she knew that like her, he wanted to find his purpose, to leave a mark in the world in his own way. While hers was with her pen, Taiwo wanted to be at the front, fighting on behalf of those who could not fight.

Her thoughts returned to the gulf between her parents' aspirations for her and Taiwo and their own dreams. Sometimes it felt like because their father had grown up wanting more, he needed to live vicariously through her and Taiwo. One of his favourite verses from the Bible was *"Honour your father and your mother and your days will be long"*, and to be honest she and Taiwo had heard it so many times that it subconsciously drove all her decision-making. At what point did putting her own thoughts before those of her parents become dishonourable, and where was the balance between living her life for herself and living her life in honour of her parents? Deep down she knew that her parents only ever wanted what was best for their children, but was having their own dreams synonymous with ingratitude for what their parents had sacrificed?

Taiwo's predicament was still better than hers, she thought, as she sliced into an onion. She almost laughed out loud at the thought of him wanting to run off to join the Army – he could be so fanciful sometimes. She would take being a lawyer over being a third wife any day. But things were already difficult enough at the market, inflation was higher than ever and Kehinde knew that her parents stayed up most nights whispering conversations they thought she couldn't hear. Too proud to ask for help, she knew that her father would rather come up with what he thought was the best plan for his family in the face of impending danger.

With Kehinde married and with Mr Ogunjobi's gifts, they would not be solely dependent on their fish sales to survive and put Taiwo through the rest of his education. From that perspective the marriage made sense, for everyone except her.

For once in her life, she wanted to be selfish and do what she really wanted, not what her parents thought she should want. Sighing, she picked up the chicken that Taiwo had plucked and placed it on the chopping board beside the diced onions. As their mother measured out a cup of rice, Kehinde hacked away at the chicken, wondering what the future held for them all.

Chapter Two

By that afternoon, the rain had stopped and given way to a cool breeze. Kehinde did not consider herself to be particularly superstitious, but as she watched the palm trees on their street sway in the setting sun, she imagined that good weather must be an auspicious start for one's eighteenth birthday. Humming under her breath, she changed into her new oleku, made from a deep blue adire, with a pattern of white swirling circles. She wondered what Mr Ogunjobi's wives looked like as she lined her eyes with her tiro. Did they all look the same? Like a set of Russian dolls, stacked within each other, each new one slightly different from the last but with the same general appearance.

Taiwo hopped around behind her as he changed into the buba and sokoto she had laid out for him in the same print, having returned from the racecourse with barely enough time to change. His inability to plan and be anywhere on time always made Kehinde wonder how he would ever survive without her.

"Captain Mackenzie said that I'm better off coming to Zaria

with him immediately when the war starts," he said, as he tied the belt of his sokoto.

"And today would have been a terrible time to tell Mummy and Daddy that."

"Why is everyone refusing to understand that Nigeria is going to war?"

"The British Empire is going to war; it doesn't mean Nigeria is."

"Keke, you're not stupid enough to believe that."

Kehinde smarted at his tone, knowing that he was right, and even more irritated at herself for how much she had sounded like her mother had that morning.

"Can't you at least wait till school is over?"

Taiwo stood behind her, meeting her eyes in the mirror as she replaced the lid of her tiro. His buba sat upright on his broad shoulders and the colour of the material against his complexion reminded Kehinde of an iroko tree. Looking at him in the mirror always made her feel like she was looking at a version of her face she was as familiar with as her own. They both had their mother's slanted eyes and their father's full lips, but where Kehinde had inherited their father's personality, as cool as still water, Taiwo's personality was more like fire, quick to flare up but easily tamed with practice. He had also inherited their mother's smile, the kind of smile that lit up not just the face of the owner, but the whole room.

"What's the point of finishing school? It's useless," Taiwo said, picking at a loose thread at his collar.

"Useful enough to get you a job."

"Being in the Army is a job. And right now, I feel a lot more strongly about defending the Empire than I do about sitting around sharpening pencils in class."

Kehinde sighed; her brother could be such a dreamer. She

blamed Captain Mackenzie and although she had never met the man, she was growing to dislike him more with each passing day.

"Our reality will soon be impossible to ignore," Taiwo continued.

"We aren't at war yet."

"But when we are, I'm going to enlist. I don't care what Daddy, or anyone, has to say about it."

"I told him about my offer today," Kehinde said, ignoring the image of Taiwo's raised eyebrows in the mirror.

"Let me guess, he told you to decline and get married. The sensible thing to do for a sensible girl such as yourself," Taiwo said, cocking his head to the side.

"I'm not getting married, at least not yet," Kehinde said, adjusting her head tie so it sat more firmly on the peak of her hairline.

Taiwo sighed, like he was talking to a toddler.

"Keke, when have you ever not done what they've said you should," he waved his hand in the direction of the parlour. "Before your offer came in, you were more or less resigned to becoming Mrs Ogunjobi. What was it you said about defending Daddy's honour?"

"Well, the offer changed everything," Keke said, annoyed at how her brother always managed to make her feel like a lost sheep.

"So, he said you should take the job?"

"It wasn't an outright no," Kehinde said, turning to face Taiwo and hating how he smiled knowingly at her answer. "I'm still going to accept; I'm just giving Daddy a bit of time to come to my side. Which is exactly what I'm advising you to do as well."

"Unlike you, I know what I want and I'm ready to fight for

it. I'm going to tell him tomorrow morning, before he gets the ferry to Ikorodu," Taiwo said, shrugging his shoulders.

Kehinde watched the determined look on her brother's face with a mixture of pride, fear and jealousy. How she wished she could be more like him – more able to stand up to their parents without feeling the sting of their disapproval. What was the worst that could happen if she told them she wasn't getting married and put her foot down? They would be upset for sure, but when she started earning an income, they would see that they were all better off with her in a good job, not sitting at home knitting, or whatever it was Mr Ogunjobi's wives did in their spare time.

"Fine. I'll tell him I'm accepting the offer tomorrow morning as well."

Taiwo's eyebrows shot up again.

"It's always easier to talk to him in the morning, before Mummy is up," Kehinde continued, unwilling to admit to herself that it would be easier for her to be firm, to stand up to her father, if Taiwo was there beside her.

"Yes, Keke!" Taiwo stamped his foot as he gave her a mock salute.

Kehinde suddenly squealed and hopped as a cockroach raced across their room. This was another reason why she hated the rains; all the creepy crawlies of the world seemed to congregate in Lagos and there was nothing she despised more than insects and rodents.

"Believe it or not, I'll miss you when I go. Just a bit," Taiwo said, laughing as he watched her shrink against the wall.

"I won't miss your snoring. I wonder what it's like to sleep without the sound of a marching band in my ear," Kehinde said, bending over to get her sandals out from beneath her bed to defend herself. The cockroach disappeared under their bedroom door before she had a chance to use her weapon.

"Don't speak too soon. Your Mr Ogunjobi looks like he can snore for all of Lagos with that big nose of his. If you end up in his house, trust me, you'll beg to have my snoring back," Taiwo said, laughing as he ducked just in time to escape Kehinde's hurtling sandal.

"Kehinde! Taiwo! The photographer is here!" their mother called from the parlour as Taiwo ducked again, barely missing the other sandal.

Their father had asked a photographer friend that worked at the *West African Pilot* to stop by the house to take a picture of Taiwo and Kehinde. He was crouched in the middle of the parlour, arranging his equipment by the dining table. As he looked up at them, Kehinde noticed the long tribal marks on each side of his face. Their father stood beside the photographer, watching him unpack his equipment with an almost boyish look of excitement on his face.

Standing still was the hardest part. Kehinde felt stiff and unsure of herself as the photographer asked her to place a hand on her hip. She had only ever posed for one photograph years ago when she was still a little girl, and that was with most of the congregation at church for a visiting British journalist. Taiwo, on the other hand, appeared to be loving every minute of it as their mother cheered him on.

"My handsome boy!" their mother said from where she was standing behind their father's armchair. "Kehinde, smile with your teeth, you look so much prettier when you smile properly." Her mother bared her teeth in a failed attempt at what a real smile should look like.

"She looks beautiful, just as she is," her father said from his armchair. Kehinde beamed at him.

"That's it!" said the photographer, capturing Kehinde's smile as the light from his camera flashed. He shook hands with their father once he was done, wrapping away his camera like he was swaddling a baby.

"Ò ṣe, òṛẹ mi. Won't you have something to eat?" their father asked.

"I need to leave for my next appointment. I'll bring the prints once they're ready though," he said, nodding as Aunty Laide and Uncle Ladipo arrived.

"Happy birthday, my babies," Aunty Laide said as she enveloped both twins in a hug that felt like falling into a loaf of freshly baked bread. Kehinde broke away and Aunty Laide gave one of the two bags she was carrying to each twin. Taiwo's bag had a brown leather belt with a gold clasp on it, while Kehinde's contained a book she had been trying to get her hands on, *Itan Igbesi-Aiye Emi Segilola* by Segilola, an ex-prostitute who had documented her memoirs.

"Thank you so much, Aunty Laide!" Kehinde gushed.

"It's high time you started building your own library," Aunty Laide said, winking as they ignored Kehinde's mother's frown. She, like many people in Lagos, did not approve of the infamous book. Beside her, Taiwo was trying on his new belt and making everyone laugh as he turned from side to side like a model.

Not long after Aunty Laide and Uncle Ladipo arrived, the handful of guests from the crescent started pouring in and as the evening progressed, with the sounds of the Calabar Brass Band playing from Uncle Ladipo's gramophone, Kehinde felt herself begin to relax. If war was indeed imminent, she might as well enjoy the party. Her father's favourite song, "Oba Oyibo" by Tunde King, started playing and she danced with Kunle, laughing as he protested about being dragged off his seat at the dining table. To her right, Taiwo was talking to two sisters who lived a few houses down their street. Taiwo had his hand round the waist of the curvier sister and although Kehinde could not hear what he was whispering in her ear, from the way the girl was giggling she knew that it probably was not a conversation their mother would approve of.

Her father and Uncle Ladipo were sitting at the centre of a cluster of men in the middle of the parlour, while her mother held court in the kitchen with the women, wearing a pink shift dress with a rose pattern, one of the three dresses in her Sunday best collection. Kehinde watched her arrange the dùndú and chin-chin on two trays as the other women stood around her in various acts of pretending to be useful while they gossiped about whose child was doing what, with who and when. Kehinde averted her gaze and turned her back to her mother before she was summoned to join the kitchen ranks.

"Kehinde, my mother said you're to be the next Mrs Ogunjobi," the sister not being held by Taiwo was saying. She had a hooded brow, framed by shaggy eyebrows above beady eyes and a pointed mouth, like a wild bird. Kehinde could almost imagine her pecking away at a tree as she nodded.

"You lucky thing. I heard he sent his second wife a trunk of all kinds of gifts the night before their wedding. Lace from Switzerland, chocolate from Belgium, and yards of ankara," the sister gushed.

"My mother said he's very generous," said the other girl, Taiwo's hand still around her waist. Her features were daintier than her sister's, and her hair had curled ends that stood stiffly around her face as she spoke. "Our mother said he saw you in church one day and went to meet your father the next day! With a face and a figure like yours, I can't say I'm surprised!"

"And you're just the kind of woman rich men like, aren't you. Pretty, quiet, always smiling, so agreeable. Do you ever get angry?" wild bird sister said, smiling in a way that Kehinde knew she didn't mean as a compliment.

She had heard comments like this many times in her life, and often wondered if people thought her looks gave her some kind of superpower over the rest of the world. And yes, she did get angry. In fact, she was angry as she looked at the two sisters with their silly smiles who thought she was weak just because she didn't like to be rude.

"Where is Mr Ogunjobi anyway?" Kunle asked, saving her from having to respond.

"Speak of the devil, and he appears," Taiwo said, nodding towards the door.

Mr Ogunjobi stood at the door, wearing a white agbada with coral beads around his neck and a green fila on his head – overdressed for a small house party, Kehinde thought. As he made his way in, the small group of guests stopped talking to greet him, women bobbing in curtseys and men extending their hands to shake his. Kehinde was wondering whether to make a run towards or away from him when her mother appeared at her side.

"Oya, go and meet him at the front door. Make sure you greet him well," she said in what could only be described as a stage whisper.

A small man in white buba and sokoto carrying a parcel wrapped in shiny paper followed closely behind Mr Ogunjobi. He must be Kayode, Kehinde guessed. Her father had told her that he was Mr Ogunjobi's aide and bodyguard, but she doubted this harmless-looking man could be him, even though the frown on his face was scary enough to keep anyone from coming too close.

"My flower. Happy birthday, how are you?" Mr Ogunjobi said when he spotted Kehinde. She bowed in a low curtsey, her eyes falling on her reflection in his polished black shoes. His feet were the biggest she had ever seen, they looked like they belonged to the giant in *Jack and the Beanstalk*. She looked up to see that he was gazing at her like she was a plate of jollof rice and chicken. The juice she had been drinking suddenly felt like a tsunami threatening to burst from her mouth.

"I've brought you something for your birthday," he continued. That was another thing she had noticed, he never waited for her answer when he asked how she was or about her day. She wondered what he would do if she had replied, *"I'm fine, but I'll never be your wife and just the thought of living with you makes me feel like I have malaria."*

Kayode thrust the parcel he was carrying in her direction, the scowl on his face deepening, making Kehinde wonder if he was able to read minds. Everyone had gone quiet around her, and she caught Taiwo's eye from the corner of the room. He looked like he was trying not to laugh, his eyes telling her, *"Don't mess this one up, sis."*

"Thank you so much, sir," she said, keeping her eyes downcast as she rose from her curtsey, noticing Mr Ogunjobi's eyes land and remain on her chest. She heard her mother's sigh of approval behind her; she had passed the test of being the respectful prospective wife who knew how to greet her husband. The noise level around her rose again, in a collective exhale of relief. Her father, with Uncle Ladipo now standing beside the gramophone, smiled at her as he raised his glass to his lips. Mr Ogunjobi slapped his big hands together in delight.

"My dear, you're welcome!" he said, beaming, his eyes now firmly on her face as he licked his lips.

"Mr Ogunjobi! Ẹ káàbọ̀! Kehinde, go and bring some food!

Mr Ogunjobi can't be standing here like this when there's so much to eat and drink," her mother said beside her. She made a shooing gesture as she grabbed Mr Ogunjobi's arm with her other hand, steering him in the direction of the sofa where the men were sitting.

Kehinde made her way through the guests in the parlour, past the kitchen, towards her room. She wanted to look at her present before she dished up Mr Ogunjobi's food. Kehinde guessed the parcel contained a book; she felt the solid weight in her hands and wondered if it was a Bible. The wrapping paper was purple with pink flowers on it. *Pink flowers for his little flower,* she thought, with a fresh wave of nausea.

Beneath the wrapping paper was a black box with *Kehinde* engraved on the bottom right-hand corner of the lid. Sinking down to her bed, she opened the lid to reveal a leatherbound notebook, also engraved, with a black ink pen attached to the side. Not a Bible then. The box had the tangy smell of new paper and as Kehinde turned it over in her hands, she was caught off guard by his thoughtfulness.

On one of the few occasions she had met Mr Ogunjobi in the past, she had mentioned that she sometimes wrote her thoughts down on scraps of paper, scolding herself afterwards for not telling him that she liked to cook instead. It was true, she loved to cook, and that would have been much more acceptable than telling him she liked to write. Her mother would have thrown her hands up in despair if she had heard her, all those hours in the kitchen over the course of her lifetime seemingly wasted.

"Eya, what a sweet gift!" Taiwo said, appearing in the doorway of their room, as he blew a kiss. He was holding a new bottle of beer she was sure was his third of the day.

"Will you ever stop following me?"

"You were smiling, clutching that box to your chest like it was the key to your heart,"

"I see you've finally peeled yourself off ... what's her name? The one with the big hair?"

"Her name is Sola! You've met her enough times to at least pretend to remember her name, snob!" Taiwo said, ignoring her protests as he sat beside her and grabbed the box. "This is nice!" he whistled.

"It is, right?" Kehinde said, gathering up her old sheaf of scribbles and pen on the side of her mattress and placing them in the black box beneath her new journal. The new pen did not look like the pens Mama Tosin sold at the stationery store in the market, that was for sure. This one was elegant and smooth, with a black point, and she could imagine writing with it, the black ink flowing out on the paper like a dolphin at sea.

"Who buys a birthday present for one twin and not the other though?" Taiwo said, interrupting her thoughts. Growing up, it was a running joke that anyone who got presents for only one of them had only brought half a present. The sound of a raised voice from the parlour distracted them and laughing, they both hurried out.

The mood had shifted in the short time that they had been in their room. Night had fallen outside, the dim lamp lights in the room cast shadows across the floor, and the music playing from the gramophone had stopped. Kehinde felt guilty as she saw that someone else, probably her mother, had already served Mr Ogunjobi. He was sitting beside her father, eating fried rice as they listened to the older man that had stood to speak.

"The Emergency Food Defence Act is proof that this European war will start, any day now," the man was saying.

Kehinde recognised him as Baba Seyi, the trader who sold fruit near the entrance of Ereko Market. "Why else would the British government be making feeding arrangements? And that's saying nothing about all the activity at the Department of Agriculture. They want to make sure they know everything going on, so they can plan!" he continued, his voice rising with each word.

Kehinde listened, moving closer to where the men were sitting with Taiwo. Like most readers of the *West African Pilot*, she wanted Nigeria to be independent. Yes, they were free citizens, colonialism could hardly be called slavery. But if they were free, then why did they have no say over the affairs that governed them? Why were they here taking guesses about whether or not their own nation would be at war? Why were they told where they could live and where they weren't allowed to visit, on their own land? Their economy was run by the British, and with the zoning regulations set by the colonial administrators, they couldn't even reside where they wanted to in their own country. The black Nigerians were not allowed to live in Ikoyi or Victoria Island and anyone that worked there had to be off the island by 7pm. Nigeria deserved and needed to be independent, to have the chance to decide if war was something it wanted to be a part of, not just dragged into it like an oblivious child. She would know, she mused. She was like Nigeria, silently screaming about her rights to parents who thought they knew better.

"My cousin in Ondo had to declare his cocoa sales last month, something about the governor wanting to have exact revenue and distribution figures from all the farms," said Mama Tolu, Kehinde's mother's friend from church, as she adjusted the red gele on her head.

"Food prices have gone up, look at how ridiculous the price

of palm oil is! It's all part of the colonial government's plan to use Nigeria to pay for a war we want no part of! They will bleed us dry!" Baba Seyi added.

"They never seemed to care much about my cotton sales before. Suddenly we're all under so much scrutiny," said Mr Ogunlesi, a trader friend of Kehinde's father who owned a cotton field in Abeokuta.

"When England declares war, we can hardly stand by and watch. Even if we had a choice, we should always choose to fight for justice," Taiwo said. Heads turned in his direction as he spoke, his face lit up by the lamp beside him as he stood taller in response to the attention.

"So naïve, you sound like one of those propaganda leaflets they've been sticking all over the market," Baba Seyi snorted. "Don't you know how many lives will be lost? How many families destroyed? Why should we, the people of Nigeria, be affected by the politics of the British Empire?"

"So many women and children across Eastern Europe have already been displaced. The *Daily Times* mentioned that refugees are fleeing Poland, there are already reports of Polish prisoners being taken away by the Germans. They're innocent people too and they need all the help they can get," Taiwo said.

"How sad. Imagine all those people whose lives have been affected already. It's such a blatant disregard for humanity," Kehinde said, surprising herself with the sound of her voice but not her words.

"Rightly so. We'll all be affected in one way or another." Kehinde's father nodded. Her mother, on the other hand, scowled at Kehinde; she had said too much and had disappeared for too long when she was supposed to have been helping her in the kitchen.

"But why must the affected lives be Nigerian lives? It's not like they care about us. Just because we're part of the British Empire, must we be dragged into this? The colonial authorities already want to use us till we are useless with all their rules and levies. A war will make them drain everything we have left, and what will become of our nation then? They will take all our men, there will be no family left intact. We will pay for this war, and not just financially, mark my words!" Baba Seyi said, waving his cane in the air like a harbinger of doom.

Mr Ogunjobi rose from his seat to stand beside Baba Seyi, resplendent in his white agbada in the darkening room, a glass of beer in his right hand. His presence dwarfed everyone around him, including Baba Seyi and his cane.

"Taiwo is right. If war is declared, as citizens of the Empire, we must all do what we can," he said in English, breaking the flow of rapid Yoruba and making some of the guests squint as their ears adjusted to the smooth words. He spoke slowly, looking around the room as he did so, like the colonial officials Kehinde had seen at the New Year's Parade on Broad Street.

"Mr Ogunjobi, why should we be so quick to contribute to a war we had no hand in making? To the very Empire that controls our economy and country like we are brainless muppets?" Baba Seyi said, leaning on his walking stick.

"Because, my friend, this war is more than just a senseless fight. It's a fight for freedom, from Hitler! If you think things are bad now, imagine what Nigeria would be like as a German colony. This marks a new future, a new age where the Empire will stand together for peace," Mr Ogunjobi responded, looking down at the older man, his shrug exaggerated by the sleeves of his agbada.

Kayode appeared at his side with a brown bag that he seemed to have conjured out of thin air. The bag made an unmistakable clink as Mr Ogunjobi brought out a dark bottle of what Kehinde realised was champagne from the elegant label on its body.

"You're chummy with Governor Bourdillon. You're the only one here benefitting from the colonial government, with your warehouses being the chosen ones at the ports," Baba Seyi spat out. If Mr Ogunjobi heard him, he didn't show it; instead, he raised the dark bottle above Baba Seyi's head.

"Let's toast to the triumph of good over evil, the beginning of the fight for justice!" Mr Ogunjobi boomed, nodding in Kehinde and Taiwo's direction as their mother hurried towards him with a tray of clean glasses. Seemingly distracted by the champagne and deciding that a nightcap would be more favourable than a prolonged argument, the guests in the room raised their glasses, toasting to the hope the bubbly froth hinted at. Baba Seyi sat back in his seat, muttering about the folly of youth.

Kehinde watched her father as he sipped from his glass, wondering what he was thinking. Despite herself, she had to admit that the day was ending on a much higher note than it had begun. Even if Mr Ogunjobi did not know it, her chances of writing for the *West African Pilot* had never seemed better, and there was no way her father would let her get married just as war was declared. As Kehinde took her first sip of champagne, she toasted towards a future that suddenly sparkled, full of promise.

Chapter Three

K ehinde woke up with a headache that felt like someone was pounding yam in her skull, the boom of the pestle a steady beat against the mortar of her head. Her tongue moved like a dry sponge in her mouth, and she needed water badly. As she sat up, with a jolt of pain that felt like lightning striking her body, she looked out of the window and saw the peach of the rising sun.

"Taiwo, wake up!" she hissed, pushing his sleeping form on the mattress beside hers. Taiwo rolled onto his side and looked at her drowsily, before the realisation also dawned on him. He stretched his arms like a dancer about to perform.

"Keke, I'm tired. Should we just wait till he gets back tonight?"

"No! Let's go now. I think I can already hear him in the kitchen," Kehinde said, standing up and wincing as she led the way through their bedroom door.

Their father was already dressed and pouring himself a cup of tea. His skin shone against the glow of the candle in his hand, and his lips curved into a tired smile when he saw his children approaching in the corridor.

"You're both up already? Taiwo, you still have a few hours before you have to get ready for school."

"We wanted to talk to you before you left for the ferry," Taiwo said, as he and Kehinde entered the kitchen. Kehinde closed the door behind her and took a deep breath. Her father raised his eyebrows as she exhaled.

"Why do I feel like I've been caught in an ambush?" he asked with a half-smile.

"Daddy, I've decided to enlist, to join the Air Force. I've been thinking about this a lot, and I know I'll be a great pilot, Captain Mackenzie said so himself. When the war starts, I'll begin my training in Zaria," Taiwo said, squaring his shoulders. If Kehinde hadn't heard the tremor in his voice she would have almost believed the confidence in his tone.

"Is this a joke?" her father asked, the amusement disappearing from his face.

"No, Daddy, I'm serious. I'm eighteen now and old enough to enlist," Taiwo said.

"What's gotten into the two of you? First the West African Pilot and now this? Have you both lost your minds?" he asked, his eyes going back and forth between the two of them like they were a pair of performing fools that had shown up uninvited in his home.

"This is what we want, Daddy," Kehinde said, her voice sounding a lot squeakier than she would have liked.

"And you both think you know what you want, right? What's best for you? That you can suddenly tell me what you should be doing because you've been eighteen for a few hours?"

"All over the world, people our age are making their own

decisions," Taiwo said, even though Kehinde could hear the sting of hurt in his voice that she also felt in her chest from her father's words.

"Don't tell me about the world!" their father snapped, suddenly hitting his palm against the kitchen counter. "Here I am, breaking my back to give you both a better future than I could ever have dreamed of, and you have the gall to tell me about the world! You're in Nigeria, in case you've forgotten!"

"And even Nigeria is changing, Daddy, all you have to do is open a newspaper, walk on the streets and see. There's change everywhere!" Taiwo said, his voice now charged with anger.

"Don't speak to me like that!" their father said, his nose almost touching Taiwo's in the small kitchen. It was easy to forget how tall he was, but Kehinde was reminded of who Taiwo got his height from as she watched her father move closer to her brother.

"Daddy, what Taiwo is trying to say is we just want a chance ... the freedom to determine our own paths, just like you did," Kehinde said before Taiwo could speak again. His words were escalating the situation and the last thing she needed was a shouting match that would bring their mother, the greatest defender of Mr Ogunjobi, into the kitchen.

"This is utter nonsense. I forbid it. You will not join the Air Force, you will finish school if you know what's good for you, Taiwo. You'll even be lucky if this war allows you to do that, but you will not run headfirst into the fire! And you, Kehinde, we spoke about this already. You will get married to Mr Ogunjobi, and the sooner the better. Please put any silly notions of writing for the *West African Pilot* aside!" her father said, spit flying with his words.

Kehinde's headache had taken on a life of its own. She

hardly ever saw her father this angry, and she hated to be on the receiving end of his disappointment, but this was too much.

"Daddy, you can't stop us. It's not like you can lock us in the house," Taiwo said, his voice eerily calm. The sun had risen now, the brightness highlighting the sweat on their father's brow. They all looked out of the kitchen window as an unexpected ray peeked in, an intruder on this conversation that seemed too big for the receding darkness.

"If I didn't have to get the ferry, I would give you a piece of my mind," their father said, glaring at Taiwo first before he looked at Kehinde. "We will talk about this when I get back." He picked up the jute bag of fish from the floor and stormed out of the kitchen.

If Kehinde did not feel so chastened she would have at least offered to help him carry some of his load; the ferry stop was just a ten-minute walk away. She felt ashamed but charged with adrenaline. Arguing with their parents was Taiwo's domain; she always wanted them to be proud of her, but this time, they had stood up to their father together, and they had sown the seeds for their freedom. She would be a writer and Taiwo a pilot and there was nothing anyone could do or say to stop them. But she couldn't ignore the pain and confusion on her father's face or the buzz of uncertainty that danced within her like a mosquito for being part of what she knew he would see as a betrayal. This battle had only just started, and she would have to get used to his disapproval if she was ever going to stand up for herself.

"He was really upset," she whispered to Taiwo as they walked across the short corridor between the kitchen and their room.

"Well, at least he knows now, and we can all stop

pretending. I'm going to see if I can sleep again before we have to get ready," Taiwo replied, already burrowing under the sheet on his mattress. Kehinde followed and did the same, wondering how Taiwo was able to even think about sleeping after upsetting their father like that but to her surprise, she dozed off as soon as she lay down.

When she woke up again, the sun was shining through their open window. Still clutching her head, she looked over at Taiwo, who was sleeping face down on his mattress, snoring with his mouth open.

"Taiwo! Wake up! You'll be late for school!" Kehinde said, her voice coming out as a hoarse whisper. When Taiwo didn't budge she pulled her wrapper tighter around her chest and stood to shake him. He lifted his head and looked at her through one half open eye.

"Keke? Go away," he said, as he dropped his head back down on the pillow.

Kehinde made her way to the bathroom on the side of the house to use her chewing stick, her father's words ringing in her head with the remains of her headache as she tried to get the sour taste out of her mouth. Memories of their birthday party and their fight with her father swirled in her head as she bathed in cold water. Had she dreamed it? Definitely not, the conversation had happened for sure. When she came back into the house, she caught a glimpse of their mother already in the kitchen, preparing breakfast and the fish they would be taking to sell at the market.

"Keke, kilode? You look so tired!" her mother said, as she came out of the kitchen, grabbing Kehinde's chin so she could study her face.

"I have a headache," Kehinde said. To her surprise, a smile

stretched across her mother's face as she threw back her head and let out a short laugh.

"Oh, Keke! It must be the champagne you had last night! I should have warned you, the same thing happened to me the only time I ever tasted it at Kitan's wedding years ago! Those bubbles ehn, it's like they're doing the bata dance in your head!" Her mother's laughter grated on the edge of Kehinde's brain. She let out a groan as she sank into her father's armchair.

"I'm boiling yam. That will help you feel better," her mother said, disappearing into the kitchen again. Kehinde cringed at the thought of eating anything, especially yam. She watched her mother's lithe form as she moved around the kitchen and wondered how she could move so quickly after being on her feet throughout the previous day.

As the starchy smell of the boiling yam filled the dining room, Taiwo emerged with impeccable timing, rubbing his eyes and sniffing. He did not look like the champagne or his multiple beers from the night before had affected him at all. Kehinde ignored him and sipped her glass of water, wishing she could crawl back into bed. The thought of going to the market with her mother was more than she could bear.

"There, something solid to hold your stomach," her mother said. "We need to go; you know how busy the mornings can be. Eat up, let's set out before the sun gets too hot."

As they got ready to leave, Taiwo wore his new belt with his school uniform, and Kehinde had to admit that he looked quite handsome as it cinched in his waist. As he sped off on his bicycle towards school, she and her mother headed off in the opposite direction, past the fish village and to the market.

Later that afternoon, Kehinde was sitting beside her mother in their stall at the heart of Ereko Market, swatting away a fly that was on a mission to land in her eye. The smell of blood hung heavy in the hot air as animal carcasses swayed on display at all the stalls, with everything from seafood to freshly killed goat meat for sale. Kehinde had spent so much of her life here that the smell hardly upset her, and they'd had another busy day. They had sold most of the fish from yesterday, with advance orders for tomorrow's catch. She had written down the orders for her mother to give to their father when he got home. The shade from the umbrella above their stall was barely keeping out the glare of the sun and Kehinde could not wait to be back indoors.

Kehinde still felt disoriented; her conversation with her father and her lingering headache made her want to curl up under the table, away from the noise around them. She couldn't shake the feeling of dismay. Maybe Taiwo was right, she was so used to toeing the line that she felt physically sick now that she was out of step. Was this the price of freedom? Upsetting everyone you held dear until you were left alone? She dreaded speaking with their father later, but at least the worst of it was over, she told herself. He knew where they stood, and he would have a few hours to cool off before they saw him again.

Suddenly, the loud, distant bang of the cannon in Elegbata Square blasted across the market. She and her mother looked at each other, each seeing the fear they felt reflected in the other's eyes. This was not the usual one o'clock cannon blast, and strangely, it kept going. Different traders stood around the market, murmuring as they all started to pack up for the day, driven by a collective sense of unease. Sales ended abruptly as both the traders and customers rounded up their conversations over the ominous, incessant sound.

Kehinde and her mother rushed along the path from the market to their street. Groups of people were standing under the palm trees, talking in hushed tones, the smell of sweat and anxious bodies hung heavy in the stale air. Uncle Ladipo, Aunty Laide and Taiwo were already standing in front of their gate when Kehinde and her mother arrived at home. The hem of Aunty Laide's bright pink bubu was crumpled up in her right hand, like she had gathered it up in haste, and her head scarf was coming undone. Uncle Ladipo was holding down his straw hat, speaking to Taiwo.

"It's happening, England has declared war against Germany!" Uncle Ladipo said once Kehinde and her mother reached their gate.

"They sent us home from school early," Taiwo said as they all hurried through the gate and into the house.

"I had to end my class halfway. The headmaster called an emergency meeting to make the announcement. We were all told to go home immediately," Aunty Laide said. There were sweat patches all over her bubu, and her scarf was still askew despite her numerous attempts to re-tie it.

Kehinde's mind was reeling, and she thought of her conversation with her father just that morning. Despite the mounting tension in the room, she felt a guilty excitement rise within her. Her life was about to change, she could feel it! She looked at Taiwo, and knew he was thinking the same.

"Will Nigeria be affected?" Kehinde's mother was asking Aunty Laide in Yoruba as she shut the door behind them.

"Abiola, of course the war will affect us! It's all everyone at the club has spoken about this week," Uncle Ladipo responded, speaking slowly like he was explaining economics to a child. Ikoyi Club, where he worked, had entertained many British citizens and administrators since it opened the previous year, and they had all been making plans to go home to their families and in some cases, to enlist. Kehinde looked at her mother like she had lost her mind. This news changed everything!

"Ladipo, I thought you said that even if war was declared, it wouldn't last long?" Aunty Laide said, sitting down beside Kehinde's mother on the sofa. The window was open, but Aunty Laide was still sweating, with beads of perspiration visible on her forehead.

"It shouldn't. From what I've heard, this will all be over by Christmas, next year at the latest. Hitler should be defeated in no time. He hardly has any support!"

Great, Kehinde thought. That should be just enough time for her to start her job and show her parents that she did not need to get married, at least not to Mr Ogunjobi.

"Good thing we got to celebrate your birthday before all of this," Aunty Laide said to Kehinde.

Kehinde looked through the window at the woman running past their gate carrying a small child, sure that her eyes would reveal the conflicting feelings within her under Aunty Laide's scrutiny.

"It's not necessarily bad news. Like Uncle Ladipo said, the war should be over quickly. Let me get some water for you both," Kehinde said, finding an excuse that she knew her mother would approve of as she disappeared into the kitchen to be alone with her thoughts.

She washed her hands in the kitchen sink and poured water into the glasses that she had set aside on a tray. She wished her father was here – they had so much to talk about. It must have been a busy day for him, or maybe the ferry was delayed. He should have been back at least two hours ago. As she was wondering if he had also heard the news about the war, she heard loud, frantic banging at their front door.

What now, she thought, as she made her way out of the kitchen carrying the tray of water. Taiwo was already opening the front door, and to her surprise, it was the photographer with the tribal marks. It was too soon for him to have their birthday prints with him, Kehinde thought, before she noticed that he was panting, with tears and sweat running down his face. His clothes were also wet, like he had been in a thunderstorm even though it was sunny outside. Kehinde felt her legs begin to shake.

"Your mother ... where is she? I need to see her!" he said, his eyes darting back and forth.

"Tade, what is it?" her mother said, frozen on the sofa, sandwiched between Uncle Ladipo and Aunty Laide. She sat stiffly, like if she moved her head too quickly, she would miss the words coming out of the photographer's mouth.

"It's Bàbá Ìbejì ... the ferry ... on its way back ... capsized..."

"And? Where is he now?" her mother demanded, as a cold mist suddenly wrapped itself around Kehinde's heart. She placed the tray on the dining table as she willed the photographer to speak but was unable to comprehend the words that were forming on his lips.

"He was not among the survivors ... I'm so sorry ... It was a terrible accident. Some passengers were able to swim to shore, but we are still looking for the others. We found some bodies, but no one has seen Bàbá Ìbejì," he stuttered.

Kehinde could see her mother start to tremble as Taiwo sunk down onto the floor, crumbling like a puppet in a pantomime. Kehinde felt like she was having an out-of-body experience, as if she were untethered from the earth. She dropped into her father's armchair, seeing Aunty Laide's arms close around her mother from the corner of her eye.

He was not among the survivors. The words were playing over and over again in her mind, the cold mist in her chest now drowning her heart relentlessly.

"I was there with the crew doing interviews and overheard the fishermen say Bàbá Ìbejì had boarded the ferry on the other side. They are still there … I had to come quickly … it was the least I could do," the photographer was saying.

Kehinde's mother's sobbing was getting louder by the minute as she rocked back and forth in Aunty Laide's arms. Aunty Laide held her, tears streaming down her face in a steady procession to her heaving chest. Uncle Ladipo had his hat in his hands, standing beneath the clock, his face ashen, and Taiwo remained on the floor, his eyes on his feet. Kehinde looked at the photographer, trying to remember his name.

"Mr Tade, my father is a strong swimmer, he might be trying to make his way back to shore as we speak," Kehinde asked. Her father *was* a good swimmer, he had taught many of the children in the neighbourhood how to swim, including herself and Taiwo. If some passengers had made it back to shore, he had to be there, somewhere.

"My dear … it's extremely unlikely. Men have been at shore for the last hour helping the survivors and identifying bodies," he said, looking past Kehinde like he was trying to unsee the events he had witnessed earlier. His voice could barely be heard above her mother's sobbing. Her wails filled the bungalow, bouncing back and forth between the walls. Kehinde needed her father here. Whenever her mother was this hysterical, he was the only one who could calm her.

The reality of their situation was beginning to hit home. She needed her father here, but according to Mr Tade he was never coming back. Never. Surely it could not be true. If her father was dead, she would feel something inside her core, something telling her that a part of her was gone forever, lost at sea. Instead, she felt raw, like she had been turned inside out and the most sensitive parts of her were exposed like a gutted fish.

Mr Tade was saying something about getting home before the blackout. She was vaguely aware of him standing up to leave, turning down an offered glass of water, shaking Uncle Ladipo's hand. She heard him say he would see himself out and that he would be back. Something about being sorry, Bàbá Ìbejì was a wonderful man, such a loss. Then the door shut and all she could hear were her mother's sobs. Subconsciously, Kehinde moved to the sofa and hugged her mother, her arms brushing Aunty Laide's arms as she continued to rock her back and forth on the other side. She willed her cries to drown out her thoughts and tried to focus on the clock, the sound of people hurrying home outside, the familiar smell of Aunty Laide's floral perfume, anything but the sentence that kept playing in her mind like a manic tambourine. *He was not among the survivors.*

What would happen to them now? Without fresh fish, they couldn't pay the dues for the market stall, and without the money from the sales, how would they survive? What would all this mean with the announcement of the war? How was it possible that she had received two earth-shattering pieces of news in one day and her eyes were as dry as sandpaper?

"I'm going out to look for him," Taiwo was saying, pulling on his satchel as if he was ready to run out of the door.

"Taiwo, the announcement made it clear that we are all to stay indoors this evening. Any loiterers will be arrested and taken to the police station. We must wait till tomorrow morning," Uncle Ladipo said, trying to be rational although the shock was apparent in his hoarse voice and bloodshot eyes. Aunty Laide was shaking her head, visibly trying to be strong for this family she had come to know and love. It felt like they were all actors in a bad play at Elegbata Square, each acting out a part that had no script. Kehinde felt the pain in Taiwo's eyes reach out to mingle with hers, the cold mist around her heart also engulfing his.

"We'll look for him tomorrow morning," Uncle Ladipo repeated, in this new broken voice that sounded so different from his usual timbre. Kehinde realised with a jolt of pain that Uncle Ladipo meant they would be looking for her father's body. She had been right about her father being a good swimmer. If he had survived, he would be here himself, telling them about the accident in his calm baritone.

Then darkness came, blanketing the house with a thick cloak of grief. It was agreed that Aunty Laide would sleep in their parents' room with their mother, with Uncle Ladipo sleeping on the sofa in the parlour.

Back in their room, Kehinde slept on Taiwo's bed, curled into his back the way they used to sleep as children. Silently, they both lay there, in too much shock to communicate with words. Each of them needed the strength the other would bring. How different this night was from the last one, the end of their eighteenth year, the last birthday they would celebrate with their father. The play that was her life was unfolding into an inconceivable scene – Britain was at war with Germany, her father was dead, and Kehinde had no idea what the next day would bring.

Chapter Four

Kehinde had once read that bad news travelled fast, and she remembered the saying now as she made her way through their crowded parlour with a tray of water in her hands. Somehow, everyone in the surrounding streets had heard that her father was missing and presumed dead. The same visitors that had celebrated with them just two days ago, were now bringing their condolences in the form of words, dishes full of ikokore, ewa and asaro, and barely concealed pity in their eyes.

Kehinde's mother looked like she had aged ten years overnight. Lines were etched across the previously smooth skin on her face, the brightness in her gaze replaced by a dull glint. She wore a brown iro and buba, and her hair was tied up in a black head scarf, looking like a broken doll that had been put together by a blind man. She sat on the sofa in the parlour, propped up by Uncle Ladipo and Aunty Laide, unable to acknowledge the visitors who were speaking about how great a man Bàbá Ìbejì had been, how tragic the accident was, how he would be missed.

Kehinde handed out glasses of water, more out of a sense of obligation than an actual desire to care for the people who had shown up uninvited to their home. She wanted to curl up in her father's boat and pretend they were playing a game of hide and seek the way they used to when she and Taiwo were little. As she made her way through the parlour there were murmured apologies and sighs of thanks.

"What a brave girl you are, your father would be so proud of you."

"God have mercy on you."

"You and Taiwo need to be strong for your mother."

The last comment came from Mrs Fari, a trader from the stall a few doors down from theirs in the market.

"I was barely your age when my own father passed away," she continued, adjusting the waistline of her iro when Kehinde had collected the bag of stewing beef she had brought. "I had to fend for my three younger sisters and my mother, but God was faithful. He will provide for you in your time of need."

Kehinde looked at her blankly. Where was God now? Her father had attended Bethel Cathedral every Sunday, singing and clapping during the praise and worship. Every time she knelt to pray, it was because her father was constantly reminding her that God wanted to hear from her too. He knew the Bible from beginning to end, he could recite the Book of Proverbs in Yoruba, but he had not been among the survivors. *As He giveth, so He taketh*, Kehinde heard her father's voice say in her mind and she shook her head against the words. Why had God taken her father? What had they done to deserve this? God had failed him when he needed God most. *God's plan*, she heard her father's voice again. Did God plan for them to be found wanting when they were most in need? Did God plan for the inevitability of death to continue to break the humans He cared so much for?

The worst part was Kehinde kept trying to imagine her father's final moment. Drowning was supposed to be excruciatingly painful, but he couldn't have drowned. She was convinced he had been hurt, maybe something had hit him on the head and it had been an instant blackout, with no pain. Or could he have been trapped somewhere under water, screaming silently, unable to swim out? This particular line of thinking was sending Kehinde down a tunnel she was sure would end in insanity.

Blinking, Kehinde made her way back to the kitchen to get more water, placing the empty tray and bag of meat on the counter. It was not lost on her that the last time she had seen her father, his eyes had been full of hurt and disappointment, caused by her and Taiwo in this very kitchen. Would their argument have featured in his final thoughts? She felt a fresh stab of pain as she remembered putting her father's breakfast on that same tray just two days ago.

Uncle Ladipo and Taiwo had gone out first thing in the morning, even renting a boat from one of the other fishermen to look for his body. After hours on the water, they found nothing, no trace that her father had been on the water that day, or any of the other days in the forty-two years of his life.

Now, it was two o'clock and Taiwo was nowhere to be found. He had left the house with Kunle shortly after he got back from the search, leaving Kehinde and her mother to receive the mourners: an unending, colourful stream of people in various shapes and sizes, flowing in and out of their home.

Kehinde had never felt more alone. Unlike Taiwo, Kehinde did not have a best friend that could offer a brief reprieve from the pain in her head. Before she had left school, she had always been too shy to make her own friends, choosing the ones Taiwo had chosen for them, and when they weren't there, Taiwo was all she had. Her brother had always been enough for her, her safe space, the person who knew what she was thinking before she spoke, the one who spoke on her behalf. He knew her better than anyone else, sometimes more than even she did. How she wished she had someone and somewhere else to escape to now.

Thinking of the only other place she had ever felt comforted, she slipped out of the back door at the side of the kitchen. Their cement courtyard had a small fence that overlooked Uncle Ladipo and Aunty Laide's courtyard and with a quick hop, she landed squarely on the other side. She went over to the flowerpot outside the kitchen door where she knew they hid their spare key and opened the door.

As soon as she stepped in, Kehinde was enveloped by the comforting smell of coconut oil and lemon juice, the essence of Aunty Laide and Uncle Ladipo's bright house. She walked towards her favourite piece of art on the wall in their parlour, a red and yellow mosaic of a boy whose facial expression had always been a mystery to her. His eyes looked sad, but his mouth was set in a bemused smile, like he was watching the events of the world with the pity of one who already knew what was to come. To the left of the painting was the room she was looking for, the place where she had spent countless hours, Aunty Laide's study.

Kehinde opened the door and with a sigh almost as cathartic as a sob, sank into the brown leather pouffe in the centre. Authors from around the world, ranging from George Orwell to Virginia Woolf, lined the four walls of the room from top to bottom, offering their silent words of consolation. She sunk her feet into the huge purple and green raffia mat that took up most of the floor space as she settled into the pouffe, adjusting to accommodate the lump in the middle of the cushion.

As she lay back into the soft leather, her eyes fell on the black and white picture on the mahogany writing desk in the corner. It showed Aunty Laide and Aunty Bimpe, her younger sister, their heads both thrown back as they laughed at something the photographer was saying. Aunty Bimpe had lived here with Aunty Laide and Uncle Ladipo for years while she did her midwifery training, but she had moved to London with her Jamaican husband, Uncle James.

Kehinde remembered all the upheaval her move had caused; nobody thought Aunty Bimpe should go, but she did anyway. Kehinde was only seven years old at the time, but she would never forget the sight of Aunty Laide begging Aunty Bimpe not to move to London with a man she barely knew. Aunty Bimpe was a rebel and Kehinde admired her because unlike her, Kehinde had always been too scared of the unknown to ignore the advice of everyone around her. Kehinde and Aunty Bimpe still exchanged letters, and contrary to what everyone had been worried about, Aunty Bimpe was thriving as a midwife in London. She, Uncle James and their two sons were living a great life that had been worth fighting for. With a lurch in her heart, Kehinde imagined how she would have to write about her father's death in her next letter to Aunty Bimpe – that's if Aunty Laide didn't tell her first.

"I knew I would find you in here," Aunty Laide said, startling Kehinde as she appeared at the entrance of the study. She sank down beside her on the raffia mat, stretching her legs out in front of her.

"How are we going to survive?" Kehinde asked.

"We'll get through this together," Aunty Laide sighed.

"Mum…" Kehinde started, unable to complete her sentence.

She felt her panic rise again as she thought of her newly shrunken mother. Everyone who knew their family also knew that her father and mother had been childhood sweethearts. Taiwo and Kehinde had heard the story of how they had met as five-year-olds, by the river in their village in Abeokuta, inseparable from the inception of their friendship. Years later, they had left their home behind to migrate to Lagos in search of a better life. It was the fairy tale of their childhood, a story of love that seemed hardly attainable. Love that had always been like a lighthouse, a beacon of hope, that had now been washed away, never to resurface. Kehinde hugged her knees closer to her, the white bubu she was wearing completely covering her like a cloud of cotton. Aunty Laide looked down at her hands then exhaled before she spoke.

"Your mother is stronger than you realise, Keke. We had a long talk last night."

"About Daddy?"

"Yes, and a lot more. Keke … your wedding needs to happen this week, after your father's funeral," Aunty Laide said, looking straight into Kehinde's eyes, and taking her by surprise as she knelt and took Kehinde's two hands in hers.

"Aunty Laide, please. I don't want to marry him, not this week, not ever!" Kehinde begged, imploring Aunty Laide to understand, her words tumbling over each other in her haste to get them all out at once.

"Keke, listen to me. Get married to Mr Ogunjobi, he will provide for you and your mother and Taiwo will be able to continue with school," Aunty Laide continued, gripping her hands.

"What does my mother think?"

"It was her idea, omo mi. Keke, getting married now might not be such a bad thing. No one knows what will happen with this war. At least Mr Ogunjobi will be able to protect you," Aunty Laide continued earnestly.

"Aunty, this isn't what I want," she choked out, the pain in her voice making her sound like she was croaking.

"Sometimes we must put away what we want, to do what we need to do, for the good of our family," Aunty Laide said, her eyes wet as she pulled Kehinde into a fierce embrace. Kehinde sunk into her hug, hating herself as she felt the familiar warmth of going along with what everyone else wanted. It was the easier, safer thing to do. And now that her father was gone, it all felt kind of pointless. Even if she accepted the job, her father would never come back. Neither would he come back if she got married, she felt a stronger voice scream in her head. She had lost her father, why did she have to put aside her dreams as well?

Her father had wanted her to get married and now the war he thought was coming had arrived and they were even worse off. Even if she decided to work at the *West African Pilot*, her wages would never put enough food on the table for her family in the absence of her father. His death was not something she had ever accounted for, and how could she have? And regardless of what she did or didn't do, her father would still be gone forever. What was the point in fighting at all? Kehinde felt numb as she let Aunty Laide pull her off the floor and through the front door. The picture of the boy in the parlour seemed to be smiling at her in a way that said he understood the complexities of staying alive, what it took to survive even when you could not fight for yourself.

The worst part about death was how life forced you to move on, flowing onwards like a river, propelling you forward, not caring about the bumps you had to endure along the way. She suddenly felt like she was sitting in an open barn with no walls, exposed to the storm that was brewing around her. It was the day after her father had been pronounced missing, presumed dead, and here she was already planning how to live without him. Kehinde saw her dreams floating away on a tide of despair, suddenly further from her grasp than they had ever been. She gulped for air, wondering if her chest would ever feel light again.

The wave of resentment and jealousy that rose unbidden in her chest took her by surprise and threatened to drown her. Taiwo was off, God knew where, and here she was being told that her marriage would be the only thing that could save her family from poverty. He was the older twin; he had been in the world for seven minutes before she was born. Why did she always have to be the one making sacrifices?

She still remembered the day, just over a year ago, when her parents had broken her heart by telling her the news that would change her life forever. She was weeks away from her seventeenth birthday, crouched beneath the dining table, completely still, praying that her parents would not catch her eavesdropping. She knew they were unlikely to hear her over the sounds of the street that came from the open window, but she held her breath as she listened to their exchange. She had stopped herself from sneezing by pinching her nose as she involuntarily inhaled the smell of the red pepper stew from lunch that still lingered in the air, tickling her like a teasing fairy.

"Laide, thank you so much," her father had said.

"You know I would do more if I could. Kehinde deserves this as much as Taiwo does," Aunty Laide replied.

Her father had hesitated before speaking again, clearing his throat the way he did when he was trying to find the right words to say. "And you're sure there's nothing else we can do?"

"The scholarship position is for just one student. They both passed, but you will have to make a choice about who will be taking it. Remember it's only a partial scholarship, you will still have to pay half the fees," Aunty Laide said. Kehinde could see her feet, squeezed into her smart black shoes with folds of skin bulging over the sides as she shifted her weight from one to the other. She must have come straight from the teachers meeting to their house, she only ever wore those shoes to school. Kehinde thought she could hear the sadness in Aunty Laide's voice and felt grateful for this small show of loyalty.

"Well, in that case we'll have to break the news to her softly," her father said, his voice deepening on the word softly, like he was trying to give the act of delivering the news the strength it would need.

"It's only the final year she'll be missing. She's lucky she even went to school at all," her mother said. Her sandalled feet stood placed together, as dainty as the edge of the lace tablecloth that framed the view from Kehinde's vantage point under the table.

"Abiola," her father warned.

"It's true. She would have been more useful coming to the market with me all this time," her mother continued.

"She'll be devastated, most especially because she's only one year away from getting her school certificate," her father said.

"Let me know if you want me to be there when you tell her," Aunty Laide replied.

"Thank you, Laide, you've done more than enough

already." Kehinde watched their feet move in unison as they made their way towards the front door. Her father's slippers made a slapping sound against the cement floor, while her mother's sandals glided gracefully despite the loose threads that hung off the straps. Aunty Laide's black shoes had a heavier, slower tread, the weight of the news she had just delivered yet to be transferred from messenger to receiver. Kehinde heard the door shut, as the gust of wind that had come in suddenly vanished along with her education, like a fire being blown out from a candle.

At the sound of the door clicking, she scrambled out from under the dining room table and hurried to her room. She had been lying on her bed reading *Sense and Sensibility* when she saw Aunty Laide walking up their footpath, through her bedroom window, and she knew why she was coming. It was the day Aunty Laide had gone to find out if the school could offer two places, instead of one. Things had already been bad enough in the market. With the colonial government's new tax policy and with the rise in imports in the last year, her parents had found paying their secondary school fees increasingly difficult. Then Aunty Laide had told them about the new scholarship the school had introduced. Right from the beginning they had known there would only be one place, but they had all hoped that if both children performed well, a miracle would happen. But from the set of Aunty Laide's shoulders as she had walked up to their door, Kehinde had already known.

As she lay on her bed afterwards, pretending to read while her chest splintered, she felt like the displaced Dashwood sisters. What she had heard sunk into her brain, and like water filling up a bucket, the weight of Aunty Laide's words crushed her into the mattress. She would not be finishing secondary school, Taiwo would be going on without her, the obvious choice, the child worth investing in. They had both got the same score, joint holders of the first place, but Taiwo had been chosen, not her. Not her, even though she was the one who enjoyed school more, who was better at it. Taiwo was not even there to hear the news himself, he had left earlier to watch the Calabar Brass Band at Elegbata Square. She tried to be happy for him but how could she be happy for him when he had got what she had wanted more than anything else?

Her father opened the door to her room to see her lying on her bed, the book in her hands only partially hiding the tears in her eyes. The wind from the open window above the bed blew in, rustling the lace curtains, almost pushing the door back against her father's face. She thought about her first day of school, when he had told her and Taiwo to always remember the home they had come from, to go in and make him proud. Kehinde gazed up at him, waiting to hear the words she knew were coming, watching as the lines on his forehead arranged themselves into a stoic assembly, ready to support his mouth as they bore the bad news.

The face she would never see again.

Feeling like her mind was reeling in a thousand directions, she was brought back to the present as she and Aunty Laide stepped out onto a sombre looking Malumo Street. It was different, like it had been painted over by a malicious brush with grey paint. There was an unusually cool, biting breeze in the afternoon air, almost as if the announcement of the war had conjured an atmosphere of danger. In the distance, Kehinde saw a boy on his bicycle carrying a gas mask on his back. Her father had died, but the world around her was beginning to fight a completely different battle from the one that was raging within her.

Chapter Five

The next three hours passed by in an unhappy blur, with Kehinde's mother sobbing intermittently in the parlour, visitors coming and going, and Uncle Ladipo doing most of the greeting and talking. Kehinde and Aunty Laide were in and out of the kitchen, Kehinde forcing herself to focus only on serving the visitors. She had just emerged later that afternoon with a new tray of water when she saw Taiwo alighting his bicycle through the parlour window. She dropped the tray and went outside through the back door, almost running across the overgrown grass on the narrow pathway by their house. In her haste she collided with him as he tried to sneak in through the side door.

"Tee, where've you been?" she asked, taking in the sight of him. He was wearing one of their father's fishing tunics and as he swayed on his feet, she could smell beer on his breath.

"Calm down, I've been at the racecourse with Kunle and Captain Mackenzie," he hiccupped.

"I've spent the whole morning in and out of the kitchen,

serving visitors, and listening to Mummy cry, and you've been sitting around, drinking like nothing has happened?!"

"Obviously not. I needed to get away."

"You're so selfish! You didn't even think for a second about what it would be like for me to be here on my own!"

"Hang on, I don't recall you coming with me and Uncle Ladipo earlier to look for Daddy's body. You were still asleep when we were going round in circles on the water!" His eyes were glistening, seemingly lit up by a fire behind them, his upper lip curling in a sneer. Kehinde knew that look well. He was gearing up for a fight and she was ready for him.

"How sad for you, Taiwo. As soon as you left, I had to feed the five thousand visitors that descended on us! And as usual, you did nothing to help!"

They were still alone at the side of the house, their voices muffled by the wind. The creeping plant on the wall beside them swayed gently, almost seeming to strain to hear the conversation.

"I've also had a hard day!"

"You're not the one being married off to pay the bills!" Kehinde retorted. Taiwo paused as his mouth opened in shock.

"Wait, Keke, what are you talking about?" He asked.

"Aunty Laide told me that I'll be getting married this week, to Mr Ogunjobi. After the funeral. With the war coming … without Daddy…" Her shoulders visibly sagged as she exhaled.

"No, Keke!" Taiwo interrupted, holding her. "Look, Captain Mackenzie said he can fast-track my move to Zaria. If I enlist and start my training now, I could go with him to join the Royal Air Force before the end of the year! They need the men, Keke, and my stipend would be sent to you and Mummy."

"You can't join the Army, Tee," Kehinde said with a shrug. His pipe dream of being a soldier suddenly seemed silly and childish in the face of their father's death and her impending marriage. "It's not what Daddy wanted. Can't you at least hold on till the end of the school year? You might have changed your mind by then?" she continued.

"But Daddy is no longer here, Keke," Taiwo said, still holding her shoulders.

"Even if he isn't, it was his dream for you to finish school and become a lawyer."

"His dream, not mine! You know this more than anyone!" Taiwo said, dropping his hands from her shoulders and grabbing her hands. "Keke, Daddy's gone, and there's nothing we can do about it, but this is the moment we both have to stand up for what we want. You can't sit back and let them tell you what you do, you have to start fighting back like you mean it. If you don't—"

Before he could finish, Uncle Ladipo stuck his head out of the kitchen door.

"There you are. Kehinde, Mr Ogunjobi is here to see you," he said, glancing at Taiwo briefly before looking back at Kehinde and gesturing with his hands for her to come into the house. Taiwo clammed up and followed Kehinde in through the kitchen, now looking completely sober. Aunty Laide was standing inside, waiting for them by the back door.

"Keke, your uncle and I have just spoken to Mr Ogunjobi. He has assured us that he's prepared to marry you this week, the day after the funeral. It will be a small wedding here, just us, and then you'll go to your new home with him afterwards," she said, the relief palpable in her voice.

"She can't —"Taiwo said.

"Not now, Tee," Kehinde said, wanting to get the entire interaction over with.

"He's in the parlour now," Uncle Ladipo said, pushing her towards the open door and raising his eyebrows at Taiwo.

There were only three visitors left, and although there was a low murmur of voices in the room, Mr Ogunjobi's bellow could immediately be picked out above the others.

"England will win this war against Hitler, together with the rest of the Commonwealth. There's no doubt about that," he was saying, referring to the broadcast that had announced the war.

Today he was wearing a navy three-piece suit and his low afro was parted on the side. Almost like he could sense her presence, he looked up at her and rose from where he was sitting beside her mother, the red on his tie matching the red of the sofa. Quickly, he crossed the small space towards the kitchen door, his leather shoes making a loud clip-clop sound on the floor.

"My poor flower. I came as soon as I heard," he said, his brow creasing as he looked down at her. He had beads of sweat on his forehead despite the breeze coming in from the open door and windows. Kehinde looked up at him, her knight in a suit, here to save her and her family from poverty and ruin. They would be married in mere days and yet she couldn't find the words to say to him, she struggled to believe how quickly her life was changing, spiralling, without her consent or understanding. She wanted to scream but it felt like even if she did, nobody would hear her.

"Thank you, sir," she said, not meeting his eyes.

"I've already spoken to Mr and Mrs Latinwo. I can't spend too much time here now, but I'll be back tomorrow," he said, with a quick nod at Aunty Laide and Uncle Ladipo. *To finalise our wedding plans*, Kehinde thought glumly. Beside her Taiwo greeted Mr Ogunjobi with a mumble, barely concealing the disgust on his face. Mr Ogunjobi must have mistaken his grim countenance for grief because he patted Taiwo's shoulder in response.

"Your father was a good man. He will be sorely missed," he responded, shaking Taiwo's hand. Taiwo remained uncharacteristically quiet, gritting his teeth against the hard words she knew he wanted to spit out. Kehinde felt her earlier anger towards him melt into pity for both of them. They had lost their father, and they were both now equally lost. Taiwo had spent the day grieving in his own way, while she, as usual, had let the day happen to her. *I'm such a coward,* she thought, allowing herself to sink into her self-pity. Yesterday she had been fired up about making a difference and now she could hardly think beyond the fact that her last conversation with her father had been an argument. She was too confused and afraid to think about what she really wanted, and maybe even too exhausted to care.

"Thank you again for coming, sir," Uncle Ladipo was saying beside her.

"For nothing, you're my family now," Mr Ogunjobi said, his eyes landing on Kehinde. "I must run, I left a meeting in Apapa, but I'll clear my schedule for the rest of the week."

Nodding and bowing, Kehinde and Taiwo said their goodbyes as Uncle Ladipo escorted Mr Ogunjobi out of the house. The three other visitors also stood to leave.

"We have to start going now before it gets dark," said one of the men that Kehinde didn't recognise. Although no one could guess the extent of the changes to come, the people of Lagos were already coming to terms with their new way of life, and as the penalty for loitering after dark was arrest or forced conscription, everyone was fearful of breaking the new rules.

Later that evening, Kehinde, Taiwo, their mother, Uncle Ladipo and Aunty Laide sat around the table eating amala, ewedu and fish stew, a quick dinner made by Uncle Ladipo with the last of the fish left behind by her father. The sun was setting outside, and they had a single candle lit in the centre of the table. Kehinde was surprised at how hungry she was; she had barely eaten anything since the day before, which now seemed like a lifetime ago. It was strange how your body continued to have its physical needs, regardless of the state of your mind, she thought.

"I'm glad you're eating, Keke," Uncle Ladipo said, smiling, although the dark bags underneath his eyes looked like haunted shadows as he spoke. "I'll need to go back to work tomorrow, so will Aunty Laide. Abiola," he said softly, looking at Kehinde's mother directly. "Have you given some thought to what we spoke about earlier?"

Kehinde's mother looked up from her bowl, startled, like she had been pulled out of another world. Her headscarf sloped to the left of her forehead, and her unkempt appearance was so unlike her usual pristine one that it was almost comical.

"Yes, Ladipo," she said quietly, clearing her throat. "I want to get the funeral rites over with quickly. I've sent word to Reverend Kasunmu to come tomorrow to finalise the arrangements."

"Abiola, are you sure?" asked Aunty Laide, from her place beside their mother.

"I am. There's no point prolonging this … there's no body…" Their mother paused as if gathering her strength before she carried on. "There's no body to bury. We'll say prayers for him on Friday, and that will be all. It's not like we have the money for a funeral anyway."

The table was silent as her words sunk in. Kehinde let the words register, a new phase of despair settling in her stomach. The expense of a coffin with no body in it was one they could do without, but this meant that there would never be a proper grave to mourn her father, no real ceremony to signal his departure from the world. Her father was lost forever, and they would have to forge ahead.

"And Kehinde will get married on Saturday," Kehinde's mother continued.

"Are we all just going to sit here pretending that this makes any sense?" Taiwo said, his voice sounding loud in the quiet room. He had stopped eating and as Kehinde looked down she saw that his hands were clenched into fists under the table.

"Taiwo, that is no way to talk to your mother," Uncle Ladipo said.

"Uncle, no, this is not right. We're at war with Germany! This is not a good time for Kehinde to get married!" Taiwo interrupted. Beside him, Kehinde looked down into her bowl. The stew had congealed around the amala and she had lost her appetite.

"Taiwo, calm down, you don't know more than your own mother. All this uncertainty is exactly why Kehinde should get married, at least we won't have to worry about her as well. Your mother is acting in the best interests of both of you," Uncle Ladipo said, sitting forward in his seat.

"Oh, please, Uncle," Taiwo scoffed. "She always wanted Kehinde to get married quickly, war or no war."

"Enough! You will not disrespect your mother like this!" Uncle Ladipo boomed, his voice echoing around the dark room and suddenly taking on a life of its own.

"Kehinde doesn't need to get married! I'm joining the Air Force, I'll be the one to provide for this family now, not Mr Ogunjobi," Taiwo said, looking at Kehinde pointedly.

She felt sweat pooling in her underarms as the room once again fell silent. At this point, it would have made sense for her to say something, anything, about how she agreed with Taiwo. He had given the perfect thunder for her lightning to strike. This would be a good time to stand up for herself, to say she had a job she wanted to do, that she didn't understand how it would work although she wanted to give it a try. But a fear she was yet to define kept her mouth shut and the grandfather clock on the wall chimed seven o'clock, making her jump.

"Taiwo, you're not joining the Air Force, and Kehinde is getting married to Mr Ogunjobi. That's final," Kehinde's mother said in a wobbly voice that belied the determined expression on her face. Taiwo shook his head at Kehinde, and the disappointment on his face made her eyes prickle. He got up from the table and stormed off, slamming the door of their bedroom in his wake. Kehinde made to stand up and run after him, but Aunty Laide shook her head.

"Leave him. He's just lost his father and now he's losing his sister in a different way. It's a lot to take in," she said sadly.

And Kehinde felt like she was losing her mind.

"What's all this about him joining the Air Force?" Kehinde's mother asked, the skin of her brow folding into two parallel lines beneath her scarf.

"This is the first I've heard of it as well. I can't say I'm surprised though. A lot of young men have been speaking about enlisting all summer. However, Taiwo must finish school first, I know that's what Bàbá Ìbejì would have wanted. I'll talk to him tomorrow morning before I go to work," Uncle Ladipo promised.

Kehinde continued to look down into her bowl, watching her cooling food take on a new form as the conversation continued around her. Her hunger was replaced by a hollowness in her gut. Unlike Taiwo, she didn't even know what she wanted anymore. Was she in the right state of mind to start anything new, job or marriage? She was in so much pain, and she knew she did not want to get married. But her father was gone and according to the adults who had advised her for her whole life, there was no other solution.

Kehinde's New Journal, September 8, 1939

Today was Daddy's funeral, or rather, funeral blessing. We went to Bethel Cathedral and said prayers for him, then we went to the graveyard in the small courtyard behind the church and stood by a meaningless stone with his name on it. Mummy was crying throughout the ceremony, but the second we got back home she stopped crying and just had this strange look on her face, like she had turned into Daddy's tombstone's twin. Not funny. Her silence was even scarier than the crying. Taiwo and I didn't cry at all. I held his hand throughout the prayers and when we got back home this time, he didn't disappear. He's been a bit distant since Wednesday morning when Uncle Ladipo came over to talk to him about not joining the Air Force. They were sitting on the back step outside the kitchen for hours and when they were done Taiwo looked like he had been crying. I overheard Uncle Ladipo telling Mummy that he couldn't convince Taiwo, although he begged Taiwo to go back to school next week and reconsider. Taiwo still hasn't spoken about it much and he was already asleep by the time I got to the room after helping Mummy clear up the kitchen. I also know he's angry with me for not speaking up, but this time it's different, like a sad kind of anger that also feels like pity. For the first time, it feels like I don't really know what he's thinking, and it makes me feel like an avocado cut in half. The worst part is that tomorrow I will be gone forever to Mr Ogunjobi's house and we won't get a chance to catch up before I get ready to leave.

My brain feels like a fog full of everyone else's comments about what I should and shouldn't be doing. I still can't believe this is all happening. I thought about—

Kehinde jumped as she heard her mother's door creak open, hitting her head on the cabinet beside her as she scrambled to close her journal and put the candle out.

"Kehinde, is that you?" her mother called out, making her way towards the kitchen. She hissed as she took in the scene in front of her. "It's almost midnight! We aren't supposed to have any lights on!" As she looked closer at Kehinde's face, her expression melted. "You're nervous about tomorrow," she stated, crouching down to sit in the small space beside Kehinde on the floor.

"Nervous about getting married to a man I barely know, the day after my father's funeral? Not at all." She felt mean and petty for being sarcastic, but her nerves were frayed, and her life felt like it was a crumbling piece of bread that had been squeezed too many times, soggy and of no use to anyone.

"Everything seems to be happening so quickly. Your birthday feels like it was a year ago. So much has changed in just five days," her mother sighed, adjusting the hem of her nightgown as she pulled it over her knees, her shadow expanding her small frame in the dim light.

"Mummy … can't we postpone the wedding? Can I have some more time? I'm not ready."

"Keke, we have nothing. This is the only way. Aunty Laide

took me to get my ration card, and I'm glad at least you'll be provided for."

Kehinde watched her mother's mouth set into a thin line. Like a sheep being led to the slaughter by its shepherd, she could not look her in the eyes. Her mother was supposed to be her protector, but now they had found themselves in the reverse situation and Kehinde didn't know what to make of it.

"There are things … things that happen between a man and wife in the bedroom," her mother continued. "You must do as your husband wishes, follow his lead."

Kehinde nodded, feeling numb as she blocked out the thought of being alone with Mr Ogunjobi.

"I love you so much, Keke … I hope you know that?" her mother said suddenly, putting an arm around Kehinde. "I know this is what your father wanted, and Mr Ogunjobi is a good man, he'll treat you well. I know you'll be happy."

"Yes, Mummy," Kehinde swallowed a lump in her throat as she felt panic rise within her.

"Let's get some sleep, we have to be up early," her mother said, rising and moving towards the door. Kehinde quickly pushed her journal under the cabinet, making a mental note to pick it up later to add to the bag of her belongings that would be relocating with her the next day.

Chapter Six

Kehinde woke up to her mother tapping her shoulder at dawn, forgetting who and where she was in the seconds it took for her to blink her eyes open. Taiwo's bed was empty, and before she could dwell on where he could be, she followed her mother to begin the preparation for the new day of this unfolding nightmare. How different the previous Saturday had been, the still fresh memory of her last morning on her father's boat shaking her to her core. Her parents' room still had the lingering, sea air smell that clung to her father, and Kehinde felt like she was having an out-of-body experience as her mother brushed out her tight curls and tied her hair up into a bun. She sat still as Aunty Laide slipped into the room, her hand resting on the iro and buba and aso-oke gele that Kehinde was to wear. Her mother had decided that the cream colour of her outfit was her best option; not too brash for mourning, but still soft enough to complement her complexion as the bride. The pink stripes in her aso-oke were meant to make her face look brighter but Kehinde felt as dark as night on the inside.

After her bath, her mother helped her tie the iro securely around her waist. Aunty Laide wound Kehinde's gele around her head so tightly that she feared her brain would pop out of her skull. Not that she would have minded. Her brain already felt like mud, she imagined that not being able to think would be a welcome relief. But one thought remained – before the sun set, she would be in her new home and her father would still be gone. Kehinde shivered at the inevitability of the day ahead.

"Where's Taiwo?" Uncle Ladipo asked, shortly after Aunty Laide opened the front door for him.

"I heard the door click before we started getting ready," Kehinde's mother mumbled.

"He shouldn't be out at all during the blackout! Is he trying to get arrested?" Uncle Ladipo threw his hands up in exasperation.

How could Taiwo leave her alone on this morning of all mornings when she needed him most, Kehinde wondered, shocked at the familiar taste of bitter resentment that rose at the back of her throat.

"I'm sure he'll show up soon," Aunty Laide said.

He didn't, but sure as the sun, not long after Kehinde came out of the room, Mr Ogunjobi arrived in his agbada, with a native priest in a white wrapper and Kayode the ever-present bodyguard as his witness. The traditional ceremony was a small affair, a brisk wedding blessing that ended almost as quickly as it started. Kehinde barely heard the priest intone the Yoruba words around her. Uncle Ladipo, Aunty Laide and her mother sat around the parlour, also bearing witness to what felt like a set of sacrificial rites.

Kehinde heard herself repeating the words the priest asked her to, and she trembled as he pronounced them man and wife, the latest Mr and Mrs Ogunjobi. As her husband shook hands with Uncle Ladipo after a celebratory breakfast of fried yam and eggs where only Mr Ogunjobi asked for seconds, the words *he was not among the survivors* played repeatedly like a scratched record in Kehinde's head. It was becoming the soundtrack to the play of doom that was now her life. Her father had not been here to witness this sham of a wedding and he was never coming back. Her life would continue to propel forward, her as a living ghost without him.

"Take care of our baby, sir," Uncle Ladipo said, sounding like he still had yam in his mouth. Mr Ogunjobi patted him on the back.

"You'll always have a place here, Keke, never forget that" Aunty Laide whispered as she hugged Kehinde. They were standing in front of the gate now, the afternoon sun beating down on their small party.

The lump in Kehinde's throat barely allowed her to nod in response. Her mother was standing in the door frame, still wearing black and looking like the wind would blow her away at any moment. She stepped forward and pulled Kehinde into a long hug that had her distracted enough by how much smaller her mother felt to forget about the drumming noise in her head for the moment. The goodbyes ended and suddenly, Kehinde and her new husband were climbing into his brown Austin. Kayode had already packed Kehinde's bags in the boot and was now sitting in front beside the driver. The doors slammed, closing the first chapter of Kehinde's life forever.

After what felt like five minutes but was actually more like fifteen, Mr Ogunjobi's car turned into Bamgbose Street, the sounds of the city receding as they made their way down the quiet paved road on the other side of Lagos Island. Like most streets on the island, this one was narrow and lined with trees. Unlike Kehinde's street however, the houses here were much bigger and surrounded by tall fences. Aunty Laide had told her that this area was known as the "Brazilian quarters," after the Aguda: the ex-slaves who had settled there on their return from captivity, and was now home to several upper-class Nigerians. The houses were unique in their architecture – curlicues on many of the buildings, with high ceilings and arched windows. Her father would have loved to see the houses, she thought with despair. He had always been interested in historical buildings. Maybe he had visited – surely, he must have done so before promising her hand in marriage, Kehinde thought, trying and failing at not feeling the resentment rise again, this time directed at her parents. If her father had only listened to her, she wouldn't be here, rushing towards a new life in this strange car with the warm hand of a husband she barely knew resting on her knee. But her father was gone and now she would never know what her life would have been like if he'd listened, if she had received his blessing to work at the *West African Pilot* instead.

"Welcome home, my flower," Mr Ogunjobi said, giving her thigh a squeeze as they pulled up to an imposing white house. Kehinde felt her heart rate quicken.

Kayode opened the door for her and Kehinde got her first look at her new home. It was the biggest house she'd ever seen. A wide lawn that looked like it was tended to by a meticulous gardener stretched behind the gate, and a brown wooden door stood above a flight of three broad steps that led into the main house. Her husband held her sweaty palm as he led her towards the front door, with Kayode following behind them carrying her bags.

A young girl wearing what looked like an English maid's uniform opened the door for them. For the first time that day Kehinde felt like laughing. Why would Mr Ogunjobi make his help dress like they were working for a colonial master? She had noticed his driver was also in uniform and thought it was a one-off, and not for the first time, she found herself wondering what this man she had married was really like.

They walked into a waiting area with two armchairs covered in a gold, embroidered material, with a light brown table between them. Kehinde could hear the low murmur of voices from behind another door to their right. The maid sunk down into a low curtsey as she greeted them, her movement generating a faint smell of fried onions and tomatoes that seemed at odds with her dress.

"Ẹ káàbọ̀, sir, everyone is waiting in the parlour to welcome you," she said, her eyes darting to the floor after a quick glance at Kehinde.

With a nod, her husband led her in through the door and she gasped involuntarily at how majestic the room was. In the middle of the floor sat a rug, dominated by a black and yellow pattern that looked like dancing crowns and sceptres. Four wide, arched windows on either end of the room had thick, beige curtains held back with golden tassels. Every space on the wall was covered in a painting or picture, some of them pictures of Mr Ogunjobi with various men from the colonial government, dressed in formal attire. Pots of tall house plants had been thoughtfully placed around the room, giving the air a faint smell of wet leaves as they swayed against the breeze coming in from the wide-open windows on each wall. As she looked around the room, Kehinde realised that the women and children seated on the embroidered gold sofas must be the members of the Ogunjobi household, her new family. They all stood up as the door shut behind Kehinde and her husband.

There was a middle-aged woman, the oldest in the room, who Kehinde knew must be Mama Tope, the first wife. Her skin was the colour of dark, wet sand at the riverbank, in sharp contrast with her green lace iro and buba. Her small eyes narrowed even more as they rested on Kehinde. Kehinde felt her shoes sink into the carpet as she adjusted her stance under the scrutiny of Mama Tope's gaze.

The first of the three children standing beside her was Tope, who was only a few years younger than she was and who Kehinde vaguely recognised from Sunday school. Despite the light of recognition in Tope's eyes, after a brief smile at Kehinde she averted her gaze. Beside her were two young boys who looked like they were between the ages of ten and eight, pinching each other behind their backs as they struggled to standstill.

"Welcome home, Baba Tope!" came a low voice from the other woman standing in front of the sofa to the left of the room. Her skin was the colour of a kola nut, and she was dressed in the most colourful oleku Kehinde had ever seen. It looked like what she imagined Joseph's technicolour dream coat would have looked like, with big sleeves fringed by different coloured threads hanging at her wrists. Her hair was swept up in a matching scarf, but you could still see thick black curls sprouting out from the top. High cheekbones sat above her full cheeks, making her face appear angular but soft, and when she smiled at Kehinde, there was a gap in the middle of her two front teeth that made her lips seem fuller.

Kehinde felt the warmth from that smile across the room. Beside the woman were two miniature versions of her, with big hair tied up in rainbow-coloured ribbons.

"Ẹṣe, Ayo mi. Everyone, I would like you to welcome my new wife, Kehinde, to our household," her husband announced, like introducing new wives was something he did every other day.

"Ayo, show her to her room and help her settle in. I'll be in my room resting till later," he continued, before he turned and walked through yet another brown door that Kehinde had not noticed on the far-left wall of the parlour. She felt like she had been abandoned in a lion's den by her captor and willed herself not to run back out through the front door.

Without another word, Mama Tope also left the room, this time through the door on the right side of the room, her three children following close at her heels. Kehinde was left standing in the parlour, wondering if she would ever know which door led where when Ayo walked towards her.

"E káàbọ̀, new wife," she said, grinning from ear to ear. Her two daughters had moved with her, sticking to her legs like extended limbs. "These are my daughters, Adenike and Ashabi," Ayo continued, wrapping an arm around each one. Ashabi popped a thumb into her mouth, sucking as she looked up at Kehinde.

"Thank you … It's nice to meet you all. What would you like me to call you?" Kehinde replied. She had been chewing the inside of both her cheeks all day and now they felt like two pieces of tripe as she ran her tongue over them. Ayo threw her head back and laughed.

"Call me? My name is Ayo, what else would you call me? Come, let me show you to your room," she said, still laughing in a way that made a light come on within the darkness that Kehinde thought would swallow her whole. Kehinde followed Ayo and her daughters through the same door Mama Tope had gone through. They stepped into a small corridor with a staircase at the end of it and another brown door to the right.

"That's the kitchen," Ayo said, pointing towards the closed door. "It's my turn to make dinner tonight, so I'll show you what it looks like while I cook. From next week it will be your turn though; your nights are Saturday, Sunday and Monday now," Kehinde wanted to ask her who came up with the schedule, but Ayo was already moving on towards the stairs, her daughters running up ahead of her. The stairs were covered in a thick red carpet, the walls a pale cream colour lined with more pictures, this time of the Ogunjobi wives and children.

They walked up to a small living area surrounded by six brown doors, with another flight of stairs beside the door closest to the landing. Ayo walked on the balls of her feet, her movements quick and nimble like a cat. There was a clicking sound as Ayo moved, and Kehinde realised it must be Ayo's waist beads, barely visible underneath the waistline of her oleku. Ayo opened the door as her daughters ran into the room next to it.

"This is your room, beside mine," Ayo said, standing to the side so that Kehinde could walk in.

It wasn't huge, but it was bigger than the room she shared with Taiwo, with a double bed in the centre. The only window took up most of the wall facing the front of the house, lined with the same beige curtains as the living room downstairs. On one side of the room, there was a dressing table, and stool with a mirror above it. A floor-to-ceiling closet stood on the other side of the bed with a small grey rug in front of it, where Kehinde's bags were now resting beside a brown trunk.

"The bathroom is beside my room, and Mama Tope's beside that. Tope's room is beside hers, and the boys' room on the other side of Mama Tope's. Ashabi and Adenike stay in my room with me," Ayo paused as Kehinde made her way into the room slowly, perching on the edge of the bed.

"Why do you look so sad?" Ayo asked, looking intently at Kehinde but still smiling. Kehinde almost jumped at the question. Were her feelings so easy to read that someone she had only just met could see right through her?

"I lost my father a few days ago," she responded, surprising herself with her honesty. Something about Ayo made her want to open up, to confide in her, even though she barely knew her. Maybe it was her beautiful smile, or the way she couldn't seem to stand still, like there was a spring of excitement bubbling within her.

"Oh, you poor thing!" Ayo said, rushing to put an arm around Kehinde's shoulder.

"He was on the ferry that capsized earlier this week."

"I read about that in the *Daily Times*! Nobody seems to know what happened. There are rumours that it was a German bomb planted along the bank, as if we need more fearmongering right now! So terrible!" Ayo said, visibly moved. A tendril of hair that had escaped from her headscarf dipped into the crease on her forehead as she frowned.

"It was terrible … I still don't really feel like myself," Kehinde said, finally giving up on trying to hold back, not caring if Ayo thought she was weak.

"Oh, you poor thing! I'm so sorry," Ayo said, a dark look crossing her face.

"Thank you. Thank you, for being so … nice," Kehinde said, meaning it, and letting the growing light within her spread. "So, what do I need to know about living here?" she asked, desperate to change the topic.

Ayo's face brightened up again as she stood, her big sleeves dancing with the movement. As she opened her mouth to speak, a muffled scream came from the window overlooking the lawn. Both Kehinde and Ayo went to look out at the scene unfolding on the green grass beneath them. Her husband was sitting on a chair, sipping from a glass, and a man Kehinde did not recognise was kneeling in front of Kayode.

From their vantage point it looked like the man was crying, and Kehinde gasped as she realised that his nose was bleeding. Kayode threw his hand back and punched the man again, this time making Kehinde jump as she felt a shock of fear like cold water come over her. Her husband's mouth was moving rapidly as he spoke to the man, whose shoulders were heaving as he sobbed. Ayo tugged at Kehinde's arm.

"Let's go to the kitchen now. Quickly, before they look up and see us," she said, turning around and making her way out of the door.

Kehinde had to pick up her pace to keep up with her as they made their way down the stairs, the image of the man on the lawn making her head spin. Her unease was tinged with a sense of alarm that she could almost taste at the back of her tongue, like a coin had been placed there. Who was that man? Why was Kayode hitting him? Was her husband the one who asked for him to be brought here? Why was Ayo behaving like nothing had happened?

Ayo opened the door to the kitchen. It was huge, easily three times the size of Kehinde's mother's kitchen at home. A large gas cooking range stood against the wall, with kitchen countertops running along either side above numerous cabinets, and a kitchen door leading to a courtyard at the back. Despite the questions still swirling in her head, Kehinde was distracted by the size of the room. Ayo laughed nervously at the look on Kehinde's face.

"Our husband likes to have the best. This house was designed by a British architect. We moved here shortly after he married me," she said, bending over as she brought out a black pot from a cabinet under the sink.

"Help me bring a bag of onions from the pantry," Ayo continued, gesturing at a small pantry door in the corner of the kitchen that Kehinde hadn't noticed. The pantry was stocked with more food than Kehinde had ever seen in one home. It looked like they could feed the whole of Ereko Market with the rows of yam, potatoes and onions stacked against each other, but even that couldn't distract Kehinde from the memory of the bleeding man on the lawn.

"We're making ẹja osan and agbo. I already cleaned the fish before you came. Baba Tope's favourite meal is abula but there's no time to make that one today. I hope you can cook? He enjoys his food almost as much as he enjoys his women," Ayo said, cackling at her own joke. "He makes us take turns with the meals, to make sure we can't poison each other. We eat dinner together every day, like one big happy family."

Kehinde couldn't tell if Ayo was being sarcastic or not as she dropped the tomatoes and onions on the counter. Was she pretending to laugh as she spoke about poison? Had they both not witnessed the same act of violence in this very home or had Kehinde imagined the scene?

"I cook most days, Mama Tope only cooks on Fridays. She can't cook to save her life, so she's scheduled for the day our husband is in meetings from morning till night. Lucky him, the rest of us must endure all kinds of concoctions she makes in the name of food. Chop them for me, will you?" Ayo carried on, placing a chopping board and knife beside the bag of onions.

"Ayo, what was happening downstairs?" Kehinde asked, unable to ignore the unease that had joined the cocktail of nerves within her. She glanced at the kitchen door, worried that someone would come into the kitchen at any minute. The house had a humming sound, with constant voices and footsteps echoing across the walls.

"Our husband is a kind man, but he doesn't like to be disrespected," Ayo said in a matter-of-fact way, heating up a pan of cooking oil.

"What do you mean?" Kehinde asked, dicing the tomatoes and onions, wondering if the sight of men being beaten up was something she should get used to. It certainly didn't seem to bother Ayo.

The maid who had answered the door walked into the kitchen at that moment and Ayo stopped talking. She did a general bow of greeting in their direction as she poured water from a pitcher into a glass on a tray. As she left the kitchen with the tray, Ayo glanced at the door and kissed her teeth.

"Be careful of that one. Atinuke is Mama Tope's eyes and ears in this house. She's been with her since they got married," Ayo sniffed.

"Ayo, who was the man downstairs?" Kehinde asked once Atinuke had shut the door behind her.

"He used to work at the Apapa warehouse, for our husband. I don't know the details, but I overheard Baba Tope and Kayode talking yesterday, something about him lying about the cassava being brought in by a supplier. Our husband was trying to compile a report for the governor, or something," Ayo said with a wave of her hand, like she was talking about the inconvenience of rain.

"You said something about our husband not wanting to be disrespected ... what did you mean by that?" Kehinde asked, looking at the door, the bitter taste like a coin once again spreading through her whole mouth.

"You'll see, just don't talk back to him. You look smart enough to figure him out quickly," Ayo said.

Chapter Seven

K ehinde and Ayo finished making dinner, and by the time Atinuke was back in the kitchen, Kehinde knew everything there was to know about the schedule in the house and that Ayo and Mama Tope were not friendly. She still didn't know much about her new husband, but at least Ayo seemed like someone she could trust, for now. Atinuke glanced at Kehinde like she was also trying to figure her out, before gathering plates and crockery onto a tray to set the long dining table. She followed Atinuke out with another tray of glasses and water.

The dining room was situated to the right of the kitchen, through another door that led off from the smaller parlour that Ayo referred to as the den. Her mother would love this place, Kehinde thought, as she looked around at the ornate chairs and chandelier, surmising that gold must be her husband's favourite colour. She tried to focus on the furniture around her, pretending that its glory could make her forget that her father wasn't at home in his armchair, reading a newspaper.

Atinuke laid out the food on the table as the rest of the

household filed in. Ayo's daughters were first, running up to their mother and re-attaching themselves to her legs. Next came Mama Tope's sons, their arrival announced by their thunderous footsteps as they ran down the staircase. Tope arrived shortly after, her head hanging low as she stole another quick look at Kehinde. She was followed by her mother, looking even angrier than she had before. She had changed into another iro and buba, this time in blue adire with a matching headscarf. Kehinde noticed that she had a limp and quickly looked away before Mama Tope could catch her staring.

Everyone stood behind their seats as they waited for Kehinde's husband (Baba Tope as Ayo had advised Kehinde to call him) to arrive. The children sat at the end furthest away from the head of the table with the wives on the seats closer to him, Ayo on the right and Mama Tope on the left. Ayo gestured for Kehinde to stand at the seat beside her. Standing opposite her, Kehinde noticed that once again Tope refused to meet her eyes and was reminded of her quiet form in their Sunday school class when they were children. She hadn't changed much.

Barely a minute had passed before Kehinde's husband made his entrance. He had changed into a white kaftan that billowed out around him as he walked in and took his seat at the head of the table. Once he sat, everyone took their seats and immediately bowed their heads, with Kehinde following suit. Baba Tope nodded in her direction as he started to say grace.

"Our Father, we give you thanks for our meal and for our family as we welcome my new wife, Kehinde, to this glorious household. May this food nourish us and may we continue to be blessed with your unending bounty. We ask this through Christ our Lord, Amen," he prayed.

The meal passed by uneventfully, with Baba Tope and Ayo leading most of the conversation. Kehinde noticed that everyone at the table ate with their knives and forks, the way the colonial administrators at Ikoyi Club did whenever she visited Uncle Ladipo at work. The food was delicious, the fish obviously fresh, but Kehinde found she did not have much of an appetite as the thought of the night to come pushed itself to the fore of her mind. With mounting dread, she wondered what kind of man her husband was. Ayo said the man outside had done something wrong; did he mete out the same treatment to everyone who wronged him? Surely her father wouldn't have said yes to his proposal if he was a dangerous man? She shuddered at the thought of his hands on her, and the agbo felt like a pebble in her throat as she swallowed.

"Kehinde, I hope you're settling in well?" Baba Tope said as he put the last piece of fish in his mouth.

"Yes, Baba Tope, Ayo has been very helpful. Thank you," Kehinde stuttered, calling him the name Ayo had told her he liked, still not quite believing that she was here, eating dinner as part of this household. Mama Tope glowered at her as she took a sip of her water, saying nothing.

"Very good. I'll wait for you in my room," he said, his seat scraping against the floor as he stood up.

Mama Tope and her children followed shortly afterwards. Ayo looked at Kehinde in a way that reminded her of the way her mother had looked at her the day she started her period. Like she felt sorry for her, but there was nothing she could do to stop this inevitable part of womanhood.

"Come, let's get you ready," Ayo said after a moment,

holding out her hand. Kehinde stood up and followed Ayo up the stairs, her feet dragging on the floor.

"You'll need to take a bath. Baba Tope likes us to bathe at least twice a day on the nights we spend in his room," Ayo continued as they arrived on the landing of their floor. "Did you come with a nightgown?" she asked as they stepped into Kehinde's room.

"No, I usually just wear a wrapper to sleep," Kehinde responded, confused.

"Let's check your trunk," she said and lifted the lid of the deep mahogany case, whistling as she did so.

"Our husband must have changed suppliers; these fabrics are much nicer than the ones that were in my bridal trunk," Ayo said to herself. Kehinde had not noticed; clothes had never been something she cared much about.

"Here we go, there are two nightgowns at the bottom," Ayo said, holding up a long white cotton nightgown that looked like what Kehinde imagined Jane Eyre would have slept in.

"Ẹ̀ṣẹ́, Ayo," Kehinde said. The day had been a lot better than Kehinde had anticipated thanks to her, and she was grateful.

"You'll pay me back oh. I'm going to sew some dresses for you with all this fine fabric. I'm looking for new customers, and with your figure, all you have to do is wear them to church and I'll have the whole congregation knocking on our door," Ayo said with a grin. "I'll let you freshen up while I get the girls ready for bed. When you're done, go up the stairs to Baba Tope's floor. He'll be waiting for you there." Ayo hesitated like she wanted to say more but instead she left the room, shutting the door softly behind her.

Kehinde undressed and changed into her wrapper. She gathered up her soap and sponge as she made her way across the parlour into the bathroom, still getting used to the luxury of having one inside the house. The children were gathered in the small parlour on the landing, so engrossed in their game of ayò that they barely acknowledged her.

Kehinde looked in the mirror above the sink as she placed her belongings on the side of the bathtub. There were dark circles under her eyes and lines around her mouth that she didn't remember being there the last time she had looked at her reflection, the day of her birthday. She wondered what her mum and Taiwo were doing at that moment, what time he had reappeared after the wedding, and if he regretted missing it, her thoughts painfully moving yet again to how different she wanted things to be. They would probably still be at dinner, and maybe Aunty Laide and Uncle Ladipo would have stayed as well. Taiwo and her mother had never struggled to make conversation, but Kehinde suspected that any topic would be too difficult, too raw for even the two of them to broach today and for the days to come. Deciding that she had best not keep her new husband waiting, and not wanting to find out what would happen if she did, she had a quick bath.

Dressed in her new nightgown, she floated up the stairs to Baba Tope's floor.

"My flower, is that you? Come in." Babe Tope called out.

Kehinde took a deep breath as she made her way inside. Baba Tope sat on a red velvet armchair to the side of the room beside a writing desk. Kehinde's attention was instantly drawn to the red and gold embroidered curtains on both sides of the room that was easily double the size of hers, with one set of curtains covering a small balcony area. The canopy bed in the middle of the room looked so high that Kehinde imagined she would need a stool to climb into it. Her husband saw her taking in the room and smiled.

"I hope everything is to your liking?" he asked. Kehinde was startled to see his bare, hairy legs beneath his silk dressing gown for the first time.

"Yes, Baba Tope ... your room, the whole house is beautiful," she replied, still hardly believing that this was her new home.

"No expense was spared. I modelled it after my friend Bernard's home," he said, referring to the British governor of Lagos State, who he was apparently on first name terms with.

"Come, sit with me," he commanded, patting a leather pouffe beside the armchair. Kehinde saw an open bottle of red wine with two glasses on the stool beside him as she made her way across the room.

"Thank you, Baba Tope," she said, her nerves returning in a flurry as she felt his gaze burn through the thin cotton of her nightgown. The musky smell of his cologne made his presence even more stifling.

"It's important for a woman to dress well at all times, even at night," he said, his voice sounding as thick as oil as his eyes swept over her. He reached over and poured a glass for Kehinde. Remembering her experience with the champagne from her birthday, Kehinde took a small sip and replaced the glass on the desk. This seemed to please him even more.

"My dainty little flower, so elegant. I want you to be happy here. I have a surprise for you," he said, reaching over to stroke her cheek. Kehinde felt herself shiver.

"A surprise?" she squeaked.

"Don't sound so scared, my flower," he said with a laugh, cupping her chin in his hand. "I have rented a small store for you, in Sandgrouse Market. Your father told me that you like to stay busy, and I promised him you would not be idle. I intend to keep that promise."

"A store?"

"Yes, and you can do anything you want there, sell whatever you like," he said.

Kehinde felt a rush of conflicting emotions. A store! She would have a way to make money, to do something with her time! The West African Pilot offer bobbed to the surface of her mind. If he was fine with her going out every day, to earn a living, then maybe he would be fine with her doing the job she actually wanted, a job where she could have a real purpose, to do the great things her father had told her she was destined for. To be married but still have a voice.

"Baba Tope ... there's something you should know," she started, summoning all the courage she could muster and thinking about what Taiwo would do, how he would speak without fear, ignoring the memory of her father's disapproval.

"Yes?" he asked, smiling at her.

"I've been offered a position at the West African Pilot as a writer, for their women's column," she said with all the confidence she could muster. "The editor has invited me to their office to speak about the terms of my contract next week," she continued slowly, as she watched the bemused smile on Baba Tope's face turn into a frown.

"No wife of mine shall write for that pile of rubbish that Azikiwe calls a paper. Besides, writing is a job for a middle-class man, not a woman of your station!" he retorted, his face wrinkling and his nose scrunching up like there was a bad smell in the room. His nostrils flared and with his face so close to hers, she felt like he could inhale her whole. "And there I was, thinking you would be grateful for the store," he laughed without mirth.

"I'm happy with the store ... but I thought perhaps I could

do something more meaningful," Kehinde stammered, wringing her hands in her lap. Baba Tope laughed again.

"A writer? Is this a joke? I knew marrying a fisherman's daughter would come with its challenges but surely not this?" Kehinde felt like she had been slapped in the face, what did her father being a fisherman have to do with anything?

"Baba Tope, please, don't be angry. This is something I've always wanted to do. I thought you would be proud."

"Kehinde, never mention such nonsense to me again. You should never have to consider such menial work with everything I will provide for you. Read your books, keep writing your little notes in your journal, manage your store to keep busy, but if you want me to be happy with you, I never want to hear anything about you taking on a job like that again. Especially not with the likes of Nnamdi Azikiwe," he said, refilling his glass.

Kehinde watched him as he drank from the glass, her indignation growing. From his demeanour she knew he did not expect her to say anything else, the matter was closed. Ignoring the warning that sounded like a bell in her head, she decided to try one more time.

"Baba Tope, I'm not doing this for money. Writing is how I express myself, and I want—"

"Shut up!" he shouted, making Kehinde jump as he slammed his glass down on the side table. The wine, also in shock, sloshed over the rim of the glass.

"I will not have you talk back to me! Do you know how many years are between us? Did your mother not teach you to be silent in the presence of your elders? My word is final, you will not write for the *West African Pilot* or any other newspaper and this is the last time we will speak of it! If you aren't grateful, I will take the store away from you! Find something better to do, like selling food or focusing on our children when they come. You won't even have time for the store when you get pregnant anyway," he said, sitting back in his chair, obviously done with the conversation.

Kehinde felt like she had been struck dumb as she watched him. Maybe she could change his mind? If he had already rented a store for her then he couldn't be opposed to her being independent, surely? She considered raising the conversation again another day. She had got married like an obedient lamb, but she realised she wasn't ready to give up on being a writer so easily, not when it was the perfect way for her to do more without having to change who she was completely. How else could she do something meaningful with her life? But what would happen to her if she insisted, she wondered. If she insisted on taking the job, she could be sent back home to live with her mother, in shame and poverty, and who knew where they would end up then? The last of her resolve melted away as the image of the man with blood streaming down his face rose, unbidden to the front of her memory. Would he do the same to her if she kept talking? Her father had also not wanted her to take the job – had he already known that her husband would be so against it? Her heart sank at the thought. Surely her father must not have known this man as well as he thought he did? He couldn't have.

Baba Tope turned back to her, cupping her face in his hands again.

"My flower, I don't mean to startle you. I'm just surprised that you would want to do something so degrading. How would it look if a man like me had a wife writing for a common, left-wing newspaper? Please, put such silly thoughts aside," he soothed.

Kehinde nodded and bowed her head, her hurt and

disbelief making it impossible to find her voice. She felt naïve and stupid, but also angry. Who did he think he was that he could talk to her like this? To tell her what to do? Surely if she was old enough to get married, she was old enough to take on the job she had spent her whole life dreaming about?

"Get down. In front of me," he slurred, changing the topic so suddenly that Kehinde blinked, still recovering from his tirade of words. "Bend down, and kiss my feet," he continued.

Kehinde blinked again, unsure she had heard correctly. Slowly, she followed the movement of his hands until her eyes landed on his pair of big, mottled feet. He used his hand to guide her head downwards until her lips met his toes.

"Suck them," he said, his voice hoarse as he narrowed his eyes.

She briefly considered running out of the room, but the image of the bleeding man came to her mind, sharper than the lamplight in the room. Kehinde tried not to gag as she did as she was told, trying and failing to ignore the smell of curdled cheese that engulfed her.

"Stand up," he said, after what felt like several minutes went by. Kehinde stood up slowly, standing almost directly in front of the bed, the taste of dirt still fresh on her tongue.

"Now ... take off your nightgown ... slowly," he slurred. Kehinde felt her face grow hot. At her hesitation his face hardened. "I am your husband now. Take it off," he said, leaning back in his armchair.

She had no choice, and did as he said, her face burning and her ears ringing. She lifted the gown above her head and dropped it on the floor beside her, her arms automatically reaching up to cover her most intimate areas.

"No, drop your hands ... that's it. Now turn around for me, slowly," he said, taking another sip of his wine like he was appraising a delivery of new goods. Kehinde did as she was told, forcing her mind to focus on a memory, something far away from this room. She thought of the peace of her father's boat and stayed there as her husband stood up from the armchair. She could feel his hardness as he came up behind her, dropping his robe around his feet while he grabbed her.

"Mmm, just as I thought," he murmured into her ear, his breath a hot cloud of wine and fish.

Kehinde remembered her mother's muted words the night before and closed her eyes. For years, she had heard her parents' distant cries of passion from their room, but she knew that any cries uttered from her lips in this room would be without joy. He bent her over suddenly and began to push himself between her legs. Kehinde held herself still as the tears that had refused to come all week flowed silently out of her eyes, blurring the sight of their shadows, flickering in the soft candlelight as her marriage was consummated.

Reverend Kasunmu had said her father was in a better place, and she wondered now if things like this happened in the place where he was. As her husband's ecstasy and the pain in between her legs mounted, she focused on the image of her father smiling, sitting in his boat, the break of dawn, a perfect halo behind his head.

Later that night, as her husband snored next to her, she lay awake, staring at the high ceiling. For the first time, it dawned on her that she might never amount to more than a parlour wife, doomed to please her husband as he saw fit. So much for being destined to do great things.

Chapter Eight

True to his words, Baba Tope had rented a store for Kehinde at Sandgrouse Market, close enough to the main road to make it a prime location.

As Mr Tunde, the driver, drove her and Kayode to Lewis Street, Kehinde could already see the changes the war had brought. New posters lined the walls, encouraging men to fight for the Empire, to aid the war effort, and one had soldiers of different races and colonies, smiling under a banner that read "Together – The Armed Forces of the British Commonwealth". Beside the poster, a young English man in khaki was handing out leaflets to people as they walked by and she spotted one or two colonial administrators flitting in and out of stores, buying provisions. It was rare to see them in Lagos Island; they lived in Ikoyi and Victoria Island and their servants were usually the ones to run their errands for them.

Men and women walked along the busy pavement, and store owners opened their shutters on both sides of the road. They pulled up to a little store on the corner of Lewis Street that had an iron gate bordering it off from the walkway.

Kehinde stood beside Kayode, looking up at the brown roof of her store as he offloaded the old pots that Ayo had given her with the frying oil, flour, sugar and nutmeg, thinking about the last forty-eight hours, as people rushed past her in all directions, preoccupied with thoughts of their own.

On her wedding night, she had spent sleepless hours listening to Baba Tope's snores, and the next morning, they had all trooped off to Bethel Cathedral for the 9am service. As Baba Tope had shown her off to his friends, she'd noticed that her mother and Taiwo were not there. Was that because they could not bear the thought of being there without her father? Or maybe it would be too painful to see her with her new family? Was Taiwo avoiding her? It seemed odd that two days had passed and he hadn't even tried to reach her. She was hurt. Yes, they were both grieving but why was he staying away when she needed him?

"I'm done now, Ma," Kayode grunted, slamming the boot of the car. He had arranged the pots and bags of provisions on the floor of the little store.

"Thank you, Kayode."

She watched Kayode hop into the passenger seat of the Austin before turning around to get a good look at her store. With grey cement walls, it was much sturdier than her parents' umbrella stall at Ereko Market. The entrance was set back from the main road, the iron gate now flung open, and Kayode had also given her a padlock and key which she could use to lock up when she left in the evenings.

Two little girls carrying trays of groundnut on their heads hurried by giggling as Kehinde stood at the entrance, wincing. She was still sore between her legs, the pain on the second night with Baba Tope almost seeming worse than the first. Luckily, after tonight it would be Ayo's turn to share a bed with him for the next three nights and she looked forward to sleeping alone in her new room. Women in the books she read seemed to covertly refer to nights with their husbands as something they enjoyed doing but she knew without a doubt that the precious nights she spent away from Baba Tope would be the only peaceful nights she would have in her new home. Did Ayo feel the same way? She could scarcely ask, it wasn't the kind of thing one spoke about.

With a sigh, she turned to the bags of flour, sugar, oil and yam on the floor. In line with Baba Tope's suggestion, she had decided she would sell snacks in her store, small things like puff puff, akara and dùndú to the workers heading off to their offices along the adjoining streets. More to keep herself busy than for the money; Baba Tope had made it clear that he did not have serious plans for her employment and nor should she. She almost laughed at how different it would be from working as a writer. The only way her voice would be heard would now be when she called out to her customers, destined to make great food.

"Hello, hello!" said a young woman, appearing in the doorway. "My name is Ama Alanta; I own the store next to yours." She pumped Kehinde's hand up and down as she eyed the empty shelves.

"Good morning, Ama. I'm Kehinde Ogunjobi," Kehinde said, stalling as she said her new surname.

"Very nice! This store has been vacant for so long. I've been in mine for two years and it's been empty the whole time. I sell locally made leather sandals and slippers for men and women, lots of styles and sizes!" Ama said, looking down at Kehinde's feet like she was trying to guess her size.

"This stall has been vacant for two years? Why?" she asked as Ama looked up from her feet.

"Oh, it's a very expensive space to rent, and so small too. It is a great location but who can sell anything in this tiny room?" Ama responded, then immediately covered her mouth with her hands, her eyes lighting up. She was beautiful in a way that reminded Kehinde of a cherub, with teeth set back in prominent pink gums when she smiled. "I don't mean to offend you! Please don't mind me and my big mouth. What I meant is that there just hasn't been anyone who can pay the rent for this place and who hasn't complained that it was too cramped to take all their things... Not that you're making a mistake ... I meant—"

"Ama, don't worry. I understand what you meant," Kehinde interrupted, immediately warming to her. The words seemed to be coming out faster than she could control them, and it was endearing, because Kehinde was the opposite. She instantly envied how freeing it must be to speak without reconsidering every word.

"I'm your first customer. I love akara," Ama said, pointing at the tub of akara mix that Kehinde had made that morning.

"Okay, I'll make you some," Kehinde responded, surprised but pleased.

After a few minutes of silence passed while Kehinde heated up the oil, Ama spoke again. "So, what were you doing before you came here?"

"Doing?"

"Did you work somewhere else?"

Kehinde hesitated, pausing to scoop some of the mix into the oil.

"I used to work with my parents. I sold fish at their stall at Ereko Market before I got married a few days ago."

"Congratulations!" Ama said.

"Thank you."

Another moment passed, the silence in the shop filled by the sizzle of the frying akara. Kehinde handed a newspaper wrap of four hot balls to Ama.

"Thank you! What do I owe you?"

"You're my first customer, so it's free," Kehinde said.

"I knew I would like you!" Ama responded with a fist pump in the air and they both laughed. "Well, I'll let you settle in then! Come and find me later if you get bored, I have some slippers you can try on," Ama said, smiling her gummy smile again as she made her way out of the store.

Kehinde wondered about the cost of the stall. Baba Tope had told her he had paid for the next two years upfront, assuring her that his connections at the market had given him a good deal. After church yesterday afternoon, she had gone through her new trunk of belongings. The trunk was at least three times the size of the bag of clothes she had brought from home, consisting of jewellery and endless yards of material in all colours and styles. She now had more adire, ankara, lace, aso-oke and damask than she knew what to do with. Her mother would have been so excited to see it all – the gifts were more to her taste than Kehinde's.

Her father had told her that Baba Tope owned several storage warehouses and shipping barges along the Apapa and Tin Can Island ports but other than that, she didn't really know what he did every day. Baba Tope was a generous man, that much she knew already. Apart from the gifts in her trunk, he had presented her with a brand-new gold necklace the morning after their wedding. As he clasped it round her neck, he had even asked her how she was feeling, to which she politely answered that she was fine. What else would she say? He had made it clear on their wedding night that her feelings were to be in line with his expectations and nothing more, and she was still too scared and in too much pain to find out what would happen if she did not comply. Scared being the operative word, as she still had no further clarity on why he had watched Kayode beat up a man on her first day there. He was an enigma, giving her gifts but taking away her freedom, and she found that her fear of him was also tinged with a growing resentment.

The pain in her heart was one thing; that hadn't stopped since the day her father disappeared, and she didn't think it would ever go away. The pain between her legs was another entirely, of the duties expected of her as a wife. She started mixing the puff puff batter, realising that she had nothing to do as the rest of the day stretched out ahead of her.

Kehinde got through the rest of the morning with the book Aunty Laide had given her for her birthday, trying to use it as a distraction from the thoughts flying in and out of her mind like mosquitos. A few customers dropped by and bought all the puff puff and akara she had fried, and she made a note to bring more ingredients from the house the following day. By the time Kayode came with Mr Tunde to pick her up in the brown Austin later that evening, she was already locking up the gates, feeling restless.

She felt as heavy as the bag of flour in her store at the realisation that a day like today was what her new life was to become. She prepared dinner with Atinuke, careful not to answer any of her questions too deeply after Ayo's warning. Mama Tope was still not very welcoming and Kehinde was wary of giving her any information that could be used against her. The previous morning, as they were walking out to church, Kehinde could have sworn Mama Tope had tried to trip her up. But there were so many of them that it was hard to accuse her of a crime that anyone could have committed.

At dinner, she looked everywhere but at Mama Tope, focusing instead on not thinking about the taste of Baba Tope's toes.

"Sir, a call for you, from Sir Bernard Bourdillon," Atinuke said, appearing in the dining room.

"Ah, yes, I've been expecting him," Baba Tope said, standing from his seat and moving faster than Kehinde had ever seen him walk towards the telephone in the den. "Good evening, my friend, how are you and your family?" Baba Tope said, adopting a formal tone. The door shut behind him and they could only hear the rise and fall of his muffled voice. Kehinde could imagine him leaning into the phone, trying to hear over the static.

"The governor has invited me to join a carefully selected group to preside over the war efforts in Lagos, the War Relief Committee," Baba Tope said when he returned to the table. "Kehinde, I have some visitors coming today, after dinner. I want you to be there, to serve us. Make sure you look nice," he continued.

"Congratulations Baba Tope. But these visitors are coming after the curfew?" Ayo asked, looking worried.

"It will be quick. They won't be discovered, I've made sure of that," Baba Tope said in a brusque tone.

"Iyawo parlour, that's all you're here for," Mama Tope whispered to Kehinde as she walked past her when dinner was over, on her way out of the room.

Kehinde tried not to let the insult sting as she took a bath, washing the smell of frying oil and ata rodo off her skin. It was true, that was all she was here for. To sit in the parlour, looking pretty, like a new piece of furniture that Baba Tope wanted to show off. An acquired doll to be shared with his friends, one that had been trained to remain silent, to keep smiling even when it had been handled roughly. The *West African Pilot* seemed so far away that she had to swallow the lump in her throat to stop herself from sinking lower in the bath. Was this life really what her father had dreamed for her? What her mother had agreed made the most sense? Her feet felt heavy as she walked back to her room, shutting the door behind her slowly.

Ayo knocked on her room door. "Kehinde, do you need help?" she called.

"Thanks, Ayo, I'm fine," Kehinde said, deciding that she should probably line her eyes with tiro. She hadn't lined them since her birthday, but Baba Tope had asked her to look nice.

"Okay … I've asked Atinuke to put some ẹran dídì and drinks on a tray. You can serve that to them. I couldn't buy much rice, it's already so scarce," Ayo said from the other side of the door. Kehinde wanted her to come in but also felt like she had asked too much of her already. Surely, being able to entertain Baba Tope's friends was something any woman should be able to manage on her own?

"Thank you, Ayo. I'll be down in just a few minutes."

"Okay, I'll be in my room, let me know if you need anything."

Kehinde listened to Ayo's retreating footsteps as she stood to tie her iro, knotting it firmly at her waist. As she went down the stairs, she heard men's voices coming from the formal parlour and hurried to arrange the refreshments with Atinuke. When she walked into the kitchen, Atinuke looked her up and down.

"You look nice, Ma," she said.

"Thank you. Can I take the tray through?" Kehinde asked, suddenly self-conscious under Atinuke's gaze.

"Yes, Ma. Master and his friends are in the parlour,"

Atinuke replied, giving Kehinde the tray of fried meat while she picked up the other tray of glasses and drinks. Kehinde felt like she was walking the plank as they walked the short distance to the parlour, like a piece of bait about to be fed to sharks.

"And you're sure being part of this Relief Committee won't bring you under too much scrutiny?" said a man in a black kaftan, sitting on one of the armchairs. Another man in a white kaftan and fila was sitting opposite him, smoking a cigar.

"No, if anything it makes me more trustworthy. Nobody will think to question my authority now," Baba Tope said, glancing up in time to see Kehinde and Atinuke walk in. "Ah, there you are. Babajide, Lateef, this is my new wife, Kehinde," he said, patting her thigh as she bent to put the tray on the centre table. She felt the blood rush to her face as she rose, feeling the silence in the room all over her body as all three pairs of male eyes appraised her like a horse on show.

"Your wives are getting more and more beautiful, my friend," Mr Babajide said, licking his lips as he shifted in his seat. Mr Lateef said nothing, continuing to stare at Kehinde as he took another drag from his cigar, the smoke half obscuring his face.

"Kehinde, you can sit here," Baba Tope said, patting the space on the sofa beside him. Kehinde sat, relieved to no longer be the centre of attention but cringing as Baba Tope left his hand on her thigh in plain sight.

"So, you were saying, about my, er, goods. You're sure you can get them out as usual?" Mr Lateef said, addressing Baba Tope with a sidelong glance at Kehinde.

"Of course, nothing has changed, except that my partners have said they anticipate there will be more demand now," Baba Tope said, leaning forward to pick up a piece of beef.

"How lucky you are, Lateef. I just got word today that all exports of cocoa to Germany across the Empire will be banned. As of today, the colonial government will buy all my cocoa at a set price, and then distribute it at another price to control supply and demand," Mr Babajide said, shaking his head.

"How unfortunate," Mr Lateef drawled, not looking sorry at all.

"There's nothing to worry about, my friend, that's why we're here today, to work out an arrangement. You're an old friend and business partner, I won't let you go down," Baba Tope said, his arms outstretched.

"Thank God for friends in high places," Mr Babajide laughed.

"I heard Jacob no longer works for you?" Mr Lateef asked.

"Ah, yes, I had to get rid of that snake. He stole from me and then threatened to report me to the trade office. A shame, he was a good office manager, finding another now will be hard," Baba Tope said with a shrug. Kehinde wondered if this Jacob was the man she had seen on the lawn, or if there was another man Baba Tope had "had to get rid of". She shuddered at the thought.

"Yes, a real shame, he was so sharp," Mr Babajide said as he poured himself a beer.

"Too sharp for my liking. Too big for his boots," Baba Tope said, shaking his head.

"A pity. So, we'll iron out the new arrangement at your warehouse tomorrow then," Mr Lateef said, looking again at Kehinde as he put out his cigar.

"Yes, of course. I've arranged a permit that will see you both safely home, but it won't do for you to be out late. We're all too old for forced conscription," Baba Tope said, guffawing at his own joke. The other men laughed too, the chewed meat still glistening in Mr Babajide's mouth as he threw his head back. Kehinde watched them, her disgust mounting.

"Now, before we go my friend, you need to show us how much you love this new wife of yours," Mr Babajide said with a leer.

"You naughty boy," Baba Tope said, squeezing Kehinde's thigh harder. The movement only seemed to wet Mr Babajide's appetite.

"Go on, give her a kiss before we head out," he said.

Kehinde stiffened as Baba Tope turned her face and planted a sloppy kiss on her lips. No matter how many times he kissed her, she would never get used to the instant revulsion she felt. She fought the instinct to run from the room as his hand moved up from her thigh while Mr Babajide cheered like he was at the theatre.

Hours later, as Kehinde lay in bed, the cotton of her nightgown kissing her ankles as she tried to forget the sound of Mr Babajide howling like a wolf, she wondered what her father would have thought of all this. When she was ten years old, the year she sprained her ankle, her father had been the one to take her to the hospital. He had sat there with her till the nurse had bound her leg, and he had been the one to dry her face, telling her he couldn't stand to see her in pain. But he was the one that had agreed to put her in this situation, and she hated that as the days went by, her resentment was rivalling her grief. How could her parents think this could be better than her living at home with a meaningful job? She wanted to believe it was their fear of the future that had led her here but if they really loved her, surely, they would never have agreed to this marriage? How could her father, her greatest defender, the man who encouraged her to want more, hand her over to this husband that had secret meetings and hurt other men?

One thing she was sure of was that her father would not have liked the scene that had played out in the parlour. In fact, from the little she had gathered from the conversation, the man she married was a very different one from the man her father had thought he was. If he was alive, she wondered what he would have done if she told him. As much as she hated to admit it, Kehinde was beginning to feel like the parents she had entrusted her life to maybe hadn't made the right decision for her, and it was a jarring thought that kept her awake much longer into the early hours of the next day.

Chapter Nine

The next morning, Kehinde walked to work, insisting she needed the fresh air after breakfast. She could not bear the thought of being cooped up in the car with Kayode and Mr Tunde, feeling like a prisoner on parole. She got to her store in less than fifteen minutes, the brisk walk leaving her feeling physically if not mentally better as she walked through the crowds of men and women going about their day. Her lethargy had become a muted fury. She thought of the *West African Pilot*, imagining herself discussing women's rights with Nnamdi Azikiwe – how ironic that she was now forbidden from standing up for her own rights, let alone for other Nigerian women. She would sell food and be a parlour wife, and nothing else, an onlooker to the events unfolding around her.

Kehinde was unlocking the gate of her store when Ama appeared beside her.

"Good morning, Kehinde! My new friend! How are you today?" Ama asked, wearing a brown ankara dress with a pattern of orange swirls that brought more brightness to the day than Kehinde was feeling.

"Good morning, Ama. I promise to come to your store today, I got caught up with settling in yesterday afternoon," Kehinde replied, genuinely happy to see her. As she rolled open the gates of her store, she noticed a man standing off to the side of the road.

"I still have those slippers I promised you, but let me introduce you to my brother, first. Emeka, this is Mrs Kehinde Ogunjobi, she owns the store beside mine," Ama said as he took a step forward to shake Kehinde's hand.

"Nice to meet you, Mrs Ogunjobi," he said.

When he shook Kehinde's hand, his skin felt calloused but soft. Kehinde returned the handshake, resisting the urge to pat down the top of her hair. She had tied it back in a bun, and she imagined that she had little tight curls dancing in awkward directions all over her head after her walk in the wind. Not that Emeka looked like he would mind, in fact, he looked a bit dishevelled himself, with most of his shirt coming out of the top of his trousers.

"Are you related to Mr Gboyega Ogunjobi by any chance?" he asked. As he spoke, his brown eyes lit up behind the gold rims of his glasses.

"Yes, he's my husband. You know him?" Kehinde replied.

"I would be surprised if anyone in Lagos didn't know who he was, he's in the papers every week," Emeka said, his eyes widening as he looked at her with newfound respect.

"Well, it's nice to meet you too, Emeka," Kehinde replied. Emeka looked at her curiously when she spoke, like he was carefully considering every word that came out of her mouth. It made her feel self-conscious, like she had a stain she didn't know about on her clothes.

"Join us for breakfast?" he said after a pause, lifting a black plastic bag. "We're having a quick one before I head off to work."

"Oh no, I couldn't impose," Kehinde said, already shaking her head.

"Impose keh? You're not imposing anything biko, come inside!" Ama said, grabbing Kehinde's arm and steering her in the direction of her store. "In fact, this way I can guarantee that you'll come in here today, no stories about getting too busy to visit. We still have some time before my customers start coming up this street anyway," she said as they walked into Ama's store.

Ama's huge store had *FINE LEATHER* written above the door in bold, red capital letters that stood out against the white paint of the wall. Shoes, sandals, slippers and handbags in different colours lined the shelves on the walls, with the men's on the left and the women's on the right. A long mirror that went almost from the floor to the ceiling stood beside the women's shoes, making the store look even bigger.

"This is beautiful, Ama," Kehinde said, as she walked round the padded bench in the middle of the store, inhaling the sharp scent of shoe polish and something flowery.

"Thank you, thank you!" Ama said, pretending to bow as she led the way towards a door at the back with Emeka following close behind her.

"Good morning!" the teenage girl sitting at the cashier's desk called out, pausing to look up from the nails she was filing at Kehinde. She looked vaguely like Ama and Emeka, with the same complexion that reminded Kehinde of fresh wheat.

"My cousin, Onyi. She helps with the store," Ama said. Kehinde nodded at the girl, who was now humming along to the beat of the soft jazz playing from the Rediffusion on her desk.

Ama opened the door at the back to reveal a small, sparsely furnished room with a writing desk and two chairs. The cement floor was clean, and the yellow walls had nothing but a round clock and a picture of Jesus with a bleeding heart on it. Kehinde guessed that like her store, the small door to the side led off to the courtyard that had a shared toilet for the stores on their side of the street.

"Come in, come in," Ama said, sitting on one chair and gesturing at the other for Kehinde to take a seat on. Emeka came in behind them, shutting the door. He sat on the desk and started bringing out the contents of the black nylon bag – two loaves of bread, a can of sardines and a thermos flask of tea.

"Thank you again, for inviting me to breakfast," Kehinde said.

Ama threw her head back and laughed as Emeka grinned.

"Ah, Kehinde! Has anyone ever told you that you talk like you're from London? So polite! You would think that we had invited her for breakfast at the governor's house in Ikoyi the way she is thanking us," Ama said, laughing again as she broke a loaf of bread into two. She handed one half to Kehinde. She was not hungry as she had already eaten breakfast at home, but she accepted it anyway. She didn't want Ama to accuse her of refusing food like a princess in Buckingham Palace.

"Don't mind Ama. So, what do you sell in your store?" Emeka asked, peering at her from behind his glasses as he took a bite of his food. The rest of his shirt had come undone, and he was perched on the desk in a way that made Kehinde think of her father telling her and Taiwo that tables were not meant for sitting.

"I sell snacks … puff puff, dùndú, akara, just small things," Kehinde replied, feeling slightly intimidated as she sat in Ama's storeroom. They seemed to be around the same age, but Ama was obviously more independent and accomplished than she could ever hope to be.

"That's nice, we love akara! I'll be a loyal customer." Emeka paused to pour the tea into the mugs that Ama had brought out of the desk drawer and handed one to Kehinde. "I work for the *Daily Times*, my office isn't too far from here," he continued as Kehinde's eyes opened wide in amazement.

"You're a writer?" she said, sitting forward in her seat, feeling envious, in awe and even more intimidated all at the same time.

"Hopefully that isn't too hard to believe. Do I look like something else? Bricklayer maybe?" he said, flexing the muscles in his arms beneath his shirt. Ama laughed again as she accepted her mug of tea.

"Oh no, that's not what I meant. I've just never met another writer before," Kehinde said, blushing. From the way his hand had felt when she shook his, she had assumed he did something more labour intensive, like, well, carpentry. She was finding it hard to imagine him bent over his desk with just a pen in his hand.

"Ooh, you write too?" Emeka asked.

"Yes, I do," Kehinde responded, immediately wondering why she had lied. Well, it wasn't exactly a lie but the only real writing she had done was in her journal and her submission to the *West African Pilot*.

"I'm not surprised. You look like there's more to you than just a pretty face," he said, putting the last bit of bread in his mouth.

Ama let out another peal of laughter, while Kehinde

blushed again, annoyed with herself for how happy his words made her, and wondering why she was grinning so much.

"And now I must get to work," he said, standing up and brushing the crumbs off his trousers. "Pleasure to meet you, Mrs Ogunjobi. Bye sis, see you later!" he continued as he made his way out of the door, tucking in his shirt as he left. Kehinde heard him say goodbye to Onyi before he joined the host of people rushing to work on Lewis Street.

"Don't mind Emeka, he thinks he's so funny," Ama said.

"Has he always been a writer?" Kehinde asked, still in awe.

"Yes actually, right from when we were in secondary school," Ama said, standing as she started clearing away the remains of breakfast. "How long have you been writing for?"

"All my life really," Kehinde said, taking another sip of tea. "English was my favourite subject in school, and I got an offer to join the *West African Pilot*."

"Wow! Kehinde you're so interesting! When do you start? I'll miss you! I mean, I barely know you, but I was already looking forward to having a friend next door."

"Oh, I'm not going anywhere. I'm not accepting the offer."

Ama blinked. "Why not?"

Kehinde floundered, embarrassed as she tried to find the right answer, kicking herself for mentioning the offer in the first place. "My husband didn't exactly approve," she said, settling on the truth.

Ama let out a low whistle. "Marriage sounds so delightful."

Kehinde laughed again, genuinely grateful for the outlet.

"Anyway, since you're definitely staying, will you come to the Association meeting with me later this afternoon?" Ama asked, sweeping the crumbs on her desk into one of the empty bags.

"The Lagos Market Women's Association? I haven't joined," Kehinde said.

"Why not?" Ama asked, raising her eyebrows.

"I didn't think I was eligible to become a member."

"You can join today, there's always a sign-up sheet at the door! They recently changed the rules to allow all market store owners to join, regardless of how long they've owned a store."

Kehinde clapped her hands, feeling real joy for the first time since her father's death. She knew of the Association, and admired their leader, Madam Titi, from a distance – she was a firm supporter of Nnamdi Azikiwe and Herbert Macaulay, and the *West African Pilot* had interviewed her in the past. She was one woman who didn't seem to care about what everyone else thought about her speaking her mind or fighting for her rights. Kehinde had dreamed of being able to write a piece about the Lagos Women's Association (LMWA), hoping that working at the *West African Pilot* would have given her access to Madam Titi.

"The LMWA is the best way to know what's happening in the market. Especially with the way things are now, you should definitely join," Ama continued, encouraged by the excitement on Kehinde's face, as the bell above her store door outside rang. "That's my customer. I'll come grab you for the meeting, it's a quick one today at three. Onyi can watch both stores for us," Ama said as she ushered Kehinde out to where an older man was holding a pair of black sandals.

Kehinde walked back next door, which now seemed like an empty little cave in comparison to Ama's. Feeling a bit more optimistic, she sat at her desk, imagining what would be discussed at the meeting later. Her mother had been a member of the Association, but Kehinde knew that she hardly attended the meetings. She had joined because her friends had joined, not because she had any real interest in what the Association or its leader stood for.

By the time the afternoon came round, Kehinde was practically jumping in her seat. Unlike the day before, only two customers had stopped by and Kehinde had spent the morning alone with her thoughts, unable to concentrate on the weathered copy of *Wuthering Heights* in her lap. She almost gave Ama a hug when she saw her friendly face pop round the entrance.

"Ready?" Ama asked. She had tied her hair in an orange headscarf that brought out the heart shape of her face.

"You're sure it's fine for Onyi to watch both stores?" Kehinde asked, standing up from her desk.

"Sure, I've given her clear instructions. We can lock the gate and leave a sign for anyone that comes. Onyi will be able to attend to them before we get back," Ama replied as Kehinde started locking up.

Not much to steal here anyway, Kehinde thought as she turned the key in the lock. They dropped the key with Onyi and set off north on the long winding path of Lewis Street. They walked past the stores on either side of them with traders selling their wares and customers moving up and down the busy street.

"Where are we going?" Kehinde asked, as Ama linked her arm through hers.

"Glover Memorial Hall on Customs Street. We háve a meeting there on the third Tuesday of every month. I'm sure today will be interesting. This will be the first one since the announcement of the war," Ama replied, as they paused to let two men carrying wheelbarrows laden with yams and sweet potatoes get ahead.

"And what exactly happens at these meetings?"

"Hmm, well, usually we talk about the latest government policies that affect us, anything happening in the market, and we also discuss upcoming events," Ama responded, still holding firmly onto Kehinde's arm, and panting slightly as the street started to slant uphill. Kehinde was silent for a moment. She didn't recall her mother ever talking about the few meetings she had attended; they simply sold their fish and went home.

"You're sure it's fine for me to come to the meeting today, even before I join?" Kehinde asked, as they reached the top of Lewis Street, pausing as a bus went by.

"Kehinde, you really are precious. Of course it's fine! It's open to all women with a market store in Lagos, which now includes you. Here we are! I can see a few women have already arrived," Ama said as they stopped in front of a big blue building with white pillars. *Glover Memorial Hall* was written across the space above the big brown doors.

There were about eleven women standing outside the building. They all called out various greetings in Ama's direction as she and Kehinde walked in. The hall was a big one, with some women already seated on the rows of chairs, facing a podium. They made their way to the front of the hall and took two seats on the far-right side.

"There are many people here today oh," Ama continued, pulling out a hand fan from her bag.

"There are," Kehinde said, putting her handbag on her lap as she decided against leaving it on the floor. As her mother had hardly gone to the meetings, Kehinde knew from following their activities in the news that women from all markets across Lagos were part of the Association, but she could never have imagined how busy it would be.

"People usually come oh, but I've never seen this place

packed like this. Good thing we got here early," Ama responded as the hall filled up behind them. Women were arriving and sitting in the chairs across the hall as they exchanged greetings.

"Mama Gbenga! Ẹ káásán o! Ṣ'àláfíà ní?"

"Àdúpẹ́, Ma. How is your husband now? I hope he's feeling better?"

"The one and only Ama! Báwo ni?" another woman with a sleeping baby tied to her back said.

"Iya Jola! I have your sandals oh! I know you said your feet have stretched, don't worry, these ones are very comfortable. How is my baby?" Ama asked, craning her neck to look at the baby on the woman's back whose head lolled to the side in response.

"She is fine, àdúpẹ́ Jesu. I want to sit at the back so that I can quickly feed her before the meeting starts. I just wanted to greet you first, I'll come to your shop after this to try the sandals. Ò ṣe, ọ̀rẹ́ mi," said the woman, smiling at Ama as she made her way towards the back of the hall, the baby's head bobbing with each step.

"You can speak Yoruba?" Kehinde asked Ama once the woman was out of earshot.

"Yes now. You think because I'm Igbo I can't speak Yoruba, abi?" Ama replied, sounding amused.

"Well, yes, I guess it just never occurred to me," Kehinde responded indignantly, as Ama laughed at her for what felt like the millionth time.

"Most of my customers are Yoruba, I had to learn fast. When I came here three years ago, before I started the shop, Emeka told me that the best thing I could do for myself was to start speaking Yoruba. Because you're Yoruba, you take it for granted. To do any business in Lagos you need to speak it well.

In fact, to do anything in Lagos you have to speak Yoruba," Ama said, adjusting her scarf as she leaned back into her seat.

"Can Emeka speak Yoruba too?"

"That one, if you hear him speak, you'll even think he was Yoruba. He's been in Lagos for over six years now, he came here right after he finished his school certificate, and he's been working at the *Daily Times* since," Ama said proudly.

"He must really like it here then," Kehinde said, wondering what else Emeka could do.

Ama let out a short laugh.

"Kehinde, it's not about liking it. Coming to Lagos was the best thing for his career," Ama said.

Before she could say more, Madam Titi walked up to the podium. Kehinde had only ever seen her from a distance, and mostly in newspaper pictures. In person, she was taller than average, wearing a pale yellow iro and buba and matching head tie with a hijab. She had small lines in the skin around her eyes as she smiled, with a dimple forming in her left cheek. Kehinde guessed that she would probably be around her father's age, in her early forties. She clapped her hands as she called for silence in the room.

"Good morning, my fellow market women. Welcome to our September Association meeting," she said in Yoruba, her strong voice carrying to every corner of the room as the women sitting in the chairs all sat to attention.

"That's Madam Titi, the president of the LMWA, our iya loja. She has a stall at Ereko Market. She's hardly there though, I hear her daughter runs it for her. She's much too busy with the LMWA to be there every day," Ama whispered to Kehinde. If only she knew how much Kehinde knew about her already, Kehinde thought with a smile.

"We have a busy agenda today…" Madam Titi continued,

as a heavily pregnant woman walked towards her with a sheaf of papers in her hands.

"First of all, the Lagos task force has complained about the general level of hygiene across our markets." A collective groan went up in the room.

Kehinde knew about the task force, they went around dressed in mufti, inspecting the market grounds, and issuing fines to store owners who had failed to keep their surroundings clean. Many a market trader had fallen prey to the fines they dished out.

"Iya loja, please, with all due respect, there is something that has been worrying me," said a woman standing in the middle of the hall.

"Ma, as you know, many of us here sell imported goods. Will the ships still be coming now that this war has started?" she asked, her voice shaking slightly as murmurs went up across the room. Someone else near the front row shot up her hand as she rose to her feet.

"I would also like to know if we need to increase our prices. If there are no containers arriving, none of us will have enough stock to see us through to the end of the year," she said. At this, the noise level in the room audibly rose. Everyone knew that with the ongoing inflation, prices of goods in the market were already higher than usual and customers were starting to complain.

"Even transport within Nigeria has already stalled. The Department of Agriculture has blocked the transportation of rice from Abeokuta to Lagos, why I don't know. The little rice in Lagos has doubled in price," said the woman with the baby that had greeted Ama.

"The price of salt is up too, and the other day I could hardly find any to buy," said another woman who stood at the back of the room.

"But I heard that the government will be setting prices for everything we sell in the market as part of the food control measures for the war. Will they consult us before they set the prices?" asked the first woman that had stood, now wringing her kaftan in her hands.

"They better consult us. God knows I've had enough of being pushed around by the whites around here, war or no war," shouted a woman Kehinde couldn't see at the back. After she spoke the room broke into a babble of voices, each person voicing their own concerns and fears at once.

"Enough!" Madam Titi said, banging her hand on the top of the podium until there was silence again in the hall. She cleared her throat before she started speaking again.

"We all know that war has been declared, but we need to remain calm. Right now, I've been told that there's no cause for alarm. The government has directed that we will need to close our doors by 5pm to ensure we are home well before the curfew. Regarding the price control measures, I've already been in communication with the commissioner and will let you all know as soon as I have an update," she said, her eyes daring anyone to speak up again.

"Now, can we get back to our agenda?" Madam Titi continued. The women across the hall shifted in their seats as Kehinde watched with awe. She had commanded the hall like a headmaster would control a room full of children and her words flowed out effortlessly. How Kehinde wished she had the confidence to do that! The ability to have her voice heard and listened to, a leader in every way. She listened to Madam Titi steer the meeting and imagined for a fleeting moment that she was in her shoes, herself the voice of reason, the captain steering the ship through turbulent waters.

Chapter Ten

Kehinde grabbed Ayo's gloved hand as a horse galloped close to them. Their size, speed and the peculiar smell of manure and hay that followed them, all contributed to the list of reasons why Kehinde didn't like horses. Today however, the Ogunjobi household had turned out in all their finery at the racecourse to support the head of their home.

At almost thirty-six acres, the Lagos Racecourse had a central field where the horse races took place, with smaller areas sectioned off to serve as football and cricket sections. Kehinde had heard from Uncle Ladipo that the land had been gifted to colonial authorities in Lagos by Oba Dosunmu and had become a sporting area for the expatriate settlers of Lagos and their friends, the only real recreational area until Ikoyi Club opened. The War Relief Committee had organised a fundraising event, the first of many aimed at donating towards the war effort.

The elite across Lagos were out in their numbers, and although it was a Saturday, everyone was dressed in their Sunday best, with some of the colonial officers in uniform, the medals on their chests glinting in the sunlight. Kehinde was wearing a red and white fitted dress lent to her by Ayo after she had spent the previous night taking in the waistline to make it a perfect fit. Ayo looked impeccable in a white shift dress and gloves, and a pale blue hat that matched her smart heeled shoes and purse. Mama Tope for once was not in iro and buba, instead wearing an ill-fitting floral dress that strained across her bust. The children were all dressed in various computations of English wear, the boys in waistcoats and trousers, the girls in little summer dresses.

A live band played music at the other end of the spectators' area, and the guests swayed along to the music as they helped themselves to the refreshments. It looked like there were at least two hundred people gathered there, not including the stableboys and waiters that were walking around in their black and white uniforms, serving cold glasses of freshly squeezed orange juice, zobo and plates of chin chin, fried plantain, beef skewers and puff puff.

Kehinde still could not believe she had been married for a week. Time had sped up and slowed down at the same time, and it felt like a month had gone by when it had just been a few days. Although the sharp pain in her chest had settled into a dull ache, she had moments where the reality of her father's infinite absence slammed into her, making it difficult for her to breathe. She missed home, and she was sure that if she had Taiwo with her, her grief would have been easier to bear. She still had not seen or heard from him and she had not heard from her mother or Aunty Laide either. She was looking forward to seeing them; Baba Tope had agreed that she should spend the afternoon with her family after church the following day.

From where she was standing with Ayo, she watched their

husband move through the crowd, shaking hands and stopping to make conversation with little clusters of people. He knew almost all the white civilians, speaking English with ease as they nodded at whatever he was saying. He was laughing with a big, red-faced man who looked like he had had one too many glasses of brandy. On closer inspection, the man looked like the general manager of the John Holt company. He had been in the previous week's edition of the *Daily Times* in an interview about the increased importance of palm kernel exports and how one of Baba Tope's depots had been identified as a trusted storage space for the duration of the war.

She found herself wondering if Emeka had read the article. The day after they met, she had scanned the copy of the *Daily Times* they had at home, looking for his name, surprised at the tingle in her stomach when she found it under an article about conscription in Eastern Nigeria. She had shut the newspaper, wondering why she was still thinking about a man she had only just met.

"You know this is where we met," Ayo said, her eyes also following their husband to where he stood beside the pole bearing the Union Flag dancing in the wind almost to the beat of the music.

"Where who met?" Kehinde asked, pushing all thoughts of Emeka from her mind.

"Our husband, who else would I be talking about? I had come here with my friends from Ibadan to see the famous Lagos Racecourse and he was here with some of his friends," she replied as she took a sip of her water.

"Had you arranged to meet here?"

"No, that was the first time we ever saw each other. He came up to me and asked what my name was."

"Did you know he was married already?"

"Yes, I did. It made him even more attractive," Ayo shrugged, pausing to adjust her hat. "From the minute I saw him, I knew he was my escape. I knew he would take care of me, and really, that's the best that any man has ever offered me," she continued, her voice taking on a bitter edge.

Ayo was making Kehinde see their husband in a new light, one where he was an eligible husband. Her parents had probably thought the same; they would have looked at him and seen a provider, a responsible, powerful man that would take care of their daughter along with all his other wives and children. The difference though, was that Ayo had made this choice herself, while Kehinde still felt like the choice had been taken from her. She estimated that Ayo had probably been around the same age as she was now when she got married to their husband and she wondered what it was about Ayo that made her want to be a parlour wife. What seemed like a nightmare to Kehinde suddenly appeared to be Ayo's dream. Her stomach lurched at the thought of Mr Ogunjobi's body pressed against hers. Surely, Ayo couldn't enjoy that at all? And his hands were always so cold and hard when he held her. Emeka's hands had been warm, even though they definitely hadn't felt soft when she shook them.

"I want to go to London one day, on a passenger ship. I'll take Adenike and Ashabi to see everything. Big Ben, the Tower of London, even those guards that stand outside Buckingham Palace," Ayo said with a faraway look.

"With our husband?" Kehinde asked, grateful that Ayo was forcing her to get out of her head.

"Yes now, who else will pay for our fare? That's why he asked for your details, for Kayode, to sort out your passport. He wants everything to be ready in case he decides we should all go on a family trip. He usually goes on his own at least once a year, and before I came, he even went with Mama Tope."

"Really? When?"

"Years ago, I don't think the boys were born. There's a picture of them in front of Buckingham Palace with Tope, she was a baby then. The picture is on Mama Tope's bedside table."

"Interesting," Kehinde said, unable to imagine Mama Tope on the cobbled streets of London. Baba Tope, yes, she pictured him in one of his double-breasted suits, but Mama Tope's uniform of bubus and bubas seemed incongruous with the image she had of the smart streets of London.

"Our husband can board any of the Elder Dempster ships leaving the ports, at any time. All he needs is to show his seal and signature. I don't expect any of us will be going on holiday anytime soon though, with this war going on. So bloody inconvenient," Ayo sighed.

They both looked up as the next race began, the blast of the gun sounding as Kehinde suddenly spotted Kunle on the edge of the track. She had almost forgotten that he worked here on the weekends, and she felt unexpectedly giddy to see a familiar face from her old life. He was stepping out from the stable area carrying a metal bucket of hay as he made his way towards the barricades.

"I've just seen my friend, Ayo. I'm going over to say hello before he disappears, I'll be back shortly," she said as she hurried over to where he was standing.

"Kunle! How good to see you! I should have guessed you would be here today!" Kehinde said when she reached him.

"Kehinde! Báwo? How's married life?" he asked, smiling his shy smile as he led her off the racecourse and closer to the shaded area near the stables.

"Married life is okay … I can't complain," Kehinde said, knowing that she really could not complain as it would be inappropriate.

"And how are your mother and Taiwo?"

"I haven't seen them since, but I'm going to see them tomorrow afternoon after church. Besides, I should be asking you about Taiwo, you see him every day at school."

"School? Taiwo hasn't been to school since your father died," he said. When Kehinde frowned at him, his eyes widened. "You don't know, do you? Taiwo enlisted on Monday. He's going to Zaria to train with the Air Force at the end of next week!" he continued.

The ground felt like it was turning into water despite the pounding hooves all around her. Kunle had beads of perspiration appearing on his forehead as his kind face creased into a look of pity.

"I thought you would be the first to know. I'm so sorry … I shouldn't have said anything," he reached out to hold Kehinde's arm.

The crowd cheered as the horses commenced their final lap, but as their hooves beat a steady tempo across the course, Kehinde's head roared with incoherent thoughts. She had to see Taiwo immediately and talk him out of this. Surely there was a way he could withdraw his place in the Army, at least defer it till after his final year of school. If she was at home this would never have happened, if she had spoken to him more the day after their father died, she could have put an end to this before it started, and if their father was alive, she would not even have to think about any of this.

"I'm so sorry, Kehinde. I need to get the next batch of horses ready now. It is so busy here today," Kunle said, still holding her arm as he adjusted the bucket of hay in his other hand.

"It's fine, Kunle, it was good to see you," Kehinde replied with composure she didn't feel as she stumbled away into the swirling dust, towards her new family.

"Who was he?" Ayo asked when Kehinde got back to where she was standing, the crowd paying them no attention as the horses they had bet on raced ahead.

"My brother's best friend."

"Ah, the famous Taiwo. I do hope I get to meet him one day," Ayo said, turning her attention towards the racecourse as the excitement in the crowd spread.

Kehinde watched the course but did not see the race. Taiwo had gone ahead and done it, without telling her! They never made any big decisions without telling each other, and now he hadn't even bothered to let her know. The shock she felt was tinged with the familiar taste of the jealousy she wanted to wish away. This was exactly like being left behind at home while Taiwo got to go to school. School, she thought bitterly. She had wanted that place that he was now throwing away without a second thought. Why did he get to go off and be a pilot while she was stuck here, making dinner, and smiling in the parlour, and thinking about the bare rows of shelves in her store, ignoring the emptiness her father had left in her?

Her anger and hurt simmered as she realised that Taiwo must have avoided her all week intentionally because he knew she would try to dissuade him. Bristling, she wondered if she could get to her mother's house to see him after the race, immediately knowing that would be impossible. It was already midday, and she would need to be back before the blackout. She would have to wait to see him the next day.

The crowd roared again as Power, the horse with the

highest number of bets on his back, made it across the finish line in first place. Kehinde joined the crowd, clapping on autopilot as she continued to think about her brother's betrayal.

———————

Even at the best of times, Kehinde struggled to concentrate during the service at church. Unlike her father, her faith extended to the odd prayer, usually only said when she desperately needed something, and she would not have minded if she never spent another morning sitting among the congregation of Bethel Cathedral.

There were no non-Africans in this church, and the congregation consisted of all classes. Since it opened its doors in 1901, the church had opened its arms to the likes of Mr Ogunjobi and their expansive families. After all, he was contributing to the welfare of the flock by taking care of his household; where would those women and children be today if he had not cared for them?

Kehinde tapped her foot, waiting for the closing hymn to end as the choir belted out the last verse, something about God's protection in perilous times. The sermon had preached about having faith, even in moments of uncertainty, followed by announcements requesting for volunteers to sign up at Government House. She had noticed again today that her mother and Taiwo were not present. The service ended and she spent the next twenty-odd minutes impatiently greeting Mr Ogunjobi's friends, many of them keen to see the new wife proudly displayed on his arm.

"My flower, are you sure you don't want Tunde to drive you to your mother's house? You've been walking around too much lately," he said, frowning, looking at her stomach. Kehinde immediately guessed that he was hoping she was already pregnant and crossed her hands across her body.

"Thank you, Baba Tope. There's a bus that will get me to my mother's street within ten minutes."

She walked down the church street, hoping that she was not pregnant. The thought of growing his child in her womb made her shudder even though she knew it was expected of her. Shaking off the thought, she made her way to the bus stop at the end of the road where a few other parishioners and pedestrians were also waiting.

She felt the eyes of an older woman on her dress as she patted it down. This was a new one made by Ayo that fit her snugly at the waist and flared down to her calf, one that clearly showed the lack of a baby in her stomach. Kehinde knew her mother would also be praying that Kehinde would get pregnant, at least within a year. With a sigh, Kehinde pushed the thought out of her mind more forcefully and got on the arriving bus, walking to the back.

The bus sped by the familiar streets she had passed for years on her way home from church, sitting beside her father, with Taiwo and her mother sitting on the row behind them. They would talk about the houses as they drove by, their father speaking about the history of the old Lagos streets, pointing at the exact spot on Broad Street where the King had stood when he visited. How she wished he was here beside her now, laughing at the man in front of the bus, arguing with the conductor about his disappearing fare. He would have made a comment about the newly painted high court as the bus sped past, and he would have been sad to see that the tired-looking woman who sold corn with her two small children was still on the edge of Odunsi Street. He would have been alarmed to see the number of men already walking around in khaki uniform. Could he still see where he was now? Was she in fact seeing everything through his eyes?

The bus came to a stop at the fishing village, jolting her back to the present. Still thinking about her father, Kehinde got off the bus and made her way down the familiar path towards her first home, the one week she had been away feeling more like a year. As she got to Malumo Street, she saw her mother bending over the hedge of hibiscus in their front garden. She looked more subdued, something in the limp way she pulled a weed from the ground and sighed as she stood up and dusted her hands on her lap, the cheekbones in her gaunt face accentuated by her black head scarf. Her mother made to pick up the bucket of weeds beside her when she spotted Kehinde, and her face transformed into the brilliant smile that Kehinde had been scared had gone forever, with her father.

"Keke!" she said, meeting Kehinde outside the gate and enveloping her in a hug. Kehinde felt the absence of the old curves that usually silhouetted her mother's already small frame like she was picking up a half full sack of potatoes.

"Mummy, it's so good to see you. I've really missed you … I've missed home." She felt suddenly overwhelmed with longing.

"This is not your home anymore oh, your husband's house is your home now," her mother said, stepping back to take a good look at Kehinde. "What a beautiful dress! You're looking so well; Baba Tope is taking good care of you! And of me too! Every day, Kayode comes here with bread, fresh fruit and meat. I've been sharing it with Uncle Ladipo and Aunty Laide, the food is too much!"

"But Mummy, you don't look like you've been eating. You've lost more weight."

Kehinde regretted her words almost immediately as her mother paused to look away. "Ah, Keke, I'm trying. Aunty Laide and Uncle Ladipo come over every day to check on me. We have dinner before curfew together, they make sure I eat something."

Kehinde guessed that dinner was probably the only meal her mother was eating then. She imagined her walking around the silent house during the day, torturing herself by sitting in her father's armchair, arranging his old newspapers and bulletins.

"How is Taiwo? Is he at home today?" Kehinde asked, not saying more in case her mother had been too grief-stricken to notice that he wasn't going to school.

"Keke, maybe you should come inside first. I told Aunty Laide and Uncle Ladipo to come this afternoon, let's talk before they get here," she said, leading Kehinde up the footpath and through their door.

As Kehinde followed her in she felt the absence of her father, a sensation similar to trying to drink from an empty cup. Everything was the same, her mother had not moved anything. Yet, there was clearly a lack of something integral to the very core of this home, the smell of the sea on his clothes, the earthy scent of the black soap that he bathed with. She took a seat at the dining table, pulling out the chair backing her father's armchair, wondering how her mother could bear to live here, without him. Her mother took the seat beside her, sighing as she sat.

"Taiwo has joined the Army," she said without preamble, a note of resignation in her voice as she untied the scarf on her head, her cornrows looking like deflated worms.

"Where is he now?"

Her mother blinked at her. "You don't sound surprised. He told you himself?"

"I haven't seen Taiwo since I left home. Kunle told me, I saw him at the racecourse yesterday. Where is Taiwo now?"

"He's coming this afternoon, specifically to see you. He should be here any minute."

Her mother had adopted the conciliatory tone she had always used when she was trying to mediate their fights growing up. Regardless of whatever they were fighting about, she always ended up taking Taiwo's side, Kehinde thought with growing annoyance. Her father, her defender, would not be here to speak for her today.

"Coming from where? He wasn't at church," Kehinde asked.

"The barracks, he moved there the day you got married," her mother said, not meeting Kehinde's eyes.

"Mummy, how could you let this happen?" The shock in her voice was louder than the words she spoke.

"Kehinde, don't start, I've already heard enough from Uncle Ladipo!"

"This is the last thing Daddy would have wanted. He said so himself, the day he died!"

"Your father is no longer here, Kehinde! You have no idea what it's been like this past week, no idea at all!" her mother said, standing up from the dining room table.

"Mummy, all I'm saying is that you should have tried harder to stop him. If I was at home, I would have done everything, anything, to make him see reason."

"There's nothing you could have done, Kehinde," Taiwo said behind her. He stood in the doorway wearing his khaki uniform, looking at them like he was scared to step across the threshold even with the mutinous expression on his face. The sight of him was more than she could bear, she felt like a gas cooker that had just been set ablaze.

"When were you going to tell me? I had to find out from Kunle!"

"I've told you so many times, Kehinde. You've always known, you've just refused to listen," he said, crossing the room to stand beside their mother as they faced Kehinde together. She looked at them, certain they must have lost their minds the day her father went missing.

"You … you didn't even come to see me. And why wouldn't you at least wait to finish the school year? It's so hasty, it … it makes no sense!"

"Why doesn't it make sense? The war has started, but you think I should sit in school, twiddling my thumbs because Daddy thought being a lawyer was my best option? Because you're stuck with Mr Ogunjobi since Daddy couldn't tell him no? Because you couldn't stand up for yourself?"

If his words were a hand, Kehinde felt like he had slapped the breath out of her.

"Taiwo, that's enough—" their mother started, reaching up to hold his arm as Kehinde also stood to her full height.

"You sound ridiculous. How dare you talk about Daddy like that because of this stupid war! And when it's over you'll have nothing to do!"

"And you'll still be stuck with Mr Ogunjobi, too scared to do something about it, as usual," he spat out.

Kehinde felt the tears she had been looking for all week fill her eyes as she looked at her brother. He kept talking, holding on to the bag strap across his body like a supporting staff.

"I'll remain a pilot long after the war is over. I've started my training with the Air Force already. Captain Mackenzie said I have the potential to be a great pilot one day. He thinks I'll be on the field in a few months, even by January."

"And then what? How will you ever get a job as a lawyer now?" Kehinde cut him off. He was throwing it all away, throwing away the chance of having a respectable office job, the life that she would have loved to live if only the chance had been given to her. Pushing on with his dreams even though her father forbade him from doing so. He was forging ahead, leaving her behind, so he could do the great things they were both supposed to do while she remained useless.

"That's not what I want to do! Even if Daddy was alive, I still wouldn't be a lawyer! Why can't you understand that this isn't about you! There is absolutely nothing that you, or Mummy, or Uncle Ladipo can say to stop me! Accept it or not, that's your own problem! You might not have the courage to stand up for yourself, Keke, but I do. So, stop trying to hold me back because you can't push yourself forward!"

Kehinde was as rattled as a shekere, his words the loose beads dancing against the gourd of her head. A cocktail of emotions coursed through her: shock, fear, jealousy, resentment, abandonment, some she couldn't even articulate in one word as she stood facing her brother, the sound of the clock chiming the only noise in the house.

"I'm stuck here, stuck being a parlour wife, and you still get to do what you want," she muttered.

A dark look crossed Taiwo's face as he looked at her. "You're angry that you're such a spineless pushover? And that's somehow my fault? Take the damn job if that's what you really want. What are you so afraid of?"

Now it was her mother's turn to look surprised.

"What job?" she asked.

"Kehinde got offered a job at the *West African Pilot*, which from the look of things, she won't be accepting," Taiwo said with a sneer, his words a wooden spoon in the pot of her tumultuous feelings.

"It's for the best, a wife's duties are in her home. How were you planning on taking care of your husband with a job like that? Soon you'll have babies to look after, there's no time to be running off writing at some paper," her mother said. Kehinde felt the familiar stab of irritation at her mother's words.

"I'm sure I would have managed, Mummy. But anyhow, the decision has been made and I won't be taking up the position," Kehinde said, hearing how broken her voice sounded.

"The decision has been made for you, not by you. Unsurprising," Taiwo repeated, the disappointment all over his face.

"Taiwo, shut up! Unlike you, I'm doing what's best for our family! I actually care about how my actions affect everyone else, something you know nothing about! It's always been about you and what *you* want!" Kehinde exploded, wiping furiously at the tears on her face.

"You're just too scared to stand up to your husband, the same way you were too scared to stand up to Daddy. You care so much about what everyone else thinks that you can't even go after what you want! So much for finding your purpose."

"Daddy was proud of me! He would have said yes if not for the war, I know it!" Kehinde said doubtfully.

"Yes, and look where his pride has got you. You're still here, waiting for a yes that will never come," Taiwo said, the fury in his eyes mingling with pity as he adjusted the satchel strap across his chest.

"You're so selfish, and so stupid! You go off, and fight for this Empire that doesn't care whether you live or not. Leave

Mummy and me to fend for ourselves. I hope you never come back!" Kehinde shouted, regretting her words almost as soon as they left her mouth.

"Hello!' came Aunty Laide's voice from the front door that had been left ajar. She came in with Uncle Ladipo, carrying a Victoria sponge cake. Taiwo looked back at Kehinde, his mouth hanging open.

"You don't mean that," he said finally.

"Kehinde, apologise to Taiwo now!" her mother said.

"I have nothing to apologise for. Have a good life in Zaria, or wherever you end up," Kehinde said, pushing past Aunty Laide and Uncle Ladipo, through the door as she made her way back to her new house, feeling like she had nowhere to call home.

Chapter Eleven

Kehinde walked blindly out of the house, letting her legs lead her while she focused on trying to hold back the tears that were rushing down her face like a waterfall until she could smell the ocean. A few fishing boats littered the shore, but there were hardly any fishermen walking around.

With a sigh that felt like her chest would leave her body, she kicked off her shoes and sank to the floor, wanting to feel close to her father to get some solace from his presence, but none came. She hated Taiwo and she hated herself more. She missed him already and wanted to run back home to beg his forgiveness, but she was too angry with him for leaving her. Yes, her twin, the person she had always felt closest to, was leaving her behind and it was unforgivable. And as her thoughts started to slow down, the sinking feeling that remained in her gut screamed at her that Taiwo was right. She *was* a coward. She was exactly where she was because she couldn't stand up for what she wanted. He had asked her what she was afraid of and for the first time, she really stopped to think about it.

Growing up, she hadn't liked to be scolded, being told off always left her feeling sad in a way that had never seemed to affect Taiwo. And she liked being her father's favourite, the one who always took his advice. But she was an adult now, old enough to at least try to make her own decisions so why was she shackled by this fear of not living up to her parents' expectations? Her father had been the one to tell her she was destined to do great things, surely now was the time to make that happen, and to figure out exactly what she was supposed to do with her life. It had to be more than being Baba Tope's third wife!

She hiccupped as a trio of scruffy looking seagulls walked by. At least they had company, she thought bitterly. Taiwo had made his decision to leave her behind, and that was what hurt the most. Without even a second glance, without even pretending to consult her now that everything had changed. She was all alone, and Baba Tope would be waiting for her, probably already annoyed that she had been out for so long.

———————

When she finally got back home, she made her way into her room, aware that she had missed dinner and had barely any time left to prepare for the night ahead in Baba Tope's room. She only had a few minutes to bathe and, knowing that her absence at dinner would have been noticed, she was hoping not to irritate him further by making him wait for her. She quickly took her dress off and changed into her wrapper, gathering her bathing things.

As Kehinde opened her door, she saw Mama Tope emerge from her room and position herself by the door of the bathroom. Kehinde's face fell as their eyes met. This was the last thing she needed right now.

"Good evening, Mama Tope. Please, I need the bathroom," she said, in a voice she hoped sounded respectful but firm.

"Can't you see that I'm about to enter? What do you think I'm doing here?" Mama Tope said, folding her arms and planting her feet like two solid trees on the floor. The hem of the long, brown bubu she was wearing made her look like she was rooted to the spot.

Kehinde exhaled. She didn't have time for this, but forced herself to form a polite sentence. "Please, Ma, you saw me come out of my room. Our husband is waiting for me upstairs."

"Then it looks like you'll have to keep him waiting."

Kehinde let out a slow breath to steady herself. "Ma, please. Can I just use it quickly?"

"Are you deaf? Or maybe your ears are still growing. I've told you I'm using it and you'll have to wait, abi what do you want me to do?"

Kehinde pulled up her wrapper on her chest, adjusting it as Mama Tope eyed her, squinting as she smiled. Saying anything else would give her the ammunition to accuse Kehinde of being rude to her, but she knew that Baba Tope would be upset if she spent too long getting ready.

"Please Ma, I'll only be a minute. I just don't want to upset our husband, please, I'm sure you can understand," Kehinde asked, bowing her head slightly in deference. Mama Tope let out a short laugh.

"You foolish girl. You think because we share a husband you can talk to me anyhow? What could there ever be to understand between me and a small girl like you?" she sneerèd, opening the bathroom door and slamming it behind her.

Kehinde stood in the hallway, readjusting her wrapper, humiliated and angry. She was still standing there, trying to decide what to do when the door to Ayo's room opened.

"I thought I heard your voice. How was your mum?" Ayo asked.

This small act of kindness broke Kehinde's resolve and the tears she thought she had left behind on the beach resurfaced. Ayo ushered her into her room, shutting the door behind them.

"Shhh, shhh, má ṣùkùn. What happened?" Ayo said, rubbing Kehinde's back.

The words came tumbling out as Kehinde recounted her day, from Taiwo's enlistment to Mama Tope and the yet to be used bathroom. When she got to the last bit Ayo's face hardened.

"That wicked cow. She's tried that with me before, but I quickly put her in her place."

"Does Baba Tope know she behaves like this?"

"He doesn't want to know. He would rather pretend we all got on like rice and stew. She was his first love after all," Ayo said.

Her matter-of-fact tone made Kehinde dissolve into a fresh set of tears. What kind of life was this, where she shared a husband with two women she barely understood? Yes, Ayo was becoming her confidante in the house, she had been nothing but kind to her, but this whole situation made no sense. How did Baba Tope have three separate relationships with three women under the same roof? While Taiwo fought for the Commonwealth would she continue to have petty fights with Mama Tope?

"Shh, don't worry. Let's get you cleaned up quickly, okay?

We can talk about everything else in the morning. Our husband will be wondering where you are." Ayo said, picking up a handkerchief from her dressing table to wipe away Kehinde's tears.

Ayo turned around and pulled out a bucket from beneath her dressing table, before stepping out of the room, the sound of her footsteps echoing down the stairs and then back up again as she reappeared with a bowl of water and a hand towel.

"Here, we can get you freshened up in no time," she said, dipping the towel into the bowl of water and dabbing at Kehinde's face. She washed Kehinde's feet in the basin, drying them with the towel while Kehinde dried the tears on her face with her hands.

"Ese, Ayo."

"Oya, quickly, go and put your nightgown on, it's getting late."

By the time Kehinde made it upstairs it was dark outside. Atinuke had already gone around the house, putting out the lights and drawing the curtains. Kehinde knocked on Baba Tope's door, resisting the urge to run down the stairs, out of the door and back to her mother's house.

"Come in!" he said.

When she opened the door, he was sitting in his silk dressing gown, his reading glasses perched on his nose and a stack of documents in his right hand.

"I was beginning to think you would never arrive. You must have barely made it back before curfew," he pouted.

"I'm sorry, Baba Tope. I was delayed," Kehinde said, sinking into the chair beside him.

"I hope everything is fine at home. Your mother has been receiving the food I sent?"

Everything was not fine at home, but Kehinde didn't think he really wanted to know the truth. His attention had returned to the papers in his hands, shipping documents with the Elder Dempster logo and his red seal across the front. He smiled as he shuffled them, clearly unconcerned with whatever response she would give. "Yes, thank you, Baba Tope. My mother is grateful. She sends her greetings."

"We raised over £100 at the racecourse yesterday! It was the War Relief Committee's first event, hurriedly put together at that! We're already set to make a real difference to this war," he said, beaming as he put the papers into the drawer of his desk.

Kehinde stifled a yawn that took her by surprise. She was exhausted, and she also didn't understand why the Empire needed their colonies to donate money towards a war of their choosing. Surely, they had enough money already? Why was every Nigerian obsessed with making a difference in this European war? She thought of Taiwo in his uniform and felt upset all over again.

"Bernard was very impressed. He said he would write a letter to the King to tell him about us in Lagos, imagine that! He has even arranged to have a picture of the committee taken for the newspapers. Next, we're planning bomb drills for the citizens of Lagos," he continued, pouring himself his customary glass of red wine. He sounded like a child planning a birthday party and Kehinde said nothing, sure that he would continue his one-sided conversation regardless.

"I'll ensure I have enough time on Fridays for the Relief meetings, Kayode will need to move some things around in my schedule." He paused to take a sip of his wine. "Anyway, by the time Christmas comes round we'll have more of an idea of where this war is going," he said.

Kehinde felt her disgust rise within her as she looked at

Baba Tope, obviously pleased with himself. She would go to bed angry again; it seemed her anger and resentment followed her everywhere she went, simmering beneath the surface like beans in a pressure cooker. She couldn't quite make sense of the world and the people around her anymore. Her father's death, her marriage to this strange man that seemed obsessed with keeping up appearances, Taiwo joining the Army, it was all too much. And after everything, she was still just a parlour wife. She wanted to switch off her mind, to switch everything off like a lamp and lie in the dark, alone in her room. She imagined herself in deep black water, like she was swimming in the lake by the fishing village at night.

Her father had taught her and Taiwo how to swim when they were five. They would set out early on Saturday mornings, their mother calling out warnings to be careful as they ran out of the house. He had spent weeks taking them through the different strokes, explaining how to tread water while conserving their energy, chastising Taiwo for swimming with his head above water because it was bad for his neck. She wanted to go swimming now, and stay there, alone under the black water in the silence, away from everything and everyone.

———

She woke up the next morning at the crack of dawn, before the rest of the house, and went to the kitchen. Taiwo had always said that he ate most when Kehinde was upset. Measuring out the flour, sugar, eggs and butter, she let her mind wander as she mixed and churned her feelings in the pan. After breakfast, she walked to her store, carrying the cake but still feeling wrung out, like she was coming down with a cold. She felt sad and lost, but also foolish. She and Taiwo had fought in the past, but their fight yesterday was the worst they had ever had. She couldn't see a way back from it, and more than anything, she hated the self-loathing that was growing wings inside her.

Ama took one look at her sitting at her front desk when she arrived on Lewis Street and ushered her next door into Fine Leather.

"Kehinde, why so glum? Is that a cake?" she asked, pushing Kehinde in through the front of the store.

Onyi nodded in acknowledgement as they went past, but quickly looked back down at the leaflet she was reading. The title read *"The threat of colonisation by Fascist Germany and why we need to pull together to win the war"*, and from the way Onyi's mouth hung open there was no doubt that she was feeling the threat of German invasion.

As soon as they walked into the office at the back, Ama made Kehinde take a seat and kicked her shoes off as she sat behind her desk. "So, why do you look like you just found out the world is ending today?"

Kehinde hesitated. She didn't think Ama would understand the fight she had with Taiwo or her own angst. After all, Ama was independently running her own store, far away from home, and she doubted she was used to taking orders from anyone but her customers.

Ama's face softened when Kehinde didn't laugh. "Kehinde … I know we met not too long ago, but I really want you to know that you can trust me. I might be able to help."

"I'm not even sure I can explain it all if I'm being honest," Kehinde said.

"Try me," Ama said, reaching out and taking her hand.

So Kehinde started speaking, telling Ama everything, the way she had spoken to Ayo the previous night, but this time, also going into detail about her father's death and how much she felt trapped. As she spoke, it felt like the rock that had lodged itself in her chest was starting to ease, slowly but surely.

"Oh, you poor thing. You've been through so much in the last few weeks," Ama said, when she had finished.

"You don't think I'm a pushover?"

"I mean, I would have done a few things differently if I were you, but I know it's easier said than done."

Kehinde felt the self-loathing expand, and Ama must have seen it in her eyes because she quickly spoke again as she grabbed Kehinde's hand across the table.

"No, Kehinde, I'm not agreeing with your brother that you're a pushover at all. So much has happened to you, and if you don't like fighting, I can see how you would have struggled to stand your ground and not make the obvious choice."

"The obvious choice?"

"Not to get married! And to take the job!"

"If only it was that simple," Kehinde muttered.

"And why isn't it?"

"Who would have taken care of my mum?"

"You, and Taiwo. You would have figured something out, Kehinde," Ama said, still squeezing her hand.

She looked like she was about to say more when the bell in front of the store rang and they heard Onyi greeting a customer at the door.

"Ugh, just as we were settling down," Ama sighed, standing hurriedly. Kehinde followed Ama out of her office and heard Onyi gasp as Ama got to the shop floor ahead of her.

"Good morning, Ma! What an honour to have you in my store today!" Ama said.

Kehinde looked up to see who it was that had got both Ama and Onyi so excited. To her surprise, the woman standing in the middle of the store wearing a blue iro and buba with a matching hijab was none other than Madam Titi, the president of the Lagos Market Women's Association. She looked amused as Ama stumbled over her words.

"How can I help you, Ma?" Ama said.

"Ẹ káàárọ̀. Mrs Asaye tells me you sell good sandals. I need to get a pair, I'm afraid my old ones are now worn out."

"Yes, Ma, I know Mrs Asaye very well! You've come to the right place! We sell the finest Nigerian-made leather goods here. Onyi, quickly, bring some sandals for Madam to see. Please Ma, take a seat here. Can I offer you something to drink, Ma?"

Kehinde watched as Ama and Onyi ran around the president of the LMWA. Up close, she was still formidable, and she sounded imperial as she spoke her Yoruba-infused English slowly. Around her wrist was a brown subha which hung low beneath her sleeve, and Kehinde remembered Ama explaining that the Association meetings were never on a Friday because Madam Titi spent her Friday afternoons praying at the Koranic Central Mosque.

"You look familiar, do I know you from somewhere?" Madam Titi said in her deep voice as she turned to look at Kehinde.

"Ẹ káàárọ̀, Ma, I was at the Association meeting with Ama on Tuesday. Perhaps you remember my face from there?"

"No, that's not it. Come closer, what's your name?" she asked, peering at Kehinde as she beckoned her over.

"Kehinde Ogunjobi, Ma"

"And your father's name?"

"Fola Ilesanmi, he recently passed on."

"Exactly! That's where I know you from!" Madam Titi said, clapping her hands together. "I knew your father, every trader in Ereko Market knew him! There's something about your face that reminds me of him! I was so sorry to hear of his accident. How's your mother?"

"She's well, Ma," Kehinde lied. What else did people expect her to say when they asked her that question? More interestingly, how had her father failed to mention that he was acquainted with Madam Titi, of all people? Kehinde would have loved to have met her much sooner than today, under better circumstances.

Onyi came out of the back room, with four shoe boxes piled high in her arms. Ama took them from her and turned to Madam Titi.

"Ma, I've brought you the latest styles we have," Ama said, as she knelt on the floor to bring the sandals out.

"How did you know my shoe size? I didn't even get a chance to tell you," Madam Titi said, the amused look returning to her face.

"Ma, all I have to do is look at your feet, and I'll know," Ama said, grinning as Madam Titi tried on a pair of brown leather sandals that appeared to fit perfectly. Ama stood back as she walked towards the mirror with a slight limp.

"Not bad. Do you have black ones in this style?"

"Yes, Ma, in this box. There's another pair of black ones in another style that I think you'll like. Let me go and get them from the back myself," Ama said, grinning at Kehinde behind Madam Titi's bent back as she hurried off towards the storeroom.

"Your father was a good man. I was deeply saddened to hear of his accident," Madam Titi said to Kehinde in Yoruba.

"Yes, Ma, we miss him very much," Kehinde replied, touched.

"And what are you doing now? I heard you recently got married to Mr Ogunjobi?"

"Yes, Ma, I've been married for just over a week now. I sell food in the store next door."

"I'm surprised, your father always said you loved books. He was very proud of you, you know," she said as she sat to take the sandals off. Kehinde felt the blood rush to her face as Ama reappeared with the second pair of black sandals.

"Your friend here is a good saleswoman. I came in to buy one pair of sandals, but it appears that I'll be leaving with two," Madam Titi said, smiling at Ama, who was still grinning from ear to ear.

"Please have these packed for me, I'll take the black pair over there and the brown ones I tried on," she said as she looked through her purse. Once Ama had stepped away, she glanced at Kehinde again.

"My associate and secretary for the LMWA is heavily pregnant. She's due to give birth any day now and she's moving to Ibadan with her husband after the baby comes. I'm going to need a replacement for her. Someone who can represent the LMWA, and that can read and write English well. Would you be interested?" she asked.

Kehinde blinked at Madam Titi. Was she dreaming?

"You need not worry about your store. It's a part-time position and to be honest, most of the work I will need you to do for me can be done from wherever you choose. You see, I can't read or write very well but a lot of what I do requires reading and writing, in English. I'll need someone smart and capable. It doesn't pay much, but it's an exciting role that I think might suit you well."

Kehinde's heart sang for joy. It wasn't the *West African Pilot*, but it would still mean she could write and make a real difference for the women of the LMWA! But Baba Tope wouldn't approve, the voice of doubt whispered in her head. He would be angry with her for even asking, the same way he had been upset when she had mentioned the *West African Pilot*. Madam Titi continued to look at her, the fire in her eyes burning into Kehinde's thoughts as she waited for a response.

Aunty Bimpe had said something to her, when she was five, that she would never forget. Kehinde had been with her and Aunty Laide, and she had asked a question about the meaning of life, and whether each person had a purpose. Aunty Bimpe had explained that God gave people options, and they chose their own paths, while praying that their choice would align with His will for them. And Kehinde had clung to that, the way she held on to her father's belief that she and Taiwo were destined to do great things. It had been the driving force in her life, to have more courage than she thought she possessed, to speak up, and to find her voice even when she was afraid of what that would mean in light of the expectations of everyone around her. But she hadn't always been brave, and lately, she hadn't had the strength to summon the courage to stand up for herself.

Ama had since brought the sandals to Madam Titi and was watching Kehinde. She remembered what her new friend had said earlier about making the obvious choice. *This is a chance that will never come again*, a small voice, whispered in Kehinde's ear, pushing away the doubt. Much like the position at the *West African Pilot* that she had thrown away forever, this was another chance to do something meaningful, to take her life in her hands and actually do what she wanted for once. And this time, she wouldn't be stupid enough to ask for permission.

Baba Tope barely knew how she spent each day as it was, and what he didn't know certainly wouldn't hurt him. Her name did not have to appear anywhere in print if she did not wish it to. The thought of her father swimming indefinitely towards a shore he would never reach made up her mind. Taiwo was wrong about her. She was not a pushover, and she would take the job. No one at home had to know, Baba Tope would never find out.

Kehinde cleared her throat.

"Ma, I would be honoured to be your secretary. When can I start?"

PART II
November 1940–December 1940

There are three qualities a virtuous wife must possess:

1. Like a clock, she must keep time and consistency.
2. Like a snail, she must be wise and stay within her home.
3. Like an echo, she must speak when spoken to; but not always expecting to have the last word.

Cassandra's Column, *The Daily Times**

* Panata, S. 2020. "'Dear Readers...': Women's Rights and Duties through Letters to the Editor in the Nigerian Press (1940s-1950s)," *Sources. Materials & Fieldwork in African Studies*, no. 1: 141-198. Paris: Sources Journal

Chapter Twelve

CENTRAL LAGOS, NIGERIA

November 3, 1940

The brown Austin pulled up to the edge of a forest that had tall, dark trees covering the earth like a canopy. The humidity and shade coming from the forest engulfed Kehinde and Baba Tope as they got out of the car.

"Ose, Tunde. You can park the car here, we'll come out when we're done," Baba Tope said. They had come from church, and he was still dressed in his agbada and fila. Beads of perspiration started to form on his forehead as he stepped into the darkness of the closely packed trees. He held Kehinde's hand, pushing away any thoughts she had of fleeing.

They had driven for about two hours, the buildings getting less dense, the landscape giving way to more trees and red sand as they drove further and further away from Lagos. Although she guessed they were somewhere in Ogun State, Baba Tope had not told her where they were going. The night before, he had simply stated that they would be visiting a native doctor after church.

Kehinde had already guessed why he wanted her to see this particular doctor, not least because of her mother's worries.

"You must secure your position in your household," she had said to Kehinde during her visit home last week. "Without a baby, he will start to think there's something wrong with you. What if he sends you back?"

This had become the core of her conversations with her mother, a source of contention, a shared open wound that her mother continued to poke with a stick laced with self-pity and anxiety. What would they do if they lost Baba Tope's favour? What would people say if Kehinde had to return home, like a faulty kitchen appliance sent back to the market? Every week when she visited, her mother would look at her stomach as she arrived at the door, not bothering to hide her disappointment.

Kehinde was beginning to dread her visits home, only ever excited when Aunty Laide and Uncle Ladipo could drop by. It was also easier to pretend that things were fine between her and Taiwo when there were other people there. She hadn't heard from him in a year, and the only reason she knew about his whereabouts was because of the letters he wrote to her mother, Aunty Laide and Uncle Ladipo. She knew he had finished his training at Zaria and was now part of the Royal Air Force for the Empire stationed somewhere in Burma, and although she missed him, her pride would not let her write to him. They were at an impasse, and she knew he was waiting for an apology from her that she had not yet been able to give.

The tall grass kissed her ankles as they stepped into the forest. Kehinde heard water running nearby but could not locate its source as she looked around, her eyes adjusting to the darkness within the trees. The air smelled earthy, like cut leaves and mud mixed with something more primal, like a mass of unwashed bodies. Her feet sunk into the wet grass as they made their way deeper into the forest, Baba Tope's steps surefooted as he led the way ahead. Kehinde did not need to ask if he had come here before. She almost laughed at the irony of her church-going husband having a Babalawo that he visited outside Lagos, one that he was now bringing his newest wife to in search of answers. What would his colonial administrator friends think of that?

They reached a clearing in the forest where the trees were less dense, the grass more sparse and much shorter. In the middle of the clearing was a mud hut with a thatched roof above it. Beside the hut was what looked like a clothing line hanging from the edge of the hut to the closest tree, with various trinkets and ornaments swaying on it, making a tinkling sound as they danced in the wind. As they got closer, a small man dressed in a white, sleeveless kaftan came out of the hut. His head was bald and smooth like an egg and he had no shoes on his feet. Tribal tattoos in symbols that looked like sea animals and star constellations lined his arms, and his face was smothered in white chalk, his red-rimmed eyes a deep contrast to the paleness of his skin as he regarded them silently. When they were about five paces in front of the man, Baba Tope prostrated, lying flat on the floor. He tugged Kehinde on the way down, gesturing for her to kneel beside him.

"Great elder, it is me, your humble servant, Gboyega Ogunjobi. I've come to seek your help over a matter concerning my young wife," Baba Tope said, his voice muffled as he spoke into the ground. Kehinde kept her eyes downcast as she noticed another pair of bare feet appear on the ground beside the Babalawo's. These ones were much bigger and darker, with toes that pointed in different directions. After a moment, both pairs of feet moved towards them. Kehinde felt a cool hand land on her head.

"What's the matter?" asked a deep voice that rumbled out of the trees like a clap of thunder.

"My wife is barren. I humbly seek your help, great elder," Baba Tope said beside her, his voice shaking on the word barren. Kehinde felt like a child that had been brought to the headteacher after failing an exam. The cool hand on her head felt more speculative than reassuring, a hand trying to get to the bottom of this empty vessel.

"Rise!" the deep voice said.

Kehinde and Baba Tope rose, giving her another chance to look at the men before her. The second man that had appeared was tall, with a broad, muscular chest, left bare over a pair of white funtua cotton shorts. A black ring of lion's teeth was tattooed above his right breast, and he held a granite bowl in his hands. He stood beside the bald Babalawo, watching Kehinde and Baba Tope with a blank expression on his face.

"Come closer, child," the Babalawo said.

Kehinde moved forward, the soft mud beneath her feet sticking to the soles of her sandals like quicksand.

"I'll need to examine her. Bankole, prepare the hut!" he said to the tall man beside him, who nodded and set off towards the hut in the centre of the clearing.

"Wise elder, will that be necessary?" Baba Tope asked. He wiped the sweat across his brow with a handkerchief. Kehinde gulped as she imagined what this 'examination' would entail. Baba Tope also seemed a bit startled; she didn't know what he had been expecting but clearly this was not it.

"Do you question my ways, Gboyega?"

"No, wise elder. Please forgive me."

Bankole reappeared and whispered into the Babalawo's ear. He nodded and looked at Kehinde, extending his hand towards her.

"Come with me, child. Gboyega, you must wait outside," he said.

Baba Tope looked like he wanted to protest again but he shut his mouth in a tight line as he watched Kehinde follow the Babalawo into the hut.

She had to duck to avoid hitting her head on the door frame as she entered the low hut, and she was greeted by a metallic, fishy smell, like old blood. The only source of light was a square cut out where a window should have been on the side of the hut, and there were more trinkets and beads hanging from the ceiling. Babalawo pointed at a raffia mat in the middle of the floor.

"Lie down there, and raise your skirts," he said in a voice that did not leave room for negotiation.

Mortified, she did as she was told. The Babalawo knelt in front of her, muttering under his breath as Bankole stood silent at the door. If he was embarrassed, he did not let on. Instead, his gaze remained steady as he stood holding the bowl.

The Babalawo continued to mutter what sounded like a chorus of disparate vowels and consonants as he looked beneath Kehinde's skirts. Kehinde held her breath. She closed her eyes, anticipating the worst, but to her surprise, after a brief look, he stood up again.

"When do you have your monthly bleeding?" he asked.

"At the middle of the month, usually," Kehinde lied.

"Let's go outside," he said, as he pulled her skirts down.

Stunned, Kehinde stood up and followed the Babalawo and his assistant out of the hut. Baba Tope jumped from the bench when he saw them as he rushed forward, an anxious look on his face.

"Wise elder, I hope the examination went well?" Baba Tope asked, his eyes going back and forth between Kehinde and the Babalawo.

"Physically, your wife is fine," he responded.

Kehinde was surprised at the relief she felt at his words. Although she thought this was a load of rubbish, she was still apprehensive. Since her father's death, she secretly worried that there might be something wrong with her internally, something that had broken along with her heart. Her periods came sporadically and unannounced, more irregular than the rains in the dry season. She hadn't told anyone; she suspected it would only make matters worse for her if she did.

"The problem is in the spiritual realm," the Babalawo said, closing his eyes and twisting his mouth as if the words were painful to say. "Your enemies have conspired against you, Gboyega. They are jealous of your success, and they have put dark forces together to ensure you do not have any new joy in this world," he continued. The sky above the trees had darkened and the wind around them seemed to corroborate the ominous words of the Babalawo.

"What shall I do, wise elder?" Baba Tope asked. Kehinde almost did a double take. Surely Baba Tope must know better than to believe this man? There was no evidence that his words were true.

"A sacrifice must be made. A sacrifice of blood," the Babalawo said with a nod.

Kehinde tried not to roll her eyes. Her father had told her of men like this, men who fought spiritual wars on behalf of their fellow physical beings.

"Anything, wise elder, what must I do?" Baba Tope asked, his hands clasped in front of him.

"Every last Friday of the month, I will sacrifice a goat as an offering to Sango. His power will strike off your enemies one by one, their forces shall be destroyed by the blood that is shed," he declared.

Kehinde watched as Baba Tope nodded along to the words, his lips pressed together in concentration. Bankole remained silent as he watched the exchange, blending into the background with the trees.

"Yes, wise elder. You have never failed me in the past. I will make the necessary arrangements to have the goat brought to you, at the appointed time, along with a small donation of course," Baba Tope said. Kehinde was not surprised to hear this. She had suspected for some time now that her church-going husband wasn't faithful. After all, he was a firm believer in having insurance. Kehinde looked up at the trees, trying hard not to laugh at the thought of Baba Tope instructing Kayode to arrange the monthly purchase and delivery of the poor goat.

The Babalawo inclined his bald head towards Baba Tope. "Your contribution to the cause is accepted as always. After at least twelve sacrifices, your wife should conceive a boy child. It may take longer, but I will do my best to make the petitions on your behalf. You must continue to plant your seed at regular intervals in the month to ensure the success of the sacrifice."

"Thank you, wise elder," Baba Tope said, also bowing his head.

On the ride home they were both silent, but Kehinde could feel the heat of his anger as he pretended to read the *Daily Times* in his lap. Throughout the past year, it had become harder for him to hide his disappointment that she was not yet pregnant. She wasn't disappointed at all; she still dreaded every night she spent in his bed although she had learned to bear it.

She added it to the list of things that had become her cross to carry. One, her father was dead. Two, her twin was far away and not speaking to her. Three, she was unhappily married. Four, she might never have her own children, which was sad, but not terrible considering that having children for a man who had become nothing more than the gaoler that kept her clothed and fed, was unbearable. From all she had seen of how Ayo fussed over Ashabi and Adenike, she knew it was the kind of love she would welcome one day. But she knew she did not love Baba Tope, and she at least wanted her child to be confident about her love for his or her father, the way she and Taiwo had never doubted their parents' love for one another. Ayo kept telling her that she would grow to love their husband, but Kehinde did not think it was that simple. He disgusted her, and all she really felt for him was fear.

She had to admit that her marriage had at least exceeded her expectations on a material level. When she was in church, she was greeted like royalty, and she never had to worry about money. He sent her mother a weekly stipend that exceeded her needs and Kehinde never had to spend any of the money she made in the market. Ama had taken her to the First Bank head office and shown her how to open a bank account. All the money she made in her store and at her job with Madam Titi went in there, and she had amassed almost £95 over the last year. The allowance she received from Baba Tope went towards her toiletries and she usually had some left over. But being materially well off would never be the same as being emotionally sound, and Kehinde knew that her marriage was significantly lacking in that department. She and Baba Tope would never have the kind of love her parents had, or the understanding that helped them communicate without words.

She sat back and looked out of the window, thinking about all the things she was actually grateful for instead, like going to work the next day and spending time with Ama and Emeka.

"You need to start eating more oranges," Baba Tope said suddenly, bringing her back to her ever-present reality of being his wife. She turned away from the window to look at him. He was still looking at the newspaper in his hands.

"Excuse me, Baba Tope?"

"Should they have checked your hearing too? I said, you need to start eating more oranges. It says here that women are taking it to help with fertility. The vitamin C is good for you and the baby," he said unnecessarily loudly, pointing at the text he was reading. Kehinde pretended to study it.

"Thank you, Baba Tope. I will ask Ayo to add more oranges to the household shopping list," she responded, stifling a laugh as she thought of Ayo's face when she heard about this.

The journey back to Lagos seemed shorter than the journey out of it and Kehinde was grateful to see the familiar sight of the Marina as their car drove over Carter Bridge. She was surprised to feel a sense of relief as they pulled into their driveway; she never imagined that she would come to think of this house as her home.

Ayo was waiting for her in the kitchen when she walked in. She had just placed a pot of beans on the stove to boil and dried her hands on the kitchen towel when she saw Kehinde arrive.

"Well, how was it?" she asked, after checking to make sure Atinuke was out of earshot.

"It was okay, strangely enough he said there was nothing wrong. Just enemies in the spiritual realm that must be fought with a monthly blood sacrifice and donation. And more oranges."

Ayo let out a bark of laughter. "You mean you went all the way there to hear nonsense? You could have just gone to the bar at the end of Customs Street for that."

"I should probably see a real doctor though," Kehinde said, thinking again about her irregular cycle.

"Oh, Kehinde, I've told you, sometimes it takes time for a baby to catch. I'm not complaining though, if you had your own children now who would help me with Ashabi and Adenike?" Ayo said.

Kehinde laughed at that. It was a running joke between them that Kehinde had joined the Ogunjobi household to help Ayo take care of her children. They had very quickly realised that Kehinde was the better hairdresser between the two of them, and she had taken over as custodian of Ashabi and Adenike's tresses. They now spent Saturday mornings after breakfast in Ayo's room, Ayo tapping away at her sewing machine while Kehinde did Ashabi and Adenike's hair in the style chosen by their school for the week. Kehinde loved it, she was fond of the girls, and she was a natural hairdresser. She also helped the girls with their homework on most evenings, especially Ashabi, who struggled with her maths. She reminded Kehinde of Taiwo in a way; although she was smart, she wanted to spend all her time playing outside and it was difficult to get her to stay still and concentrate. Adenike was a lot more conscientious, and she looked up to Kehinde, basking in her approval when she remarked on how well she had done her writing. Kehinde was beginning to think of Ayo and her daughters as the sister and nieces she never had.

"Let's hope I give birth to boys with no hair," Kehinde

replied. She saw pain flit across Ayo's face and immediately knew she had said the wrong thing.

"Let me start dishing up the food. Baba Tope will be hungry after being on the road all day," Kehinde said quickly.

It was not something they had ever explicitly spoken about, but she knew that Ayo had wanted a boy badly and was still hoping to have one; she had been praying for one since Ashabi had been born seven years ago. Her lack of a son was the card Mama Tope used to taunt her, telling her that her boys were Baba Tope's favourites. It didn't help that he took his sons everywhere with him and spoke openly about them being the heirs of his businesses. Ayo knew that for Baba Tope to truly see her as an equal to Mama Tope she needed to produce a male heir.

"Maybe I should also see this doctor. But he might tell me I have to shave my head and start speaking in a deep voice if I want to conceive a son," Ayo said, breaking the ice.

Laughing, Kehinde measured three cups of boiled beans into the dish they were using for dinner. "Probably. How's the dress coming along?"

The "dress" was a gown Ayo had been working on for weeks for the wife of one of Baba Tope's colonial administrator friends. They were going back to England, and she wanted something distinctly African to take back with her. She had given Ayo three different adire fabrics and had told Ayo to make whatever style she wanted, but each time the lady came over to be fitted, she had a different issue with it and Ayo had to go back to the drawing board.

"I wish I never started making the damned thing. I've even started seeing it in my dreams, it's like I can't escape."

"Maybe you should tell her you've given up," Kehinde said, only half joking. She couldn't imagine having the kind of patience required to go back and forth on something as frivolous as a dress.

"After Baba Tope already told them he's married to the best dressmaker in Lagos? No chance," Ayo said laughing.

Kehinde laughed too, but her laugh rang hollow. It wasn't jealousy she was feeling. Far from it. She just felt herself longing for the kind of marriage that Ayo seemed to have with her own husband. The type of marriage where your husband was proud of how you spent each day and told his friends about it. Baba Tope hardly asked about her shop, except when it was time to give her the stipend he paid her for its upkeep. Besides, if he knew how she really spent each day, he would be livid.

"You hardly talk about your store in the market, by the way. Not even to me. It's almost like it doesn't exist. When I ask you how your day has been, you only talk about the time you spend with your friend, Ama," Ayo said, like she could read her mind.

Despite how close they were, Ayo knew nothing about her involvement with the LMWA. Kehinde had kept it from her, firstly to protect her in case their husband ever found out, and secondly, she knew that Ayo would try to talk her out of it. And third, she had always been a terrible liar. But she didn't want to lie to her now, and Ayo had been nothing but kind with her. Surely, she could trust her with this?

Atinuke came into the kitchen, carrying the trays she would use for their dinner. Kehinde's mouth shut faster than the door. If she wanted to tell Ayo, this would have been a terrible moment, the worst thing that could happen would be Mama Tope finding out. Maybe this was a sign she shouldn't tell Ayo, she thought. After all, secrets were best kept when not shared.

Chapter Thirteen

The next morning, Kehinde and Ayo cleared away breakfast, the clatter of plates merging with the sounds of the children running up and down the stairs as they got ready for school. Kehinde left shortly after the children, enjoying the cool breeze from the previous night's rain. She no longer had to convince Baba Tope to let her walk in the mornings. The petrol rationing that had begun earlier in the year meant that motor transport was prioritised for essential activities, and he could hardly justify the cost of driving Kehinde to and from work.

A tall man in khaki walked past her and she almost did a double take – he reminded her so much of Taiwo that it hurt to look away. He smiled at her as he hurried along, and Kehinde focused on the road ahead. Instead of going to Sandgrouse Market, she turned onto Lewis Street and walked down the path to Ama and Emeka's apartment.

Humming, she walked up the stairs until she got to the third floor and knocked on their door.

Emeka opened the door, and she felt the familiar skip in her stomach at the sight of him.

"Kehinde! Perfect timing. I just put the eggs on the table."

"Great!" Kehinde said, walking in as Ama came out of the kitchen carrying a teapot.

Ama's eyes lit up when she saw her.

"Please tell me you brought akara?" she asked, nodding at the bag in Kehinde's hand.

"I did indeed," Kehinde replied, swinging the still warm bag in Ama's direction.

"I was just telling Emeka that I was craving your akara, the one with okra and prawns inside!" Ama squealed.

"Fresh from the pan," Kehinde said, grinning as she watched Ama open the bag and arrange the akara on a plate beside the dish that had Emeka's signature vegetable omelette on it. Kehinde had deliberately eaten little at home just so she would have enough space for the Monday breakfast with Emeka and Ama that she had come to look forward to as the best part of her week.

Kehinde loved coming to their apartment. She loved the way the front door opened up to the small living and dining area, and the way they had both left their mark around the two-bedroom apartment overlooking Simpson Street, with Ama and Onyi sharing one room and Emeka the other. The parlour, dining room and kitchen made up the majority of the flat, with one bathroom beside the kitchen. In the corner of the parlour was a writing desk and sofa where Kehinde had spent many hours with Ama and Emeka in the past. The colours and personal touches were what made the space feel like another home for Kehinde. Ama had apparently spent years working on the purple and green raffia mat between the sofa and the dining table with their mother, and a similar quilt on the bed in the room she shared with Onyi. Emeka's watercolours and sketches of the landscape in their childhood home hung on the walls and brought even more character to the room.

"You look nice," Emeka said over the rim of his mug when they were all seated.

"Thank you," Kehinde said, still smiling. She was wearing a blue velvet pinafore with a white lace shirt, and she had done her hair into two big cornrows that framed her face. As she'd done her hair that morning, she'd pretended to herself that she wasn't anticipating the usual way Emeka stared at her when all her hair was swept away from her face, like he couldn't look away.

Ama dished up the eggs on the three plates, cutting a slice of bread for each of them. "Sorry there's no butter. Yesterday's bomb drill took so long that I didn't have time to buy any."

There was still a heavy cloak of tension in the air. With the Nazi invasion of France earlier in the year and the constant threat of air raid attacks from Dahomey, the war felt increasingly closer to home. Although Lagos was yet to be attacked, they all lived in fear of being bombed and the government had responded with frequent drills that were fast becoming a nuisance.

"That's fine, it looks like we have more than enough," Kehinde responded, placing a piece of akara beside each of the portions Ama had dished up.

"What's on the agenda today?" Emeka asked her.

"Madam Titi wants me to take the minutes of the meeting with the officials of the LMWA. Ben Makinde is coming, he's drafted a petition for us to present to the commissioner of Lagos," Kehinde said.

Her job as Madam Titi's secretary had made her happier than she could ever have imagined after her father's death. She wrote all of Madam Titi's letters for her, including reports that were sent to the commissioner's office. The reports usually meant she had to interview the women in the market, to hear their concerns about the war and their petitions to the colonial government to let them set the prices for their own goods. It was exhilarating, and she felt like she had finally found her purpose. Sure, it wasn't the *West Africa Pilot*, but she was making a difference in these women's lives in her own way, and she felt more confident than ever. Despite what Taiwo said, she was doing something for herself. She had kept the biggest secret of her life for over a year, and it was worth it. She went to her store each morning and within the first two hours she had cooked all the food she planned to sell each day. She'd made an arrangement with Ama, and Onyi did a great job of attending to her customers while she was at Madam Titi's office. Kehinde spent Friday afternoons while Madam Titi was at the mosque in Fine Leather helping Ama, as those were her busiest days and it was working well in their favour. Feeling useful outweighed her fear of being discovered, and she made sure she was always home in time for dinner.

"Who's Ben Makinde?" Ama asked.

"Herbert Macaulay's Associate. Thank you, Emeka," Kehinde replied, accepting the cup of tea he passed to her.

"I heard about the proposed tax bill. Doesn't sound like the government will take no for an answer. I'll ask at work if I can cover the story as it builds, it would be great to interview Ben," Emeka said.

"That's a good idea," Kehinde said, already imagining the angle he could take.

"I don't know why they don't want us to make money. I'm already struggling to get some of my raw materials. Do you know how expensive shoelaces are now? It doesn't help that the government dictates what prices we can charge our customers. They might as well come and run my business for me," Ama grumbled.

The greatest source of hardship was the rationing, Kehinde thought. Basic things like garri and salt were in short supply, and the price of everything had gone up. The prices of exports were now strictly regulated by the colonial government, meaning that some of Baba Tope's regular customers at the warehouse had become bankrupt from selling at a loss. Just two days ago, Kehinde and Ama had tried to buy sardines from the convenience store down the road and there had been none left.

"It's not about making money. It's more about contributing to the war effort," Emeka said as he wiped oil from the side of his mouth. Kehinde watched a breadcrumb hang perilously off the edge of his moustache, a survivor against the odds. She tried and failed at keeping her gaze off his lips as they moved.

"I might scream if I hear one more person say war effort. It's all anyone talks about," Ama said.

"Well, it's what's driving most of the decision-making with the colonial government," Emeka said with a shrug.

"It's been over a year already, and it only seems to be getting worse. Anyway, I need to go," Kehinde said with a sigh, forcing her thoughts away from Taiwo fighting alone, somewhere in Burma.

"I'll walk with you. I'm conducting an interview at the High Court on Broad Street, so I'm heading in the same direction," Emeka said.

"Okay, let's go," Kehinde said, unable to hide her excitement.

"I'll stay and tidy up for a bit. I already told Onyi to tell your customers you're not in today," Ama said, standing up and pushing in her chair.

"Thanks, Ama, see you later," Kehinde said, thinking that this friendship was at the top of the list of things she was grateful for.

She and Emeka stepped out into the morning sun, joining the crowd of civilians on Lewis Street as they made their way to their various destinations. Groups of school children in their uniforms, women carrying babies, women headed to the market, holding bags of their wares, and men in suits with briefcases hurried past them. The smoky aroma coming from the corner of the street where a man stood selling roasted groundnut and corn hung like a fog in the air.

"Nice day, at least it isn't raining," Emeka said, kicking a dusty pebble as they crossed to the other side of the street.

"Walking in the rain always feels so miserable," Kehinde agreed.

Two boys who looked like brothers ran by in their school uniforms, their bags bobbing on their backs as they half walked, half jogged. After a moment Emeka spoke again.

"I always wondered what it would've been like to go to school in Lagos."

"Why?"

"I don't know, it just seems so busy. I can't imagine walking on the streets with all these adults, fighting my way through to get to class."

Kehinde laughed at the thought of a little Emeka pushing through the crowds of Lagos Island. It was difficult to imagine. He was so calm that she pictured his childhood as a steady stream, with him drifting along through it.

"What was it like going to school here?" he asked, looking

at her in the way that always gave her goosebumps, like he could see beneath her skin and read the thoughts she was too scared to speak.

"Well, I grew up here, so I never thought of it as busy. I also always had Taiwo walking to school and back with me so I guess he must have fought through the crowds on my behalf."

Emeka laughed at that. "From everything you've said about him I can't imagine he would have let you face the crowds on your own."

"He didn't, anyone that wanted to speak to me had to go through him." She could never talk about school, or Taiwo, without feeling nostalgic, and sad about what should be.

"Thanks for reviewing my article on the female cocoa farmers in Ondo by the way. You've got a great eye for detail," Emeka said.

"You're welcome, I enjoyed it." Kehinde replied, basking in the glow of his praise.

"I remember you saying you were a writer, the day we first met," Emeka said, his arm brushing hers lightly as they shifted to the side of the street to let a man leading two children walk past. Kehinde felt the brief jolt of electricity that came at the merest touch from him rise and subside almost immediately, replaced by joy that he also remembered the first day they had met.

"I was, or am, although I'm not really," Kehinde said with a shrug. "I got offered a job at the *West African Pilot*, to write for their women's column."

Emeka stopped walking and looked at her with wide eyes.

"Kehinde, that's amazing! You never mentioned! Why didn't you take it?"

"I told Ama, I guess maybe she just never told you. My

husband thought it would be a distraction," Kehinde said, almost wishing she had not said anything at all. She didn't want Emeka to think of her as a little girl who had been forbidden from doing what she wanted which was often how she thought of herself when she recalled those early days of her marriage.

"That's interesting, I reckon you would have been great at it. I've seen you trying to negotiate with your customers a few times, you're not that good at selling food. You're much better at writing letters and price lists," he said, shrugging his shoulders and looking at her sideways.

"Hey!" she said, punching his arm.

Laughing, he ducked away from her second punch. "At least Madam Titi is lucky to have you as secretary of the LMWA." They both stopped again as they waited for a man on his bicycle to ride past. "I would never have pegged you as a revolutionary though," Emeka said when they continued walking.

"Who said anything about being a revolutionary?"

"The *West African Pilot* is for the revolutionaries of Nigeria, isn't it? Housing the likes of Nnamdi Azikiwe and his followers trying to kick the colonial government out."

"I wouldn't call myself a revolutionary, but I do find their articles interesting. Besides, these days it looks like they've put all anti-colonial sentiments aside. All anyone writes about is coming together to win the war," Kehinde said, thinking again of her father who would spend hours debating the articles with her.

"The *Daily Times* is a lot more kosher. You know, the gentlemen writers like me sit there, sipping tea and eating scones while we write, not like those hooligans at the *Pilot*. I hear they stand on their desks, shouting about independence over modern slavery and extortion."

"I can't imagine you standing on a desk if I'm being honest," Kehinde said, giggling at the thought.

"Neither can I! Why don't you come over to the office? I could show you around?"

"I would like that," Kehinde said, feeling like the sun was shining directly on her.

"Maybe around lunchtime today? Just ask for me when you get to the front desk."

They got to Broad Street quicker than they both would have liked.

"Well, this is me," Emeka said, pointing in the direction of the High Court. He hesitated, like he was about to say something else, then stopped.

"I'd better go up, the meeting will be starting soon," Kehinde said, suddenly feeling awkward. Emeka's face broke into his mischievous smile as he waved at her before turning to walk away in the other direction. Kehinde watched his retreating form, a patch of sweat appearing on his lower back, making its way through his white cotton shirt. Blushing, she turned and stepped into Glover Memorial Hall to the sound of raised voices.

"It's against our culture!" a man was saying.

"Ben, I know. We've discussed this already. We must be very strategic about the way we handle this. We don't want a repeat of what happened in the 1929 Aba riots," she heard Madam Titi say. Kehinde entered the room and saw Madam Titi standing with a man she did not recognise. They both turned to look at her as she came in.

"Ah, Kehinde's here. Ben, meet my secretary, Kehinde.

Kehinde, let me introduce you to Ben Makinde," Madam Titi said.

"Good morning, Ma, good morning, sir," Kehinde said, bobbing a curtsey in Ben's direction. She had met his boss, Herbert Macaulay, a few times – he and Madam Titi were old friends. Herbert Macaulay had started off as Madam Titi's customer at Ereko Market and had been instrumental in installing her as the head of the LMWA. He had recently founded the Nigerian National Democratic Party – known as the NNDP – and he and Nnamdi Azikiwe were at the forefront of the movement to make Nigeria independent from colonial rule.

"It's a pleasure to meet you," he said, already turning back to Madam Titi. "We must refuse to comply; they can't force us."

Kehinde guessed that by 'they' he meant the British colonial government. For months there had been rumours that the colonial government would be taxing the market women as a source of revenue for the war, and no one was happy about it. Kehinde thought of Baba Seyi's words the night of her eighteenth birthday and realised he had been right about the colonial government using the Empire to pay for the war. If the tax bill went through, it would be the first time that women would be paying any form of tax in the Western region of Nigeria. Last week, Madam Titi had told Kehinde that she had received confirmation from Governor Bourdillon that the income tax for female traders would indeed be introduced before the end of the year.

"It's an abomination. With the new taxes we'll be taking barely any income home," Madam Titi responded. Her voice remained calm even though Kehinde could see she was agitated from the way she kept adjusting her head scarf. "We'll need to plan our actions carefully. If we do this the wrong way things could get ugly," Madam Titi continued.

Again, Kehinde remembered her father. He had been the first person to tell her about the women who had died in the 1929 Aba Riots. She had imagined how their families had felt saying goodbye to them in the morning, only to hear that their wives, mothers and sisters would not be coming back.

As Madam Titi spoke, the other expected attendees of the meeting walked into the hall. They exchanged greetings as they took their seats around the table. Kehinde sat next to Madam Titi, arranging the papers and pen she had brought to take the minutes of the meeting.

"Madam Titi, we need to act now. I've just left the store of a young woman who got word this morning that her husband perished in India. She can barely survive on the stipend they sent to her! It's bad enough that they're killing our men in these strange places, must they make our women at home poor too?" Mrs Bamidele, the welfare manager, said without preamble.

The women in the market were feeling the pressure. Kehinde had heard of women who had returned to their home towns to take over farming and harvesting from brothers who had gone to fight in Burma and India. She felt the usual stab of anxiety in her chest as she pushed the thought of Taiwo fighting out of her mind.

"It's not like we get a say in any of the politics around here, or anywhere for that matter. We can't vote, they don't ask for our opinion, they just expect us to smile and take whatever comes next. Every day I wake up and hear there's a new law that nobody has asked me about, in my own country," Iya Dara, their public relations officer said, wringing her hands in the air. The nose ring that Kehinde had not previously noticed caught the light in support of her indignation.

"Their argument is that British women pay tax, but they are significantly more well off than we are," Mrs Coker, their treasurer, said in a clipped voice, adjusting her glasses as they slid down the slippery slope of her perspiring face.

"This is just another example of why we should be asking for our freedom, to be an independent nation. Free of the British Empire for good!" Ben said, slapping the table and making all the women jump.

"Steady now, Ben. As you all know, I've invited Ben here to tell us exactly what we need to say and how to position ourselves to make sure we're successful in stopping this tax from going ahead," Madam Titi said, looking round the table.

"The women across all the markets in Lagos are ready to do as you say, Ma," Iya Dara said, fanning herself with a large fan. Kehinde watched her sympathetically, as not for the first time she wished that there were more windows in this room. Whenever they had meetings here things heated up quickly and she could feel sweat pooling in places she did not even know housed sweat glands. "I only have to say the word and we'll rally around you," Iya Dara continued.

"So, let's begin then. I have a first draft of our petition based on the letters Kehinde shared. Now I want to refine it and ensure its ready before the end of this week so that you can present your cause to the government. We need to strike while the iron is still hot," Ben said, hitting the table again on the word hot. Kehinde started, wondering if slapping the table was his version of a full stop.

They spent the next hour refining the petition, going over the points they wanted to make and how to make them. Despite her excitement, Kehinde could feel a gnawing dread eating away at her. What if Baba Tope found out about the planned protests and her involvement? She quickly dismissed the idea. This was important and the women needed her, Madam Titi needed her. If Taiwo could risk his life, surely the least she could do was show up at a protest? She would go and keep her head down; being absent was not an option.

Chapter Fourteen

After almost two hours, the meeting was finally adjourned with a tentative date for the protest fixed in December. As Kehinde left the hall she thought she saw Atinuke cross the street, but when she looked again, she couldn't see her. Mama Tope sent her to pick up things from the market sometimes but Mama Tope's store wasn't nearby so it was odd to see Atinuke here. She was probably imagining things, her head still ringing from all that banging Ben had done on the table. Kehinde put the thought aside and made her way to the *Daily Times* office on Forsythe Street, suddenly feeling shy. What if Emeka had forgotten he'd asked her to come? What if she stood there like a lemon while he wondered what she was doing there? Maybe he felt sorry for her? And why did she care so much? He was sitting at the front desk when she arrived, laughing with the receptionist, and immediately stood up as she walked in.

"You came!"

"I've been looking forward to it all morning," Kehinde said, instantly annoyed with herself. Why had she said that?

"Well, I hope it lives up to your expectations," Emeka said, smiling and placing a gentle hand on her back to usher her through the double doors to the right of the front desk. The doors opened up to a large open floor office that smelled of ink, fresh paper and cigars – the same smells she had come to associate Emeka with. Men and a few women sat at rows of long desks, bent over typewriters, some on the phone, a few running from one end of the floor to the other, with printed articles in their hands. The press was being operated by two men to the far left of the office floor. A white man came out of the office at the back with another man gesticulating as he spoke, but Kehinde couldn't hear what they were saying over the noise. It was chaotic and she loved it.

"Emeka, who's the lovely lady?" called a man sitting at the desk closest to Kehinde. He had a book open in front of him, and another sheet of paper where he was taking notes.

Emeka pretended to stick out his tongue. "I'm not telling you. She's all mine."

"Ooh, I'll find out for myself then," he said, standing up to shake Kehinde's hand. "Ugo Mba, reporter at the *Daily Times*. What's a pretty lady like you doing with my ugly friend?"

Emeka let out a howl of laughter. "She's here to look around, silly. She owns the store beside Ama's in the market."

"Ah, the puff puff and akara lady? I think I'm addicted, Emeka brings your akara to the office almost every day. I've heard a lot about you," he said, looking pointedly at Emeka. "What's your name again?"

"Kehinde Ogunjobi, it's nice to meet you," Kehinde said, wondering what he had heard, and simultaneously annoyed with herself for the glow she felt at the thought that Emeka had been speaking about her.

"Let me rescue you before Ugo says anything else to get me

in trouble," Emeka said, pulling her away as Ugo laughed and waved them off.

Emeka took her around the floor, introducing her to the other journalists, the advertising team, a graphic designer and the men operating the press. Kehinde gasped at the amount of strength required to operate the machine, and she watched in awe as the rows of printing paper were squeezed out of the slit on the other side.

"What's it like working here?" Kehinde asked at the end of the tour.

"It's great, I really love it. Makes me feel like a genius, without actually having to do much."

They both laughed, and Kehinde was surprised to realise she wasn't envious. She loved being here and could still imagine herself as a writer, but she was fulfilled by her work with the LMWA. She was making a real, tangible difference in women's lives and with the upcoming protests, she hoped she would be leaving an imprint in the history of Nigeria in a way she could have never done as a writer.

"We do a lot of printing for the colonial government. Mostly propaganda to build unity in Nigeria, to encourage everyone to do their bit for the war. That sort of thing. You know, Nazis eat black people and we're doomed if Hitler wins the war."

Kehinde laughed then covered her mouth when a few heads in the printing hall turned in her direction. Emeka grinned at her. "We've started printing a weekly bulletin that just covers up-to-date reporting on the war – victories, battles, losses and diplomatic manoeuvres."

"I know about that bulletin, I read it," Kehinde said. She read it because of Taiwo mostly, even though his letters to her mother were a lot more insightful about his actual wellbeing.

"Great! At least all that paper isn't going to waste."

They both laughed again.

"Have you always known you wanted to be a journalist?"

"For the longest time I wanted to be an artist, actually."

"Why didn't you do that instead?" Kehinde asked, thinking of his beautiful paintings that hung around his and Ama's apartment.

"Writing was more acceptable to my father. He still hasn't forgiven me for not running Fine Leather's Lagos branch. It's a good thing Ama does such a good job at it."

When Emeka mentioned his father, a cloud passed over his usually cheerful face. Kehinde suspected there was a story there but decided it would be rude to pry.

"Well, thank you so much for having me, I'd better head home now."

"Should I walk you home?"

Kehinde so badly wanted to say yes but the thought of Mama Tope, or even Baba Tope, seeing her with a strange man brought her back to her senses.

"No, thank you. You've spent so much time with me already and I wouldn't want to delay you."

"Thanks for coming by," Emeka said, reaching out for her hand then dropping his arm before he could make contact.

"Thanks for having me," Kehinde replied, trying to stop the warmth she was feeling from showing on her face. *What is wrong with me*, she thought as she walked back out onto the busy street. She was acting like a besotted schoolgirl, not a married woman, and she chided herself as she walked home.

When she got to the house, a woman she didn't recognise was on her knees, sobbing in the small parlour while Mama Tope sat on the sofa in front of her, counting out a stack of one-pound notes in her lap. She looked up at Kehinde as she paused in the doorway.

"This doesn't concern you, get out of here and mind your business," Mama Tope hissed. Kehinde did as she was told, closing the door before she fled upstairs.

"Ayo, what on earth is going on downstairs?" she asked as she burst into Ayo's room.

"With Mama Tope and Sade?" Ayo responded. She was sitting at her sewing table, her foot tapping away as she hemmed the edge of a pink lace buba. Adenike and Ashabi were sitting on the floor in the corner of the room, lost in the final act of their play with two dolls dressed in newspaper dresses.

"Is that her name? Who is she? Why is she here?" Kehinde said, relaxing as she inhaled the familiar smell of cotton and lavender in Ayo's room.

"Unfortunately for her, she's the shop assistant at Mama Tope's store. The one that she owns but hardly visits," Ayo said, pausing to cut a piece of thread with her teeth. "Sales haven't been good recently. As you can imagine, barely anyone is trying to buy overpriced, imported lace with the small money they have these days. As if anyone has anywhere to wear outlandish fabric during a war. Mama Tope told Sade that if she was a better shop girl then there would be more customers. She's withholding most of her salary this month."

"Poor woman. Things are only going to get worse for her with this upcoming income tax. I wonder who she'll blame then – that's if we can't stop it from going ahead," Kehinde said, more to herself than to Ayo.

"If who can't stop what from going ahead?" Ayo asked. Her foot had stopped tapping on the pedal beneath the table and a piece of white thread hung from the corner of her mouth as she studied Kehinde's now still form.

"Adenike, Ashabi, leave the room please. Mummy needs to talk to Aunty Kehinde alone," Ayo continued, her eyes still on Kehinde.

Kehinde squirmed. Adenike and Ashabi hurried out of the room, with Ashabi stopping to give Kehinde a hug on her way out, like she was afraid Kehinde was about to be told off by her mummy.

"Kehinde, what's going on?" Ayo asked, the concern on her face breaking Kehinde's resolve. She made her way to the bed in the centre of the room and sat on it, her hands squeezing the edge of the quilt as the once comforting smell of lavender threatened to suffocate her. Ayo was too smart to not notice Kehinde's slip-up, and Kehinde had been so careful but of course the day had finally come when she had to confess. Ayo had been too kind to her, she couldn't lie to her face. And she trusted her. It was now or never.

"What would you say if I told you that I had a second job, one that Baba Tope knows nothing about?"

"Kehinde, what are you talking about?" Ayo whispered. She stood up and joined her on the bed, her eyes wide like Kehinde had just told her she saw the banana tree in the garden walking on her way in.

The words came tumbling out, about how Kehinde had been working with Madam Titi and the LMWA for over a year now, how she had written countless letters and petitions, how she finally felt like her life had some purpose, and how with the help of Ama and Onyi, she had been able to pull it all off. Ayo's mouth hung open the whole time, her eyes widening even further when Kehinde spoke about the protest march against the income tax bill scheduled to happen before the end of the year.

"Kehinde, you must not, you cannot be part of this," Ayo said, shaking her head.

"Ayo, this is exactly why I didn't tell you anything about it before."

"Seriously, Kehinde, you must be mad. Baba Tope will kill you if he finds out. This is exactly the sort of thing he can't stand!"

The threat of the man lying on the front lawn lay between them, a solid, silent reminder of Kehinde's first day in the house that seemed to take up its own presence in the room. The day that Ayo had told her that Baba Tope didn't like to be disrespected. She was sure that what she was doing would fit his definition of disrespect, but this was so much more important than the mystery of the beaten-up man and she pushed her terror behind her.

"You won't tell him, right?" Kehinde said, a stubborn crease resting between her eyebrows.

"That's not the point! Of course I won't say anything, but do you realise how angry he'll be when he finds out?"

"He's never going to find out, I'm being careful. You only just found out today and I've been doing it all year!"

"Because *you* told me by accident! Our husband has eyes and ears everywhere! It's only a matter of time before you're found out and disgraced! What will happen then?" Ayo had stood up and was pacing the room now, agitated in a way that Kehinde had never seen before. There was a knock on the door and for a moment their eyes both met in dread.

"Mummy, Daddy is back. He said he's ready for dinner," Adenike's voice called out from the other side of the door. Ayo and Kehinde both breathed a sigh of relief.

"We'll talk about this later. Let's get dinner on the table," Ayo hissed.

Downstairs there was no sign of Sade or Mama Tope in the den, just Tope helping her brothers with their homework and Adenike and Ashabi continuing the game they were playing. Baba Tope was sitting on the armchair beside the telephone, watching his children with an indulgent smile.

"Baba Tope, good evening," Ayo said first, with Kehinde echoing the greeting with as much enthusiasm as she could muster.

"Good evening, my wives," he beamed.

Ayo grabbed Kehinde's hand as they walked into the kitchen. After a quick look to make sure Atinuke was not there, she slammed the door behind her.

"Kehinde, how could you be so stupid?"

"No one in this house knew what I was up to until a minute ago! I would say I've been extremely careful, thank you very much!" Kehinde retorted. Ayo's panic was causing a fast-spreading fire amidst the roots of trepidation already embedded in her heart.

"You know what I mean! Baba Tope won't like this at all, not one bit!"

"Ayo, with all due respect, why are you defending him? Why do we have to live our lives exactly the way he tells us to?" Kehinde wiped her brow, wishing she had gone ahead to take a bath instead of walking into Ayo's room.

"Because he is the head of our home! He takes care of us all! The lives we live are thanks to him! That's why! Think about what would happen to you, to your mother, if he found out!" Ayo was slamming pots on the kitchen surface as she spoke.

"Shh, Atinuke will hear you!"

"I don't think she's back from whatever errand Mama Tope sent her on. Kehinde, this can never end well."

"For the last time, Ayo, he's not going to find out!"

"I hope you're right, Kehinde, I really do. If he finds out, we're all in trouble."

"Why are you so afraid?" Kehinde asked, knowing this was about much more than she could possibly understand, much more than even her own fear of him. She still thought about the bleeding man from her first day in the house, but she hadn't witnessed any further acts of violence here. Baba Tope was definitely running some kind of underhand business at the ports with Mr Babajide and Mr Lateef but other than that, his bark appeared to be stronger than his bite.

Ayo paused and let out a sigh. She seemed to deflate as she turned around to face Kehinde, her hands and back still resting on the kitchen counter.

"Because I have so much to lose, Kehinde ... I have nowhere to go if Baba Tope sends me away," she said.

Kehinde watched her, confused. Ayo had told her that she had grown up as an only child with her single mother in Ibadan but she never said much else about her childhood. Unlike Kehinde, she only ever spoke about her life after she had become a wife and mother, which Kehinde had always thought of as a bit odd but never directly asked about.

"I'm not like you, Kehinde. I don't have aunties and uncles or even a caring mother to turn to," Ayo continued, turning around to pour the amala flour into the pot of water on the stove. "I've barely spoken to or seen my mother since I came here. I never met my father, and it felt like my mother was taking out all her frustrations on me. Every miserable day that I lived with her, she would remind me that I was unwanted and unloved. Baba Tope saved me; he gave me a life I had only dreamed about before I met him."

Not knowing what to say, Kehinde simply put an arm around Ayo as she continued speaking.

"Even up until the night before my wedding, my mother continued to insult me. It was such a relief to finally be free of her. The last time Baba Tope and I went to see her, all she did was ask him to pay for her leaking roof. She hasn't even met Adenike and Ashabi. I've written her letters, but she has never replied to one. I send money to her neighbour who checks in on her, but she has never uttered a word of thanks to me."

"Ayo, I'm so sorry. I had no idea."

"There's no way you could have known," Ayo replied.

Everything made sense now, why Ayo seemed to be the perfect wife, how she had tolerated Mama Tope for all these years, why she kissed the ground their husband walked on. Kehinde felt suddenly ungrateful for taking her own life for granted. She might not have grown up with much wealth, but she had never known real pain up until her father died, and since then things seemed to be falling into place for her, even if it wasn't the life she had imagined for herself. She squeezed Ayo's hand.

"Ayo, I promise I'll be careful. Baba Tope will never find out about the LMWA," she said.

Ayo looked at her like she didn't believe her, and after a brief pause, she smiled in a way that didn't reach her eyes. "Well, you better stop distracting me and let me turn this amala well. If it's lumpy, Baba Tope will know that something is wrong."

Chapter Fifteen

Beetroot salad used to be Kehinde's favourite meal. Her mother had a way of seasoning the beetroot, fresh from her garden, with vegetable oil infused with lemon and thyme. Beetroot had a halcyonic quality to it, a reminder of the days when she would sit at the dining table with her parents and Taiwo. They would all eat the salad, their mother smiling as she watched her family enjoy the meal she had not only prepared, but grown – nurtured from a place in the earth and harvested specifically for this purpose. When Kehinde was old enough to reach the kitchen counter, she started making it her own way, adding spring onions and a dash of ginger to the recipe, basking in her mother's begrudging approval when their father declared that Kehinde had surpassed her teacher.

Now, as her mother placed a plate of beetroot salad on the dining table, she felt a wave of nausea rise within her. Beetroot was no longer the essential ingredient of a simple meal. Instead, it had become her mother's solution to what she referred to as Kehinde's 'fertility challenges'. Her weekly visits to her mother's house had become a strain on her conscious efforts to push forward, to find happiness.

"How was the visit to the Babalawo then?" her mother asked as she sat opposite her on the dining table, holding a cup of tea.

"It was fine. Everything is fine," Kehinde replied, the fork in her hand doing a dance with the salad in front of her.

"You look well enough; you've even put on weight. Your husband is taking good care of you," her mother said again, taking a sip of her tea as her eyes moved over Kehinde, landing on her stomach. As she moved her mug the smell of the peppermint brew filled the room, adding heat to Kehinde's rising irritation that turned to pity as she caught her mother stifle a sigh.

In the past year, Kehinde had expected her mother to wither into an empty shell, adrift at sea in the absence of the love of her life, the core that had held her together. But after those initial months, their mother's mouth had set into two parallel lines. She laughed less, she had lost weight, and her eyes had a primal look, not of hunger, but of a determination to survive. Gone were her mother's stories of her friends' conquests, their failures, and the latest gossip on Malumo Street. Now she spoke about how she had started selling the flowers that she grew in her garden, how the food Baba Tope sent her was more than enough, so much that she had a cool clay pot now in the kitchen for leftovers. She was saving up to buy a refrigerator, with plans to start charging a small fee to keep food for the other families on the street.

"Did you hear that Kunle is being taken to Burma?" her mother asked after a moment of silence.

"What? No, I hadn't heard! He enlisted?"

"Not enlisted as such, it was more like a forced voluntary

conscription. Some soldiers appeared at the grammar school earlier this week, asking for boys to sign up. Aunty Laide said they're all still shocked."

"I don't understand. Why didn't he say no?" Kehinde asked. Kunle was the least likely person she could imagine fighting, let alone wielding a gun.

"I don't imagine he had a choice with the way Aunty Laide described them showing up, with guns and all, in the classroom, can you imagine! She said they took the whole senior class, and that they'll be training this week and shipped off by the end of the month!" her mother said with a hint of her former gossipy tone.

"His mother will be devastated!" Kehinde replied. Kunle was his parents' only child. After seven years of marriage and countless miscarriages his parents had apparently lost all hope that they would ever have a child of their own. He had been treated like an egg his whole life.

"Yes, I imagine his mother will be devastated, poor thing. She'll survive, we all do," her mother said, finishing the rest of her tea as her mouth turned downwards.

"Well, at least he and Taiwo will be together," Kehinde said.

"You still haven't written to your brother, have you?" her mother asked, instantly reminding Kehinde why she should not have brought the prodigal son up.

"I'm not writing to him."

"You've never fought like this before. After everything that's happened, you still don't think you should apologise to him?"

"Why do I always have to be the one to apologise to him first? He could also write to me, but I don't hear anyone saying that," Kehinde said, gripping her fork. It was true; growing up, she always said sorry first. Well, he was about to learn that things had changed.

"Every time Aunty Laide writes my letter to him we always end with a request for him to write to you. And besides, you're a woman, we are the peacemakers. If you're waiting for a man to tell you sorry, you'll wait forever."

Kehinde stopped herself from rolling her eyes. Her mother's answer for everything was "you're a woman". When Kehinde had started her periods and told her mother that she was having cramps she had told her to bear it because she was a woman, and pain was theirs to hold with grace. When her father had first told her about Baba Tope's proposal, her mother told her that most women didn't marry for love and she should be happy that she would at least want for nothing. Always because she was a woman, she would have to be silent while the men in her life did whatever they wanted.

"Well, this man happens to be my brother, and maybe I'm ready to wait for his apology forever." Kehinde tasted the bitterness she felt on the back of her tongue, suddenly making the beetroot taste more like efo. Her mother looked at her and shook her head.

"How is your husband? Your senior wives and their children?" she continued, changing tack. Her mother switched from one topic to the other so abruptly these days, it was hard to keep up.

"They're all well, thank you, Mummy."

"Help me thank your husband again for his generosity and thank Ayo for the dress she made for me, although I don't know when I'll wear it," her mother said. In a previous life, her mother would have worn the dress to church, but her mother hadn't been to church since her father's passing, and her religion, or lack of it, was a topic they were yet to broach, a river that was not yet safe to cross. Once upon a time she would sit, smiling as their father read them Bible stories, sometimes even asking her own questions. Kehinde had thought her mother looked most beautiful in those moments, watching her husband read from God's own book, hearing the words she could not decipher herself, and believing them, the way she believed every other word that came from his mouth.

"And he's treating you well?" her mother asked, her eyes lit up with concern.

Kehinde's shoulders softened. At the back of her mind, she knew her mother only wanted the best for her, in her own way. She was too traditional to believe Kehinde could have any dreams separate from what her parents or husband wanted for her, and Kehinde couldn't help but feel sorry for her. How could she expect her mother to understand why she wanted more? She had had much more than her mother ever did over the course of her lifetime. She imagined her confusion if she told her that she was going behind the back of the husband who was taking care of her to do a job he didn't approve of. She would be nonplussed, especially as Kehinde knew that with her father gone and with Taiwo away fighting, Kehinde's stability was the one thing her mother took comfort in. She loved her in her own way, Kehinde thought, remembering what Ayo had said about her own mother. The least she could do was to let her think she was content.

"Yes, Mummy. He's taking good care of me," Kehinde said.

"But Kehinde, you are too old for me to be begging you to eat like this," her mother said, kissing her teeth.

Feeling like a ten-year-old, Kehinde finished the rest of the salad quickly.

They moved to the parlour, their mother settling into her father's old armchair. Kehinde felt a jolt of shock as she realised that the memory of him sitting there was already beginning to fade. She could imagine his silhouette as he tuned the Rediffusion, leaning forward in his seat, but the memory was fuzzy, the colours faded, her father merely an apparition. Seeing her mother sitting in the chair, in solid form, did not look unnatural, but it also did not help her fading memories. It was like he had been displaced for good. Her mother picked up the brown envelope she kept all Taiwo's letters in and handed two folded pieces of paper to Kehinde. Taiwo's bold, cursive scrawl was visible through the thin paper.

"I have a new letter from Taiwo," her mother said, handing it to her.

Kehinde would never admit it, but she loved reading Taiwo's letters to her mother when she visited. His words were the collective ray of sunshine in a field of beetroot. It was the only way she could feel close to him without reaching out to him herself. She missed him – he was annoying, and she was not ready to forgive him for making her feel so small and abandoning her when she needed him most, but she would never stop loving him. Her hands shook as she tore open the envelope.

Dear Mother,

I trust you are keeping well.

The jungle here in Burma is a monsoon rainforest, and when we march, it is through knee high water, slashing through the tall grass with our cutlasses. The climate here is much harsher than it is in Lagos. Some of my comrades have died just from the living conditions, and I learned recently that many perished even on the journey here. May their poor souls rest in peace. The Japanese soldiers are wicked, they come with their insufferable language and take joy in seeing men fall. Captain Mackenzie continues to take me with him on his flights and I am almost ready to fly my own fighter jet. I will be sent out on the battlefield on my own soon.

Fear not, sweet mother, for I am well and in good spirits. Your letters bring me hope and memories of better times. Although things are hard, I do not regret my decision to come here. I am with my brothers in battle, fighting for the Empire and although I miss home dearly, I hope that I will indeed be granted some leave days to come home soon. Once I have a date, I will let you know.

I hope Aunty Laide and Uncle Ladipo are also well? I have a comrade here who says he worked at Ikoyi Club with Uncle Ladipo for some months before the war, what a small world it is! You may ask him if he knows a Gbadebo Adewole, he was a cleaner at the tennis courts and has spoken fondly of Uncle Ladipo. He also agrees with me that Uncle Ladipo's fried rice is the best he has ever tasted. Please tell Aunty Laide that I am trying to keep up with my sums and reading as promised, it is not easy but rest assured that I am doing the best I can!

Please also give my love to Kehinde. I know she is still angry with me and I don't blame her, I know I hurt her feelings but I had to come here, there was no other way.

I pray for you every day my sweet mother and look forward to the day that I can see your smile once again.

Yours faithfully,

Your son, Taiwo

By the time Kehinde got to the end of the letter her mother had tears in her eyes.

"My dear boy, how I miss him so," was all she said, her words muffled by the handkerchief she pressed against her mouth.

"Burma sounds horrible," Kehinde said, thinking that the rationing, inflation and fear of bombs that they were dealing with in Lagos paled in comparison to what sounded like a swampy nightmare.

"I hope he gets some leave to come home soon," her mother said, dabbing her eyes with her handkerchief.

"I hope so too, it would be nice to see him," Kehinde said, feeling tearful as well. She would come here to see him whenever he came home on leave, she decided. He hadn't said sorry, but he had apologized in his own way. She would tell him in person that she had forgiven him for leaving her, because she knew she had, she was just too proud to write it in a letter.

With the letter was a postcard that had a picture of an aeroplane on it. It was a small one, the kind that she knew the Royal Air Force in England used as fighter jets from the pictures Emeka had shown her in the *Daily Times*. Taiwo had spoken so much about aeroplanes since they were children, those mysterious shells of metal that lifted themselves into the air and stayed there. He had drawn so many pictures of aeroplanes all over his school notebooks that they had looked like they would take flight on their own.

Kehinde sighed as she held the letter, closing her eyes as she imagined Taiwo bent over whatever desk or bunk he was sitting on, scribbling away furiously with his left hand, his eyebrows knitted in concentration the way he always did whenever he was writing. The left hand that had caused so much trouble over the years. He hadn't been allowed to do anything with that hand growing up, as their mother was convinced that anyone who let their left hand dominate was doing the devil's handiwork. Kehinde secretly thought it made Taiwo special. It was the reason why he just got things, why he was so good at his arithmetic without trying, why he always saw things from a different perspective. Whenever they were alone, he reverted to the full use of his left hand, with no one to judge him.

The way he wrote had changed. There was a maturity and hardness to his words that had not been there before. Kehinde wondered if perhaps his speech was just more formal on paper than it was in person, and she longed to find out. Her other half, her best friend – she was incomplete without him physically there with her. She missed him. Their birthday this year had felt lacking, with him being across the country and her celebrating with her new family. She had woken up early with Ayo to bake a cake, fry puff puff and chin chin, aware that her birthday also marked a year since she had last seen her father.

Kehinde left her mother in the armchair as she folded up the letter, standing up to place it with the others in the brown envelope on the side table. They were all evolving, she could feel it, and it frightened her because she did not know what it meant or what to expect. Her father had been right; with war came all kinds of changes that she could never have predicted.

Chapter Sixteen

Kehinde watched the vegetable oil bubble in its cauldron as she waited for her puff puff mix to rise. She had a full day ahead of her in the store today as Madam Titi did not need her, so Kehinde was settling down to fry a new batch, this time with cinnamon. Uncle Ladipo had told her that he had made cinnamon puff puff for the Ikoyi Club Ladies Progressive Club war fundraising party, hosted by Lady Violet Bourdillon the other day and she was keen to try out the recipe. Apparently, it had reminded the colonial administrators' wives of the mulled wine they drank at home at Christmas time.

"Does your pot tell the future?" Ama asked from the door.

"It does, but only if you pay me £50," Kehinde said, grinning as Ama stepped in.

"Even for friends and family?" Emeka asked, coming in behind her.

"Even for them. How's your day going?" Kehinde asked both of them, noticing that Emeka had got a new haircut, but left his beard and his moustache. His facial hair had a way of accentuating his lips, like a soft frame around a beautiful picture, especially when he smiled. She blushed when she realised she must be staring and quickly looked back into her pot.

"Slow day," Ama said, taking a seat on Kehinde's desk. "After that big order I had for boots, I haven't had much traction. Not many customers are stopping by these days. It might be easier to sell raw hide and skin to the government."

"That's a shame."

"Not slow for me. I actually just came to say hi, I'm on my way to interview Ben Makinde now," Emeka said, hovering in the doorway.

"Oh, that's today?" Kehinde asked.

"It is, we wanted to do it in the close to the protests, to get readers interested. Thanks for organising it."

"You're welcome. Let me know how it goes."

"I will," Emeka said, holding her gaze for a heartbeat longer than seemed normal to Kehinde before waving at them and leaving. But she was probably imagining it, because she was convinced she had an overactive imagination where Emeka was concerned.

"I've thought about dropping my prices, but with everything else being so expensive and the factory in Enugu struggling to get quality leather, it's all so hard," Ama continued when he had left. "Have you finished making the puff puff? I could smell it from my shop and it made me hungry. I need something to cheer me up."

Laughing, Kehinde brought out the bag of leftover puff puff from the previous day that she had saved specifically for this reason. Ama always found a way into her store looking for something to eat.

"This is from yesterday's batch. You can wait if you want

some fresh ones though," Kehinde said as she handed the bag to Ama.

"You're the best! Thank you! How are things at home now? Have you told your husband about the LMWA or the protests?"

"No, and I never will," Kehinde said, pausing to scoop the mix into the hot oil.

"I find it so strange how you can hide such a big secret. I can't imagine being married and my husband not knowing how I was spending each day; it just seems so odd. If it was me, I know I would blurt it out," Ama said, munching on her puff puff.

"Well, there are many things odd about my marriage as you know," Kehinde said, trying not to be irritated. Ama meant well but she could be so annoying with her probing. To be fair, she had been a great friend and confidante; she was the person closest to Kehinde now. She told Ama everything that she couldn't tell Ayo and she listened, judgement free. She was the best friend she had always wanted and somehow never managed to have, but sometimes Ama looked at things in such a simple way. Kehinde knew by now that nothing was ever that simple. There was never one story, but multiple stories with different versions. Besides, she was not at risk of 'blurting' anything out, because she hardly spoke to Baba Tope. Between the shared meals, serving his friends in the parlour and sharing his bed, she mostly listened to what he had to say, not the other way around. She might as well be mute when she stepped into the house. She had no voice there and was not expected to have one.

"Like your maid – that's another strange one. I used to think that only colonial administrators had maids you know, until I met you," Ama continued, ticking off the second thing on the list of oddities with her free hand. The puff puff in the cauldron sizzled and popped as Kehinde turned them over with her spoon, the sweet smell of frying sugar and dough filling the little store like a mist. "What do the children do then? Don't they have morning duties?"

"Not really. I mean, Tope helps with dinner sometimes, and Adenike and Ashabi clean Ayo's room with her but I think that's it. The boys don't do anything," Kehinde admitted. In most homes, the children woke up early and had assigned chores they had to complete before going to school, like grinding pepper for the meals to be made during the day and cleaning rooms. Baba Tope had declared that his children would not live like peasants, so Atinuke did most of the work.

"Must be nice," Ama said, sounding wistful.

"Ama, you of all people should know that it's not as glamorous as it seems," Kehinde said, as she watched the puff puff turn golden brown.

"Oh, I know, you're convinced your husband is a murderer and he's old and fat, but surely it must be nice to get driven around in a car? To live on Bamgbose Street and to have a maid like a colonial administrator's wife?"

"I would trade places with you any day," Kehinde said, meaning it. Ama was only two years older than her but she already owned a business, and she was living her life exactly the way she wanted to. Sure, she ran the business for her father, but she had full autonomy. She had her own voice, not the voice everyone else thought she should have.

"But your life is hardly bad. I mean, you're still doing what you want, in a strange secret double life sort of way, but you're doing it! You do your LMWA work with Madam Titi and you get to make delicious food," Ama said.

"Unlike you, I barely got a choice."

"What's that saying, 'you can't eat your cake and have it'. I would know, my mum loved saying it so much, I must have heard it every day of my life while I lived in Enugu," Ama said, pulling a face.

Laughing, Kehinde passed her the bowl with the fresh batch of puff puff. "How are your parents?"

"Fine, threatening to come to Lagos to drag me back home to find a husband but they're only joking. My dad likes telling his friends that his daughter is running the Lagos branch of Fine Leather."

"They sound so nice."

"They are, hopefully you can meet them some day. If your husband lets you come with us next time we're going back to Enugu. Unlikely."

They both laughed at that.

"Emeka said I should invite you to come with us when we travel for Christmas and the new year, but I told him there was no way you could get away."

"That's kind of him," Kehinde replied, trying to appear nonchalant as she looked away, pretending to study the now empty cauldron. But she couldn't ignore how happy she was at the thought of Emeka wanting her to meet his parents in the childhood home that she had heard so much about.

"He's never asked me to invite any of my other friends home," Ama said with a smirk.

"Oh, it's probably just to say thank you for all the editing I've helped him with," Kehinde replied quickly.

"I'm sure that's it," Ama said, grinning. "I'll never understand why the two of you love writing about Nigeria so much. Politics is so boring."

"I don't understand how you can't be interested in it!

Especially now that the colonial government churns out a new law almost daily."

"I just want this war to end. Everyone is so miserable all the time," Ama said with a pout.

"Good afternoon!" came a woman's voice from the doorway. Kehinde looked up to see a familiar-looking woman standing at the entrance of her shop.

"Iya Jola! Long time no see!" Ama said, standing up to embrace the woman.

"Nice to see you. How is business?"

"We are managing! How is Jola? And your husband?"

A shadow crossed the woman's face for a moment. "Well, Baba Jola is getting on as best as he can. I came to get some puff puff for him actually."

"Where are my manners! Kehinde, this is Iya Jola," Ama said, turning back to Kehinde.

"I remember her from the LMWA meeting, the first one we had after the war was announced," Iya Jola said, smiling at Kehinde. *That was it*, Kehinde remembered. She was the woman who had come with a baby strapped to her back.

"Yes! How is your baby?"

"She's fine, thank you, Jola is a big girl now. She's with her father … I don't like to leave them for too long, it's just that he's craving puff puff."

"I won't hold you up then, how many would you like?" Kehinde asked, turning to the fresh batch in the bowl.

"A bag of ten will do."

"Here you go," Kehinde said, wrapping ten big ones in an old newspaper.

"Ese," Iya Jola said, smiling as she paid and left.

"Poor woman," Ama said, once she was out of earshot.

"What happened to her?" Kehinde asked, smiling to herself

as she put the lid back on the bowl of puff puff. Ama could be so dramatic sometimes, she thought, as she remembered how Ama had referred to an older man who had fallen and sprained his ankle outside their stores the other day as "almost unable to walk ever again".

"Oh, you don't know?" Ama said, her eyes wide in her face.

"Well, I hardly know her to begin with."

"Her poor husband got back from Burma a few weeks ago, blind!" Ama said, covering her eyes for added effect.

"Actually blind?"

"As a bat. Apparently, he got shrapnel in his face and is lucky to even be alive!" Ama said.

"Oh dear, that's horrible. I was wondering what she meant when she said she didn't like to leave her daughter alone with him." Kehinde said as she sat again, feeling cold as she thought of Taiwo, and Kunle for that matter, fending for themselves in Burma.

"She's had to run her shop and take care of him, together with their small daughter! She's really worried about the idea of being taxed, she's making barely enough for her family as it is! She can't afford to attend the protest next week, but right now it's her only hope that the tax won't go ahead."

Kehinde sighed. Iya Jola was one of many women of the LMWA who were banking on the work she had been doing with Madam Titi and Ben on the protests. She had spent countless hours perfecting written petitions, leaflets and logistics and they were finally prepared to face the colonial government. She hoped all their work wouldn't be in vain – from what Emeka had told her, the government was determined to raise the revenue generated in Nigeria to help pay for the war. "I hope they listen to us," was all she said.

"They better! Anyway, Burma sounds terrible from what Iya Jola said. Have you written to your brother now?"

"No, not yet. I'm hoping he'll be home on leave soon," Kehinde said, feeling guilty. Iya Jola's husband had come home from Burma blind, and many had died, but her brother was alive and they weren't speaking.

"Hopefully he comes back soon! I better get back now. Thanks for the puff puff! I love whatever it was you added to it this time! See you tomorrow!"

"Cinnamon. See you tomorrow," Kehinde said, waving at her friend as she watched her step back out into the street, turning to smile her gummy smile once more before heading into Fine Leather.

When she got home later that afternoon, she found Atinuke on all fours at the foot of her bed.

"Atinuke?"

Atinuke jumped like she had just been whipped by an invisible belt. It would have been comical if Kehinde wasn't so shocked to find her there.

"Sorry, Ma, I just came to clean your room."

"But you usually clean on Saturdays?"

"Yes, Ma … I found a rat, er, downstairs. So, I quickly came to make sure all the rooms were clean," Atinuke said, already standing and dusting herself down. "I didn't see anything. I'm going downstairs now to er, help Madam Ayo."

As Kehinde watched her run out of the room, she couldn't ignore the feeling that something was amiss. She kept wondering if it had been Atinuke she had seen in the market the other day, and now this? She made a mental note to talk to

Ayo about it later when she went down to get ready for dinner.

Sitting on her bed, she picked up the new book she was reading. Aunty Bimpe had sent her a copy of *Little House on the Prairie* from London and felt glad that she wasn't on duty with Baba Tope that night. The letter that Aunty Bimpe had sent with the book promised that she would enjoy it, the way Aunty Bimpe had enjoyed it even though the state of London was much worse than it was in Lagos. Kehinde said a quick prayer for Aunty Bimpe and her family's safety while she settled into the chair by her window to read. She was barely three pages in when she heard a knock on her door.

"Come in!" Kehinde said, annoyed, thinking it was Atinuke again.

To her surprise, Tope poked her head around the door.

"Oh, Tope! Is everything fine?" Kehinde said as she sat up hurriedly. Tope had never come to her room before and she was worried there was some kind of emergency. Was the house on fire? She couldn't smell anything, so surely that wasn't it. Hopefully none of the children were in danger?

"Oh, it's nothing serious," Tope said, glancing over her shoulder before she took the final step into the room and shut the door behind her. Kehinde must have still looked alarmed, because she shook her head again. "Sorry to have bothered you, this can wait really."

"No, no, it's fine. Joko," Kehinde said, gesturing at her bed.

Tope hesitated then sat on the edge of the bed, close to the door, as if scared to get too close. "Well, I know you like reading, and I wanted to ask you if there were any books I could read about life in England?"

"Life in England?" Kehinde asked, trying not to laugh. What a strange request. Tope was always so awkward around her that she knew laughing would make her flee the room, so she tried her best to arrange her face into a companionable smile.

"Yes. I'll be going there, once the war ends of course," Tope said with a small smile, but still avoiding Kehinde's eyes. She had a lazy right eye that tended to move on its own and Kehinde had noticed she would rather avoid looking at anyone directly, probably so her eyes would not be the focus of attention. *Poor girl,* she thought.

"Going there on holiday? How lucky!"

"Oh no, going there for my schooling. I might do an accounting course, and maybe go to university as well. My father is still deciding but it's certain that I'll be going once the war ends, my mother told me," Tope said, now smiling and looking straight at Kehinde. Her joy was contagious and Kehinde couldn't help but feel happy for her.

"That's wonderful! I've never left Lagos myself so I'm not sure I'm the right person to give you advice though," Kehinde said with a laugh.

"I thought perhaps you had read a book that could help?"

"Oh yes, you said so. Hmm, let me think about it. Maybe *Cold Comfort Farm*? But it's a parody, so maybe not. Ooh, *Mary Poppins* is a nice one to start with!"

"How do you know so much about books? My mother said you barely went to school."

Kehinde felt the heat go to her face. What else had that woman said about her? "I only missed the last year of secondary school."

"That must have been so disappointing! I can't imagine what I would do if I couldn't go to school," Tope said, looking genuinely concerned. Kehinde smiled at her, realising not for the first time that, although there were only two years between them, their lives were worlds apart.

"It was bad at first, but my Aunty Laide, our neighbour, gave me lessons for free. She's a teaching assistant at Breadfruit Grammar School."

"No wonder you're so proper! My mother said you've been getting by on your looks but I find that hard to believe," Tope said.

Kehinde raised her eyebrows as Tope looked away, pursing her lips like she wanted to eat her words.

"I'm sorry, that came out sounding funny."

"It's fine. I know your mother doesn't like me. I do hope we can be friends though," Kehinde said, meaning it. They were so close in age and it would be a shame if they couldn't get along.

"I would like that," Tope said, her left eye looking directly at Kehinde now.

"Great! So, start with *Mary Poppins*. Aunty Laide has a copy, I'll get it for you the next time I visit my mother. You're probably better off just wandering around Ikoyi to get a real sense of what it's like in England to be honest. Mind, you would be at risk of being mistaken for a maid or cleaner so maybe take the car with you."

Tope let out a loud laugh at that.

"Tope!" came her mother's voice from across the other side of the door. She must have heard Tope laughing in her room.

"I better go," Tope whispered, standing up quickly. "Thank you so much … Aunty Kehinde. See you at dinner," she said, disappearing from the room as quickly as she came.

Kehinde laughed as she fled the room, but underneath her amusement was pain, and hurt. Mama Tope despised her because they were married to the same man. Ayo had told her that when Mama Tope and Baba Tope had got married, she had thought he was the love of her life. His affairs had broken her, and the polygamous home she now found herself in was far from what she had dreamed of. But Kehinde could not understand why she was making her suffer for a situation she had not put herself in by choice? Unlike Ayo, she didn't want to be here, couldn't Mama Tope see that? It was like blaming a shrub for a gardener's decision to uproot and replant it. Mama Tope was the kind of woman she preferred to avoid, women who blamed and punished other women for men's actions, instead of holding the men accountable. Kehinde vowed she would never become that woman. She would always fight to be a woman that made other women's lives better, even Tope, through her words and actions.

In a way, she was jealous of Tope. Her father was alive, and wealthy enough to send her to England for school. Kehinde's father had loved her, but despite how much he tried, he had never been able to consider educating her more than he had, and even if he had lived, Kehinde would probably still be here as a parlour wife. The most she could hope for was that her work with the LMWA would continue to give her life some purpose, and that maybe one day she could go on holiday to England. As it was, she had never even left Lagos and no matter how many books she read, she would always wonder what it would look like through her own eyes.

Chapter Seventeen

December 16, 1940

The crowd of women outside Government House threatened to take over Custom Street. From Kehinde's estimation, there were at least one thousand women there, and half that number had signed the petition written by Ben Makinde which Kehinde clutched in her hand. They were there in their colourful outfits, contrasting with the green lawn and trees on both sides of the road. Although it was a Monday, most of the market stores across Lagos had been closed for the day and the women stood as one under the hot, early afternoon sun. Everyone present looked like they were melting, with many of the women's hands going back and forth on their faces with handkerchiefs like windshield wipers on a car. Ama and Onyi were standing next to Kehinde in front of the crowd, holding a brown cardboard sign that said "NO TAXES FOR LAGOS WOMEN" that Onyi had written with red paint.

Despite the heat, Kehinde felt exhilarated, the fire burning within her as the adrenaline rushed through her veins like electricity. Madam Titi stood on Kehinde's right as they waited for the chief commissioner, Mr Lawrence, to come out of his office.

When the women arrived, they had been told by a sheepish-looking guard that Mr Lawrence was just finishing his breakfast and would be out shortly. They had now been waiting for over an hour and the crowd was getting agitated.

"Tell that man that if he doesn't open the door and come out, we'll tear this place down!" a shrill voice shouted from the back against an assenting chorus of murmurs.

Kehinde saw Emeka on the edge of the crowd, standing with Ugo and a handful of other reporters and journalists. As he caught her eye, he gave her a smile which she returned before looking away quickly, the rising butterflies in her stomach dancing with the restless energy she had been feeling all morning.

There was a perceptible shift in the crowd as the front door opened slowly for none other than Chief Commissioner Lawrence himself. Kehinde had never seen him before, although she had heard a lot about him. He looked like any other English man to her, with a brown mop of short hair and a bushy moustache that curved out on either side of his face like apostrophe marks. He appeared startled by the crowd gathered in front of his office and his mouth turned downwards as his eyes fell on the line of reporters.

"Good morning, Commissioner Lawrence. We, the women of Lagos have come to greet you today," said Madam Titi as she stood to her full height at the foot of the steps.

"Good morning to you too," he replied in clipped tones as he regarded her, his nose wrinkling like there was a bad smell in the air. Kehinde felt mortified on her behalf, but Madam Titi did not appear to mind; instead, she seemed emboldened by his hostility.

"Sir, without further ado," Madam Titi continued, speaking in English slowly and clearly for all to hear. "We have come to present our petition to you. We stand united, against the introduction of the taxes that are to be levied on the market women of Lagos. Indeed, it is an abomination in our culture, and given the rising inflation and the ongoing war, our pockets are getting lighter. This tax will only serve to make them featherweight." There were a few laughs in the crowd at this, with many of the women nodding as she continued.

"We implore the colonial government to abolish this tax, as it will make life significantly harder for the women of Lagos," Madam Titi finished. The women around her clapped, but as Kehinde watched Mr Lawrence, she saw that his lips were pressed, disappearing altogether into a thin line as the clapping got louder. He waited for the cheers to subside before he opened his mouth.

"The tax legislation will not be rescinded. Women all over the world pay taxes, there is no reason why the women of Lagos should not," he said, looking like he was about to turn around and walk back into his office.

"Women all around the world have money! British women have money, more money than we have here! Our women have already lost husbands and sons in India and Burma, some all across the world, fighting for the Empire! We, the women of Lagos, are now the breadwinners feeding our families. This tax threatens our means of feeding our children. As it is, many of us are barely getting by," Madam Titi responded. Although she still sounded calm, there were rivulets of sweat pouring out from the base of her hairline, visible under her head tie. "The women of Lagos don't get to vote on what is happening to us. Nobody asked for our opinion before deciding they would introduce this tax. So, Commissioner Lawrence, we ask that on the basis of all I have said today, the income tax be overturned, and we can all go back to trying to survive in these trying times. Kehinde, please give him the petition."

Kehinde felt her arm shake as every single pair of eyes in the crowd watched her present the signed petition to Mr Lawrence. He glanced at it briefly, his brown eyes colder than water on a harmattan morning. Kehinde held her breath as she watched him turn over the page, his gaze narrowing as he skimmed over the rows of signatures.

"Let me be clear. A considerable amount of thought and consideration has gone into this tax legislation. We will not overturn it just because some of you have signed this sheet of paper," he wrung the sheet of paper in his right arm as he said this, like a counterfeit note. "We will go ahead as planned with the introduction of the income tax from January 1941, and you would all do well to abide by it. That will be all, good day to you," he said, and with a nod, he turned around and walked back into his office. The door slammed in his wake, leaving a stunned audience behind him.

The silence in the crowd was only interrupted by the rustling of leaves in the wind that continued, unperturbed by the unease in the air. The silence felt anti-climactic, almost laughable, until a babble of complaints started up at once.

"All that standing around for nothing! Those colonial administrators are so wicked, Commissioner Lawrence didn't even flinch when he told us to get out," Ama said beside her.

"He barely even looked at the petition we signed," Kehinde said, feeling a cloud of disappointment descend on her.

"At least you'll be fine either way," Onyi said.

"What do you mean?" Kehinde asked, surprised as Onyi hardly ever said much.

"It's not like you really need the money," Onyi said, sounding envious. "The rest of us don't have rich husbands to lean on."

Kehinde looked at her, speechless for a second. If only Onyi knew what it was really like to have a "rich husband to lean on". Kehinde felt the consternation in the crowd flowing within her body. The tax bill would affect her to some extent as the income she made from her food sales was already so tiny, any further subtractions would make her disposable income negligible. However, unlike most women gathered here, she also received a substantial income from Baba Tope. But that was not money she was proud of, money she had worked for. What right did the colonial government have to take away any of their income? Besides, she had spent hours with Ben and Madam Titi planning the logistics for the day. Had all that gone to waste?

"Onyi, don't be rude," Ama hissed. "Don't mind her, Kehinde. She doesn't know what she's talking about."

"He can't be serious! What is wrong with that oyinbo man?" a woman wearing a black kaftan and hijab shouted from the back before Kehinde could respond to Ama.

"This income tax will destroy me, what are we going to do?" another woman, with a crying baby balanced on one hip, wailed, sounding close to tears.

"We can't just give up like this!" Ama said, her face unusually creased in a frown as she flapped her cardboard sign up and down in front of her like a makeshift fan.

"She's right, we can't give up just like that," Madam Titi replied. Her voice was like a cooling balm on a new burn and the crowd fell silent. "We certainly will not stop here, we will rally and go on to the house of the governor himself tomorrow," she continued, her voice rising over the now cheering crowd.

Kehinde felt her stomach lurch. The house of the governor! In the past year that she had been married she was yet to meet the governor, as most of Baba Tope's interactions with him had been over the phone or at external meetings, never in their house. But she knew it was only a matter of time before she did meet him, and her secret would be out. The chances of him seeing them together one day were very high, and what if he told Baba Tope that she had been with the women of the market, protesting? They all joked that the colonial administrators thought they all looked the same and could barely tell one Nigerian apart from the other, but she couldn't take that chance. There was no way she could not go though, Madam Titi would expect her there. What reason could she possibly give for missing something so important? But this could easily end up being a disaster of epic proportions. She broke out in a sweat as the cheers got louder.

"Every market in Lagos will close again tomorrow. We will storm the house of the governor and he must pay attention to us. They will know that the women of Lagos have spoken!" Madam Titi shouted, her fist raised in the air.

Kehinde, Ama, Onyi and the crowd of women made their way back to Glover Memorial Hall. Long after everyone had gone home, with mounting fear, Kehinde spent the afternoon taking the signatures of more women, the voices of Ben Makinde and Madam Titi the frantic soundtrack for her thoughts.

"Ese, Kehinde. Always so efficient," Ben said when she handed him the sheet of signatures. "You're an example to all the young women out there. You've shown it's possible to manage a home and still serve your country."

"Oh, Ben, you sound like an old man. There are many married women who work," Madam Titi said.

"Yes, I suppose. Let's hope your husband doesn't keep you at home when you start having babies," Ben said.

Kehinde smiled, grateful for the distraction when Iya Dara asked to speak with Madam Titi alone outside. For all of Ben's help, his occasional comments showed that like most men, he expected that her real place was in her home, caring for her husband and children.

"Kehinde, we'll need to set out early tomorrow. The commissioner would have already told the governor, so we need to get to his house before he has a chance to leave," Madam Titi said, returning with Iya Dara. "You can meet me here and we'll go together with Ben," she continued.

"Thank you, Ma. See you here tomorrow then," Kehinde said, nodding at Ben as she packed up her things in her satchel. He smiled at her, lifting his hand to wave goodbye as she walked out of the hall.

Kehinde decided that she would stop by her store to confirm she had locked it up, especially now that she knew she wouldn't be there the next day as well. To her surprise, Emeka was standing in front of her store when she got there.

"Is everything okay?" Kehinde asked Emeka, her anxiety melting away as she gave into the elation she felt at seeing him.

"I was hoping you would come here before you headed home. I just wanted to say well done for today. I know it didn't go as planned but this was a great first step. I'll be writing a piece on some of my views in light of past riots, like the Aba

Women's Riots in 1929. Maybe you can read it," he said, smiling down at her.

"There I was thinking you just wanted to see me," Kehinde said, surprising them both with her boldness. It must be the adrenaline from the day's activities that had left her feeling so brave, she thought, as she watched the unmistakable spark that sprung into Emeka's eyes.

"Well, that too," he said, taking half a step closer to her.

The sun had turned orange and men and women hurried past the store, some from the protest, and others returning home after their day at work. Time seemed to come to a standstill as they stood there, oblivious to the sounds of the market. *What am I doing*, Kehinde thought as she felt the air around her shift. She watched Emeka's lips part, wondering what it would be like to kiss him. Would his lips be soft like his eyes, or calloused like his hands?

"There you are! I was wondering if you would stop by or go straight home. Sorry about what Onyi said earlier, I hope you're not upset?" Ama said, stepping out of Fine Leather.

The spell was broken as Kehinde and Emeka jumped apart.

"Right, yes," Emeka said at the same time that Kehinde said, "I'm not upset at all!"

"Why are you both being so strange?" Ama asked, looking from one to the other.

"Am I being strange? I must head home now, to get dinner ready," Kehinde said, almost tripping on the side of the gutter as she hurried down the street.

She half ran, half walked home, arriving with enough time to have a bath before joining Ayo in the kitchen.

"Ẹ káàlẹ́. Nice of you to join me," she said to Kehinde over her shoulder, already dishing the cooked agbo into a serving bowl.

"Ẹ ṣe, Ayo. I would have come down sooner if I had realised you had started dinner."

"Yes, with or without you, this household will still need to eat," she said with a grunt, shifting on her feet as she poured the beef palm oil stew from the pot on the fire into another dish, her back still turned to Kehinde. The set of her shoulders was tense as her arms moved back and forth between the stove and counter.

"Ayo, have I offended you?" Kehinde asked, still hovering by the door of the kitchen.

Ayo paused before she turned around to face her.

"You think I don't know where you've been all day? Kehinde, after I told you to stay away from those LMWA people!"

"What?"

"Oh please, I know you went to the protest. All I had to do was make a trip down to your store to check if you were there and of course you weren't. How could you be so careless?"

"Ayo, Baba Tope still doesn't know," Kehinde said in a pleading tone. She had crossed the kitchen and was holding Ayo's hands in hers now, her eyes begging Ayo to understand.

"All he has to do is to walk into your store one day and he'll find out!"

"It's not like I attend a protest every day!"

"Kehinde, you're on very thin ice here—"

Ayo stopped speaking suddenly as they both saw a shadow cross the kitchen. It was Atinuke, coming in to take the dinner dishes to the dining table. She mumbled a greeting as she picked up the tray and carried it out of the kitchen.

"Do you think she heard anything we said?" Kehinde whispered.

"I don't know," Ayo whispered back.

"I feel like she's been following me lately. The other day I saw her in my room. She said something about looking for a rat, but it didn't make any sense."

"Kehinde!" Ayo's two hands dropped the spoon and landed on the top of her head. "If Atinuke knows, you're in big trouble!"

"How would she know? I hardly have LMWA campaign flyers in my room."

When Ayo didn't laugh, Kehinde reached out and put a hand on her shoulder.

"Ayo, I promise I'll be careful," she said, not adding that she still had one more protest to attend the next day, one she hoped would be the last. It was a lot easier to do her job in secret when she was writing minutes and reports from the safety of the four closed walls of Madam Titi's office. She loved the energy she had felt, being in the crowd earlier, but she had also felt so conspicuous, like a chicken waiting to be slaughtered in an open field. The next protest would have to be her last for sure. She was taking too big a risk, and Ayo was right. If anyone found out, only God knew what Baba Tope would do to her.

They both heard his voice as he greeted his children in the den, with each child letting out a squeal of excitement as he called them individually by name. The sound of Mama Tope's descent down the staircase was the final sign that it was time to move to the dining room for dinner. Ayo grabbed the last dish of efo-riro on the side of the kitchen counter as they made their way out of the kitchen.

"I heard there was unrest in the market today, I hope you weren't affected, my flower," Baba Tope said once they had all sat down and prayed.

"No, Baba Tope, thankfully I wasn't disturbed," Kehinde said as she passed him the dish of agbo.

"I also heard the women involved were quite unruly," he said.

"Those women that get involved with all that rubbish are so badly behaved. Politics is for the men to worry about, I don't know why any well brought up woman would get herself involved with such nonsense," Mama Tope said from her seat beside their husband.

"Quite right, no woman from a good home would be caught dead with such a useless group of troublemakers," their husband said as he cut through his beef.

"Daddy, why is it wrong for women to work in the market?" Ashabi asked, looking confused. The children all looked up from their end of the table, pausing to hear their father's answer.

"It's not wrong for them to work in the market, my dear, that's not what Mama Tope said. She and Kehinde have decent, honest jobs in the market. What is wrong is women getting involved in the affairs of men," he said.

"Why is it wrong?" Tope asked, unusually participative in the conversation.

"Because it's the natural order of things, as God made it to be. God made men to rule the world, and women are to listen and follow the instructions of their fathers and husbands in submission. It's only badly behaved women who don't submit to the men God has put in charge of them," he said, the purveyor of knowledge on one of his favourite topics.

Oh, the things men said and did in the name of God, Kehinde thought. It was the kind of thing she would have laughed about as she wrote in her journal later if she didn't feel like a cold hammer was beating away in her chest.

"Yes, dear, the Bible clearly states it. Wives, submit to your husbands, and in the same way, women who don't have husbands must submit to the men of authority in their lives," Mama Tope replied, with a rare smile directed at Kehinde on her face.

"Well said, Ma. Baba Tope, how was your day at work?" Ayo said, trying valiantly to change the topic.

"It was fine until I got in my car and saw women from the market holding signs on the way home. Who do they think they are? With us being in the middle of a war too. They're lucky Lagos isn't being bombed like London is, that's why they have time to do this nonsense," Baba Tope responded, shaking his head.

Kehinde felt a pool of sweat start to form in her underarms and on her back. Ayo glanced at her again as he continued speaking.

"The worst part is that these women go around demanding things, so entitled and oblivious to what is going on around them. If only they knew what we are dealing with at the War Relief Committee! The Empire is fighting every day to keep us safe, yet they are running around like brats. There's a reason why women don't vote, men think more rationally about the rules than they do."

"So, it isn't right for women to ask for what they want?" Tope asked again. She was leaning forward in her seat, her skinny arms taut as they rested on the dining table.

"Women can ask for what they want, but in the right way. They should always be polite, asking men in a ladylike manner. They must never demand, and if the man they ask says no, they should understand that it's for the best," he said.

It sounded like the kind of thing her parents would say, Kehinde thought. But unlike Baba Tope, her parents were kind, guided only by what they thought were traditional values and the Bible. Baba Tope just loved to have power and people he could control, she thought in disgust.

Mama Tope nodded, opening her mouth to speak before Ayo jumped in to cut her off.

"Speaking of the War Relief Committee, how's that going?" she asked, in yet another attempt to change the topic to a safer path, one where Kehinde's head was not rolling around like a football. Kehinde smiled at her weakly. The excitement at being part of the protest suddenly seemed irrational in the face of her terror at being discovered.

"It's going well. We've been able to raise more money for the colonial government. It doesn't look like this war is going to end anytime soon unfortunately," he said, sitting back as he rubbed his stomach.

"That's a shame. I had hoped things would get better, at least by Christmas. None of my customers are buying new dresses," Ayo said, picking up her cutlery. Like Kehinde, she had barely touched the food on her plate.

"It's the same thing in my store, the fabric I have is the same stock I've had for months," Mama Tope said, agreeing with Ayo.

The conversation continued about how the war had changed their lives from Ayo and Mama Tope's perspective, their husband smiling and chipping in. These were his favourite moments it seemed, where he could sit at the head of the table and watch the household he had built. Kehinde felt his gaze land on her stomach and saw the shift in his expression go from content to annoyed.

"My flower, you need to be careful with all this unrest everywhere. It's not safe and certainly not good for your health," he said.

"Thank you, my husband. I'll be careful," she said with a distracted smile. The mix of emotions she had experienced all day were beginning to make her feel giddy, not to mention the nightcap of worry served at dinner.

As she wrote in her journal when she was safe in her room later that night, she reminded herself to remain calm – tomorrow promised to be even busier, and despite her fears, this was the final chance the LMWA had to end the idea of this ill-conceived tax.

Chapter Eighteen

The next morning, Kehinde left home, pretending to go to the market as usual before taking a sharp turn towards Madam Titi's office, looking over her shoulder to make sure that no one that looked like Atinuke was following her. The babble of voices got louder as she approached the office, and as she turned the corner, she saw a crowd bigger than the one that had gathered the day before. It looked like every female trader in Lagos had come out and Kehinde had to squeeze through the closely packed bodies to the front of the crowd where Madam Titi, Iya Dara and Ben were standing. As she pressed on, she felt a hand on her shoulder and turned around to see Emeka, with Ama standing beside him. Her skin felt instantly warmer, the way it always did when he was near her.

"We were shouting your name as soon as we saw you, but you couldn't hear us over the noise," Emeka said, the hairs curling around his mouth as he spoke.

"I could never have guessed that this many people would show up," Kehinde said, raising her voice above the bustle around them.

"All the markets in Lagos are closed today! I told Onyi to stay at home, no point in her sitting in the store idle," Ama said.

The familiar explosion of cold anxiety went off in Kehinde's chest and into her head like fireworks. If Baba Tope found out the markets had been closed all day, he would ask her where she had been. She would have to think of a story to tell him before she got home.

"I better go to Madam Titi; she was expecting me about ten minutes ago. See you both later," Kehinde said, putting the thought behind her as she continued to push her way to the front. She almost lost her footing a few times as her legs connected with other legs, her feet shuffling against shoes and sandals. When she finally made it to the front, she felt like she had been sent to the frontline of a battlefield.

"There you are, Kehinde. It's very unlike you to be late; I hope all is well?" Madam Titi said, her eyebrows furrowed.

"Yes, Ma, I'm fine. I just got held up in the crowd," Kehinde said, not mentioning how she had spent almost half an hour making sure she timed her departure with Atinuke's laundry schedule.

"It's a big crowd. A fine turnout indeed. Governor Bourdillon will have no choice but to listen to us. It will be impossible to get all of us to his on foot though, Ben has organised a few buses with the help of the NNDP. Those will get us to Obalende," she said.

At that moment, the crowd cheered as about nine buses pulled up on the edge of the street. They were the brown public transport buses that Kehinde herself had been in many times in the past. She never imagined that she would ever think those buses weren't big enough.

"Some of us will still have to walk," Iya Dara said, echoing Kehinde's thoughts.

"Yes, I'll lead the rear end of women who can't get on the buses. I've already sent word to Mr Macaulay to see if we can get at least two more," Ben said.

"Come on then, we don't have time to waste," Madam Titi said, leading the way to the first bus.

As they climbed on, the driver looked at them wearily. The women settled down in the bus, with a buzz of excitement in the air like a team of mosquitos. It felt like they were going on a school trip, united in their pursuit of justice, a formidable force against the colonial government. Many of them had already lost brothers, sons and husbands in a war whose cause they could not explain, and they were determined that their income would not be under threat as well.

A woman sitting in the middle of the bus in an orange iro and buba started singing in a loud, throaty voice. The lyrics of the song were easy, and as the bus moved the other women joined in with their medley of voices, with some beating the backs of the seats in front of them.

> *"We will not take it, no we shall not!*
> *Taxes for women, no we shall not*
> *Lawrence said no, to Bourdillon we go*
> *We will not take it, no we shall not!"*

Beside Kehinde, Madam Titi joined in the singing, the wind from the open windows making the hijab and scarf on her head billow out around her face, softening the sharpness of her cheekbones. Kehinde had never heard her sing, and her profile seemed almost youthful as it was softened by the movement. Kehinde joined in too, ignoring the guilt and fear that gnawed at her. She was here for a reason, a cause bigger than herself. She was born to do great things, like this. Baba Tope would be fine, she would make sure he never found out.

The bus lurched to a stop once they reached Obalende. From there, they would walk the short distance to the governor's house on First Avenue. As they climbed off the bus the driver tried and failed not to look too relieved, taking his hat off as he exhaled.

Obalende was as busy as you would expect on a Tuesday morning, with pedestrians getting on and off buses and bicycles as they made their way to their various places of work. Many were dressed in domestic staff uniforms, going to the homes of the expatriates and colonial administrators in Ikoyi to work as maids, cooks, cleaners, tutors and so on. They looked on with interest at the women dismounting from the buses, some even stopping to ask what was going on.

The crowd surged forward, gaining momentum as some of the pedestrians at the bus stop joined the market women as they walked to First Avenue. The women around her continued singing, and Kehinde walked briskly, trying to keep up with Madam Titi, determined not to lose her in the crowd. The sun beat down on them as they marched, the trees swayed in the morning breeze and the gravel on the floor crunched beneath their feet. The harmattan haze in the air settled as dust in their hair and in the cracks of their skin. It felt like nature itself had yielded to their cause as they moved as one, onwards to the governor's house and before Kehinde knew it, they were standing at the top of First Avenue. She looked around, trying to see if Ama and Emeka were close by but there were too many faces.

Kehinde looked on in awe as they rounded the bend of the street – they were on the edge of Ikoyi, overlooking the surrounding Five Cowries Creek. A mild smell of compost floated in the air, but it was almost completely masked by the fresh scent of the leaves on the surrounding trees. Her father had always called the creek the gateway to the Atlantic, and apparently it looked most magical at sunset. This was home to only English men and women, mostly colonial administrators and their families, and her father had come here a few times to make special deliveries. This breathtaking view was only for the colonial administrators and their families to see; even the wealthiest Nigerians were not allowed to own land here, or live here, and Kehinde felt a sense of injustice. The best parts of her city were not available for her countrymen and women to enjoy as they deemed fit. The colonial government were the real owners of this land, not them. As she stared across at the open water, she was reminded of her father's boat on the open sea and how he always looked happiest on water. The same water that had taken his life. She quickly pushed away the unexpected stab of grief, reminding herself why she was here.

"His house is just over there," Ben said beside her, pointing in the direction of a white building about one hundred metres away. The house was set back against a green lawn, with a low, white fence. Two security guards in the Nigerian Army uniform of red shorts and an open waistcoat looked at the group of women as they moved towards the house like a wave to the shore. As they got closer, the wide-legged stance of the guards indicated they had been expecting them and were not pleased, the way you would regard an annoying relative that had shown up in your parlour.

"Good morning, brothers. We're here to see the governor of Lagos, Sir Bernard Bourdillon," Madam Titi said with a confidence that Kehinde didn't feel.

"And what makes you think he wants to see you?" the bigger guard replied.

"Oh, I think this is something he'll want to talk about. You can tell him the women of the LMWA are here with a matter close to all our hearts," Madam Titi responded. The guard let out a bitter laugh.

"My sister, he already told us not to let you in. Go back to the market and your husbands, please," he said, not unkindly.

"Then we will stay here until he comes out," Madam Titi said in Yoruba, crossing her arms over her chest as she did so. The women cheered from the back, some of them beginning the song again.

> "We will not take it, no we shall not!
> Taxes for women, no we shall not!
> Lawrence said no, to Bourdillon we go
> We will not take it, no we shall not!
> Bourdillon no want hear, so we stay here
> We will not take it, no we shall not!"

Kehinde joined in, raising her voice with the other women. She had not snuck out of the house only to get turned away; she would do everything in her power to stay here, where she belonged. The two security guards looked alarmed as the women grew more boisterous. Someone had brought along a talking drum and was drumming at the back as new songs were composed, the lyrics taking on a life of their own. Kehinde thought she could see a curtain twitch at one of the windows at the front of the house.

After what felt like three hours but was in fact only forty-five minutes, a smartly dressed butler came out of the front door and walked towards the gate. At the movement of the door the crowd quietened down, with everyone anticipating that the governor was making an appearance, but the noise soon picked up again at the sight of the imperial-looking black man. He held his head up as he tried to maintain his dignity against the group of women in front of him.

"Good morning, how can I help you today?" he asked in perfect English from the other side of the fence.

"Boss, these women say they want to see Governor. He already told me not to let them in," said the security guard.

"And rightly so. Sir Bernard is having breakfast and the noise you are making is most unpleasant," the butler said, his nose in the air like he could blast them all away with one exhale.

"Are you not ashamed of yourself? Our sisters are here, fighting for the rights of not only the market women, but for the rights of every Nigerian, and meanwhile you're here dressed up like a doll, speaking like you're better than us!" Ben hissed.

"Ben, calm down. Sir, we merely seek an audience with the governor to discuss issues he is already aware of, peacefully. We're not here to fight, we just want a friendly discussion," Madam Titi said.

"He has asked me to send you away. The noise you're making has not only troubled him, but is troubling our neighbours as well," he continued, with a weary look in Ben's direction.

"We've all come from different parts of Lagos. Ẹjọ, my brother, ask him to listen to us," Madam Titi said in Yoruba.

A softness appeared in the butler's eyes as he looked over the crowd.

"Let me see what I can do, Ma," he said, bowing his head as he retreated towards the front door. About twenty minutes later he came back, walking briskly as he headed towards the gate.

"The governor will not come out," he started. A collective groan went up from the crowd. He held up his hand, asking for silence. "However, he has requested that the leader of your Association, along with another member of her choice, be let into the house to see him," he said apologetically to Madam Titi.

"Ẹ ṣe, my brother. Oya, Kehinde, let's go," Madam Titi said, already walking towards the now open gate.

"Me?" squeaked Kehinde.

"Yes now, quickly, before he changes his mind," Madam Titi said with a hint of impatience.

Kehinde hurried after her through the gates. She had banked on the governor only seeing her from a distance, rather than up close. Kehinde's pulse raced faster than the sounds of the crowd receding behind them as she and Madam Titi followed the butler into the governor's home.

Chapter Nineteen

As soon as they stepped inside the house, Kehinde felt a rush of nostalgia, like she had been there before. This house reminded her of the Ogunjobi household, but without the garish gold and ornate furniture Baba Tope had chosen. Rather, it was stately but muted, with pale yellows and whites enhancing the walls and fabrics. It even smelled different, like baked bread with freshly churned butter and a hint of cigar smoke, whereas hers always smelled of onions and ata rodo – the base for the spicy food Baba Tope favoured.

They had stepped into a large waiting area where the thin green lines on the wallpaper reminded her of a vine, creeping up on the surrounding walls. The sound of crockery scraping a plate came from the dining room as the butler led them further in. Kehinde's feet echoed on the wooden floor, still not louder to her than the sound of her beating heart. He signalled to them to wait outside. Kehinde looked at a tall potted plant by the door as she tried to stop herself from dissolving into a puddle of nerves on the floor. It didn't help that she felt like she needed to pee, and she obviously couldn't ask to use the bathroom now.

"Sir. Madam Titi and her associate are here," the butler said.

"Let them come in," said a deep voice that sounded like the war broadcasts from the imperial government that Kehinde had heard on the Rediffusion in the den.

They stepped into the room, Kehinde keeping her eyes downcast and her head low. She suddenly wished she had left the house with something to cover her head, something that would make her more unrecognisable.

"Good morning, ladies, how can I help you today?" Sir Bourdillon said in a jovial tone, like he was discussing the weather.

Kehinde looked up in surprise. He was actually smiling, seated at the head of a long dining table with a breakfast of poached eggs, toast and marmalade laid out in front of him. He had a copy of the *Daily Times* folded on a tray beside a white china pot of tea, probably from a bigger set of kitchenware bought by his wife. Kehinde had heard from Emeka that she was a real English lady who drank her tea from a dainty teacup with her little finger sticking out to the side when she hosted women's lunches. She had followed her husband from colony to colony, carrying her chests of china and dinner gowns.

Although Governor Bourdillon looked to be over forty years old, the cheekbones in his face still sat high and prominent, with a narrow nose in the centre. His dark brown, thinning hair had been swept over to one side and he sat back in his chair now, regarding Kehinde and Madam Titi with sharp, pale eyes.

"Good morning, sir. I think you know why we're here,"

Madam Titi said, matching his tone. Kehinde knew they had met before but unlike Baba Tope, she did not believe they referred to each other as acquaintances.

"Do have a seat," he said, nodding in the direction of the upholstered chairs on his left. Kehinde waited for Madam Titi to sit, then took the seat beside her furthest away from the governor, although not as far as she would like.

"Segun, get these women some water. They must be parched from standing outside for so long. Hot day, it looks like," he continued, speaking to the butler over the news playing on the Rediffusion. "The chief commissioner tells me you want the tax bill repealed," he said, picking up his cup of tea.

"I'm glad you've been brought up to date with our affairs," Madam Titi said, after she had taken a sip of the water Segun put in front of them.

"Well, I'm afraid to tell you that we simply cannot oblige on this occasion," Sir Bourdillon said, a hardness suddenly appearing in his eyes, like a lake freezing over. "You see, given the current state of the economy, everyone has to pull their weight. You women should have been paying taxes for a long time now."

"The current state of which economy?" Madam Titi asked, anger creeping into her voice. Kehinde felt her palms moisten as she smoothed down her skirt.

"The economy of the Empire. It's time for the women of Nigeria to play their part."

"A part of what? Citizens who cannot vote, who have no say in the affairs that command them," Madam Titi hissed in Yoruba.

Sir Bourdillon blinked, appearing startled at the switch in her tone and language. Kehinde knew that when Madam Titi got flustered, her thoughts and words came in Yoruba, no matter how hard she tried. After a brief moment of shock at actually having to speak, Kehinde recovered enough to hastily repeat the sentence in English for him. As she spoke, he looked at her more closely, like he had just noticed she was in the room.

"Now, you can hardly say that the women have no say in these affairs. After all, we know how you women, especially the traders such as yourself, have contributed to the economy. Your market practices have been designed by you, no?" he said, cocking his head to the side, his hands placed together in a steeple grip.

"Indeed, they have, and we have worked too hard to have you come and scatter everything we have worked for!"

"Madam Titi, you're mistaken. We're on the same side," Sir Bourdillon said, sitting up straighter in his chair.

"Then why are you trying to impoverish us?"

"That, of course, is not our desire."

"We're paying for your war! And once the war ends, we'll all have nothing!" Kehinde translated this quickly, not matching the fiery tone that it was said in. She had the urge to open the window wider – the air in the room was still and she kept forgetting to breathe. She definitely needed to pee, but she wanted to clap for Madam Titi, and she also wanted to throw up. She fought to keep her composure. Everything Madam Titi had said was true and she hated what this war was doing to everyone and everything around her.

"I know these are difficult times for all of us. We've all lost something, or someone, but this is the time to stand together. The tax bill will stay, and that is final. You will all have to comply."

"Then every market in Lagos will remain shut! Let us see

how your precious economy fares without the very women you are trying to oppress!"

As Kehinde translated this, Sir Bourdillon's face turned ashen. For the first time since they had walked into his home, he looked truly worried. He rose slowly from his place at the dining table, and walked towards the open window overlooking his lawn. And for a few minutes the sound of the women beyond his gate could be heard over the Rediffusion. Their cheering had turned raucous, the talking drum beating sporadically, like the women were at a festival.

"You drive a hard bargain, Madam Titi," he said finally, his back still turned to them.

"All I'm asking for is some consideration. Many of our women have lost husbands and sons in Burma and across Europe. They're the sole breadwinners of their homes. Any further loss of income will cripple them," she responded slowly in heavily accented English, like she was teaching a child who did not understand the consequences of his actions.

"When I moved to Nigeria from Uganda, I didn't know what to expect. I was told that the Nigerians were stubborn and proud, more overbearing than the Ugandans. More demanding. It's admirable really," he said to the window, talking more to himself than to the women in the room.

"I'll see what I can do," Sir Bourdillon continued after a few minutes had passed. To the surprise of both women, he had a sad smile on his face. "I'll send word to you about when we can reconvene, and until then, please reopen the markets. And for God's sake, no more protests. Please."

"No more protests, and the markets will reopen tomorrow. We look forward to receiving good news from you," Madam Titi said, wincing slightly as she stood. Kehinde kept her head downcast as Sir Bourdillon leaned over to shake her hand, and then the butler showed them out of the house.

Kehinde felt like a wrung-out bedsheet. It wasn't a landslide victory, but at least some progress had been made. It was barely noon, but she was too emotionally spent to go back to her store today. The adrenaline from the morning and her fear of being caught had left her body like a wave from the shore. All she wanted was to go home and lie in bed.

"What happened?" Ben asked as soon as the gate closed behind them.

"He said he needs time to think about it," Madam Titi said, with a tired smile. Kehinde knew that she had little faith in the conversation they had just had. "I've given him my word that we will reopen the markets in the meantime."

"These English men are not to be trusted," Ben started.

"Ben, I know. Will you teach me, someone who is old enough to be your mother? Let's go and rest, our work is done for today."

There was a rumble of disappointment across the group of women still gathered at the gate, but Kehinde heard a few sighs of relief. Keeping the markets completely closed would be cutting off all their noses to spite their collective face. As it stood, they lived to fight another day and as the women got back onto the waiting buses, they were all silently praying that their efforts today would not be in vain.

Kehinde walked through the gates of her home, exhausted and desperately in need of the toilet. All she wanted to do was sit in a bathtub full of warm water and maybe even take a nap before it was time to prepare dinner. Despite her exhaustion, she couldn't ignore the surge of hope within her. She had done something big, she had been brave, and used her voice to help women she didn't even know. Her father would have been proud of her, she was confident about this. And even though she couldn't tell her mother, she knew she would have been grudgingly impressed. Maybe it was finally time to write to Taiwo, even before she saw him. She wanted to tell him: *See, I'm not a pushover, I'm not at home feeling sorry for myself. I did something big today, I spoke up, I made a difference.*

As Kehinde walked into the compound, she noticed Baba Tope's car parked in the driveway, with Mr Tunde and Kayode speaking beside it. *Strange*, she thought as they greeted her. Baba Tope was never home this early. As the front door shut behind her, Ayo came running towards her in the waiting room, the whites of her eyes stark against a bruise on the side of her cheek.

"Kehinde, he knows! I don't know how he found out, but he knows everything!"

"Knows what, Ayo? What happened to your face?"

"Is that her? Kehinde! Come here! Come here right now!" Baba Tope bellowed from the formal parlour. Ayo gripped the doorknob and Kehinde saw the fear swelling in the pit of her stomach mirrored in the tightness of Ayo's mouth. The bruise on her cheek appeared to darken even more within seconds as she let out a sob. Kehinde felt alive with dread, with every nerve on high alert – like a bucket of cold water had been poured on her, instantly washing away the exhaustion she had been feeling.

"I said, come here now!"

"I'm coming!" Kehinde responded, her lips trembling as she opened the door to face her husband. He was sitting on the sofa, his cheeks puffed out as beads of sweat rolled down his face. In his lap was a book. *God*, please no, Kehinde thought, a waterfall of horror engulfing her as she recognised the engraving on her journal.

"Ayo, go back upstairs," he said. "Get out!" he continued, when Ayo didn't move, and this time, she scurried off like a wounded dog. Apart from the sound of her retreating footsteps the house was eerily silent, the children not yet back from school and Mama Tope nowhere in sight.

"What do you have to say for yourself?"

When she said nothing, he sat up taller. "Mama Tope, in her wisdom, came to me this morning and explained that you were involved in activities I would not approve of. She was worried you would be a bad influence on Tope, and rightly so!" he spluttered. Spit sprayed from his mouth like holy water to absolve her of her sins.

Of course it was Mama Tope! With horror, Kehinde realised she had forgotten to lock her room door as she'd hurried to leave that morning. Atinuke must have retrieved her journal then and given it to Mama Tope. Each thought flitted in and out of her mind's eye as she thought of the day she must have seen Atinuke close to the hall, the day she had found her cleaning her room before dinner. She must have been sent by Mama Tope. There was so much incriminating information in her journal – he would know everything. She felt violated, like her clothes had been stripped off her in the middle of a show where she was the main character. Her bladder was painfully full, and she started to shake as she stood before her judge.

"You have nothing to say for yourself? When I gave you this book, I never dreamed that you would use it to deceive me. How could you do this to me?" His mouth hung open, his lower lip one wobbly line and his forehead creased into three. "Say something!" He slammed the journal down on the table beside him, making the vase of flowers on it shake. The house was still quiet – even the bricks seemed to be holding their breath, waiting for Kehinde to speak.

"Baba Tope … you don't understand—"

"So, help me understand. What's all this rubbish about you working with the women of the Lagos Market Women's Association?"

"I didn't tell you because I didn't think you would approve."

"And rightly so! But you went ahead, behind my back, working with Titi, that crazy woman! Running around town with those shameless women? Half of them are prostitutes. My God," he was clutching his chest now, his large hand dark against his agbada. "After everything I've done for you, this is how you repay me? I rent you a store, I make you a respectable woman, and yet you run off with a bunch of charlatans!"

"They're respectable women, we all are," Kehinde said, her hands clasped together. She hated the way her voice sounded, so shrill and penitent, choked with fear.

"Shut up! I've told you several times that you should never interrupt me! I'm your husband and your elder! You should respect me!"

"I do respect you—"

"You don't!"

Kehinde watched him sullenly, her hands still clasped together before her. And he was still clutching his chest like he was about to have a heart attack. Not that she would have minded. She realised in that moment that she felt absolutely nothing but resentment for him. He was right, she didn't respect him. She had been afraid of him, and she was still shaking, but she thought so little of him at that moment, it was all she could do to pretend to be sorry. Yes, she was so scared she thought she would pee on herself, but she wasn't sorry about anything. The only regret she had was leaving her room open for Mama Tope to find her journal.

"What kind of example are you setting for the daughters of this house? What kind of woman leaves her home to do rubbish across the streets of Lagos?" he said, speaking to himself although he was looking at Kehinde. He reminded her of Reverend Kasunmu, shouting rhetorical questions to the congregation at church during one of his sermons. "And all this time, I thought you were selling food. How can a woman like you, my wife, be involved with the likes of that Titi woman? This is a disgrace, a smear to my name! Of course you're not pregnant yet, how could you be when you spend your days like this!" He was foaming at the mouth now, working himself up into a fit.

Kehinde stood watching him, her fear and disgust making the responses in her head swell until they became inappropriate. She wanted to defend herself, but what could she say in the face of his rage? Ayo had told her before that when he was angry it was best to let him talk it out. Saying anything to him now would only enrage him further, so she remained silent, praying for his anger to subside. Ayo, she thought with rising panic. Had he hit her? Was that why her face was bruised?

Baba Tope rose to his feet, still holding her journal in his left hand. She opened her mouth to beg his forgiveness, hating how scared she felt, but before she could form the words, the palm of his hand connected with her cheek and she staggered backwards. Before she could recover, he slapped her again, followed swiftly by a punch to her stomach as she fell to her knees.

"I will teach you to respect me!" Baba Tope shouted, as he clutched her by the neck.

"Please … please," Kehinde spat out.

He removed his hand from her neck and instead grabbed the ends of her cornrows as he hauled her to her feet. Kehinde's head jerked as she ran, stooped, to keep up with him while he dragged her outside, the heavy wood door slamming behind them before they took a sharp left towards the edge of the lawn. She thought she tasted blood in her mouth and, as her tongue instinctively felt over the insides of her mouth, she realised her lip was cut. The banana tree loomed over them, its branches waving sorrowfully at Kehinde. *Maybe this is it*, she thought, the moment he would kill her, the same way he had killed the man on the lawn.

"Kayode! Bring me the matches," Baba Tope shouted in the direction of the gatehouse. Kayode came running out, and if he was surprised at the sight of Kehinde kneeling on the lawn with blood in her mouth he didn't show it.

"You didn't know how to behave before but now I must teach you," he said, his voice calmer than it had been inside. Kehinde felt a cold, fresh wave of fear wash over her as she watched him throw her journal to the ground. As the book landed, sheets of paper flew from it in a final attempt to break free. Kehinde scrambled towards them as they hovered in the swirling wind, not caring that the hem of her skirt was creating a hurricane of dust around her. She had been entering her thoughts into that book since the day he gave it to her, over a year ago. It had everything in there. Her childhood memories of her father, and the thoughts she'd had the day he died. Her words, the voice of her soul, were in there in fine print.

"Baba Tope, please!" she cried.

"You're lucky this is all I'm doing. You're very lucky I'm a gentleman," he said, looking at her like she was a worm he wanted to stomp on. "Hold her!" Baba Tope shouted to Kayode, who immediately dropped to the ground, clutching her in an undignified heap with her hands still reaching out ahead of her. The black book sat in sharp contrast with the green grass as it awaited its fate.

"Please! I'm sorry! Please, just leave my journal!" she sobbed, watching as he lit a match, the flame a tiny speck in the afternoon light, the white house gleaming behind Baba Tope's sturdy frame.

Ignoring her, he dropped the lit match directly on the book. The flame seemed to have pity on Kehinde as it danced slowly around the journal, but the pages eventually caught. Baba Tope immediately lit another one, dropping it into the growing inferno. As Kehinde's sobbing turned into incoherent screams, he gathered the loose sheets of paper, and threw them in. It was just a book, but it had become her best friend.

"You will never go behind my back again, Kehinde. You will respect me the way you are supposed to as my wife, and you will do as you're told. This is the last time you will ever defy me. Next time you disobey me, I will send you back to your mother," he said calmly, watching the fire swallow the book. Kehinde felt limp as Kayode stood up and left her to drop to the ground like the paper swirling in the flames. The smoke filled her lungs and she felt her bladder give way as she watched the fire eat away at her words, her skirt immediately getting soaked. A loose page with her handwriting folding in defiance swayed on the edge of the furnace against the inevitable.

"First thing tomorrow morning, Tunde will drive you to meet that crazy woman, Titi. You will resign from your position immediately, and you will have nothing further to do with her henceforth. You can keep your store, I'll let you do that much, but you are to have nothing to do with that Association again. Maybe now you will focus on being a real wife and mother. You will not go behind my back again, do you understand? If you disrespect me again, mark my words, you will be sorry," he said, looking down at her, his eyes ice cold despite the heat of the fire.

"I understand," Kehinde mumbled, her chest still heaving. She lay there in a wet heap, inhaling the smoke from the fire as he walked away with Kayode in his wake.

As Kehinde watched the rest of her journal turn to ashes, she realised that for the first time since she got married, Baba Tope had not called her his flower. And she couldn't feel less like a flower if she tried. She felt like broken wood. It was enough, she was done being a flower that could be trampled on, expected to sit prettily, smiling at everyone who watered her. She was strong, too strong to kneel here crying like a baby without a mother. Today would be the last day she would cower in fear in the face of injustice. Like wood, she could be mended, like wood, she could evolve, and like wood, she would last to find and fulfil her life's purpose. Baba Tope might not know it, but he could never break her spirit. She would make sure of that. She would be much more than a parlour wife. She had already shown she could do more, this was just the beginning, not the end. And as Kehinde watched the last of her journal dissipate, she vowed that from now on, she would put fear aside and put herself first.

Chapter Twenty

The next morning, Mr Tunde drove Kehinde as close as he could get to Madam Titi's stall at Ereko Market. Kehinde got out of the car and was hit by the familiar smell of blood and fish as she stepped into the enclave of stalls. She walked the rest of the way through the throng of shoppers buying their meat for Christmas, the dust clinging to her sandals as she moved through the crowd. Men and women went by carrying baskets and buckets, pointing at the cuts of meat on display. A butcher was slashing the leg of a cow as a portly-looking matron watched. Children of all ages ran in and out of the stalls, between the customers, some of them hitting their legs like they were swatting away flies. Madam Titi's stall was in the middle of the market, near the fishmonger's section, not too far from where Kehinde's parents' stall used to be.

She was sitting on a low stool, watching one of her daughters haggling with a customer. As soon as she saw Kehinde she started to wave.

"Ah, Kehinde! What a pleasant surprise. Báwo?" Madam Titi said, rising to her feet. She had her hair covered as usual in a white shawl, long enough to cover her shoulders. The shawl glinted against the green and yellow iro and buba she was wearing, resplendent against the bodies of fish around her.

"Good morning, Ma. Please can we speak?"

Madam Titi took in Kehinde's swollen lip, and after a quick word to her daughter, she stepped out of the stall and held Kehinde's arm. "We have space at the back, let's go there."

Kehinde followed Madam Titi round the back of her stall, past a line of other traders to the back of the market where there was an open, shared compound for the traders to rest. The floor of the compound was made of concrete, with three wooden benches arranged around the middle. Buckets and sacks belonging to the traders were scattered across the floor, and even here the smell of blood hung heavy in the air. Madam Titi pointed to the bench in the far-right corner beside a clothing line.

Kehinde followed her, slowing down as Madam Titi limped towards the bench. She winced as she lowered herself down and tapped on the seat beside her for Kehinde to sit.

"So, tell me. What brings you here? You hardly ever come to my stall so I know this must be serious," she said, looking at Kehinde intently. Kehinde felt the heat rise to her face – she never came here because it reminded her too much of her father.

"Ma … my husband says I can't work with you anymore. He doesn't approve," Kehinde said, feeling a lump rise in her throat. She felt the lump more than she felt the pain in her mouth, her cheek, and her stomach. The lump had been there since the night before – it had stopped her from speaking to Ayo when she was brought back into the house, it had prevented her from eating breakfast, and now it threatened to choke her as she looked into Madam Titi's warm eyes.

"What changed his mind?" Madam Titi looked more concerned than surprised.

"He never knew, and he only just found out yesterday. He would like me to stop my work with you ... immediately," Kehinde said, trying not to think about the anger and disappointment in his eyes as he threw the match on her journal. Madam Titi continued to look at her bruised lip, saying nothing. A gentle breeze blew round the circular compound, rustling a pair of trousers that hung on the other bench like the legs of an invisible man.

"I never told you about the day my mother died," Madam Titi suddenly said after a moment. "I was about your age, and although I had never been to school, I already knew how to survive in Lagos. I thought that if I could work hard, I could work my way to the top. I kept to myself, always wanting to go my own way. My mother had been sick for a few months by this time, she was coughing up blood, you see. Now that I think about it, she probably had tuberculosis, but we didn't know, and we couldn't afford to call a doctor. As she lay on her mat the day she died, she said to me "You must surround yourself with the best people, no man or woman is an island.". I didn't understand it then, but as the years have gone by, it is the mantra I follow." She paused to look at Kehinde, placing a hand on her cheek.

"You're the best secretary the LMWA has ever had. It will be difficult to replace you. I wish there was a way to change your husband's mind, but I know the kind of man he is. Men like him will never understand why women need to have their own voice. I wish you all the best, Kehinde, and if you ever change your mind, you know where to find me. You will always be welcome on my team of women," she said with a sad smile.

"Ma, I never said I would be leaving," Kehinde said, reaching out and grabbing Madam Titi's hand. "I would love to keep working for you … but my husband can't know. He can never find out this time. And I think I know how."

Madam Titi's eyebrows shot up so much they almost disappeared under the shawl on her head.

"Ma … the women still need me. To help with their letters, their price-setting, all the things I was doing, I can continue to do," Kehinde said, ignoring the remnants of fear in her chest that had refused to completely disappear.

"But your husband—"

"We will do things differently this time. I'll still be at my store, selling snacks. So, instead of them coming to meet me at the office, they can come to my store, and I will help them there. Who would know the difference?" Kehinde said. This way, if anyone came snooping, they would find her exactly where she was supposed to be.

"I have friends who can help deliver documents to you, without me having to come myself," Kehinde continued. "I want to keep working with you Ma, please, let's at least try this way."

Madam Titi sat back and exhaled.

"My my, Kehinde, I wouldn't want to incur the wrath of Gboyega Ogunjobi."

She held out her hand when Kehinde looked like she was about to protest. "But, like I said, you're the best secretary I've ever had, and I think your plan is at least worth trying," Madam Titi said, smiling so hard that the crow's feet around her eyes lifted in a beautiful pattern.

Kehinde let out a squeal and hugged Madam Titi. "Thank you, Ma."

"No, thank you for your bravery. Not many women would

do what you're doing, and the truth is the LMWA needs you now more than ever. Now, let me get back to my stall, and we'll start our new arrangement after Christmas."

Kehinde nodded, still tasting a hint of anxiety beneath the immense exhilaration bubbling within her. She stood and helped Madam Titi up, hugging her again. She could hardly believe they were now on hugging terms, but she could also hardly believe that she was ignoring Baba Tope. This time, she would make sure he never found out. He had taken away her freedom once, and she wouldn't let it happen again.

Mr Tunde had left her at Ereko Market under the guise that she would go to her store alone to pick up a few things and then walk home. She went to her store, and she did pick up a few things, but instead of walking home, she turned on the corner of Lewis Street. Kehinde knew Ama and Onyi had already gone to Enugu earlier that morning, but she needed to ask Emeka if he would be the courier of her documents to Madam Titi. And she knew he would say yes, but she just needed to see him, a friendly face, someone who believed in her and could reassure her that she was doing the right thing.

The landlady let her in without hesitating. She knew Kehinde's face and if she was shocked to see her, she said nothing. She stopped at the door of apartment nine and knocked. The door opened almost immediately.

"Kehinde?" Emeka looked pleasantly surprised even though he was wearing a vest and shorts, and clearly not expecting any visitors. A plate with half a loaf of bread sat beside a newspaper and coffee mug on the dining table, and as Emeka closed the door behind them, Kehinde longed for one of the many happy breakfasts she had had here.

"You know Ama and Onyi aren't around?" he asked, as he stepped aside to let her into the flat.

"I wanted to see you," Kehinde said, her voice catching, suddenly overwhelmed by his kind face.

"Is everything okay?" Emeka asked. "Oh God, Kehinde, your lip is swollen? What happened?"

The worry in his tone was the final straw that broke her resolve as she walked into the flat and sunk down on the sofa. From where she was sitting, she could see the curls of his chest hair above the neckline of his vest as he sank down beside her.

"My husband found out about the LMWA last night," she said.

Emeka's face hardened as his gaze moved from her lip to her eyes. "He hit you?"

Kehinde nodded as a tear escaped her eye. She could no longer keep her feelings in check; she had to let the pain and humiliation of what he had done to her out before it consumed her.

"That bastard!" he said, shaking his head. "Kehinde, I'm so sorry," he said, placing a hand on her cheek, his gaze still on the part of her bottom lip that was swollen.

"It's my fault, I wasn't careful enough,' Kehinde said, shivering at his touch. She thought of Ayo's bruised face and all the times she had warned her and felt another tear trickle down her face.

"This could never be your fault, Kehinde. Nothing you could have done would have deserved this," Emeka said, looking at her with the warm brown eyes that Kehinde had thought of so many times. "I'm so sorry this happened to you," he continued. "You can't let him get away with this. Have you gone to the police?"

"To tell them that Gboyega Ogunjobi hit his wife? They would ask me what I did and simply say sorry," Kehinde said, laughing despite the tears on her face.

"Gosh, I feel so helpless. Can I get you something? Ice?" Emeka said, shifting like he was about to stand up.

Kehinde held his hands to stop him from moving.

"I'm not quitting. I just told Madam Titi that I'll still work with her."

"But Kehinde—"

"I'll be more careful this time. I can still do everything I do for the LMWA, but from my store instead. I'll just need your help with deliveries to Madam Titi and back. I hope that's okay?" Kehinde was suddenly nervous. She hadn't considered that he might not want to be involved in this and she didn't want to ask Ama. It would be more obvious if Baba Tope decided to investigate if Ama was the one making frequent trips to Madam Titi. Emeka's job as a journalist was the perfect cover.

His gaze softened as he listened to her. "Of course I'll help you, Kehinde. That goes without saying. But are you sure? What if your husband finds out?"

"He won't find out; I'll make sure of it. This is much bigger than me, Emeka. I didn't take the job at the *West African Pilot*, and I won't let him take this from me too," Kehinde said, exhaling as she held on tighter to his hand.

Emeka paused, and looked out of the window, his jaw ticking. Kehinde watched his profile, overcome with the need to place her hand on his cheek, the way he had just done for her. She noticed that his glasses were on the writing desk beside a sheet of papers. Without his glasses on, his profile looked vulnerable, softer almost, like it was missing a shield. Kehinde felt the lump in her throat reappearing with another tighter feeling in the pit of her stomach.

"Kehinde, you're one of the bravest, smartest people I know. Please, don't let this ... your husband, make you think he can take that away from you…" he said, his voice trailing off as he looked at her again. "Kehinde, you have no idea how special you are," he said, looking down at her. The brown of his eyes turned to a liquid tan that matched the feeling coursing through her.

Kehinde was sitting so close to him, so near that if she lifted her hand it would land on his face. The air around them suddenly felt still, like the clock at the centre of the earth had stopped and the entire universe was waiting for something to happen. Seconds passed as his gaze dropped again on the swollen part of her lip. And then he bent his head down as she lifted her chin.

As their lips met Kehinde felt her body contract and expand at once. His mouth tasted like a glass of water, a cooling balm for her lip. His hands felt strong as they met her waist and skimmed the curve in the small of her back. She kissed him back, surprising herself when her tongue pushed against his, sighing as he sought her out in response. His beard tickled her cheek, and it sent sparks flying all over her like a firework display.

Kehinde felt like she was swimming in the lake after a hot day, her body submerged but light, relaxed but taut. His body was everything she had not allowed herself to imagine and more, and this time, she let herself give into the pleasure of him.

Emeka's hands moved upwards, skimming every inch of her as if questioning, pausing as he waited for confirmation. She heard the voice of reason tell her to stop and for once, she switched it off completely, acknowledging that there was a part of her, many parts that had longed for this moment. Her body moved closer to his, inhaling the scent of the shea butter and coconut oil on his skin, her movements quicker than the signals from her brain as she hummed and throbbed in response to his touch. She helped him as he lifted his vest, impatiently unzipping the back of her dress. Her hands fumbled at the waistline of his shorts breaking away from her lips briefly as he did so. His lips met hers again, hungrily, his hands continuing to squeeze gently, lovingly. He broke away, looking at Kehinde, seeing his desire matched in her eyes.

"Kehinde…?" he asked, uncertainty flitting across his face as his lips parted.

Kehinde met his eyes full on before she held the back of his neck, pulling him closer and meeting his lips in full acquiescence of her mind, body and soul. He stopped kissing her, pausing to pull her down to the raffia mat beneath them. Like dancers in a choreography, they moved in tandem as Emeka lowered himself, Kehinde bending her knees as he gently pulled away her slip and the last of her underwear. For a fleeting second, she felt self-conscious. Baba Tope was the only man she had been intimate with. But this was different, this was Emeka, the man she had come to trust so much that all her pain, anxiety and fear melted away beneath his hands. The hands she had imagined on her skin so many times that being here with him felt almost nostalgic.

He started to kiss her gently, on her knees and on her thighs until she started moaning softly. Her voice got louder as he continued his journey up, his lips tenderly kissing her at the centre of her very being. Kehinde felt a rumble she had never felt before, slowly building like water coming to a boil. When she could take no more, Kehinde pulled him up, needing him with an urgency she was mentally at a loss to explain to herself. This was a new sensation. She felt like she would explode, like there was a bomb waiting to go off inside her and Emeka was her only chance of survival. She ignored the roaring sound in her head. She needed him in a way that felt so raw it was primal, too strong to fight. She refused to think, each thought of her parents, Taiwo, the LMWA, Baba Tope, Ayo, what anyone would think, what the consequences would be, she pushed them all away. For once, she would choose her heart over mind, she would choose pleasure over pain and give in to her desire. As he entered her, she felt like she had been transported to another world, a place she had heard of but never thought existed. Rocking softly together, their cries blended in harmony as the bomb within Kehinde was released, shaking her body to its very core, until she felt a freedom within her that no imagination could have conjured.

PART III
October 1942–June 1943

Every passing day brings Nigerians closer to the darkness the citizens of the British Empire face in this war.

*West African Pilot**

* Korieh, C. J. 2020. *Nigeria and World War II: Colonialism, Empire, and Global Conflict.* Chapter 1. New York: Cambridge University Press

Chapter Twenty-One

CENTRAL LAGOS

October 1942

Kehinde and Ayo huddled closer together as the woman ahead of them in the queue started to cry, her sobs ringing out against the rain falling around them. The sun had barely come up, but the market already hung heavy with the smell of tightly packed bodies and wet earth.

"I left my children at home, they'll be looking for me," the sobbing woman said to no one. Kehinde tried not to catch her eye. It had been a difficult morning already, with her and Ayo having to walk an extra mile to Obalende in the hope that they would find more food there. The distant rumble of thunder in the air confirmed Kehinde's fears that the rain would get heavier. The ration queue stretched round Obalende market, and from what Kehinde could see, she and Ayo had at least fifty men and women ahead of them.

"How can they treat us like this? I've been waiting here for one hour now. Do they expect us to just stand in the rain? We're not animals," the woman wailed.

Food in Lagos was scarce, and the ration queues were getting longer. Although the LMWA had reached a partial success, so only women earning over £200 annually would have to pay income tax, Captain AP Pullen had introduced a price control scheme shortly after that. In the last eighteen months, the market traders had been made to sell food at fixed prices, set by the colonial government in a bid to curb the inflation driven by a war that seemed to have no end. To make matters worse, food and raw materials were being managed to ensure adequate supplies were sent to England for the troops across the Empire. Kehinde and Ama had watched a man get arrested across the road two days ago for stealing rice.

The wailing woman turned, and with a start Kehinde recognised Sola, the girl from her eighteenth birthday party who'd had Taiwo's arm wrapped around her all night. Gone was her bouncy hair, and in its place, she had tight cornrows that pulled the skin of her forehead, lifting her eyebrows and giving her face a startled expression. Kehinde looked away quickly before she could recognise her as well.

Suddenly, a man dressed in uniform with one arm in a sling appeared at the side of the distribution kiosk. From where Kehinde was standing she could see that his eyes were a pale grey and his lips were pressed together as he made his way to the front of the queue.

"No meat today! No garri either. Come back again tomorrow morning," he shouted.

A cry went up across the queue.

"What will my children eat today oh, what will I give them!" Sola cried. Other voices shouted above the crowd.

"Come on, let's get back home quickly, before it gets rowdy," Ayo said beside Kehinde.

Some people continued to wait, peering at the kiosk like it

would suddenly open if they looked hard enough. A small group was forming around the desolate Sola, some of them offering words of advice.

"Má ṣùkùn, my cousin told me they're bringing meat tomorrow."

"I know somewhere else you can get the meat, you'll have to pay though," said a man dressed in a white kaftan that looked like he had just travelled down from the north.

That last comment piqued Kehinde's curiosity, but Ayo was already hurrying away from the crowd, towards Broad Street, where they would walk home through the rain and mud. Ama had told Kehinde that there were black-market traders, bold ones, that came to sell their wares at night in secret locations. They sold meat, milk, garri, vegetable oil and sugar, at prices they set themselves. Kehinde had never seen them herself but today it seemed like the man in the white kaftan could be one of them.

The fine for buying or selling on the black market was a hefty sum of £10, money that Kehinde was not willing to part with. Although her store's location put her in close proximity to the workers and labourers going to work every day, hardly anyone was buying street food. Telegrams with news of lost men were arriving daily, news of bombing from Dahomey were in the newspaper and everyone was afraid that Lagos would be the next target. With the tension in the air, no one lingered on the streets or bought anything unnecessary. Besides, Kehinde's meagre rations meant that she had hardly any ingredients to cook her snacks with, and most of the work she did for the LMWA now was for free.

"We'll have to make beans for dinner again then. I hope they'll have meat tomorrow," Ayo sighed.

Kehinde knew that she was worried about giving Baba

Tope beans for the third night in a row, but she didn't care. She was too excited about her plans that afternoon with the man who actually cared about her, to worry about whether Baba Tope had meat to eat.

It was Wednesday, and on Wednesdays Emeka finished work at 1pm, giving them four undisturbed hours of bliss before Kehinde had to go home. They still saw each other in the mornings when they had breakfast with Ama, and they spent Emeka's lunch hour together on the days he could get away, but Wednesdays were special. On Wednesdays Emeka had the apartment to himself, and those afternoons were the highlight of Kehinde's life; she thought about him all day, every day, and sometimes the butterflies in her stomach kept her up all night.

"You're smiling to yourself again," Ayo said as they turned the corner on Broad Street.

"Was I really?"

"Strange, given that we're walking back in the foulest weather after not getting any food. Or is there something you know that I don't?"

"Not at all, except maybe the thought of Mama Tope's face at dinner yesterday."

"Ah, yes, she was a sight. Although I do feel bad for poor Tope."

Their husband had announced yesterday that Tope was to be betrothed to Mr Babajide. Tope had just turned nineteen, and Mr Babajide had recently celebrated his fiftieth birthday. The alliance was a business deal rather than a union of love. Mr Babajide's cocoa and cassava farms in Ondo state were doing much better than Baba Tope's warehouses due to the global increase in demand for cocoa and cassava exports, but he needed more space in Lagos to store his goods. Baba Tope welcomed the additional income but given the competition from other warehouses in Lagos he had thrown in an additional perk, his teenage daughter, ripe for the plucking.

"I feel sorry for her too," Kehinde said, thinking about the irony of the situation they both now found themselves in, and feeling even sadder that Tope's dreams of going to England would now never come true. She had a wicked mother, but she was a sweet girl and didn't deserve this.

"Mr Babajide is a horrible man. He's never been married but he's a known womaniser. He groped me one day when he was visiting the house, Baba Tope didn't know and of course I didn't tell him. What good would that have done? But I've kept my distance since," Ayo said, angling the umbrella she was carrying higher as the rain got heavier.

"So that's why you don't like him! I had noticed how upset you looked whenever he came over," Kehinde said, moving closer to Ayo. They both quickened their pace as they walked the last stretch of the path to their street.

"Yes, and I've told Adenike and Ashabi to stay away from him as well. Poor Tope will have to live with him, and I know he has no intentions of changing his ways! Anyway, I wish her all the best."

Mama Tope's mouth had hung open at the news at dinner, the unchewed eba glistening like a grey mountain, as she heard about her daughter's betrothal for the first time with the rest of the family. Kehinde felt sorry for Tope, but she found it hard to muster any sympathy for Mama Tope. It had been two years since the protests, but she would never forgive or forget her hand in her discovery.

Kehinde said nothing, feeling bad for Tope but thinking again of Emeka. After her father died and she was hastily married, all her hopes of finding a love like this had been washed away, but now she felt giddy with joy and full of expectation. If she had not got married to Baba Tope and got the store beside Ama's, she would never have met Emeka. Their affair was hardly ideal, and she wished they could be openly together, but it was the only thing that brought her real joy. Well, that and her work for the LMWA.

They stamped their feet on the foot mat as they reached their front door, the mud falling off from their sandals like ants. The rains had been relentless this year; it was almost as if the heavens were mourning the state of the world. The war was no longer just a 'European war' now that the Allied nations were involved, and no nation was unaffected. Recently, Taiwo's letters had taken forever to arrive, and when they did, a lot of his words were blacked out. Some letters were so heavily edited that they were hardly coherent. She still had not written to him. She had tried, but it felt awkward whenever she picked up her pen. It wasn't that she hadn't forgiven him, but she was unused to making up with him in letters and she would much rather just wait until he came home, and she told her mother as much. It had been almost three years since she last saw him, and as much as she missed him, she took solace in the thought that Taiwo was somewhere on this earth, alive and well enough to write to their mother.

"I have to come back and mop this place. By the time the children go to school and come back there'll be mud everywhere," Ayo said as she placed the battered umbrella in its caddy by the door.

Kehinde and Ayo went into the empty kitchen. Atinuke had left months ago, joining the hordes of women who were having to return to the farms as fewer men came home from the war, and more had to join up to replace them. Her father's only two sons were away fighting, so she had joined him on his cattle farm in Ibadan to keep his business running.

Baba Tope didn't come down for breakfast, something else that had been happening with increasing frequency, and that meant that the plates were cleared away quickly and the children out of the door in no time. Kehinde spent the morning at her store, selling food to her handful of regulars and helping Iya Jola with writing a new price list for her convenience store. As soon as it was noon, Kehinde locked up and went to Fine Leather.

"I wanted to show you two leather samples that just arrived but I know what you're like in the afternoons," Ama said with a wink when Kehinde appeared in her office.

"I promise I'll look at them when I'm back!" Kehinde had dropped the keys on Ama's desk and was already on her way out of the door.

"Oh, don't rush back on account of me. I wouldn't want to upset my brother!"

Kehinde laughed despite herself, feeling light as she half ran up the street. She let herself into the flat using the key Emeka had cut for her and started to fry the akara batter she had kept for lunch. Her love for him had taken her completely by surprise, like stumbling across a spring in a desert. After everything she had been through, real love was not something she had imagined would be hers. Growing up, she had never had a boyfriend, or serious relationship. Taiwo had had a string of flings, but she had never felt drawn to another person romantically, and had always wondered if she ever would. One of her earliest memories was sitting on the floor of Aunty Laide's parlour, listening to her and Aunty Bimpe talk about how her parents had been madly in love for as long as they had known them. Her mother always insisted that it was a boring love story, but Kehinde thought there was so much beauty in the simplicity of it all. She liked to imagine her father would have loved Emeka if things were different, if she had brought him home as a prospect, if Baba Tope didn't exist. He would have liked his straightforward manner, the way he always spoke his mind, his sense of humour and his wit, the way he saw art and beauty in everything. She knew they would have got on well, and her mother would have been charmed by him. But her mother would never meet him. If their love was to continue, Emeka had to remain a secret.

She often thought of Emeka as before and after. Before, when he was Ama's brother and she couldn't, wouldn't, acknowledge her growing feelings for him, and after, in their now, when he was her whole world. Before, he liked akara, and now he loved akara that had okra in it, but not as much as the ones with prawns. She also knew that he looked up to his father but had been scared of him growing up because he had a cane he disciplined his children with – never Ama though; much like her and Taiwo, Ama was her father's favourite. He thought his mother was a sweetheart and laughed about how much she loved shoes and bags. Now, Kehinde knew about the birthmark on his upper thigh, the one that was shaped like a pear. Now, she knew that the light brown of his eyes had layers, shades of golden hues that looked almost green in the sun. And most of all, she knew that he loved her, more than anyone else ever would.

She heard a key turn in the door and felt Emeka in the room before she turned to see him. She stayed facing the window, sighing as she felt his arms come round her.

"Today felt long, I could hardly wait to get away. Mmm, the akara smells heavenly," he murmured into her neck. "I've been dreaming of akara all day, even the clouds started to look like akara."

Giggling, Kehinde turned to kiss him and the akara was soon forgotten. Later, they were lying in bed, the afternoon sun making golden parallel lines on their intertwined bodies. Emeka's light-skinned thigh beside her dark one felt entirely natural, where Baba Tope's thigh had always seemed like an intruder invading her safe space. Emeka propped his head up on one elbow.

"You seem more tired than usual today."

"Ayo and I still couldn't buy any meat earlier."

"If someone had told me three years ago that things would be this bad, I would have bet money on them being wrong. Ugo is covering a story about the women in Abeokuta fighting over garri and it reads like fiction. Apparently, some of them even got hurt."

"It felt like a fight would break out this morning," Kehinde said, remembering the haunting sound of Sola's wails.

"Did Iya Jola tell you that she had to choose between paying a fine of £5 or spending a month in jail?"

"She did, poor woman, all because she sold sugar above the government's price. What's she supposed to do, having to fend for her daughter and husband now. It's terrible." Kehinde fell silent as she thought about how tired Iya Jola had looked in her store that morning. Madam Titi continued to meet with the colonial government, with the latest struggle being over the tightly controlled prices in the market.

"Have you seen this?" he said, hesitating before he turned over the side of the bed to pull a newspaper from his satchel, the *Daily Times* edition for that day. "EIGHT PROMISING PILOTS FROM ACROSS THE EMPIRE JOIN CAPTAIN MACKENZIE IN LONDON", the headline read. Kehinde's felt instantly nauseous as she squinted at the grainy, black and white picture. There he was in his uniform, taller than the other seven, standing next to the English man she assumed was Captain Mackenzie.

"Oh God."

"I thought it was him, he looks exactly the same as that picture of the two of you from your eighteenth birthday," Emeka said, concern etched into the lines on his forehead.

"He didn't mention this in his last letter to my mother," Kehinde sat up, feeling like her limbs had turned to ogi. What was Taiwo doing in that picture? Surely he was supposed to be in Burma?

"I doubt he had much notice himself. It might be for a special operation that he couldn't write about." Emeka sat next to her, crossing one leg through both of hers. "Keks, I think it's time you wrote to him," he said softly.

"We've spoken about this already. I'm waiting to see him," Kehinde said, ignoring the rising panic in her chest.

"Even now?"

"I hardly have an address to send letters to him, now do I?"

"Your mum will be given a forwarding address for him soon, I'm sure."

"Well, I'll wait for that," she snapped, feeling disjointed, the way she always did now when she spoke about Taiwo. Suddenly the hair on Emeka's legs felt like thorns against her skin.

"All I'm saying is—"

"You and Ama keep telling me to write to him and I keep telling you I'll speak to him when I see him!"

"Don't take it out on me, Keks."

"I think I'm going to leave now." Kehinde was already sitting up, pulling on her dress.

"You do this every time I bring him up."

"Well, maybe you should stop bringing him up."

"I can see how much this is hurting you!"

"Stop nagging me about it, I'm old enough to make up my own mind."

"Fine, I'll stop. But can't you stay a bit longer?" he said, his hand outstretched towards her.

Kehinde looked at his hand and felt the fight go out of her. She was trapped in a cage but he didn't have the key, and she didn't want to keep lashing out at him for trying to set her free. She was her own captor here, and she knew it was ridiculous, but she couldn't seem to get past the mental barrier that told her she could only apologise to Taiwo in person. Besides, he hadn't written to her either! At least if she was going to be the bigger person let it be on her own terms. But now he was supposedly in London and Burma had been far enough. Who would ever have thought that the gap between them could feel wider than the Atlantic Ocean? What if it took forever for him to come back home? Maybe the war would end, and he would come home for good finally? She held on to that thought as she let Emeka take her in his arms again.

Chapter Twenty-Two

When Kehinde got home that evening, she was about to go upstairs when she noticed that the door of the den was closed. A muffled sob escaped from the room as Kehinde opened the door to see Tope, sitting behind the sofa, her shoulders moving up and down as she tried to be quiet.

"Tope, what happened?" Kehinde said, rushing to sit beside her. Tope was still in her school uniform, twisting the skirt in her hands until the hem looked like a long green rope. She looked at Kehinde as another sob escaped her mouth.

"My father just told me that I won't be completing the school year. Mr Babajide wants to get married right away, and when I asked if I could finish school even after we got married, my father laughed! Imagine, he laughed in my face!"

Kehinde knew exactly what that felt like. It was like being told by her father that only Taiwo would be completing their final year of secondary school all over again.

"Did he say anything else?" Kehinde asked, as she put a hand round Tope's shoulder.

"He said I'm lucky to have even got to the final year of

school! What happened to all his plans to send me to England? When I asked Mummy, she didn't say anything, she was too angry to speak." Tope dissolved into a fresh set of tears.

"Oh, Tope, I'm so sorry," Kehinde said, feeling genuinely sorry for her, and surprisingly for Mama Tope, who she knew was also helpless. Tope had really been looking forward to the accounting course she was supposed to be doing at a college in London, but that was no longer to be. Tope had joined Kehinde, her mother and the hosts of women who would soon find out that their dreams coming true was a privilege, not a given.

"I'm so sorry," Kehinde said again, holding Tope close.

"My mother said you would be happy," Tope said, looking at Kehinde under hooded eyelids. "She said I should stay away from you, that you don't wish me well."

Kehinde let out a long sigh. "Tope, I wish you nothing but the best, and I wish your mother knew that."

"I told her. You've been so kind to me, and I'll always remember that," Tope said. They heard the boys running down the stairs. "I'd better go wash my face. It will be time for dinner soon."

"Yes, Ayo is probably wondering where we are," Kehinde said, standing then extending a hand to pull Tope up. With Atinuke gone, all the children now had chores around the house and Tope was always in the kitchen at dinner time. Besides, with her impending marriage, Ayo and Kehinde were doing everything they could to at least prepare her to satisfy her husband's appetite, if nothing else.

As they stood together, cutting a small tuber of yam while Ayo fried the oil for the stew, Kehinde felt her outrage at life bubbling up again. Every day, Kehinde saw women who stood by helpless while decisions were made for them, powerless to stop the instigators. At least she had taken back some control, but she was still here, married to Baba Tope while she had to sneak around with the love of her life. Where did it all end?

"You both look like you heard the war will continue for ten more years," Ayo said beside her as she arranged the dinner tray.

"God forbid," Kehinde muttered. Tope remained silent, still looking like she would burst into tears at any moment. Ayo looked at Kehinde, her eyebrows raised in a question. *I'll explain later*, she mouthed over Tope's bowed head.

At dinner, Tope continued to be morose. If her father noticed, he either didn't care or chose not to show it.

"This yam has no salt," he said, pushing his plate away.

"There's hardly any salt to buy in the market, Baba Tope," Ayo said, placing a hand on his to placate him. It worked, but the target of his angst was redirected.

"Kehinde, when you boil yam, you leave it for too long. I always know it was you that made it whenever I eat such soft yam. You're cooking food for adults, not babies, but then again, you wouldn't know since you haven't had to cook for babies yet," he said, looking past Ayo to where Kehinde sat.

The yam had, in fact, been made by Tope, but there was no point saying so; he would have found something else to criticise. This was something he did often now, and she could sense it was because she had turned out to be a disappointment. He would make comments about Kehinde's appearance, complain about the food if he knew she had made it, say she was too quiet or was talking too much. Kehinde knew he was still paying for the Babalawo's monthly sacrifice of goat after fruitless goat – he'd mentioned them the last time he asked Kehinde if she was finally with child.

"Tell your mother I would like to pay her a visit, this coming week or maybe the next one," he said.

Kehinde fell silent, ignoring Ayo's pointed look. She hadn't told Ayo she was still working with Madam Titi, more for Ayo's own protection, than for a lack of trust. She never wanted to put Ayo in a position of danger again. But Ayo worried that Kehinde wasn't making more of an effort to stay in Baba Tope's good books. And they all knew he never visited her mother to make small talk. The only other time he had visited was after he discovered Kehinde's work with the LMWA, and it was so that he could report her. It had worked – Kehinde's mother's sobbing and begging on her behalf had shown Kehinde exactly how much her mother had come to depend on Baba Tope, and she felt sick at the thought of what her father would have said. She and her selfishness alone would be to blame if her mother was left to starve.

Across from her, Tope looked into her plate of yam like she was searching for an escape door, and Mama Tope beside her looked glum, not even remembering to be triumphant in the face of Kehinde's humiliation. The children carried on eating, now used to the tension in the air. The dynamics of their dinner table had changed – what was once a merry gathering was now a silent rite of passage to bedtime, and Kehinde knew that Baba Tope blamed her.

"I'm going to bed early. Ayo, come to my room tonight," he said, the legs of his chair scraping the floor as he stood to leave the table.

"I wish you would try harder with him," Ayo said to Kehinde, later, when they were washing up.

"I haven't done anything to offend him," Kehinde said. All she had done was to try to be more than a parlour wife, to try to contribute to the changes around her, to have a voice, and Baba Tope would not even allow her that.

"You're so stubborn, Kehinde. I wish you would just listen to me."

"I have been listening to you."

"No, you haven't. He's never been able to forgive you since the protests, and you don't help by talking back to him. Can't you even just pretend to look happy?"

"I'm not happy though."

"No one is happy, Kehinde! We're in the middle of a war for God's sake!" The foam on Ayo's hands seemed to froth with her words. "I've been thinking, maybe we should go to see Doctor Gbagi together tomorrow morning. If you were pregnant, I think Baba Tope would be nicer to you."

Doctor Gbagi was the family doctor and had trained in King's College London before coming back to Lagos to open his clinic – a narrow, green building visited by the Nigerian elite of Lagos. He had attended to both Mama Tope and Ayo during their pregnancies and childbirth, and Kehinde had been at his clinic once in the previous year with a worried Ayo when Ashabi had malaria. Ayo was still seeing him now as she continued in her quest to conceive a son.

"I'm not sure who's worse, Doctor Gbagi with his big English or the Babalawo with his fallen goats," Kehinde said.

"I'm being serious! I think you should come with me when I go to see him."

"I'm serious too. Baba Tope hardly wants me in his bed now. Most of my nights, like tonight, he asks for you instead," Kehinde said. Not that she was complaining. Now that Emeka had shown her what real passion was supposed to feel like, her rare nights with Baba Tope had become even more unbearable.

"He's a man, Kehinde. He wants you to apologise, beg him. Tell him you're sorry."

"But I'm not sorry."

"Kehinde! He wants to send you back to your mother's house!" Ayo said, throwing her foamy hands up in frustration. A door upstairs slammed, and they heard Ashabi's laugh followed by the sound of scurrying feet.

"He said so?"

"Not in as many words, but I know him, and I think he's considering it."

"Maybe that's what he wants to talk to my mother about," Kehinde mused.

"That's why we need to do something, and fast!"

Kehinde said nothing, drying a plate with a towel, her mind doing rotations with the movement of her hands. Being sent home would mean her freedom! She could be with Emeka, properly now! She could openly work with Madam Titi and the LMWA, and maybe even the *West African Pilot* if they would still have her. Her mother would burn with the shame of it all, but she would get over it, and Kehinde would find a way to earn enough to keep them fed and dry, they would survive somehow, even if she had to withdraw all her savings. Taiwo would come back from the war, and they would be a family again, even if her father wasn't here. She knew he would want her to be happy, and if he knew the kind of man Baba Tope really was, he would have welcomed her back home with open arms. She loved Ayo and had grown fond of Tope, Adenike and Ashabi, but she hardly needed to stay here to maintain a relationship with them. No, she didn't need to do anything at all, she would continue as she was in the hope that Baba Tope would send her packing. It suddenly all seemed so simple.

"I need to think about it."

"I know you well enough now to know what your silence means! You want to be sent home!" Ayo said to her, her mouth hanging open in shock at the realisation.

"I didn't say that."

"You're not denying it either."

"Fine, Ayo, I'll go to Doctor Gbagi's clinic with you tomorrow. We've both had a long day, and besides, you need to get ready for Baba Tope. I'm going upstairs to check on the girls," Kehinde said, putting the last plate away in the cupboard and moving towards the door before Ayo could say anything to stop her. She didn't want to worry Ayo, so she would say nothing for now, but as the thought of not having to stay in the Ogunjobi house took shape in her mind, the more she wanted to hold on to the hope it brought.

The next day, after a trip to Doctor Gbagi's office where she had been poked and prodded and blood was taken from her like she was a lab rat, Kehinde walked to her mother's house. She was surprised to see her already at the front door of her old home, looking bright in a pink bubu as she waved at Kehinde.

"Keke! Come quickly, I've had a letter from Taiwo!" she said, jumping up and down in the doorway like a child waiting to open presents on Christmas day. Kehinde hurried up the path and was barely in the house when her mother thrust the letter at her.

> *My Dearest Mother,*
> *I am pleased to tell you that I have been selected to join the*

Royal Air Force in London, along with seven other pilots across
the colonies. Captain Mackenzie has trained us specially for this
mission, and as I write to you, we are waiting for a flight to take
us to London from Burma. By the time you receive this, I will
already be out in the field. I cannot share further details as you
can imagine, but have no fear, any letters you write in the
meantime will be forwarded on to me at my new location. I will
write to you as soon as I can with my new address.

Please give my love to Kehinde.
Yours faithfully,
Your dear son

"Aunty Laide read it to me just before she left this
morning," her mother said, gripping the back of the armchair
she sat in. "Just imagine, Kehinde. Our Taiwo! Going off on a
special mission! Oh, how proud your father would have been."

Kehinde watched her mother, stopping herself from
reminding her that her father had not wanted him to enlist in
the first place. But her father could never have imagined the
scale of this war, the extent to which it was being felt across the
world and here in Lagos.

"God keep him safe for us," her mother said, her hands still
clasped in her lap.

Kehinde felt shame wash over her. She had lost her father,
she saw women who had lost brothers and husbands every
day and yet she kept making excuses about writing to Taiwo.
He was out there, getting on with his life and she suddenly
couldn't remember why she was so angry with him. Was it
because he had left her, or more because she was jealous of him
for being brave enough to do what he wanted most, something
she was slowly learning to do herself? Him leaving didn't
mean he had abandoned her. The things he had said to her had

been painful, but true and she was no longer the scared girl that couldn't stand up for herself. She wanted to be more like her brother, she realised, and she would not let her envy and hurt keep them apart any longer. Kehinde held on to the letter as she watched her mother put tea on the table, and she knew without a doubt that it was finally time for her to write to a letter to Taiwo.

Dear Tee,

Happy belated birthday! It feels so odd to be writing to you, I don't think I've ever written a letter to you actually. I miss you, and I'm so sorry it has taken me this long to write. The things I said to you were terrible and you really hurt my feelings, but this war has shown me that life is too short to spend any of it not talking to you.

A lot has happened since you've been gone, and I honestly can't write most of it in this letter, but you'll be as proud of me as I am of you. You were right. We could not have spent the rest of our lives waiting for Mummy and Daddy to tell us what to do and I'm so glad it took you a shorter time to realise that.

What's London like? Anything like it's described in A Tale of Two Cities? Probably not, as that book is so old. I can't wait to hear all about it.

I don't know what else to write even though I have so much to tell you, so hurry up and come home.

Love,

Keke

Chapter Twenty-Three

Kehinde woke up in a pool of sweat the next morning, panting and disoriented. Her dream had started with her father swimming towards her in the lake, but instead of legs, he had a large fin beneath his waist. He was mouthing something to her, his hands waving frantically in the water as the bubbles around them multiplied, blocking him from her view. She had swum towards him, kicking as fast as she could, only for him to disappear when she reached the swirl of bubbles. Kehinde had then been thrown out of the water by the bubbles onto the shore, where she had joined Ayo and Ama, huddled under a rock, hiding from the bombs shaped like green bottles that fell from the red sky above them. Taiwo ran past the three of them and he was shouting something to the plane dropping the green bottles. He didn't see her and when she screamed his name, he kept running further away until he became a speck of dust. A bottle was hurtling towards her when she woke up in the safety of her bed.

Sighing, she got up and grabbed her toilet bag as she made her way to the bathroom. She was exhausted and the day had just started. Her dreams were becoming more and more ridiculous, with her father and Taiwo as the recurring characters in each one. The other day she had dreamed that Uncle Ladipo was making a giant loaf of bread to be shared for all the soldiers of the Commonwealth, and she and Taiwo were looking for a knife in the Babalawo's forest that would be big enough to cut it. Her father had been the governor of Lagos in another dream, his voice announcing on the Rediffusion that the war was over and all the colonial administrators had returned to England. When she had told Ama about the loaf of bread dream, she had laughed so hard that Onyi had run into the back office to check if she was choking.

At least she had finally written the letter to Taiwo. She would post it on her way out before she had second thoughts. Putting the dream out of her mind, she focused on the motion of scrubbing herself in the bath. She had a busy day ahead. Ayo and Baba Tope were going to Ibadan to visit her mother for the day, a trip that Ayo had been dreading but was now necessary because she had received a letter from her mother's neighbour saying she was ill. Kehinde had promised Ayo that she would take Adenike and Ashabi out for the afternoon after school to give her one less thing to worry about.

The house was full of the usual morning cries and shouts – the boys fighting, Tope's voice interceding, Adenike and Ashabi's high-pitched squeals from behind Ayo's door. Kehinde jumped as Mama Tope suddenly came out of her room before Kehinde could make it down the stairs. She looked smaller than usual as she stood in the doorway, her indigo wrapper tied firmly across her chest. Her face was hard to read, her eyes appearing softer, but her mouth was set in its usual straight line.

"Ẹ káàárọ̀, Ma," Kehinde said, tightening her grip on the staircase railing.

"Káàárọ̀, Kehinde. Tope told me you ... have been speaking with her? I appreciate your, er, kindness."

"You're welcome," Kehinde replied, taken aback.

With a nod, Mama Tope stepped back into her room and closed the door behind her as quickly as she had appeared.

Mama Tope was such an enigma, Kehinde thought, as she descended the stairs. She could be so nasty, yet she had moments like this, usually where Tope or the boys were concerned, where she seemed caring, motherly almost. She was like an onion, tightly packed with so many layers, and Kehinde wondered if she would ever get to her core.

Tope and her brothers were already downstairs at the table when she got there. Tope was dishing out bowls of ogi, the dull brown colour triggering a wave of nausea in Kehinde's stomach as she sat beside Adenike and Ashabi. They heard footsteps descending the stairs and to Kehinde's surprise, both Baba Tope and Ayo appeared in the doorway of the dining hall, dressed in the same blue and white adire material, with a batik print of white leaves all over it.

"My family, good morning. Ayo and I will be going to Ibadan this morning," he said, squeezing Ayo's hand as she looked up at him with a small smile. Ashabi ran from her place at the table and grabbed her mother's legs.

"No, Mummy! Don't leave us!" she cried tearfully.

"Shhh, my baby. We spoke about this already. Your father and I will be back tonight. You'll be in school all day, it will be like nothing happened," Ayo soothed.

"But I want to come with you!"

"I have a treat planned for you, Asha," Kehinde said quickly. The little girl turned around to face her, her eyes bright with expectation. "I'll pick you and Adenike up from school myself, and then we can go for a little adventure," Kehinde said, smiling.

"Thank you, Aunty Kehinde!" Adenike squeaked beside her, as Ashabi jumped up and down.

"Ese, Kehinde. Come on girls, we'll drop you at school on our way," their husband said, smiling. Still beaming, he looked at Tope and her brothers. "Tope, my boys, I'll drive you in the car tomorrow," he continued. The boys squealed in excitement, forgetting the mess of ogi in front of them as they danced in their seats.

Mama Tope had also come down and had taken a seat beside Tope, who as usual was reticent as the activity around her swelled. Poor girl, Kehinde thought. She knew how it felt to be a bride in waiting during the days leading up to a wedding you were hoping would be cancelled.

After saying goodbye to Ayo and Baba Tope, and parting ways with Tope and the boys, Kehinde walked to the market. It was a cool morning, and because of the heavy rain the day before, the trees lining their street looked greener. Everything looked brighter, and it was difficult to imagine that there was any fighting going on in the world as she nodded at other pedestrians walking to their destinations.

At the post office, she wondered how Taiwo was doing in London. The green bottles falling from the sky in her dream suddenly appeared in her mind's eye. Was her father trying to send her a message about her brother? She focused on the fact that she had finally written to him! She was elated, and the sense of relief that came when she handed over the stamped letter to the mailroom attendant made her want to do a dance. She couldn't wait to see him. Surely this war must be ending soon, now that the allies were involved? Or at least Taiwo would be granted leave shortly?

Optimistic, she walked the rest of the way to Fine Leather. Onyi greeted her from behind a copy of the *West African Pilot*, the title of the cover page reading in bold font "WEST AFRICANS ARE READY TO LAY DOWN THEIR LIVES FOR SURVIVAL TO MAKE LIFE WORTH LIVING FOR OUR DEAR ONES AT HOME AND ABROAD".

Swallowing the lump in her throat at the thought of Taiwo being one of those West Africans, she opened the door of the back office to Ama and Emeka both sitting at the desk, in the middle of a conversation, with two mugs of tea in front of them. They both looked up as the door swung open.

"You're just in time. I was telling Emeka that I need to start my stock count. The factory supervisor is already here from Enugu," Ama said, standing up from her desk.

"And I seem to have forgotten the bag he's taking back home for Mummy," Emeka said sheepishly.

"Ugh! He's only here for a few hours this morning! I can't wait till you're done with work!" Ama cried, throwing her hands in the air.

"I'll go back for it now!"

"I'll come with you, that way you won't need to head back in this direction before you go to the office. I can bring it back for you, Ama," Kehinde said.

Ama raised her eyebrows till they looked like they would disappear into her hairline. "You're going to our flat first thing in the *morning*?"

"To stretch my legs! And to help *you*!" Kehinde said, blushing.

"You just walked here from your house so your legs must be fine, but sure," Ama said with a grin.

Kehinde rolled her eyes and Emeka laughed as they stepped out into the street. He reached out to hold her hand, then dropped it immediately, both feeling self-conscious in the daylight. At least Mr Tunde was away, driving Baba Tope and Ayo to Ibadan, and Kayode was off God knew where. She felt as free as a bird.

"Don't mind Ama. I'm glad you decided to come," Emeka said, his hand still brushing against hers as they crossed the road to make a right onto Simpson Street.

"I'm glad too," Kehinde said shyly. Emeka was so forthright with his emotions, in a way Kehinde had never been, and was still learning to be.

They walked the rest of the short distance to Emeka and Ama's apartment. Simpson Street was so close to Lewis Street that it made it easy to slip here during the day, and although it also had a few stores, it was relatively quiet. Two gentlemen wearing bowler hats greeted Emeka as they got to the door of the apartment building, one of them giving Kehinde a second look as they left.

"You know, they asked me about you the other day," said Emeka, holding her hand firmly now that they were in the safety of the building as he led her up the stairs.

"Who are they?"

"Two brothers that live on the ground floor. They've seen you here a few times, thought you were another cousin from Enugu. One of them asked if they could take you to the fundraising dance at Glover Memorial Hall on Friday. I had to tell them that you're married, unfortunately," Emeka said, winking as they got to his floor. He opened the door of the apartment and stood aside for Kehinde as she stepped in.

Kehinde said nothing. She didn't like to be reminded that she was married when she was with Emeka, or when she thought about him, and definitely not when she was standing so close to him, alone in his flat. She found it difficult to concentrate in church lately – how could she, being the sinner that she was?

"Hey, I was joking," Emeka said, placing a hand on her cheek.

"Where's the bag?" Kehinde said, not meeting his eyes. He looked at her for a moment, then walked into Ama and Onyi's room, returning shortly after with a small, tan leather bag. He extended it to her and held her hand when she tried to grab the bag without touching him.

"Are you still upset about what I said the other day, about Taiwo?" Emeka asked.

"No, no, it's not you. I just wonder sometimes, what's the point of this?" she asked, moving her hands in a circular motion in the air.

"The point of what?"

"You know what."

"I love you, Kehinde. I wish we could get married, and be together properly," Emeka said after a moment, still looking at her, holding both hands now.

Kehinde felt her voice catch in her throat. She knew he loved her, and she knew she loved him, but she would never say it. Saying it could only do more harm than good. Unless Baba Tope sent her away, and even then, it would hardly be that simple to get married immediately. They would have to leave Lagos at least.

"I finally wrote to Taiwo by the way," she said, changing the topic.

Emeka's eyes went wide before he pulled her in for a hug.

"Kehinde! I'm so proud of you!"

"It wasn't a very long letter though," Kehinde said, feeling the ray of hope swell in her chest again, already looking forward to reading his reply.

"I'm sure he'll be happy to hear from you," Emeka said, looking genuinely joyful.

"I really wish we could be together properly too," Kehinde said, holding his hand, emboldened by the hope she felt at a reconciliation with Taiwo.

Emeka looked at her, like he was about to say something, then stopped.

"I do have to run though," he said, pulling away gently. "I have an editorial meeting at 9am. If I leave now, I can still make it. Can we have lunch together today? Here?"

"I can't today, I already promised to take Adenike and Ashabi out after school."

"Then we can take them out together. Let's go to Elegbata Square."

"And when they ask who you are?" Kehinde asked, worried about what Baba Tope would say if he found out about her taking his daughters to meet a male friend.

"Tell them I'm your best friend's brother. That's who I am, after all," he said, his mischievous smile returning.

"See you later then," Kehinde said, squeezing the strap of the bag in her hands as she felt her heart constrict. It would be nice to spend the afternoon with him, and she would find a way to make sure the girls didn't say anything about it at home.

―――――

Kehinde waited outside the school gates for Adenike and Ashabi as she watched row after row of children walk by in their uniforms, the boys in their white shirts and shorts, the girls in their pinafore dresses. The Anglican Missionary school was run by the Anglican Sister's community in Lagos, attached to the Lagos Island diocese that had been building a cathedral since 1924. Although the war had slowed down the building project, from where Kehinde stood beside the school gate she could see the tall spires set against the impressive blue and white domes partially hidden by the scaffolding.

Three girls ran out of the gates singing the song that the children of the Ogunjobi household and every child in Lagos had been singing since the start of the war.

"Adolf Hitler ma se o!

Ani ko ma se ani ko dara o ranri

Abe o titi iwo se tire o –"

"Aunty Kehinde! Aunty Kehinde!" Ashabi came crashing into Kehinde's legs, with Adenike following close behind her, their voices drowning out the singing and noises of the children around them

"Hello, girls! How was school today?"

"I don't like maths," Ashabi said, pouting.

"We spoke about this, dear. Remember, not liking maths isn't the same as not being able to do it, and you most certainly can do it. Did you have maths today?"

"Yes, we have maths every day," Ashabi said, still sticking out her bottom lip.

"Where are we going, Aunty Kehinde?" Adenike asked.

"Well, I thought we could take the bus to Elegbata Square. A friend of mine is meeting us there," Kehinde said.

"Yayyy! Let's go, let's go! We can buy boli and groundnut!" Ashabi cried, jumping up and down.

"Yes, I don't see why not. Let's hope the woman who sells it is there today," Kehinde said. The last time she had walked by the square it looked empty, devoid of any food traders.

Kehinde and the girls walked along the path to the bus stop, where they boarded the bus. About fifteen minutes later, they got off behind a family of three. The mother was wearing a wide-brimmed hat and a yellow sun dress that made Kehinde think of a huge sunflower, and she bounced a baby boy on her hip that smiled at her and the girls as they dismounted.

Kehinde had visited Elegbata Square a few times as a child with her family, Uncle Ladipo and Aunty Laide, to watch plays and to listen to live music. Although the square was quiet today, when Kehinde was younger there were musicians who would sit with their instruments, playing music. The square was surrounded by tall trees that gave the air a fresh smell that often mixed with the burning smell of roasted corn and fried plantain. The first time she had seen a live performance of the Jolly Orchestra was in this square with her father, and Taiwo and his friends from school were always playing football here. It was opposite the Lagos Supreme Court, a huge, white building where lawyers in their wigs could be seen walking around in the open ground floor. Kehinde's father's face would always take on a dreamy look as he spoke about how the lawyers looked so smart in their gowns and wigs, but Kehinde had never really been able to imagine Taiwo walking around there with the others. He seemed much more at home in the middle of the square with his football.

Emeka was on the other side of the square, sitting on a bench reading when Kehinde and the girls got off the bus. He was still wearing the chequered shirt and navy-blue chinos he had been wearing that morning, and his head was bent low, his forehead creased in concentration over the book in his hands. He looked up to push his glasses up on the bridge of his nose and caught Kehinde's eye.

"That's my friend over there," she said to the girls as she returned Emeka's smile.

"I don't like boys very much," Ashabi said, frowning.

"He's a nice boy, you'll see. Come on, let's go meet him," Kehinde said, taking Ashabi's hand as they made their way across the square. "And this is our secret treat, I don't want your mummy or daddy to worry about me taking time off work in the middle of the day," Kehinde added hastily.

Emeka rose, putting his book away in his satchel as he made his way over to meet them. "Girls, this is my friend, Mr Emeka Alanta. I met him at the market," Kehinde said, feeling suddenly self-conscious. Beside her she felt Adenike stiffen and Ashabi moved closer to her. Emeka must have sensed their reluctance because he crouched down in front of them.

"Hello, Ashabi and Adenike, what an absolute pleasure to meet you! Your aunty Kehinde is very proud of you, she talks about you both all the time," he said.

"She's never spoken about you," Ashabi said from behind Kehinde's skirts.

Emeka let out one of his loud, deep laughs.

"Well, that makes me sad. Not even a little?" he said, pretending to be upset as he pouted his lips.

"No, she only talks about Aunty Ama. She sent us sandals for Christmas," Adenike said.

"Aha! Aunty Ama is my little sister!" Emeka grinned, making Kehinde laugh again at how much he was trying to make a good first impression.

"I like my sandals," Ashabi said, taking the final, tentative step out of the curtain of Kehinde's skirt.

"She also made the shoes I'm wearing now actually," he said, standing up and sticking out his left foot to show off his brogues.

"My mummy said the best shoes come from London, my daddy has a supplier who ships them to us," Adenike said, with the air of a precocious child who paid attention to enough adult conversations to have a valid opinion.

"Indeed, but some of the leather used to make those imported shoes comes from the manufacturers here, in Nigeria. Same thing with the cotton used to make the clothes in the fancy ladies' shops all over the Empire. So, you could say that without us, the British would not be known as the best producers of quite a few things," Emeka said. At this point the girls were staring up at him in awe, lapping up his every word as Kehinde tried not to explode with pride.

"I think I can see the woman who sells boli over there. Shall we get some? Or would you rather keep talking about leather and cotton?" Kehinde asked with a grin.

"Yes please! I'm hungry," Ashabi said, rubbing her tummy and sniffing the air as she looked in the direction of the food vendor.

"Boli is one of my favourite things to eat as well," Emeka said, as Ashabi put her hand in his, nodding along to the wisdom of his words. Adenike moved to his other side as the four of them walked to the end of the square.

Kehinde watched the same vendor that had sold food at Elegbata Square since her childhood wrap four, still-hot pieces of roasted plantain in old newspapers for them. She measured out the groundnut into nylon bags, her face lined with years of hard labour, and then counted out her change.

"Thank you," Kehinde said to her, smiling as she gave an extra bag of groundnuts to Ashabi.

As they walked back to the bench Emeka had been sitting on, Kehinde saw the family that had been on the bus with them posing for a picture. A photographer had set up his camera in the middle of the square, with the Supreme Court in the background of the frame, and he was trying and failing to get the baby to smile. He saw them walking by and called out.

"Pictures, get your family pictures! Printed and delivered within a week!"

Kehinde felt the heat rise to her face as she realised the photographer thought they were a family. Her eyes met Emeka's in panic as she shook her head furiously.

"Yes, please! Let's take the picture," Emeka said.

"I like pictures!" Ashabi said, already running in the direction of the photographer with Adenike on her heels.

"Emeka, we can't take a family picture," Kehinde whispered.

"Who said anything about taking a family picture? I just want to capture this moment, I'll keep the picture, you never even have to see it," he said, leaving Kehinde as he ran after the girls laughing.

The other family had finished taking their picture and now stood aside as Kehinde, Emeka, Adenike and Ashabi stood in front of the photographer's camera. Kehinde felt herself stiffen as the photographer looked up. It was Mr Tade, the same photographer that had taken the picture of her and Taiwo at their eighteenth birthday, the same one who had come to the house to deliver the news of her father's disappearance. As she studied the familiar tribal marks on his face she saw the recognition dawn on him.

"Kehinde Ilesanmi?" he asked, stepping away from his camera.

"Mr Tade! How nice to see you again!" she said, then looking at Emeka she quickly added, "This is my friend, Emeka Alanta, and these are Adenike and Ashabi, my nieces."

"How nice to meet you all! How is your mother? And Taiwo?"

"All fine, thank you. Taiwo now serves in the Army, and my mum is well."

"You must be proud of him, fighting for the Empire; may God keep him safe always."

"Amen. Do you still work for the *West African Pilot*?"

"I do, but as a freelancer now. I work for a few newspapers, and I also come here in the afternoons to take pictures. I recognise this gentleman here. Do you work at the *Daily Times*?" he asked Emeka.

"Yes, sir," Emeka said, looking surprised.

"I thought so. I've seen you in their office a few times when I've delivered pictures. Good to see you all, now, let me take your picture," he said, stepping back to stand behind his camera lens.

"Okay, now on the count of three, one, two, three!" he counted as they all smiled, the flash of the camera a muted 'puff' sound. Adenike and Ashabi clapped their hands in excitement and the family beside them laughed.

"You're all so lovely to look at, such a beautiful family!" the woman with the baby gushed at Kehinde.

"Oh, we aren't a family," Kehinde said quickly. Emeka, oblivious to the comment, had paid the photographer and was telling the girls what it was like to work at the *Daily Times*.

"You could have fooled me! Have a lovely day then," the woman said, as she walked off with her husband, the baby still looking over her shoulder at Kehinde as they retreated.

Kehinde stared at them as they walked away, hearing Adenike and Ashabi laugh as Emeka pretended to cry at something they had said. The longing in her felt as sharp as being poked by a stick. How she wished they were a family, a real one, with Emeka as her husband, carrying their child on a day like this. The longing was replaced with a deep sadness, knowing that it was something she would probably only ever dream about, an alternate reality that looked nothing like her current one. She allowed herself to dream that she was the woman with the wide-brimmed hat, and she was walking away in her yellow dress against the afternoon sun with Emeka, just another day at Elegbata Square, with the love of her life.

Chapter Twenty-Four

CENTRAL LAGOS

November 1942

Tope's wedding day came round quickly and although Tope and Mama Tope grew increasingly withdrawn as the day got closer, Tope's brothers did not appear to know that change was imminent. They were as boisterous as ever, their footsteps pounding on the staircase forming the never-ending soundtrack of the house. Baba Tope drank even more now, mostly local palm wine or a bottle of whisky that he started on at dinner, carrying a glass with him as he retired into his room. In addition to Mr Babajide and Mr Lateef, he now also had visits from strange, rough-looking men that came to speak to him, flanked by Kayode, in the formal parlour. Sometimes they came just before dinner, but mostly they arrived at night, after the curfew. Ayo and Kehinde tiptoed around them, staying out of the way as the family prepared to say goodbye to its first born.

Ayo had spent many sleepless nights sewing the wedding dress; a white fitted bodice with a flowing skirt that made Tope look even younger than her nineteen years. Mama Tope had asked for so many adjustments to be made to the dress, even until the night before the wedding. Ayo, in a rare gesture of patience, accepted each new request with nothing but a nod and Kehinde had gone shopping with Tope, visiting the market with her to get the items she would need for her wedding trousseau. She had also spent weeks on finding the ingredients for the wedding cake, and was proud of what she had been able to make with all their egg and flour rations, including some of Ama and Emeka's. It seemed there was an unspoken agreement between the wives that they would all do everything that they could to make this easier for Tope.

Tope looked lost in the sea of dress as she walked down the aisle of Bethel Cathedral on the arm of her father, her eyes darting around the church like she was looking for a lifeboat. Mr Babajide stood at the altar beside Reverend Kasunmu, wearing a navy-blue suit and smiling like a shark going in for the kill.

"Poor Tope," Kehinde whispered to Ayo for what seemed like the millionth time. They were sitting on the second pew, beside the children of the Ogunjobi house, behind Mama Tope. Kehinde could barely see past Mama Tope's green gele, which had been tied high up on her head, a petition on its way to heaven.

"She looks like she's about to faint," Ayo tutted.

Kehinde felt like she herself would faint. The church was unbearably hot, and besides that, Kehinde was always so tired these days. She chalked it down to spending hours in the morning waiting in line in the ration queues. She stifled a yawn as Reverend Kasunmu opened the wedding ceremony.

Mama Tope's shoulders visibly slumped as Tope and Mr Babajide inched closer to the point of no return. How different this was from her own wedding, Kehinde mused. Her mother had been too sad to be emotionally present, and the whole thing had happened so quickly that Kehinde barely remembered any of it. She remembered arriving at the Ogunjobi household but everything before that had been a blur of spoken words and promises.

"...to have and to hold, in sickness and in health," Tope was saying, barely audible even from the front of the church.

"That husband of hers is already sick enough," Ayo whispered.

"Are you sure Mama Tope can't hear us?" Kehinde whispered back as she shifted closer to Ayo, their hips touching.

"Not with you being so close to my ear. Besides, I don't think she can hear anything right now, the poor woman."

Kehinde felt a shot of anger and indignation bolt through her body, louder in her ears than the chords of the piano as the hymn started. Even Mama Tope, a senior wife and mother of three, had no say in the life of her child. Kehinde thought about the stray dogs that sometimes wandered the streets near the fishing village. *Even they have more freedom than we do*, she thought as she clenched her fists beside her. Her wave of anger was followed by nausea and a stirring feeling deep within her. *What is wrong with me*, she wondered. She would have to see Doctor Gbagi again – it was possible that she had some strange illness that was making her feel so odd these days.

"I now pronounce you man and wife!" Reverend Kasunmu said to Tope and her new husband. Mr Babajide grinned at the clapping congregation, looking around the church before planting a kiss on Tope's cheek. Kehinde knew that he had much grander plans for her later, when they were back in his bedroom, and the thought of her own first night as a married woman made her shudder.

As the ceremony ended, everyone rose as the new couple walked down the aisle to the tune of the "Wedding March". Although most of the preparations had been done the night before, Ayo and Kehinde hurried between the pews, exiting through the side door as they headed back to the house. The two women who would cook the party jollof rice and fried beef for the guests had arrived at dawn with a black pot that looked like it could cook a whole cow at once.

"How many guests do you think will come back to the house?" Kehinde asked Ayo, as they slipped out.

"Probably about twenty or so. Baba Tope didn't tell many people about the reception, you know how he is, he's worried about the food not being enough. Mama Tope had said Mr Babajide was only coming with his older sister and her family. The sister, her husband and two children travelled down from Ondo yesterday, apparently," Ayo shrugged.

"Strange that he invited just a handful of his family. I would have thought that being his first marriage and all he would have wanted a much grander event."

"He's stingy. Even with all the women he sleeps with, he doesn't like to spend money. He's using the excuse of the war, saying he doesn't want to celebrate too much when people are losing their lives," Ayo said, shaking her head as they turned into their street.

"Well, he does have a point. It seems a bit odd to have any party at all. I expect that for many of the guests this will be their first party in at least the last three years."

"I suppose so, but war or not, life and all its parties must go on," Ayo said, as they approached their gate.

Ayo had been talking about life a lot more lately, Kehinde

had noticed. Ever since her visit to Ibadan to see her mother she kept making references to life like it was an elusive spirit that she was understudying. Apparently, her mother had been very ill and Kehinde suspected that Ayo thought her end was near. She wondered if the loss of a parent was something so irrevocable, so unforgettable that it solidified the transient nature of life in your brain forever, making you focus more on the here and now. She knew she definitely thought about life differently since her own father had died.

The gateman opened the gate for them, and they walked onto the transformed lawn. Wooden benches and chairs from the dining room had been laid out around five tables in front of the house. Kehinde could smell the spicy jollof rice and frying beef as the firewood smoke from the black pot infused the air. The best part about today was that the Jolly Boys Orchestra would be playing live on the lawn. Kehinde and Taiwo had danced to their music in Uncle Ladipo's living room, playing the record over and over until it was scratched beyond repair. Mr Ogunjobi had a friend that was a distant cousin of Ambrose Campbell and he had asked him to play at the reception. As Kehinde and Ayo walked past the patch of lawn where the band stood rehearsing, Kehinde cast a quick glance at the lead guitarist. He wore a cap low enough to cover the top half of his face which was bent down in concentration as he strummed out a few notes, backed up by another band member playing the tambourine as they warmed up their instruments.

"Ma, the palm wine is here. I don't know if it will be enough," Kayode said, appearing in the doorway as they reached the front step.

"How many kegs are there?" Ayo asked, pausing at the step to take off her hat.

"Just three, Ma," Kayode said. He had cast aside his usual

white buba and sokoto and was wearing a blue ankara instead. It was probably supposed to look festive, but he looked uncomfortable in bright clothes.

"Is there any beer left? There should be at least one crate at the back," Ayo said, running her hand through the matted spot the hat had left in her hair.

"Yes, and two old bottles of wine from Master's cellar."

"That should be enough, right?" Kehinde asked.

"It will have to be. Shame there's no champagne. Baba Tope hasn't been able to get his hands on any since the war started. We'll serve the beer first, then the palm wine, and the wine can come out last when hopefully everyone is too drunk to notice that there aren't any drinks left," Ayo said, walking into the house with the air of someone who had walked five hundred miles. These days the management of the house seemed to be wearing her down, and Kehinde could feel her frustration simmering off the pores of her skin whenever they spent yet another morning in a ration queue. Even cooking was less fun now – how could it be fun when they had to measure grains of salt and peel yam like it would cry if it lost too much skin?

Once inside, they walked through the kitchen to the backyard where the women were standing, turning sticks that were at least four feet high in the black pots. Their sweat dripped down their faces as they stood over the steaming pots, the smell of onions, garlic and ginger becoming one in the air.

"Ẹ kú iṣẹ́ oh!" Ayo called out to them from the doorway. "Kayode, make sure they have something to eat and drink before they go."

"Ẹ ṣe, Ma, God bless you, Ma!" the women called out to Ayo.

In the kitchen they could hear guests arriving outside as the band went from rehearsing to performing. The party had

officially started, and despite herself, Kehinde felt the first
strings of excitement within her. Her body swayed to the music
of its own volition, and she laughed out loud when Ayo started
to shimmy her hips from side to side as "Atari Ajanuku"
started playing.

It ended up being a nice afternoon, if one could look past
the fear in Tope's eyes as she danced with her new husband,
almost tripping over her dress on several occasions. The food
and drink went round, the music made the palm wine sweeter,
and as the sun receded into the sky all the guests tried to
pretend that the curfew was not looming on the horizon.
Tope's brothers ran round the compound laughing in their
smart shirts and trousers, and Adenike and Ashabi were
adorable in their pink flower girl dresses. Kehinde found
herself wishing Emeka was there to dance with her, a thought
she kept to herself as she savoured enough details to share
with him when she saw him next.

As the sun started dipping in the sky, Kehinde was coming
out of the kitchen after dropping a stack of used plates when
she almost collided with Mama Tope coming down the stairs.
She looked like she had been crying – her eyes were red and
small like ladybugs.

"Sorry, Ma, I didn't see you there," Kehinde said, preparing
for the sharp retort she knew must surely come. To her
surprise, Mama Tope blinked as a leftover tear rolled down her
face.

"I'm so sorry, Ma," Kehinde said, as she ushered the older
woman into the den, dropping the plates on the sideboard by
the kitchen and shutting the door behind them. She sat beside
Mama Tope and watched her cry, unsure of what to do.

"I'm sure you're happy," Mama Tope sniffed, looking up at
Kehinde through those red, sorrowful eyes.

"Happy for Tope?"

"Happy to see me crying, to see me brought down so low." Mama Tope blew her nose into a handkerchief that was crumpled in her hand. Her gele had remained immaculate throughout the day and it sat on her head like a beacon of hope for what was left of her dignity.

"I could never be happy to see you cry," Kehinde said, meaning it.

"Please, I've been nothing but wicked to you since the day you came here," Mama Tope scoffed. The words swirled around in a whirlpool that opened between them, waiting for who would be brave enough to dive in first.

"I haven't always been like this, you know. I was young, and beautiful like you once. Life has a way of humbling a woman," Mama Tope said, with a short, bitter laugh. "When I got married, I had so many plans, so many dreams. Did you know that Tope was supposed to go to Cambridge University, in England? When she was six, she had read the whole Bible, from back to front. We were so proud of her," she said, her now dry eyes looking at the rug at her feet.

Kehinde followed her gaze, at a loss for words. Of course, she knew Tope was supposed to go to university, they had spoken about it many times, but in the three years she had been married, this was the longest conversation she had had with Mama Tope and she didn't know how she was expected to respond.

"Men. They promise you the world, and once they have you, poof." Mama Tope put both of her hands in the air, her ten fingers expanding on the word "poof". "They move on. I've warned my Tope, I hope your mother warned you too."

Kehinde started to wonder if maybe she had had too much to drink, or if the heat was getting to her. With the heavy lace iro and buba Mama Tope was wearing, she could have heatstroke. She rambled on.

"We're all the same at the end of the day. Pawns in the hands of these men, with no way out of this game we've found ourselves in. Ẹ ṣe, Kehinde. Let's go outside before our husband starts to look for us."

Kehinde helped Mama Tope stand up. She knew it was the closest to an apology she would ever get from her, for all her mean words, for revealing her secret about the LMWA, for all the times she had treated Kehinde like a cockroach that refused to die. Mama Tope had finally acknowledged that in this world, they were equals of a kind, both at the mercy of the same man. Kehinde understood, and she forgave her.

"You called him 'our husband'," Kehinde said with a small smile.

"Yes now, are we not both his wives? Oya, let's go," Mama Tope said, opening the door for Kehinde.

It wasn't long before it was time for Tope to leave. Her brothers were quiet, suddenly sombre at the realisation that their beloved sister was leaving the house for good. The handful of guests who were neighbours stood in front of the gate with the Ogunjobi family as they watched Tope climb into the passenger seat of Mr Babajide's black Buick. She was crying and had cried throughout the hour of prayers that preceded her departure. Ayo and Kehinde were also crying openly now as they stood beside Mama Tope.

"Make sure you come and visit us oh!" Baba Tope called out. Mr Babajide lived in Ebute-Metta, and although that was still in Lagos, she would have to come across Carter Bridge every time she wanted to see them.

"Yes, Daddy," Tope replied, her voice cracking.

"I'll take care of her very well! Now, let's get going so we can make it home before the blackout!" Mr Babajide said through the car window as he turned his steering wheel.

Kehinde stood with the group in front of the gate as they waved through the swirl of dust at the retreating car that carried Tope away to her new life, leaving her family feeling slightly off kilter.

———————

"Sounds like the day went well, then," Kehinde's mother said the following Monday, as she emerged from the kitchen carrying a tray laden with three teacups and a teapot.

"Mostly," Kehinde said, accepting a teacup and placing it within arm's reach on the dining table. Unable to visit on Sunday because she was clearing up after the wedding, she had stopped by her mother's on her way home from her store.

"Poor Mama Tope, it sounds like she's not taking it well at all," Aunty Laide said as she stood up to pour the weak tea that looked like it had been strained multiple times.

"I don't know why she should have been so sad really. With all the men away fighting, she should have been happy that there was an eligible bachelor ready and able to marry Tope," Kehinde's mother said from the head of the table.

"He could hardly be called eligible though, could he," Aunty Laide started, stopping as she caught Kehinde wincing. "How are things in the market, dear?" she asked instead.

"Slow. Most days I sit around doing nothing really," Kehinde replied, ignoring the stab of guilt as she thought about the LMWA and Emeka. Her days could hardly be called slow.

"No new letters have arrived from Taiwo," her mother cut in, gripping the sides of her cup. She looked at Kehinde as she spoke, like Kehinde could summon her brother through the tea leaves, and to be honest, Kehinde wished she could. She was also waiting for his response to her letter.

Kehinde knew that the Elder Dempster shipping lines were back in operation; she had seen the letters on Baba Tope's desk. Now that America had joined the war as an ally, the Atlantic was relatively protected from the German U-Boats that had sunk so many ships in the previous year. She had overheard Baba Tope talk about the submarines that escorted both the passenger and cargo ships that left the Apapa port, and she knew that the War Relief Committee had sent and received letters from England. She sometimes stayed up late worrying, and although Emeka had told her that Taiwo was probably fine, every time she saw news of a British plane going down, she had a moment of gut-wrenching fear that Taiwo had been in it. She knew he must be alive though, she had not had that visceral feeling of pain yet, so he must be safe. When they were eight, Taiwo had broken his arm when he was with his friends. They had been jumping down from the first floor of a building on Onorinde Road and he had fallen on his arm. Kehinde was at home with her mother when it happened, and she knew instantly that something was wrong. When he was brought home an hour later by Kunle and his parents, she had known that must have been the sense of alarm that she had felt. So, she knew he must be alive out there in the world somewhere. But where was he, and why had he stopped writing?

"His letters are probably just delayed," Aunty Laide said, her deliberately casual tone at odds with the apprehension in her eyes.

"But this has never happened before. Since he left, he has sent us at least one letter a month," her mother said.

"Mummy, Aunty Laide is right. The shipping lines only just

reopened, there might be a backlog. I won't be surprised if we receive a batch of letters at once," Kehinde said, almost believing her words.

Her mother said nothing but continued to stare at the cup between her hands, squeezing it like she could break it. *God please let Taiwo be fine*, Kehinde prayed silently. After the loss of their father, losing Taiwo would be much more than they could bear. She would no longer want to exist in this world.

A sharp knock on the front door made them all sit up. With a sinking feeling of déjà vu, Kehinde rose slowly and went to see who it was. To her surprise, it was the messenger boy from the Obalende post office, with Uncle Ladipo standing beside him.

"I had gone to post our letters on my way back from the club and saw him," Uncle Ladipo said, the white of his eyes stark against his face. Kehinde knew without looking down that the messenger boy was holding a telegram from the War Office.

"Ladi?" Aunty Laide called from inside.

The poor messenger boy, who couldn't have been older than fourteen, extended his arm towards Kehinde.

"Thank you," Kehinde whispered, as she took the sealed envelope.

With a nod, the boy ran off down the footpath and jumped on his bicycle, speeding away the way Taiwo and Kunle used to.

"We'd better go inside," Uncle Ladipo said.

Chapter Twenty-Five

Kehinde stepped into the house with Uncle Ladipo's hand heavy on her shoulder. Her mother saw the envelope in her hand and started screaming. This feeling of foreboding and despair was too familiar, Kehinde thought, as she watched Aunty Laide fold her arms around her mother, Uncle Ladipo moving to stand beneath the grandfather clock on the wall.

"Open it, Keke," he said, although she saw the words form on his lips more than heard them. She ripped open the sealed envelope, seeing the rigid font of the telegram, the neatly spaced lines, reading the message but unable to comprehend the words.

"Keke, what does it say?" Uncle Ladipo asked, his voice raised above her mother's keening. "*The Royal Air Force regrets to inform you that your son, Second Lieutenant Taiwo Ilesanmi, has been reported missing in action since 20 November 1942, over France. If further information is received you will be duly notified,*" Kehinde recited, like she was reading about someone else, not Taiwo. Because that was the only way she could relay the information in the telegram without crumpling to the ground like a piece of discarded paper.

"He's not dead! It just says he's missing!" her mother shouted, her eyes wild as she looked around the room.

"Abiola—" Uncle Ladipo started, his face ashen.

"No, he's not dead! Can't you see? They only said he's missing in action! My son is missing! He can still be found!"

Kehinde watched Uncle Ladipo and Aunty Laide exchange a look, a look she knew meant they thought Kehinde's mother was finally losing her mind. She refused to understand it; she had to hold on to whatever embers of hope were still coming from the wildfire of her life. She had to hold on to her certainty that she would know it in her gut if Taiwo was hurt. Her hope remained that if Taiwo was dead, she would know.

"We'll go to Baba Tope. He'll know what to do! He can write to the governor himself! Or the War Office, he'll know someone there, I'm sure!" Kehinde's mother said, freeing herself of Aunty Laide as she stood up.

"Abiola … it's getting late," Uncle Ladipo started.

"You will not silence me! Not this time! I will go now to speak to Baba Tope about my son," she said, grabbing her handbag from the dining table chair.

"We'll come with you," Aunty Laide said, exchanging a look with Uncle Ladipo.

The three of them followed Kehinde's mother to the bus stop at the end of Malumo Street, near the fishing village.

"Come and get your hot, fresh corn and coconut!" shouted the corn seller as she moved through the people walking on the footpath, away from the fishing village. The sweet smell of the corn made Kehinde's stomach do a flip and she tried not to gag as unexpected nausea rose within her. Fishermen walked past them with their pails and hooks, some nodding at

Kehinde and her mother as they went by. The wind howled around them; it was always strongest this close to the water, but at least it wasn't raining. A young woman with a toddler at her side stood at the bus stop with them, and the toddler looked up at Kehinde with a crooked smile, the orange glow of the early evening sun forming a halo behind her head.

If only she could return the smile, but she feared she was incapable of smiling again. Taiwo had just gone to London, why had he been in France? Was this the special mission he had referred to in his letter to her mother? Where was he now if he was missing? Was he injured? Had he received her letter? What was happening when he went missing? Was he alone? How could they send such a stupid telegram with no details, did the War Office not realise how many lives they were affecting? How they had smashed her heart, a heart that was already patchwork, like it had been stitched under Ayo's sewing machine after each heartbreak. Her mother was right, Taiwo had to be alive. The alternative was simply unbearable. She felt a sob rising in her throat and pushed it down to the churning within her. Her mother's hysterics were enough – she would not add to them, she could not add to them now.

Kehinde's mother tapped her feet impatiently as they waited for the bus, and when it arrived after what felt like the longest ten minutes of their lives, they got on and sat in the seats closest to the door. Kehinde watched the corn seller walk past, thinking of simpler times when her father would take her fishing, when they would walk along this very road home. Home to meet her mother and Taiwo, home to their complete family, home where her heart no longer was and now never could be.

They got off near Bamgbose and walked to the Ogunjobi house, Kehinde's mother leading the way at a trot. Mr Tunde greeted them as they walked past the car, and Kehinde noticed that Baba Tope's briefcase was still in the backseat. He must have just got back and was probably looking forward to having dinner and going to bed.

Ayo opened the front door and her eyes widened when she saw Kehinde standing there, with her mother, uncle and aunt. "Good evening, everyone! Please, come in!" she said, ushering them all through the waiting room and into the formal parlour.

"We're here to see Baba Tope," Kehinde's mother said, looking shrunken in the middle of

the house plants and high ceilings.

Ayo looked at Kehinde, hesitating before she spoke again. "I'll get him, please just wait a moment."

Kehinde watched Ayo walk through the door leading into the rest of the house, the smell of leftover jollof rice and fried meat from the wedding following in her wake. To think that this house was now so familiar to her, the new home that had been forced on her. Uncle Ladipo and Aunty Laide sat on either end of her mother on the biggest sofa, looking uncomfortable as they waited for Baba Tope. Unable to sit, Kehinde stood, chewing away at her cheek.

"My family! To what do I owe this pleasure?" Baba Tope said, arriving from the side door. He was wearing the white kaftan that he only wore at home, and although his arms were outstretched, his smile did not reach his eyes. They had disturbed his rest and Kehinde knew him enough by now to know that he was irritated at their unexpected visit.

"Baba Tope, it's not good news I'm afraid," Uncle Ladipo said, rising to shake his hand.

"It's not bad news Ladipo, don't talk like that," Kehinde's mother snapped from the sofa. Aunty Laide's hand around her shoulder now looked more like a restraint than an embrace as her knuckles strained against Kehinde's mother's bubu. "Taiwo has been reported missing in action," she continued from her seat.

For a moment, Baba Tope looked like he was trying to remember who Taiwo was and Kehinde felt all the hatred in the world for him as she watched the recognition dawn in his eyes. "I'm so sorry to hear that! This war has taken so many young men from us, it's such a shame!"

"He's not been taken from us, he's just missing," Kehinde's mother said, her voice shrill. Baba Tope looked from Kehinde's mother, to Kehinde, then at Uncle Ladipo and Aunty Laide. No one said anything for a moment, as Kehinde's mother's voice seemed to echo around the room.

"Baba Tope, ẹ jọ. We need you to use your influence to find out exactly where Taiwo is now," Kehinde's mother continued.

"My influence?"

"With the governor, with the colonial government. You can write to the War Office. So we can find out more, so we can find Taiwo," her mother continued, sliding out of Aunty Laide's grip and landing on her knees as she sunk into the plush carpet. Seeing her there made Kehinde want to retch, it was too much. She reached out a hand to steady herself against the wall.

"Speak to the governor? About Taiwo?" Baba Tope asked, for once forgetting his manners before recovering himself. "The governor has too much on his plate right now to be bothered with this."

"He'll write to the War Office, they'll give us more details," Kehinde's mother cried.

"He will do no such thing," Baba Tope said, his patience wearing thin as his fake smile left his face.

"Sir, we're hoping you can ask him to make inquiries on

our behalf," Uncle Ladipo interjected, still standing beside Baba Tope.

Kehinde watched Baba Tope's lip curl. She knew what he was thinking. That these simple people did not know how the War Office worked – he was the knower of all things war-related after all because he attended the War Relief Committee meeting once a week. Her apathy caught the flames kindled by his disinterest and became a hatred for him that seemed to take on a life of its own, like a ball of puff puff in hot oil.

"You don't understand. If a telegram was sent saying he's missing in action, then he's probably already dead," Baba Tope said with a shrug. The word "dead" hung in the air like the carcasses at Ereko Market. How could he talk about her brother like that? To pronounce him dead with a shrug? Like he was talking about a dead rat found in the streets? In that moment, she knew he felt nothing real for her, he couldn't possibly think of her as anything more than his iyawo parlour, the pretty flower, useful only for her aesthetic value like the other plants that decorated his home.

"Baba Tope, please find it within you to write to the governor at least, just to be sure," Kehinde managed to choke out, surprising herself with her acting skills.

Baba Tope looked at her like he had just realised she was in the room. "Very well then, but I doubt Bernard will have any time to look into this."

How callous of him to refer to the governor with his first name, Kehinde thought. A reminder that he was friends with him but obviously not acquainted enough to ask for a favour. Uncle Ladipo nodded, his head bowed as he looked at Aunty Laide again, speaking their secret language.

"Thank you, sir. We'll go home now, so we can make it back before the curfew," Uncle Ladipo said, extending a limp hand to shake Baba Tope's. Aunty Laide gathered Kehinde's mother up as she led her out of the door like a bag of clothes.

Kehinde saw them off, simultaneously wishing she could go with them but grateful she had an escape, and some privacy to process her own well of feelings. When she returned to the parlour, Baba Tope had already gone to the dining room where she could hear the rest of the family gathering for dinner. Ayo had laid out the food – leftover jollof rice, fried meat and beans – and Kehinde sat in her place.

"Bless us, oh Lord, and these thy gifts, which we are about to receive from thy bounty, through Christ our Lord," Baba Tope intoned. Kehinde looked at him, her appetite gone. How could he sit here and pray, and shovel food into his mouth, like her brother had not just been pronounced missing?

"Ayo, this is delicious," he said.

Ayo nodded, with a small smile. No one else said anything, but Ayo squeezed Kehinde's hand beneath the table. She had obviously overheard at least some of the conversation earlier.

"Ayo, you will sleep in my room tonight," he continued, his cutlery scraping against the plate.

Mama Tope looked directly at Kehinde, her eyes full of such deep sympathy that Kehinde wondered if she also knew that Taiwo was missing. But then it hit her, Mama Tope understood what it was like to be the discarded wife, out of favour. Well, unlike Mama Tope, she was done. She would not beg for scraps from the table, she was tired of being treated like she had no rights or feelings.

After dinner, when everyone else was upstairs and Kehinde was left in the kitchen, Ayo gave her a hug.

"Keks, I'm so sorry. I hope your brother is found," she said, confirming that she had heard everything. "Give Baba Tope some time, I know he'll speak to the governor eventually. I'll remind him."

"Thank you, Ayo."

"I kept this for you all day. It arrived when you were out, hopefully it's good news. I'm going to get ready to go to Baba Tope's room now, but I'll be praying for you," Ayo said, pulling out a folded note from the waist of her iro. The note had Doctor Gbagi's clinic seal on the front. Kehinde opened the letter as she heard the door of the kitchen click behind Ayo.

> *Dear Kehinde,*
>
> *I am pleased to inform you that your symptoms are in line with the early stages of pregnancy. I suspect you will be close to the end of your first trimester. Please arrange to come with your husband to see me at my clinic at your earliest convenience.*
>
> *Yours sincerely,*
> *Doctor Femi Gbagi*

Kehinde felt like her heart would finally give way, because surely, surely, this was too much for it to bear.

Chapter Twenty-Six

"Are you sure you want to go to the market today?" Ayo asked.

They were in the kitchen again, after Kehinde had spent a sleepless night in her room, washing the breakfast plates while Adenike and Ashabi made a game of clearing the table.

"I need a distraction."

"Keks, I'm so sorry, I know how close you were to him."

"He might still be alive," she said, meaning it, because he had to be.

"He must be. The telegram would have said if they suspected he was dead surely? Speaking of telegrams, what did the note from Doctor Gbagi say?"

For a moment, Kehinde considered lying to Ayo, but she was too tired.

"I'm pregnant."

Ayo let out a squeal. "Oh, thank God! Some good news at last!"

"Please don't tell Baba Tope yet. I want to tell him myself."

"Of course! Oh, this is so exciting, a baby in the house!" Ayo whispered loudly, doing a little dance out of the kitchen.

Big news seemed to come in twos, Kehinde thought as she walked to the market, not seeing the road ahead of her, her thoughts racing faster than her legs. She felt like she was a special guest in one of her crazy dreams. The last time she had felt like this, the war had been announced and her father was gone, forever. Now she was pregnant and her brother was missing. And she'd refused to write to him for so long. Had she learned nothing from her father's death? Or the war? Why had she assumed he would come home?

She tried to focus on the cobblestones, on the leaves of the trees lining the path, and the shrill sound of a boy's bicycle bell as he narrowly missed her. Almost instinctively she reached down to her stomach. It was undeniable, her lower belly had a firmness that hadn't been there before, or had it? In addition to her unusual tiredness lately, her unreliable period had been completely absent for four months now, the longest stretch ever. How had it not occurred to her that she might be pregnant? Doctor Gbagi would soon send a letter to Baba Tope to congratulate him, or even come to the house himself, and then she would be trapped forever. Because if Baba Tope thought this child was his, he would not send her back home. But she knew that she was in the biggest trouble of her life, for Baba Tope would know that this child was not his, because he had barely touched her in months.

If she was pregnant, only one man could be the father and the baby would not be welcome in the Ogunjobi household. She almost tripped over a fallen tree branch as the panic rose within her. Baba Tope would kill her for sure this time. The shame and disrespect would be unforgivable, her worst offence yet, and even if she ran to her mother, the disgrace would be too much. Her mother would not welcome her home with open arms. This return as the prodigal daughter would be more than any parent could bear.

Baba Tope had barely looked at her at breakfast that morning, avoiding her eyes and pointedly only speaking with Mama Tope and Ayo. What if the baby arrived and looked like Emeka? He looked nothing like Baba Tope, they couldn't look more different if one was a banana and the other charcoal. Her heart hammered away in her chest like a woodpecker attacking a tree and it was all she could do to keep moving towards her store.

As she walked past the bakery on the corner by the Lewis Street bus stop, the realisation that she was at a turning point hit her sharper than the smell of bread wafting out of the window. She was not prepared to let her pregnancy be taken from her too, not after everything she had lost already. And this time, she wasn't going to wait for Baba Tope to find out and punish her however he saw fit while she begged for mercy. She was done with sneaking around and hoping he would one day send her away. It was time to fight for herself, to make a difference in her own life for once. She had to survive, she had to choose happiness for herself instead of making do with whatever circumstances she found herself in. She had to give herself a chance. Her father's death would not be in vain, Taiwo's sacrifice would not be for nothing, and every time she had fought against the injustice of being controlled would not go to waste. She found herself in Fine Leather, barely acknowledging Onyi as she stumbled into the office at the back.

"Ehen, Kehinde. I was just telling Emeka that I think the sandals should be on display in front, instead of the court shoes," Ama said from behind her desk. Emeka almost burnt his mouth with his tea at the sight of Kehinde.

"Kehinde?" he said, standing up and placing his hand on her elbow.

"Taiwo is missing."

"Oh God," Ama said, standing up so quickly that the table rattled.

"Oh, Keke. I'm so, so sorry," Emeka said, folding her into a hug. The safety of his embrace almost broke her resolve, but she held onto the tree of hope growing within her.

"Was it a telegram? Or a letter? Oh, your poor mother! Did they say anything else?" Ama asked.

"Ama, stop with the questions," Emeka whispered.

The bell outside Fine Leather rang. "Ugh! My customers always have such terrible timing!" Ama said, throwing her hands in the air. "Kehinde, don't leave before I get back."

As the door shut, Emeka pulled Kehinde closer, planting kisses on the top of her head, rubbing her back, like he wanted to erase all the pain she had ever felt. "I don't want to be here anymore," Kehinde said, struggling to breathe.

"Shhh, you're still in shock."

"I mean it, Emi. This is it. I can't take any more of this. I have to go."

"We can go to my flat now if you want? I can send Ugo a note to cover for me at work."

"I don't mean your apartment … I mean Lagos," Kehinde said, her eyes red but dry, her voice firm as she looked up, searching Emeka's face. He stared back at her, looking confused.

"You want to leave Lagos? Because of the news about Taiwo?"

"Because of … everything," Kehinde hesitated.

Taiwo going missing was one thing, and what she saw as the final act of Baba Tope's evil another, but this child growing within her, Emeka's child, had pushed her to see that she no longer had a viable future here. As he looked at her, she knew she wanted to start this new life with him, a new chapter where she was choosing herself, and not always trying to do the right thing for everyone else. But she wanted him to choose her too, not out of a sense of duty for his unborn child, but because he loved her. He had said before that he wanted them to be together, properly, but now that it came down to it, would he risk his safety to be with her forever?

"I want to leave the past behind, and start a new life with you," she said with all the courage she could muster. If he turned her down now, she was on her own, at least until this baby came to join her.

Behind his glasses, Emeka's eyes blinked rapidly, like they were trying to assist his ears in hearing. "Are you sure?" he whispered.

"I'm sure this is what I want … unless you don't want to?" Kehinde said, feeling her boldness faltering.

"Kehinde, you know I want nothing more than to spend the rest of my life with you. Let's go to Enugu! We can run away! Leave Lagos, all of this behind, and be together without the fear of being caught," he said, speaking quickly as he paced back and forth in front of her.

"You think we'll be safe there? If we go, my husband will look for us. He knows people, all over the country!" Kehinde said, her elation at how quickly Emeka had said yes dissolving in the mounting realisation that she would never be free anywhere in Nigeria, as long as Baba Tope lived.

"We can hide! He doesn't know Enugu better than I do!"

Emeka said, his words coming slowly now as he inhaled Kehinde's anxiety.

"And live our lives as fugitives? Emeka, we're not safe here. He'll have us both killed!"

As she watched the indignation in Emeka's face solidify she realised with growing certainty, she wanted this life, with this child and this man. She wanted to be a real family, to have a chance at the kind of love her parents had, to take pictures in a park together, to raise a child with memories of love and a halo of joy. She would rather die trying than not try at all. The same way she would rather die than accept that Taiwo was gone, without trying to find out for herself where he was, with or without Baba Tope's help.

"We can't run away to Enugu, but there's somewhere I think we can go. Somewhere we can disappear forever. Somewhere I can find out about what happened to Taiwo."

"Where?"

"London," Kehinde said, as a plan began to form in her mind.

"Kehinde, I love you, but getting to London right now seems a lot less feasible than going to Enugu," he said, sitting on the desk, looking defeated.

"I think I know how we can get there, but we're going to need Ama's help."

"And good thing that woman finally left so I can hear what you need my help with!" Ama said, coming back into the office.

"Who said your customers had bad timing? I think this one knew the right time to leave," Emeka said.

"So, what do you need my help with?" Ama said, sitting behind her desk, suddenly looking serious.

As Kehinde and Emeka spoke, holding hands opposite

Ama, she listened, not moving, or interrupting with questions for once, her hands clasped under her chin as her eyes went back and forth between them.

"I always saw this coming, you know," Ama said, once Kehinde had finished speaking.

"What? How?" Emeka asked.

"I knew it was only a matter of time before you would decide to leave your husband. Not that I can blame you, with everything he's put you through," Ama said, pulling a face at Kehinde. Kehinde felt the knot of tension in her chest give way as she reached out to hold Ama's hand.

"The only thing now is, how are you planning on getting to London? What about your mother? Especially now, with Taiwo missing? And how are you going to make sure your husband doesn't find you?" Ama asked as she squeezed Kehinde's hand back.

"This is where we'll need your help," Kehinde said, as she began to speak of the plan that was taking shape in her mind.

———

When Kehinde got back home that afternoon she ran upstairs to Baba Tope's room, taking the stairs two at a time. He was not back yet and Kehinde only had a few minutes to look for what she hoped she would find. Ayo was already in the kitchen cleaning the fish for dinner while she waited for her.

Kehinde went to her Baba Tope's desk, her heart beating against the new, solid feeling of resolve in her stomach. As usual, the heavy mahogany desk had been cleared away, there was only a sheaf of blank writing paper and a pen at the top. The three drawers beneath the table were locked. Swearing under her breath, Kehinde could visualise the key, tucked away in Baba Tope's pocket. She knew he kept a spare somewhere, but where? Forcing herself to think like him, her eyes zeroed in on his bedside table. She moved towards it swiftly, opening the single drawer. There was nothing in there but a pair of reading glasses and a Bible, and she felt beads of sweat forming on her forehead. Looking around the room one last time, she checked underneath Baba Tope's pillow. To her joy, a bunch of keys lay there, beside a cluster of cowry shells that resembled the ones the Babalawo in the forest had been wearing on his neck all those years ago.

Trying not to think about the cowry shells, she grabbed the keys and walked back to the desk by the window. Her hands shaking, she tried the top drawer, exhaling as she felt it slide out. There, she found the first thing she was looking for. Baba Tope's wax seal of authority that would get her aboard any ship leaving the Apapa port. Now she had to find the other, more important item. She opened the second drawer and found a stack of pound notes, closing the drawer then changing her mind, she reached into it and took a handful of notes before closing it. A sharp knock on the door made her jump.

"Aunty Kehinde, Mummy is calling you," came Adenike's voice. The door clicked as Adenike started to turn the handle on the other side.

"Just a minute! I'm looking for my brooch, I must have left it in here," Kehinde called back, hoping her voice sounded more confident than she felt. To her relief, she heard Adenike's footsteps retreating, and she turned her attention back to the last drawer.

There it was! The Elder Dempster shipping schedule for that week! Kehinde scanned the list, her eyes running over the words impatiently. Her eyes fell on a line item, and she felt her lungs soar with adrenaline. There was indeed a ship leaving that week, the *Abassa* was scheduled to leave on Thursday December 10 at 9am! No other ship was due to leave for the rest of the year. She only had a few days to get the rest of her plan in motion.

With her heart continuing to hammer in her ears like a canary in a locked cage, she quickly packed up the things she needed and placed them in the bag she had brought with her. She had just thrown the bag under the bed in her room and run out when Ayo appeared at the top of the stairs.

"There you are! I was beginning to wonder if you had fallen asleep!"

"Sorry, Ayo, I was looking for my brooch. I've found it now though!" Kehinde said with as much excitement as she could muster.

"Baba Tope will be home soon, we need to get dinner ready," Ayo said, already turning to go down the stairs.

In the kitchen Kehinde gutted a mackerel, slicing it into chunks beside Ayo as her thoughts continued to race. Running away meant she might never see Ayo and the girls again, and she felt a moment of deep sorrow. Ayo had been so kind to her, and she would miss them, but this was the only chance she would have to get away and she had to go. She had never done anything like this before – it was both exhilarating and frightening. She would write to her mother to let her know she was safe, because she knew that her mother would be distraught when she found out that she was also missing. And Madam Titi! She thought of her and the women of the LMWA that she would be leaving behind. They would miss her too, but she knew they would understand. If everything went according to plan though, no one would know she was missing until the ship had sailed, and by then, there would be nothing anyone could do about it. She and Emeka would be long gone on their journey to freedom. The hope she felt made her more certain that she would find Taiwo. Emeka would know what to do when they got there. He had said he knew people at *The Times* in London that could help with getting information on missing soldiers. With a happy, nervous sigh, she continued with the dinner preparations, trying her best to look like her life was not about to change.

Chapter Twenty-Seven

December 10, 1942

Kehinde perched on the edge of her bed, a small bag beneath her feet and her heart in her mouth. The day was finally here, and although it was still dark outside, she only had twenty minutes to get to the ferry, where she, Emeka and Ama would be making the short trip across the river to the Apapa port so she and Emeka could board the *Abassa*. She still felt like she was in a dream, a sort of trance where her alter ego was making decisions the real Kehinde would never have made. They had left nothing to chance, but Kehinde still felt horrible. She had thrown up every day for the last six days, from the pregnancy or her nerves she wasn't sure. The secrecy and lies had made her feel physically ill, and although she was prepared for her new life with Emeka, the reality of what she was about to do was weighing down on her like a harmattan fog.

She had stolen one of Baba Tope's letters, and copying his

handwriting, had written the rite of passage for her and Emeka.

> *Dear Captain,*
>
> *I hope this letter meets you hale and hearty in these troubled times.*
>
> *I write to you today to allow my good friend, Emeka Alanta and his wife, Kehinde Alanta on your passenger ship. Emeka Alanta is a renowned leather trader and he takes with him some of the finest leather to be used as a sample for the boots of our Imperial soldiers. They are to be given room and board, with a promise to settle the fees in good time. Based on my years of dealing with your line, and my long-standing reputation at the Apapa port, I humbly ask that you honour my request.*
>
> *Yours sincerely,*
>
> *Mr Gboyega Ogunjobi*

Kehinde had signed the letter, slowly copying out Baba Tope's sprawling signature, and sealed it with his red wax seal. She had returned both the seal and the stolen letter to his drawer.

The day after, she had written two final letters. One to Ayo, and a longer one addressed to the police, detailing everything she knew about the meetings Baba Tope had been conducting with Mr Babajide and Mr Lateef. With Ama's help, she had gone to First Bank on Broad Street to withdraw all her savings. In addition to the notes she had taken from Baba Tope's desk, she now had a total of £135 to her name. She left half of it with Ama in an envelope with a letter to give to her mother long after she was gone – that at least would give her some kind of income when Baba Tope stopped sending her money. Kehinde left the rite of passage with Emeka. It wouldn't do for such a letter to be found in her room, just in case anyone went snooping.

Kehinde wondered what her father would have made of all this. Taiwo was the only member of her family who she knew would approve of her actions, but she couldn't think about him now. She had to stay strong. Her mother might never forgive her for the shame, but whenever she tried to imagine her father's advice in this situation, she came up blank. Maybe doing the right thing was not always a straightforward decision.

Then there was also the issue of whether the rite of passage would be accepted or not. She knew that over the years she had been married, Baba Tope had written many such letters for other traders, but she didn't know if the traders had been accepted on the ships, or if they had made it to London. London was a place that only existed in the novels she read, a flat, two-dimensional realm, not one she could imagine herself living and breathing in. But if Taiwo had done it, so could she, and the thought of finally being free was enough motivation to go on this mad journey.

Emeka had friends in London who could help them with lodgings. He had said they would stay with one of his childhood friends who was now a bus driver in Lambeth. Emeka was confident he would take them in, and Kehinde was banking on the good will of this stranger. They had decided it would be best if Emeka did not give any notice at the *Daily Times*, better not to raise any suspicion in case Baba Tope dug deep in his investigations. Kehinde had no doubt that he would look for her, scour the streets of Lagos and everywhere in Nigeria before he gave up. Ama would stand in for her, lie that Kehinde had been there all day if she had to. Ama had also agreed to tell Madam Titi the truth after they had left, and

Kehinde knew that she could trust her to stay silent if Baba Tope thought to question her. She felt as prepared as she could be.

Kehinde stood up, forcing the rising panic down her throat as she picked up her bag. She had only packed a handful of clothes, and a few essentials, including the picture of her father and the picture of her and Taiwo from their eighteenth birthday that now seemed like another lifetime ago. When the inevitable search started, she didn't want it to look like she had planned to run away. Fumbling in the dark, she walked towards her room door for the last time, turning the knob slowly as she let herself out.

To her utter shock she saw the form of a body on the sofa in front of her room. As she stepped out, the form turned and looked in her direction. At first Kehinde felt relief, then dismay as her eyes adjusted to the dark. It was only Ayo in her nightgown, looking equally confused at Kehinde fully dressed, her eyes landing on the bag in her hand.

"Kehinde?"

"Ayo … Ẹ káàárọ̀. What are you doing here?"

Ayo sat up and adjusted the shawl around her shoulders. "I couldn't sleep. I left Baba Tope's room to come down here, but I knew that Adenike and Ashabi would wake up if I walked into my room. Where are you going?"

Of all mornings, it had to be this one, Kehinde thought as the taste in her mouth turned sour. Ayo's eyes narrowed. She stood up and moved closer, feeling the sleeve of Kehinde's velvet dress, the thickest one she owned.

"Kehinde, you didn't answer me. Where are you going?" she repeated, a note of panic in her voice.

"London."

"Is this a joke?"

"Please don't tell Baba Tope."

Ayo staggered towards the sofa. "What do you mean 'Don't tell Baba Tope?' Kehinde, what's going on?" She had taken a step back, her hand still outstretched like she was scared, but ready for battle and she shifted to the side, blocking the staircase, the gate between Kehinde and freedom.

"There's a lot to explain, but please trust me when I say I know what I'm doing and this is the only way," Kehinde said in a jumble of words.

"You can't be serious," Ayo said, her voice sounding eerily sharp against the darkness of the room. Kehinde felt a sob rising in her throat. "The only way for what? Kehinde? What about the baby?"

"Ayo, please, you're going to wake up the whole house," Kehinde whispered desperately. "I need to leave now, please, Ayo, I'm running out of time."

"What will Baba Tope say when he wakes up and doesn't see you?"

"I already left a note saying that I had to go to the market early."

"And in the evening when you're not back?"

Kehinde looked at her, mutinously silent.

"You can't be serious," Ayo repeated, shaking her head. It was hard to tell in the dark, but Kehinde thought she could see tears in Ayo's eyes. "Why would you leave us like this?"

"Ayo! You've been like a sister to me, I'm not leaving you," Kehinde cried, dropping her bag on the floor, and taking a step towards Ayo, knowing that she had meant "how can you leave *me*", not us.

"If I wasn't here, you wouldn't even have said bye!"

"I already left a letter for you on your sewing table!"

"After three years, after everything we've been through together, all you leave is a letter?"

"Ayo, please … please don't make this harder than it already is."

"This is about that man, isn't it?" Ayo hissed, after a brief pause.

"What man?" Kehinde felt the sweat in her underarms clinging to her sleeves.

"The one you took Adenike and Ashabi to Elegbata Square with! You think I didn't figure it out? I never asked because honestly, I was hoping my suspicions were wrong. You're running away with him, aren't you? Is the baby his?"

Kehinde felt her blood turn cold. "Ayo … please, let me explain later, but right now I really, really have to go."

"You're leaving us, your family, for this man?" Ayo looked so hurt that Kehinde thought her heart might explode.

"Ayo, I love him, and he loves me. And I have to see if I can find Taiwo. This is my only chance. If you care about me as much as I think you do, then please, let me go,"

They both jumped as the sound of Mama Tope's door opening cut across the tension in the air like an axe for the kill.

"What's all this?" she asked, her eyes taking in the scene unfolding before her.

"Mama Tope … please…" Kehinde started begging.

"Kehinde is going to London … Her mother sent her … to inquire about her brother at the War Office. Our husband doesn't know, she's trying to spare him the pain and worry of thinking of his little flower on that big ship all by herself," Ayo said after a brief moment of silence.

Kehinde held her breath, watching Mama Tope as her eyes narrowed, a look she knew too well. She wasn't sure if she had heard their conversation – but she must have, and now

Kehinde was doomed for sure. Kehinde felt her future slipping away with the morning mist as she saw Mama Tope's features arrange themselves into a smile.

"In that case, she'll need much warmer clothes than what she has on," Mama Tope said, disappearing back into her room.

"Why did you lie for me?" Kehinde whispered to Ayo.

Ayo looked at Kehinde silently as tears streamed down her face. Mama Tope reappeared holding a coat that looked like a dead animal.

"Here, take this with you. London at this time of the year is very cold," she said, stretching her hand out to Kehinde.

"Thank you, Mama Tope ... I don't know what to say," Kehinde said, holding the fur coat against her.

"Don't say anything. I'll let Tope know you're fine. She'll ask for you, the way you've always asked for her. She won't tell anyone where you are, and neither will we. You should go now, before Baba Tope wakes up." She gave Kehinde a tap on the shoulder and walked back into her room, closing the door firmly behind her.

"She's right, you should go now," Ayo said, her voice sounding like she had a blockage in her throat as she wiped the tears that were now streaming down her face like a waterfall. "Take care of yourself," Ayo said as she pulled Kehinde in for a fierce hug.

Unable to speak through her tears, Kehinde hugged her back, then ran down the stairs, and out of the gate, as she left the Ogunjobi house behind. She ran without stopping until she got to the jetty at Marina Bay. She could just about make out Ama and Emeka standing by the ferryman as she got there.

"I thought you weren't coming again," Emeka said, as he took her in his arms like he would never let go.

"I had to beg the driver to give us a few more minutes, he's been threatening to leave us!" Ama said, flapping her hands like a bird as she ushered Emeka and Kehinde onto the ferry.

Apart from three sailors and five dock men, they were the only other passengers on the ferry as it pulled away from the jetty against the orange of the rising sun. Kehinde huddled closer to Emeka, still trying to catch her breath.

"I was so worried you had changed your mind," Emeka murmured into her ear.

"I could never, ever change my mind. You know that." Kehinde said, looking up at his earnest face.

"You've been crying?" he asked, sitting back to look at her as a worried expression crossed his face. The hat he was wearing cast a shadow across his brow, exaggerating the brown of his eyes.

"I didn't realise how hard it would be to say goodbye," she said, stroking the brown fur coat on her lap as she thought of Ayo's heartbroken face.

"Lovebirds, if you look now, you can see the back of your ship over there," Ama said, pointing in the direction of the vast Apapa port looming closer over the water's waves.

Kehinde had never been here before, and although it had been described to her many times her breath caught as she looked at the rows of barges, containers and ships that lined the port, completely blocking out the rest of the city on land behind it. There were containers of different colours and brands, some labelled with writing in languages she could not read. Bare-chested men and boys were standing everywhere, carrying heavy-looking sacks and boxes, and lifting them into boats headed for cargo ships. The *Abassa* stood tall and proud, a long, black structure that sat on the ocean like a whale, ready to gobble her up.

"You remembered the passage letter?" Kehinde asked.

"Yes, I have our papers and passports here," Emeka said, raising a brown envelope in his hand. The bag of leather samples sat on the floor between him and Ama. Kehinde tried to quell the feeling of panic and nausea rising within her. They were here, everything was in order, the ship was ready. She told herself to calm down and concentrated on the thought that in just a few hours, she and Emeka would be sailing into their new life together. Then she would find Taiwo, and all would be well.

Emeka took her hand as they got off the ferry, placing his hand on her waist to steady her as she stepped onto the busy jetty. A truck laden with a red container drove past them, bringing with it a gust of wind that almost blew off Emeka's hat. All around them shirtless men were hauling bags and crates of all sizes onto waiting cranes and trucks. People were moving back and forth on planks leading to the ships, and the port air was buzzing with the endless activity and smell of the ocean that made Kehinde think of her father.

"Right, let's get you both on this ship! The gangway is just over there," Ama said, pointing towards the *Abassa* that looked even larger in person.

"Please remember the letter to the police," Kehinde said over the hammering in her chest.

"It's already in my bag. I'm going to drop it off as soon as I leave here," Ama said, the grin on her face rivalling the rising sun.

"Ama, thank you so much. For everything," Kehinde said, feeling like crying all over again. Ama had been the best friend she could have asked for, and she would miss her too, dearly.

"For my brother and sister? Don't mention it. I'm just sad

I'm not joining you! I can't wait to see Onyi's face when I finally tell her," Ama said.

"Remember to tell her not to tell anyone," Emeka said, not bothering to say she should not tell Onyi at all, knowing his sister.

"Of course. Now get on the ship before it leaves you!" Ama said, hugging them both before pushing them in the direction of the gangway. "I'll wait here to wave you off!" she called out to them, the wind half carrying her words away towards the ocean.

A sailor with a red face that stood out against his white and navy uniform was checking the papers of each passenger at the foot of the gangway. He nodded to them in greeting as they approached, reaching out for their papers. The sailor read the letter, looking up at both Emeka and Kehinde as he read.

"Passports, please," he said brusquely.

He studied both and handed them back to Emeka. "One moment," he said, disappearing into the ship behind him.

"What's happening?" Emeka asked Kehinde.

"I don't know," Kehinde replied feeling the sweat in her underarms cling to her velvet dress. Another sailor stepped in to replace him, checking the papers and passports of the woman behind them, waving her in as Kehinde and Emeka stood to the side. Kehinde's mind was racing. Had Baba Tope already found her missing and was he trying to stop them? Surely it was impossible, he couldn't have found out so quickly. The first sailor came back out of the ship, his mouth set in a grim line.

"I'm afraid we just have space for one more passenger. We only have a single bunk available," he said.

"I don't understand, the letter asked for two passengers," Kehinde said. This sailor clearly had not read it properly, she thought, her anxiety making her sound more annoyed than scared.

"Yes, ma'am, but unfortunately Mr Ogunjobi gave us no prior notice. Usually, he would have called days in advance to let us know. The letter is just a formality really," he said with a shrug.

Fear spread over Kehinde like a cold fire that threatened to blot out her mind, burning every thought in her as she stopped herself from dropping into the water. She was going to be sick, violently ill across the deck and the fine shoes of the passengers that walked past her, confident of their place on this ship.

"Sir, please, there must be a way. We both need to go," Emeka said, sounding hoarse.

"This is a much smaller ship, we need to reduce our chances of being spotted by those damned U-Boats, forgive my language, ma'am. We only have room for one additional passenger at this time," the sailor said apologetically.

Kehinde's legs began to shake. How could she be stupid enough to think that it would be so easy?

"Can I speak to my wife quickly?" Emeka asked, regaining his composure.

"Of course, but be quick, we are set to depart within the hour," the sailor said, gesturing to the side, already turning to the officer in uniform standing behind them.

"Kehinde, you have to go," Emeka said immediately.

"No, I can't leave you!"

"We don't have a choice, my love."

"Yes, we do! We can wait for the next ship!"

"And then what? You get your husband to call in advance next time? Kehinde, I'll have to come later. This is the only way we can be together one day! We're lucky that there's even a space left for you! Plus, the sooner you get to London, the higher your chances of finding out what happened to Taiwo."

Kehinde's tears streamed down her face for the second time that morning. Why was life so unfair? Would she never be happy? Emeka embraced her as the sobs racked her shoulders.

"It's not forever. I promise. I'll be on the first ship I can get on. We'll be together in no time, I promise."

They both glanced at the sailor again as he cleared his throat. It appeared that all the other passengers had boarded the ship already.

"I love you," Kehinde said to him for the first time. She wanted him to know, because she was scared – afraid she would never see him again, that this beautiful love that she had known would be all that she would know in her lifetime, and that her child would never know its father.

"You know I love you too," Emeka said, grinning. "Wait for me, I'll be right behind you," he said, tugging at her hand as they walked back to the sailor.

"Well?" he said, looking at Emeka.

"My wife will go ahead of me, with the, er, the leather," he said. "Can I at least carry the bag onto the ship for her?"

"No need sir, we've got porters for that." He whistled, and a boy appeared almost immediately. He picked up Kehinde's bags and stood ready for the next instruction.

"Take these to the third deck please, room sixty-nine," the sailor said. "Right, ma'am, you can follow him, he'll show you to your room. We'll be departing shortly."

Chapter Twenty-Eight

MERSEYSIDE DOCK, LIVERPOOL, ENGLAND

January 2, 1943

K ehinde watched as the shadowy outline of land came into view. The small city that was the ship moved towards its destination as passengers crowded on the deck to look and point with excitement. She had made it to England, the motherland, the centre of the British Empire, the great country that she had read so much about but never seen. She squinted as she tried to see the grey outlines of the buildings through the dense smog.

"We'll start dismounting soon, ma'am. The trains for London will be just opposite the dock," the sailor from the gangway said to her, nodding before he walked towards the other end of the ship. His name was Pete, and he had been nothing but kind since she got on the *Abassa*, making an extra effort to look out for her over the last twenty-four days. He told her she reminded him of his wife, at home in Cornwall. He had been serving with the British Navy since the start of the war and he missed her and their two boys. He could not imagine his little wife on a ship all on her own, he had said to Kehinde. She had assured him that her husband, Emeka, would be joining her in England soon, at least she hoped he would.

She had stayed on her narrow bunk, staring at the ceiling for most of the journey, the rocking motion reminding her of every moment she had spent on her father's boat. The four walls of her cabin seemed to close in on her as she spoke to herself. She would find Taiwo. Emeka would join her. They would start their family and live happily ever after. These declarations had to be true, she refused to entertain the other thoughts that stood on standby, waiting to take her down to the depths of despair, a place deeper than the ocean. As she looked at the land before her, she refused to panic. She had made it! She would not, could not, lose hope now. She would get her train tickets at the station, and board the train for London. She had the address for Emeka's friend's house in Lambeth but the last thing she wanted to do was show up at the house of a man she didn't know. There was only one person she knew in London, and she had to try her luck there first.

Kehinde felt her emotions churn within her as she placed her hands on her belly. She shivered against the gust of wind that blew in her face as she pulled Mama Tope's fur coat closer around her shoulders, grateful for its warmth. This was it, there was no going back now.

"Looks a bit grim, doesn't it?" said Mrs Potts as she came up beside Kehinde. She was an older woman from Sierra Leone who had joined the voyage when the ship stopped at Freetown, instantly latching herself to Kehinde as the only other black woman travelling on her own on the days when Kehinde made it to the dining room. Mrs Potts was returning home to London, where she lived with her husband and three children. She had come to Freetown for the funeral of her sister who she had not seen since she moved to London fifteen years ago. Kehinde would be getting the train to London with her and Kehinde was grateful that she had taken her under her wing. She had also been glad of her company, especially on Christmas Day and New Year's Day, when everyone else seemed to have someone to celebrate with.

"When I first came here with my husband I was appalled! I thought England was supposed to be beautiful, but all I saw were old buildings everywhere! Took some getting used to, it did!" she said, nodding in the direction of the grey port ahead of them.

"Is it always like this?" Kehinde asked.

"Yes! We're even lucky it's not raining! The cold is another thing though, you just wait for the end of January," Mrs Potts responded with the relish of one imparting knowledge. "Right, let's get our things together. There'll be a scurry to disembark, best to beat the rush."

When they came back up, the ship had been positioned by the pier, and the now lowered gangway had a line of passengers wrapped in all manner of coats and scarves lining up to get off the ship. Kehinde dragged her bags along with her, wishing she could leave the bag of leather behind. She let out a sigh of relief when she saw that it was Pete once again checking papers at the end of the gangway.

"Contact address, ma'am," he asked, smiling, after handing her papers back to her.

Kehinde blinked, hesitating before she spoke. "Number 3, Liverpool Street, London," she said, hoping that the made-up address wouldn't draw any attention to her. Leaving the real address she was going to would only make it easier to find her if Baba Tope decided to look for her in London.

"Okay, ma'am. You can get a train to Euston from the station, right there on the other side of the dockyard. Goodbye ma'am, and good luck. I do hope your husband can join you soon enough," he said before he turned to the passenger behind her.

Mrs Potts was waiting for her at the foot of the gangway, holding a big brown bag which she dragged along behind her. Merseyside dock was busier than the Apapa port had been, with more men here offloading cargo from the rows of ships lined up against the pier. There were shouts as the labourers carried bag after bag into awaiting vehicles. Although they were speaking English, Kehinde struggled to make out what they were saying, their accents were so strong.

She walked along the cobblestones beside Mrs Potts and the other passengers headed for the railway. Some of the passengers looked happy while some looked weary, but no one said anything to Kehinde as they hurried by.

"Looks a lot worse than it did the last time I was here," Mrs Potts said, looking in the direction of the street beyond the station. There was smoke in the air, and some of the buildings looked like they were only partly constructed.

"There was a Blitz here last year. No, it wasn't last year, it was May 1941, that's it. Those bloody Germans raided all of Merseyside. So many people died," she continued, shaking her head. Kehinde had read about it and thought about Taiwo then, wondering if he was part of the people wrecking the same havoc in enemy territory. The thought had made her sad, that her brother could be causing the same type of pain they were feeling all over the Empire. What was the point of reducing the whole world to rubble? Would the victor pick up the pieces afterwards?

They hurried towards the overhead station, where Mrs Potts muscled her way through to the crowd to the ticket stand. "Two train tickets to London please," she said loudly, making the man behind the ticket counter blink.

"Coach or first class?" he asked, glancing at Kehinde before looking back at Mrs Potts.

"Coach, please."

Kehinde was grateful for how Mrs Potts had taken command of the situation, focusing on the present and not what she would do when she got to London. She followed Mrs Potts to the platform where they boarded their train and settled down in their seats. Almost immediately after the train started moving, Mrs Potts fell asleep. Kehinde, on the other hand, watched the rolling countryside, wondering about this country that seemed to have so much grey, green and brown.

Once they arrived in London, Kehinde and Mrs Potts made their way to the bus stops that were lined up outside Euston station. Kehinde again was overwhelmed by the people of all shapes, colours and sizes that hurried past her. Everyone walked so fast, like they knew exactly where they were going and could hardly wait to get there. Station workers shouted announcements through a loud speaker and the noise of it all made her head spin.

"You're sure you know where you're going, dear?" Mrs Potts asked Kehinde. They had reached the bus stops and although Kehinde was getting on the number 11, Mrs Potts had to wait for the 82, which would take her home to North Finchley. The streets here were wider than the ones in Lagos, with more cobblestones than sand, and there seemed to be an ever-present smell of smoke in the air. The pumps and stockings she was wearing were no match for the cold and her ankles felt like they were freezing into ice blocks.

"Yes, Mrs Potts," Kehinde said, her voice wobbling in the wind, stepping aside as an older man brushed past her to get on his arriving bus. The buses here were so imposing, big and brown, like moving houses. She wanted to run home with Mrs Potts and cry again for how foolish and naïve she had been, for thinking that this had ever been a good idea.

Before she could convince her alter ego to retreat into whatever black hole it had emerged from, bus 11 pulled up, bringing with it a blast of cold air that seemed to knock some sense into her.

"Thank you, Mrs Potts, I'll write to you!" Kehinde said, hopping on to the bus with her bags before she could change her mind.

"Take care then! Come and visit me some time!" called Mrs Potts, as Kehinde fumbled in her bag for her fare. She hurried along to the back corner of the bus and sat waving to Mrs Potts as the bus pulled out of the station. Now she was truly alone.

She tried to concentrate on the roads as the bus made its way through South London. The city looked like what she had imagined, but with a dull cast her imagination could never have conjured. The people on the streets walked by looking haunted, half hidden as they huddled into their coats. The cold air rushing into the open windows of the bus smelt damp, like clothes that had not had a chance to dry in the sun. Several posters hung on the stone walls of the buildings encouraging men to enlist, calling for nurses and more disturbingly, warning about spies. Some places had clearly been recently bombed, Kehinde thought with a start as the bus wound round a collapsed building where smoke snaked out of the rubble. The war that had seemed like a faraway threat in Lagos seemed much closer here. As the bus pulled past the worst of it, a young woman came into view, crouched and sobbing on the edge of the street. Kehinde shuddered, wondering again where Taiwo was and if he had walked these streets too.

Sleepy, but too worried about missing her stop, she found herself dozing off and waking in a panic intermittently. An older lady sitting opposite her was trying and failing to hide her laughter every time Kehinde's head snapped up.

"St George's Street!" the driver finally called out, after what felt like hours. Kehinde gathered her belongings and hopped off the bus as she tried to get her bearings. It was a long, quiet street, with rows of houses packed side by side next to each other. There was a church on the other end of the street where the bus had dropped her off, and although no houses on this road appeared to have been hit directly by a bomb, the smell of smoke hung heavy in the air. Unlike the trees in Lagos, the ones here had no leaves on them, and were covered by a frosty sheen that added to the grey overcast. Shivering, Kehinde made her way down the street she had addressed countless letters to, checking the house numbers until she got to 13. She pressed the bell, and after a few minutes, she heard footsteps approaching the door.

"Good morning. How can I help you?" said the black woman peeking around her barely open door, looking Kehinde up and down.

"Good morning. I'm looking for Mrs Bimpe Thompson, please," Kehinde said, barely hearing her own voice above the pounding of her heart.

"That would be me. Can I help you?" Aunty Bimpe said, opening the door a bit wider as she came to stand on her front step. She was a taller version of Aunty Laide, and although it had been many years since Kehinde had last seen her, she was sure it was her as she spoke. She was wearing a white nurse uniform and she fiddled with her apron as she listened to Kehinde.

"Aunty Bimpe ... it's me ... Kehinde," she stuttered.

The confusion in Aunty Bimpe's face deepened for a second before the creases in her face smoothened out with the dawn of recognition. Her face lit up into a huge smile as she hugged Kehinde, pulling her and her bags into her home.

"Kehinde! My God, how wonderful to see you! Come in, come in, you'll catch your death out there in this dreadful cold!" She ushered Kehinde into the little house, shutting the door firmly behind them as Kehinde was enveloped into the warmth.

"Last time I saw you, you were this high!" she said, raising her hand to just below her hip. "What are you doing here? Is your husband here with you?" she asked, peering through the window by the door.

"No, no. It's just me," Kehinde said, her knees almost buckling with the relief of finally making it to her destination.

"What a lovely surprise! You didn't tell me you were coming! And Laide never mentioned you were coming either! Or maybe you both did, and I just never got the letters? What a mess the post has been lately, it's why I stopped sending your books!"

"Bim, who are you talking to?" called a deep voice from within the yellow wallpapered house.

"James! It's little Kehinde Ilesanmi all the way from Lagos here to see us! I should stop using your maiden name! Remind me, what's your husband's surname again?" Aunty Bimpe asked.

"Ogunjobi," Kehinde said quietly.

Uncle James appeared from what Kehinde presumed was

the kitchen from the smell of frying eggs that came with him. He looked the same as he had when he had come to Lagos from Jamaica years ago, before he and Aunty Bimpe moved to London, and he still reminded Kehinde of a teddy bear, just that he now had grey hair around his temples.

"Kehinde! Wonders shall never end! How lovely to see you!" Uncle James said, wrapping her in a hug as Kehinde's head rested under his chin. Their kindness was more than she could bear, and she finally released the dam of tears that had been bubbling in her chest since she left Lagos.

"Oh my," Aunty Bimpe said, shaking her head as she looked at her husband.

"Come in, dear, let's have a chat on the sofa, shall we? Your aunt will bring you a nice cuppa and you can tell us all about it okay?" Uncle James soothed, leading her deeper into the house with his arm still around her.

Kehinde could just about make out the dim front room as she was lowered onto the sofa underneath a window that looked out onto the street. Hiccupping and sobbing, she accepted the tissue that Uncle James extended to her, unable to stop crying even when Aunty Bimpe returned with a cup of hot tea. Aunty Bimpe held it as she looked at her husband again, their shared worry passing between them like an invisible ball.

"You poor thing. Was the journey frightening?" Aunty Bimpe said. "Kehinde dear, what's going on? Did something happen?" she continued when Kehinde kept crying, crouching down beside her. Jamal and Kevin, their sons, had also appeared by the front room door now, looking at the scene playing out in their home with wide eyes.

"Nobody knows I'm here, Aunty... I ... I ... ran away," Kehinde sobbed.

"James, take the boys outside for a walk, please," Aunty Bimpe said, standing up to place the cup of tea on a side table. She sat beside Kehinde and wrapped an arm around her, reminding Kehinde of the way Aunty Laide had held onto her mother the day they had found out her father was missing forever.

"Boys, you heard your mother. Coats and shoes on," Uncle James said in a tone that broached no argument. The boys scuffled out of the room and were back down in no time with their coats, still peering at Kehinde like she was a giraffe that had escaped from London Zoo. The door slammed behind them and Aunty Bimpe gave Kehinde's shoulder another squeeze.

"Okay, dear. I'm listening. Tell me everything," she said.

Chapter Twenty-Nine

K ehinde told Aunty Bimpe the whole story, from the beginning, every detail from her arrival in the Ogunjobi house, her job with the LMWA, the telegram about Taiwo and now her secret departure. She left nothing out, even Emeka, and although Aunty Bimpe's eyebrows shot up into her hairline when Kehinde said she was pregnant, she listened without saying anything.

"Kehinde, love, we must write to your mother, at least to tell her where you are. She'll be worried sick," Aunty Bimpe said at last, when Kehinde was done speaking and had finally agreed to take a sip of her tea.

"No, Aunty! She'll tell my husband where to find me!"

"I don't think she will, you know. Put yourself in her shoes. She's already so worried about Taiwo, think about how worried she'll be if she thinks you're also missing!'

"So, you think I should tell her I'm here with you?" Kehinde asked, rubbing her nose against her sleeve.

"I definitely think you should!" Aunty Bimpe said, looking at her in the same earnest way Aunty Laide did when she was trying to be convincing, with her eyebrows knitted together and her lips in a pout. "Write to her today, love. I certainly will if you don't!"

Kehinde looked so crestfallen that Aunty Bimpe quickly added, "Oh, of course you can stay here for as long as you want, dear, but we need to tell your mother. That's the only condition," she said.

When Aunty Bimpe had shown her to the kitchen table and forced Kehinde to sit with a stack of papers, and a pen, Kehinde settled down to write the most difficult letter of her life.

> *No 13 St George's Street*
> *Southwark*
> *London*
> *January 2, 1943*

Dear Mother,

By now, my husband would have told you that I have left his house, and I expect that before then, Ama would have left my note explaining that I had left Lagos. I know the money she gave you cannot compensate for all the trouble, but I do hope it will at least stop you from worrying about how to survive until I can send more.

Please don't be angry with me. I had to do what was best for me, and I am still convinced that this is our only real chance of finding out where Taiwo is. Only God knows when this war will end, but I'm sure that regardless of what happens, I will never go back to Mr Ogunjobi's house. I will never be a parlour wife again, and Mummy, although I am sorry for all the shame my

*departure may have caused you, I have no regrets over my
actions.*

*I met a man, who I love dearly, and who I hope will be joining
me soon in London. I know you and Daddy always wanted what
was best for me, within your resources and understanding, and I
thank you for everything you have done for me. Please believe
that the life I have chosen to live now is for the best. I pray you
will find it in your heart to forgive me. I am safe in London with
Aunty Bimpe and Uncle James, I will send you news of Taiwo's
whereabouts once I get some.*

Your dear daughter,
Kehinde

No 12 Olusola Bamgbose Street
Lagos Island
Nigeria
February 23, 1943

My dearest Kehinde,

*Home is not the same without you. First Tope, and now you,
it feels as if there is a gaping hole in the house, and it can never,
ever be filled again. Adenike and Ashabi keep asking me so many
questions, they don't understand how you could have vanished,
just like dust. Of course, I tell them that I do not know where you
are but that only leads to more questions about your
whereabouts.*

*I was so glad to hear that you arrived in London safely. Baba
Tope continues to search high and low for you. He is convinced
that you have been kidnapped for some sort of blood ritual and he
has been to see the Babalawo twice now. I do hope he will be okay*

soon; it hurts me to see him in so much distress and it certainly is not good for his health. Are you sure you will not at least tell him where you are? Whatever you decide, fear not, your secret remains safe with me.

Tope came home to visit last week and although she seemed a bit tired, she looked well, better than any of us were expecting. She asked after you, and I know your secrets are not mine to tell but I did say that I expect you will write to her. One good thing about you leaving is how it has brought Mama Tope and I closer together. She now gets up early to go to the ration queues with me, and we take it in turns to make meals, imagine that! Who knew that the departure of our youngest wife would turn us into friends?

Stay in touch, Kehinde. You were in our lives for such a short time, but I feel like I lived a whole lifetime with you. Let me know how you get on in London, and if I am ever lucky enough to make the voyage there, I do hope you will let me come to see you with the girls. I love you like a sister, and I hope we will meet again soon.

Your sister wife,
Ayo

House 3 Malumo Street,
Lagos Island
Nigeria
February 24, 1943

Keke,
I wrote as soon as your letter arrived! You can imagine my shock at hearing from you! We have been so worried, your

mother has been beside herself with fear. How could you run off like that without telling anyone? Your husband turned up here demanding answers that we did not have, you can imagine how that would have felt for us. Uncle Ladipo has been putting up posters with your face on it, he even went to the police to report you missing.

Keke, although we have all been so worried, I love you as you know, and your mother agrees that it is indeed best to say nothing about knowing exactly where you are to your husband. I know Bimpe and James will take good care of you but please, Keke, come back home. We will find a way around this. I hate to think of what your future could look like as a fugitive in London, of all places. Your mother is here with me as I write, and has said she will welcome you back with open arms, you need not worry about that.

Yours,
Aunty Laide

Daily Times Office,
172 Broad Street,
Lagos Island
Lagos, Nigeria
February 28, 1943

My love. Getting your letter filled me with more happiness and hope than I thought possible. I've been a bit unwell and was away from work for a week, nothing serious, just a bit of a cold. So, when I got to the office and saw the letter addressed to me in your handwriting I was overjoyed. My only question is why did you not go to Samuel's house in Lambeth as I had advised? I hate to think of you imposing on Aunty Bimpe and her family, and now we also run the risk of being discovered. I know you said you can trust her, but I worry that your mother will tell your husband everything and our secret will be out. I cannot bear the thought that we will not be together after all of this.

Speaking of your husband, just yesterday, Ugo got wind of a plot the colonial administrators are hatching to have him arrested. He's being accused of multiple counts of embezzlement and fraud. Ugo is still investigating, but it looks like he had a smuggling operation going on at the port. I know you always said you thought he and his friends were up to no good, but this confirms it. Was this what you wrote in your letter to the police? I wish you had told me, I would have made sure they found him sooner! After everything he did to you, I would have been glad to be the one who made sure he was brought to justice. I hope he gets what he deserves.

I am saving every penny I own to pay for my fare to come to you as soon as possible. Ama's friend at the Supreme Court knows someone who can get me a good rate on one of the Elder Dempster passenger ships, but we will have to wait a bit my love – a few months, is what I have been told.

Ama and Onyi send their love. Although I was not at the store when your husband and Kayode came round the day after you left, Ama said they asked so many questions, but they will never find you. I know it is wicked of me, but I laugh so hard when I imagine them going round in circles with their search, and I laugh even harder as I imagine his face when the police show up at his door.

I cannot wait to hold you again. Sometimes I lie awake just imagining the feeling of you in my arms, the sound of your voice, the way your little nose scrunches up when you talk about something you do not like. I miss your akara, and I miss your way with words. The thought of spending forever with you makes me grateful for life, it makes me think that God must exist indeed to have blessed me with you. I wait patiently for the day that we can be reunited as one. Till then my love, please wait for me as I wait and long for you.

Always loving you,
Emeka.

Chapter Thirty

LONDON, ENGLAND

June 29, 1943

Kehinde shifted into as much of a foetal position as she could manage. She had been tossing and turning all night, and although she welcomed the warmth that had come with the start of summer, it meant that she spent most nights in a puddle of sweat.

Aunty Bimpe was sure the baby would arrive any day now, and Kehinde had to agree with her. Every evening, she struggled to climb the short flight of stairs in the house to Jamal's room, where she had been sleeping since her arrival. Both boys now shared Kevin's room and although they did not complain, Kehinde worried about all the upheaval she had caused for the Thompsons.

Aunty Bimpe and Uncle James had insisted that she stay with them, immediately reorganising their lives around her. Uncle James worked as a supervisor in the library down the road and he brought so many books home for Kehinde to read that it was easy for her to take her mind off everything else going on. He had even gone to the War Office at Whitehall to inquire about Taiwo, but it was confirmed that no one had heard from him and the four other pilots from their squadron since they left for France.

Aunty Bimpe had warned her that being sad was not good for the baby. As a midwife, she had seen many mothers lose the fight against despair during this endless war. She had begged and coerced Kehinde to go for walks, to eat the soups and drink the tinctures she had made for her, but with no news of Taiwo and Emeka still not here, Kehinde found it hard to be optimistic. She feared the worst; she was alone in London, about to have a baby without its father and her brother was nowhere to be found. Sometimes she wished she had stayed in Lagos and palmed off this baby as Baba Tope's, at least that would have guaranteed her a future that was more certain. Baba Tope's arrest and jail sentence at the beginning of the year would have made it much easier for her to flee with Emeka if she had stayed, but then she would have lived with the constant fear of what would happen when he got out. At least Ayo and Mama Tope were fine. Ayo had assured her that despite being heartbroken, they had enough money and grit between them for the upkeep of the house.

Another sharp pain at the base of her stomach made her turn over for what felt like the millionth time that night. Aunty Bimpe had told Kehinde that she must wake her as soon as she thought she was in labour, so they could go to St Thomas's hospital, where she worked, but Kehinde did not want to disturb her. It was still dark outside, and she knew that Aunty Bimpe had a long shift ahead at the hospital the next day. She clamped her mouth together as yet another wave of pain rolled over her, this time spreading from her lower belly to the base of her back.

Panting, she stood up to see if walking around the room would make her feel better. Her feet sunk into the carpet as she stood slowly, focusing on the picture of Jamal on the wall wearing a gold medal on what must have been his sports day. As she squinted her eyes to see the picture better in the dark, her body spasmed again, making her double over. After what felt like a long stretch of time had passed, she stood, this time making her way to the door, pausing as she placed her hand on the doorknob. She had to get Aunty Bimpe because this baby was trying to make his arrival into the world.

His arrival, because somehow, she knew this baby would be a boy. She felt connected to him, feeling his every move, sometimes seeing his face in her mind's eye. If only his father was here to welcome him. The thought was quickly replaced by a new wave of pain that engulfed her like thunder hitting a roof, and she grabbed the doorknob with both hands, stifling the cry that came unbidden from her lips.

"Keke! Are you okay?" came Aunty Bimpe's voice from the other side of the door.

"I think the baby might be coming," Kehinde grunted, as Aunty Bimpe pushed the door gently to let herself in. She had a bundle of towels beneath one arm, a candle in the other hand and was already wearing her apron. Kehinde realised that she must have heard her moving around much earlier in the night and had already begun to prepare herself for what she knew would come.

"Right, love, you look worse than I thought. I've put some water in the kettle already but why don't you get comfortable while we wait," Aunty Bimpe said, leading Kehinde back to the bed and propping her up against the pillows. Kehinde did as she was told, happy to not have to make any decisions while she tried not to wake the whole house with her cries. The pain was like nothing she had ever felt before.

"Let me check how far along you are, love," Aunty Bimpe said, gently lifting Kehinde's nightgown. "Hmmm, looks like you've already dilated quite a bit, dear, not long before it's time to push. No time to get to the hospital," Aunty Bimpe said, sounding shocked.

"Is everything okay?"

"Oh yes, everything is fine, my love, it's the natural order of things. Let me pop downstairs to get the water. I'll be back in a minute."

The minute felt more like an hour as Kehinde's labour pains continued. She felt like she was rocking in her father's boat in the middle of a storm as the panic rose within her. "Shh, má sùkún, ọmọ mi," her father would say to her whenever she curled up at the base of his boat. He felt close to her now. She could sense his presence in the room, calming her, telling her to be brave.

"Right, love. Let's see how you're getting on," Aunty Bimpe said, reappearing in the room. She was sweating as she hauled a basin of water to the foot of the bed, straightening up as Kehinde cried out. The pains were getting so close together now, she was hardly able to catch her breath in between them.

"Don't worry, love, nothing lots of women before you haven't done," Aunty Bimpe said, more to herself than Kehinde.

The guttural sound of her own voice took Kehinde by surprise as she got on all fours on the bed. If this was what women had to go through whenever they gave birth, she could not fathom how anyone could do it a second time. How had her mother given birth to two at once? She felt her heart constrict as her contraction subsided. Taiwo's face against the sun at the beach came back to her so powerfully that for a second, she thought he was here with her. But unlike her father's presence in the room, Taiwo's presence felt real, she felt his life like her own, pulsing through her veins.

"Taiwo is alive. I need to find him," she blurted.

Aunty Bimpe turned around from where she was bent over at the foot of the bed, arranging the towels and rags she had brought to the room. "Yes, dear, he lives forever as all who died in the faith of our Lord Jesus Christ," she said, the wideness of her eyes indicating that she thought Kehinde might be delusional with pain.

"No, Aunty Bimpe. I would know it if he was dead."

"Shh, don't exert yourself, dear," Aunty Bimpe said, coming up beside her to place a cool hand on Kehinde's wet shoulder.

"But—" Kehinde stopped mid-sentence as another contraction racked her body, this time causing her to slide off the bed as she knelt on the floor, biting some of the blue coverlet to stop herself from screaming.

"Shhh, shhh. You're almost there, love. We'll start pushing any minute now, and then I need you to do exactly what I say, dear," Aunty Bimpe said, adopting the soft but brusque tone she took with her patients at the hospital.

Kehinde leaned her head against the mattress. She felt like she was dripping from every orifice in her body. Sweat, tears and snot from her nose flowed as she became a mass of pain and panic. She wished Emeka was here. He would know what to say, he would know what to do, he would make her feel better. She was suddenly shaken by the thought of him never coming and never meeting his child. What if he forgot about her? Despite their letters, it had been months since he'd actually seen her, what if he had met someone else? What if he'd changed his mind about coming? He didn't know about the baby, was his love for her enough to make him come? She started to cry harder.

"Shhh my love, there, there now. Okay, let's get you back on the bed, okay. I'm going to need you to put your knees up like this, okay, love," Aunty Bimpe soothed as she guided Kehinde back on to the top of the bed. Gently, she eased Kehinde's legs apart.

"You're ready now, love. On the next contraction I'm going to ask you to push, okay? And when you push, love, listen to me, stop pushing as soon as I say stop, okay?" Aunty Bimpe said.

Kehinde nodded in response. This was it, there was no running away now. The moment was here and there was only one way out. She felt the rumble growing within her as the next contraction started, bracing herself as Aunty Bimpe positioned herself in between her legs.

"That's it, love, push! Push!"

Kehinde pushed, clenching her teeth as she did so. Her father felt closer, she could hear his voice as he cheered her on. There was a saying in Yoruba, something about the line between death and life being blurred during childbirth? She could hardly focus long enough to string it together in her mind. She stopped pushing as Aunty Bimpe coached, but before she knew it another contraction gripped her.

"That's it! This baby is coming out!" Aunty Bimpe squealed.

And so it went, the tug of war that was the beginning of life as Kehinde joined the mothers of the earth in their welcoming song.

"I see the baby's head!" Aunty Bimpe said.

Kehinde pushed, her exhaustion competing with her pain as she willed it all to be over, not sure if she was willing life itself to end. Anything to make the pain stop.

"That's it, love! The baby's almost all out now! One more big push, that's it, my love, keep going, dear!"

Just when she felt like she was about to give up she heard her father's voice, clear and calm. *Keep going, Keke, that's it.* Her father was here with her, he would see her through.

"Yes, my dear! Yes, oh well done! Well done, my love!" Aunty Bimpe cried, tears streaming down her face as Kehinde's baby boy was born. He screamed as he greeted the world, hands and legs flailing as Aunty Bimpe placed him on Kehinde's chest.

Kehinde looked at her son, lost for words as she looked at his little face. Emeka's bright brown eyes peered back at her as her son took her in, pouting with the lips that looked so much like hers and Taiwo's as he scrunched up his tiny nose. He was the most beautiful boy on earth.

"Hello, little one," she said into his ear, the tears in her eyes streaming down to bathe him, a baptism absolving Kehinde of all her worries. Her son was here, everything would be fine now.

"He's a handsome one, isn't he?" Aunty Bimpe said. She straightened up to open the windows to let in the rays of the rising sun. "I think he looks a lot like your father already, you know," Aunty Bimpe continued, making her way towards the door to give the new mother and baby some time on their own.

"He does. It's like my father came back to me. He's here to guide me through the rest of my life," Kehinde murmured.

As she lay in bed feeding her son and looking out of the window, she felt calmer than she had in a long time. She thought about everyone that had brought her to this moment, the people that had helped her find her voice, that had shown her that making a real difference meant being brave. Everything would be fine now. Come war or peace, she had made it to the place where it all began, to a love she never imagined possible. Kehinde was finally home and free.

Part IV

"Show the light, and the people will find their way."

Motto of the *West African Pilot**

---

* Azikiwe, N. *West African Pilot*, Lagos, Nigeria, 1937-1967

Epilogue

October 3, 1945

Kehinde ran across the station, her feet stomping on the cobblestones as she made her way through the throngs of people. Beside her, Babatunde jogged as fast as his little legs would carry him. This was an important day, for him and Mummy, and he hurried along with his hand in hers. Aunty Bimpe had warned them to leave home on time. Now that the war was over and the streets were full again, she had anticipated there would be traffic on the roads. She and Uncle James had seen them off to the bus station earlier that morning.

"Mummy, will we be back before it's dark?" Two-year-old Babatunde had asked, as he looked up at his mother while they waited for the bus. She was still amazed at how many words her small man had these days.

"You're only going down a few streets! You would think you were going on a trip to Berlin from the way he's been going on all morning," Aunty Bimpe laughed, picking up a giggling Babatunde.

"Well, who knows? We might decide to take a trip down to Berlin," Kehinde said, laughing.

"Oh, I hope not! It's far too soon for that," Uncle James cried.

"Now now, remember, you're supposed to be helping Nana with our special tea today, so you have to get back before it's dark. How will I ever get on without the help of my little man otherwise?" Aunty Bimpe said to Babatunde with a wink.

"We'll be back home before you know it, poppet!" Kehinde said, planting a kiss on her son's head as Aunty Bimpe smiled at her over the top of his hat.

"Good luck, Keke," she said softly, looking through her eyes to the whirlpool of emotions behind them. This was the day they had spoken about, the moment that Kehinde had been hoping for every day of her new life in London.

"Thank you, Aunty. See you both soon," Kehinde said, as she tried not to choke on the medley of joy and anxiety that was coursing through her.

"Babatunde, be a good boy for your mummy, okay?" Uncle James said, as he patted the boy's head of curls.

Kehinde had got on the bus to Euston and was now here, later than expected and running to platform nine. She picked Babatunde up and put him on her hip so they could move faster. As she got closer, men and women were embracing around her, some speaking in foreign languages, others crying and shouting in English. Some of the men looked beyond repair, with wide eyes, stooped over like ghosts roaming a world they did not recognise. Kehinde gulped as she got closer to the platform, the same platform she had disembarked from nearly three years ago.

On the platform there was hardly anyone left, just a few officers stepping off the train. Her heart danced, and not because she was recovering from the run. Could there have been some kind of mix-up? He was supposed to arrive today.

And then she saw him, standing with his back to her, studying a piece of paper, his head bent towards it. She would know that back anywhere. He was leaner, much ruddier than he had been the last time she saw him, but it was him. He must have sensed her behind him because he started to swivel slowly, and when he finally turned, Emeka was smiling, a beaming smile that radiated off their bodies as they ran into each other's arms.

"Daddy?" Babatunde whispered from where he was crushed between them.

Kehinde broke away from Emeka, to see him as he saw his son for the first time.

"This is Babatunde, your son," Kehinde said, as Emeka lifted him up and looked into his own eyes in the little face with the skin that glowed golden like his and Ama's.

"My son? Keks … you mean you were…? In all your letters you didn't say—"

"Shhh, you're here now, that's all that matters."

"Oh God, Keks … I have a son! Babatunde?" Emeka's eyes were filling up as he held the little boy who was grinning from ear to ear. Babatunde grabbed Emeka's glasses in his fist and laughed.

"Oh, Keks, what a precious gift," Emeka laughed, kissing Kehinde and embracing his boy at the same time. "I have so many questions to ask, so many things to say."

"Let's talk about it when we get home. Aunty Bimpe and Uncle James are dying to meet you."

The three of them walked down the platform, Kehinde with the loves of her life. She remembered that day in Elegbata Square, with Emeka, wishing that she was a real family with him, Adenike and Ashabi, and now here she was, her dream come true. She could hear her father's voice as he quoted one of his favourite proverbs, "*Bi Esin ba dáni gúlè ã tun gun ni; If a horse fell someone, what we do is to re-climb it.*" She had fallen off life's horse a few times and had lost her way, but finally, she felt like she was on the right path. Her father had said she was born to do great things, but her purpose had been simple all along; to choose life and to choose the little moments of joy that would build the foundation of a lifetime of happiness. She had chosen love, she had found her voice, and she was free. Life, like the ocean, came in waves with joys and disappointments, but she was finally at shore, at peace in the boat that was her body.

Kehinde's new journal, gifted by Emeka upon arrival in London.

October 5, 1945

It feels odd writing in a journal again, it almost feels like writing to myself, my old self, and that self of mine has changed so much, so I will write a letter to Taiwo instead, because Taiwo feels more like the current me than the Kehinde that used to be.

Tee, I have missed you. I know in my heart that you are out there somewhere, but I wish you were here with me. I feel complete but my completeness feels like a puzzle with a missing piece.

I have a new life now, a life you would be so proud of. Uncle James got me a job working as a cleaner in the library down the road. The pay isn't much, but I am surrounded by books every day and I love it. I take Babatunde with me and sometimes he

holds books upside down, trying to make sense of them the way
Aunty Laide said we used to do. I've also decided to start writing
again, not as a journalist but short stories about Nigerian
women. I feel like our stories are so rich and I want the world to
hear us, to hear about the experiences that give us each a unique
voice.

Emeka is finally here, almost three years to the day after I left
Lagos. After I left, the Atlantic passenger routes became too
dangerous, more than two ships were bombed before the end of
the war. I didn't realise that a part of me thought he would never
come. That's what loss does to you; it teaches you to hedge
against your hope. He's here now, and he and Babatunde are
making up for all their lost time. He has a reference from the
Daily Times and we are both hoping he finds a job soon. Aunty
Bimpe's little house is bursting with all of us in it and we will
need to find a place of our own.

It's ironic that after years of complaining about the colonial
government in Nigeria I find myself now making a life in the
very heart of the Empire. It's not so bad, the white people here
treat us blacks better than the ones in Lagos, who are there to rule
over us, do. Sometimes I still get funny looks on the streets and
there are some people who still find it odd to see free black people
in London, imagine that! Even in 1945 there are people who are
so backward. Just the other day, Margaret at the library asked me
if I have to take more baths to "keep the blackness off". Uncle
James gave her a piece of his mind, and told me later that she's a
funny one and I should pay her no mind.

It is definitely a foreign land, and I don't know how you put
up with the cold weather and sometimes even colder people. I
want to return to Nigeria one day, maybe when the dust settles
and I can go back to be a real family with Emeka and Babatunde.
Ayo, Tope and Aunty Laide's letters from Mummy all confirm

that Baba Tope is still in jail, but I don't think Lagos will ever be safe for us, for as long as he lives. For the time being, London will have to be our home, but truly, the real reason I don't want to go is because I know you are closer to me here, Tee, and I don't want to leave before we are reunited. Maybe we will go back to Nigeria together and Mummy will forgive me finally when she sees us. Just imagine how Daddy would have smiled at the thought.

Till we meet again, my dear brother, I promise to keep living for both of us.

Author's Note

The idea of *The Parlour Wife* came to me in 2018, one afternoon when I was visiting my paternal grandparents. Somehow, we found ourselves talking about World War Two and to my surprise, my grandmother spoke about her memories of joining ration queues with her family. I'm obsessed with historical fiction and period dramas, but at that moment it struck me that I hardly knew anything about what had happened in Lagos during the Second World War. Unlike the people in the Western world that I had read numerous books about, I knew nothing about what the people in Lagos had experienced during that period. What were they doing when the war was announced? How were their lives affected? What aspirations did they have, and what was life as a woman like back then?

Thus began my journey down the rabbit hole of finding everything I could about life in Lagos during World War Two. As my grandfather advised, "Anyone who wants to write a book needs to be prepared to read many books.". So, many books, journals, online articles, newspapers, documentaries and videos were consumed in the process of helping me understand what life was like for the men and women living in Lagos during the Second World War, and as colonial citizens of the British Empire. If you're interested in finding out more on this subject, I've included a bibliography at the end of the book that would be a good starting point. My grandparents' first-hand accounts were extremely useful in painting the picture of what colonial Nigeria looked like, down to the meals they used to eat, and the opinions people had about the colonial government. Some of their experiences were recounted to me so vividly that I had to include them as scenes. For instance, the cannon blasts on the day the war was announced in Lagos is a sound my grandfather remembered with such clarity that I felt like I had heard them myself.

Although *The Parlour Wife* is a work of fiction, I hope it will get readers thinking and talking about how people have always wanted the same things, through the ages – to find one's purpose, to have a voice, to be free, to be useful, to love and to be loved for one's true self.

Acknowledgments

I would like to thank God Almighty, my heavenly Father, for the creativity, discipline and patience to write this novel. Thank you for my talent and thank you for providing all the resources that went into bringing my dreams to fruition. To you be all the glory, honour and adoration, now and always, in Jesus Mighty Name, Amen.

Emily Glenister, my agent, thank you from the bottom of my heart. Right from the first interaction we had, I knew that we were destined to work together. Thank you for steering me through the publishing world with kindness and empathy, for being my champion at every opportunity and encouraging me every step of the way. I am blessed to have you.

To the team at One More Chapter, thank you for your passion and enthusiasm. Thank you for treating *The Parlour Wife* like your baby and thank you for the care that has gone into bringing Kehinde's story to life. Ajebowale, my editor, I remember reading your offer letter with tears in my eyes. The way you described *The Parlour Wife* gave me so much hope, and your nuanced insight and perspective gave my characters so much more depth. Thank you for the sensitivity you gave Kehinde's story.

Renike Olusanya, I've been a fan of your art for so long and I still cannot believe how lucky I am to have had you design the cover art for *The Parlour Wife*. Thank you for the stunning cover and the months of work that went into creating this flawless artwork.

Thank you to all four of my grandparents for the endless hours spent answering all my questions. Thank you for giving colour to a time in Nigeria's history that was full of so much hope and promise. Michael Thomas, thank you for taking out the time to speak to me about what training as a pilot in Nigeria looks like. To Ms Aramide at Sandgrouse market, your advice on the governance mechanisms of the Lagos Women's Market Association really helped to inspire my story. Ms Aduke Gomez, your witty and insightful perspectives on the history of Lagos were instrumental in enriching my depiction of 1940s Lagos. Thank you so much for sharing your knowledge and time with me.

Nikesh Shuklah, my Faber Academy tutor and my course mates on the Faber Academy Writing a Novel course, class of 2022, thank you for encouraging me to take my writing seriously and for being my first, gentle reviewers. Thank you for the objectivity you gave my words in those early days.

To my egbons in the literary world, Abi Dare, Nikki May, Ola Awonubi and Sefi Atta, thank you for the phone conversations, positive messages, voice notes and wisdom. The way you took me under your wings helped me fly and I will always be grateful. To my fellow writers and literary enthusiasts who cheered me on; Jola Ayeye, Chioma Okereke, Ola Tundun, Caroline Lammond, Evie Gaughan, Rogba Payne, Corin Burnside, Rukky Brume, Chiso Uko and Koye Oyeyinka, thank you for being sources of advice and encouragement. Thank you to the Black Girl Writers community and my first literary mentor, Hannah Weatherill, for your guidance and support.

Writing can sometimes feel like a lonely journey, but my amazing friends and family never let me feel completely alone. My mum, my sister Lara, my brothers Bode and Mayowa, my girls Dafi and Edia, read the earliest versions of *The Parlour Wife* and gave me the confidence boost I needed to carry on when I couldn't find my way. Thank you to my unpaid legal advisors Dipo, Kike, Mayowa and Edia for the time spent reviewing my contracts and offers. I wouldn't be here without you.

To my friends and family who I cannot possibly list but will try to do so anyway; Dami, Ayomide, Kemi, Larry, Bisola A. Joke, Bodunde, Lamide, Bodunrin, Tofe, Toyosi, Bisola, Timi, Nifemi, Aunty Ola, Timi, Olaolu, Aunty Peju, my Dalmeida family group, Nefe, Deji, Bisola F. Wonu, Relly, Gbolawoyi, Ronke, Aisha, Sandra, Piriye, Joann, Dumbili, Anu, Christine, Damilola, Nike, Taiwo, Princess, Janar, Rupali, Jess, Yoma and my OLPH Choir family, thank you for being in my corner always. Thank you so much to all my aunties, uncles, cousins, friends, the parents at my children's school that have become friends and acquaintances not listed here for your constant support.

To everyone at my workplace, the partners and my colleagues, thank you for letting me bring the fullest version of myself to work every day.

To my fantastic parents and parents-in-law, thank you for always asking, "So when is the book coming out? How can I get my copy?" Your belief in me means so much more than you can ever know.

My Shay and my Shaz. The way you ask questions, the fresh way you look at every aspect of life, your optimism about even the smallest details have transformed the way I view the world. Thank you for being the perfect blessings for me. I love you, my Shay and my Shaz.

Finally, my Dolz, my biggest fan, my trusted companion, my best friend, the one who keeps me grounded, the person who gets the worst of me but still wants all of me, thank you for being my endless love.

Bibliography

1. Adeboye, Olufunke, "Rabi 'Alaso Oke' of Colonial Lagos: A Female Textile Merchant Commemorated in a Yoruba Proverb", *Unilagedu*, 13 Aug. 2015.

2. Akande, Segun, "Learn About the 45,000 Nigerians Who Fought Against the Japanese", *Pulse Nigeria*, 12 Jan. 2018

3. Archnet > Site > the Old Secretariat Building, "A Taste of 1930's Middle Class Lagos", *Youtube*.

4. BBC – WW2 People's War – Nigerian War Experience

5. BBC – WW2 People's War – Taking Nigerian Forces to India and Back 1945–1946.

6. Chudi, Lawrence, "West African Pilot News Debut Revives the Spirit of Zik and Pan Africanism", *Odogwu Blog*, 25 Dec. 2019.

7. Coates, Oliver, "New Perspectives on West Africa and World War Two", *Journal of African Military History*, vols. 5–39, nos. 1–2, 26 Oct. 202.

8. Coates, Oliver, "The Threat of Aerial Bombing in World War Two Lagos, 1938–1943", *Journal of African Military History*, vols. 66–96, nos. 1–2, 26 Oct. 2020.

9. Das, Manali, and Manali Das, "Nigeria's Role in World War II Unearthed | Fifteen Eighty Four | Cambridge University Press", *Fifteen Eighty Four | Cambridge University Press – the Official Blog of Cambridge University Press*, 23 Mar. 2020.

10. Deutsch, Jan-Georg, "EDUCATING THE MIDDLEMEN: A POLITICAL AND ECONOMIC HISTORY OF STATUTORY COCOA MARKETING IN NIGERIA, 1936–1947".

11. "Elder Dempster Lines", *Wikipedia*, 15 Oct. 2023.

12. "Events of 1940 – WW2 Timeline (January 1st–December 31st, 1940)".

13. "Feeding the Troops: Abeokuta (Nigeria) and World War II on JSTOR", *www.jstor.org. JSTOR*.

14. Findmypast. "'A Fair Share for All'; Rationing in Wartime Britain", *1939 Register | findmypast.co.uk*, 19 Dec. 2019.

15. Fryer, Peter, *Staying Power: The History of Black People in Britain*, United Kingdom, Pluto Press, 1984.

16. Global Nonviolent Action Database, *Lagos Market Women Campaign to Remove Income Tax*, Nigeria, 1940–1941.

17. Grass Roots Organizing: Women in Anticolonial Activity in Southwestern Nigeria on JSTOR, *www.jstor.org*. *JSTOR*.

18. Herbert Macaulay, *Wikipedia*, 9 Feb. 2024.

19. "Home", *Pilot News*, 9 Apr. 2022.

20. "INFLUENCE OF BRITISH ECONOMIC ACTIVITIES ON LAGOS TRADITIONAL MARKETS, 1900–1960".

21. Kamm, Emily, "Price Control, Profiteering, and Public Cooperation: the Lagos Market Women's Association and the Limits of Colonial Control", *University Honors Theses*, Paper 309.

22. King-Keazor, Muni, and Ed Emeka Keazor, "History Through the Headlines", *Premium Times Opinion*, accessed 13 Feb. 2021.

23. Kirk-Greene, A. H. M., "Nigerian Politics and World War II – the Second World War and Politics in Nigeria 1939–1953, by G. O. Olusanya, London: Evans Brothers, (for the University of Lagos), 1973. Pp. Ix + 181, Bibliography. Cased £2.50, Limp £1.25." *The Journal of African History*, vols. 334–336, no. 2, 1 Apr. 1974.

24. Korieh, Chima J., *Nigeria and World War II – Colonialism, Empire and Global Conflict*, Cambridge UP, 2020.

25. Korieh, Chima J., "The Home Front", *Cambridge University Press eBooks*, vols. 111–163, 31 Mar. 2020.

26. "Lagos: Towards a True Democracy (1940–1949)", *YouTube*, accessed Aug. 2021.

27. Leith-Ross, Sylvia., *Stepping-stones*, London: P. Owen, 1983.

28. Liverpool: SS *John Holt* (John Holt and Company Ltd) Travelling From Lagos to Liverpool | the National Archives, 12 Aug. 2009.

29. Losh, Jack., "Britain's Abandoned Black Soldiers", *Foreign Policy*, 6 Aug. 2019.

30. "Masterpiece, 'World War II Major Events Timeline", *Masterpiece*, 13 Nov. 2023.

31. McDowell, Linda, "Coming Home: The Heart of Empire", in *Working Lives: Gender, Migration and Employment in Britain*, John Wiley and Sons, 2013.

32. MSW, "Port of London: The Second World War", *Weapons and Warfare*, 23 Feb. 2020.

33. NF, "Owe Yoruba: 100 Yoruba Proverbs and Their Meanings", *Nigerian Finder*, 5 Oct. 2019.

34. "Nigeria | History, Population, Flag, Map, Languages, Capital, and Facts", *Encyclopedia Britannica*, 11 Feb. 2024.

35. "Nigerianostalgia", *Tumblr*, 8 Jan. 2013.

36. Nwafor, "Nzegwu: First Nigerian Military Pilot", *Vanguard News*, 31 Aug. 2018.

37. Okogba, Emmanuel, "We The Citizens Can Take Our Country Back", *Vanguard News*, 18 June 2017.

38. "Old Lagos", */Nik-nak/*, 22 July 2015.

39. Omipidan, Teslim, "The National Congress of British West Africa (NCBWA)", *OldNaija*, 24 Mar. 2021.

40. Omipidan, Teslim, "This Is Why Every House in Ibadan Had to Switch off Outdoor Lights in 1941", *OldNaija*, 2 Nov. 2023.

41. Panata, Sara, "'Dear Readers…': Women's Rights and Duties Through Letters to the Editor in the Nigerian Press (1940s–1950s)", *Sources*, 6 Mar. 2023.

42. Poppy, "Searching for Histories of Black Women's Service Across the Seas in the Second World War", *History Workshop*, 13 Jan. 2023.

43. RAF Museum, "Liberator Flight Lieutenant Emanuel Peter John Adeniyi Thomas", Pilots of the Caribbean: Heroes and Sheroes, RAF Museum, accessed April 25, 2024.

44. "'Salt Is Gold': The Management of Salt Scarcity in Nigeria During World War II on JSTOR", *www.jstor.org*. JSTOR.

45. Sawada, Nozomi, "THE EDUCATED ELITE AND ASSOCIATIONAL LIFE IN EARLY LAGOS NEWSPAPERS: IN SEARCH OF UNITY FOR THE PROGRESS OF SOCIETY", *University of Birmingham, United Kingdom, Centre of West African Studies School of History and Cultures College of Arts and Law University of Birmingham*, July 2011.

46. Shashore, Olasupo, "Journey of an African Colony: The Making of Nigeria", *Netflix*, accessed Aug. 2022.

47. Shashore, Olasupo, *A Platter of Gold. Making Nigeria, 1906 – 1960 (Revised edition)*, Quramo Publishing, 2018.

48. Somotan, Halimat T., "Lagos Women in Colonial History: A Biographical Sketch of Alimotu Pelewura. Vestiges: Traces of Record Vol 4 (2018) ISSN: 2058–1963", Columbia University, 2018.

49. Swiggum, Sue, Elder-Dempster Line.

50. "Tafawa Balewa Square", *Wikipedia*, 14 Oct. 2023.

51. "The Changing Face of Alfred Rewane Road Ikoyi – Daily Trust", *Daily Trust*, 30 July 2018.

52. Chamberlain, Announces Britain Is at War With Germany, *www.BBC.com*.

53. "The Colonization of Africa and Why It Came to an End", *Think Africa*, 1 Jan. 2023.

54. "The Effects of WW2 in Africa", *South African History Online*.

55. The Guardian, From Diary of the Years of Occupation © 1993 by the Board of Trustees of the University of Illinois, "Neville Chamberlain's Declaration of War", accessed 13 Feb. 2022.

56. "The *Nigeria Daily Times*, Volume 7, Issue 2243", *Digital Commonwealth*.

57. "U-boat", *Wikipedia*, 12 Feb. 2024.

58. Vaughan, Megan, "A Research Enclave in 1940s Nigeria: The Rockefeller Foundation Yellow Fever Research Institute at Yaba, Lagos, 1943–49", *Bulletin of the History of Medicine*, vols. 172–205, no. 1, 1 Jan. 2018.

59. Welle, Deutsche, "Africa in World War II: The Forgotten Veterans", *dw.com*, 7 May 2015.

60. "West African Pilot", *Wikipedia*, 29 Sept. 2023.

61. "West African Pilot Essay", *Course Hero*, accessed Feb. 2021.

62. "What You Need to Know About the Battle of the Atlantic", *Imperial War Museums*.

ONE MORE CHAPTER

YOUR NUMBER ONE STOP
FOR PAGETURNING BOOKS

The author and One More Chapter would like to thank everyone who contributed to the publication of this story...

Analytics
James Brackin
Abigail Fryer
Maria Osa

Audio
Fionnuala Barrett
Ciara Briggs

Contracts
Sasha Duszynska Lewis

Design
Lucy Bennett
Fiona Greenway
Liane Payne
Dean Russell

Digital Sales
Lydia Grainge
Hannah Lismore
Emily Scorer

Editorial
Arsalan Isa
Charlotte Ledger
Bonnie Macleod
Janet Marie Adkins
Ajebowale Roberts
Jennie Rothwell

Harper360
Emily Gerbner
Jean Marie Kelly
emma sullivan
Sophia Wilhelm

International Sales
Peter Borcsok
Bethan Moore

Marketing & Publicity
Chloe Cummings
Emma Petfield

Operations
Melissa Okusanya
Hannah Stamp

Production
Denis Manson
Simon Moore
Francesca Tuzzeo

Rights
Vasiliki Machaira
Rachel McCarron
Hany Sheikh
Mohamed
Zoe Shine

The HarperCollins Distribution Team

The HarperCollins Finance & Royalties Team

The HarperCollins Legal Team

The HarperCollins Technology Team

Trade Marketing
Ben Hurd

UK Sales
Laura Carpenter
Isabel Coburn
Jay Cochrane
Sabina Lewis
Holly Martin
Erin White
Harriet Williams
Leah Woods

And every other essential link in the chain from delivery drivers to booksellers to librarians and beyond!

ONE MORE CHAPTER

One More Chapter is an
award-winning global
division of HarperCollins.

Sign up to our newsletter to get our
latest eBook deals and stay up to date
with our weekly Book Club!
<u>Subscribe here.</u>

Meet the team at
<u>www.onemorechapter.com</u>

Follow us!

 @OneMoreChapter_

 @OneMoreChapter

 @onemorechapterhc

Do you write unputdownable fiction?
We love to hear from new voices.
Find out how to submit your novel at
<u>www.onemorechapter.com/submissions</u>